The Arc of Blood

un Roman en Anglais (mostly)

Elizabeth Mostyn

THE PHENOMENOLOGICAL DETECTIVE

ISBN 978-1-7394052-2-9

Cover design & typesetting by Raspberry Creative Type

1

2019

Cedric Lindholm turns up dead on the second Friday in January. Paris is sniffling under a blanket of snow and stifling central heating. Few Parisians who have the option choose to venture out. He has manifested on top of a snowbank, as if dropped from an aeroplane, and someone rang the police just before midnight. There is almost no blood, except that congealed around where his silvered head is efficiently bashed in.

Patrice Lanier, *commissaire* of the *Police Judiciaire*, stands gazing at the body, not touching, as he waits for the scene-of-crime team to arrive at about 05.00. He pulls his overcoat closer around him and tries to work his leather-gloved hands into his sleeves. He wishes that the forensic science department would hurry up.

The scene-of-crime officers have now arrived, and then the pathologist, Dr Marc Rousseau, who starts by looking at the body's position and outward appearance. Others from the night duty team are examining the scene, some entering the hotel building from which the victim is likely to have fallen. René Mercard, day shift, is already trying to find a witness who saw the American emulating Icarus. He is not having any luck.

Patrice walks over to the pathologist, thinking in a triumph of hope over experience that he might get an opinion ahead of the post-mortem.

Rousseau is looking as cold as he is, although he has a thick knitted scarf tucked over the lower half of his reddened face. Rousseau turns towards the *commissaire* and grunts the words:

"He is dead."

Patrice, who knew that, says "Humph." The doctor confirms that he didn't die from the fall, which Patrice also knows. The expression "blunt object" is mentioned as Rousseau instructs his assistants to remove the body and leaves the scene with the usual comment that Patrice will be the first to know what he finds when he gets Lindholm on the table. Patrice says thanks and the doctor says it is nothing.

Patrice tells Mercard, who is passing on his way to talk to someone else, to confiscate any CCTV footage from nearby cameras, and gets ready to leave at 06.15

***

Back at the *Trente-Six,* headquarters of the *Police Judiciaire* in Paris, Patrice's team is considering the why and wherefore of the killing of Monsieur Lindholm, and whether the window was open or closed when he went through it. Team members Fleur Olivier, René Mercard and Clémence Godard are joined by Henri Bonnetain, a senior officer from Lille, nearing retirement, who will be exercising a supervisory brief over Patrice's team during his absence. Patrice has asked Henri to give them a rundown of the story so far, the usual straightforward framing of a murder case.

"The Reverend Cedric Philip Lindholm – how do we know his name? – fell out of, or was pushed out of, the window of Room 607 in the Hôtel des Jardins, whose aperture remained open when Madame Olivier reached it." He smiles at Fleur Olivier, who has worked out where the reverend exited, by dead reckoning from the street.

"According to your Doctor Rousseau, the fall of six floors did not result in his death. Which had already been rendered by a gigantic blow to the head with a brass table lamp, *quoi*?" He looks again at Fleur, waiting for her to tell him that the pathologist has yet to confirm that the brass lamp had indeed been used – even though it was obvious and covered in the sticky stuff. Mme Olivier does exactly as expected.

René Mercard says that he could find no witnesses at all, even though someone must have seen the reverend land on the snowbank. Obviously, no one wants to become involved, but there is a little CCTV footage. M Bonnetain asks, again, how do we know the name of the deceased?

Fleur Olivier gives a cigarette cough and says that we know him already. From before.

"He was slightly implicated in the case of the Russians last summer."

"*Oui*," says Patrice, casting a glance at the chair which had been occupied, then, by Pucelle. "He was one of Pucelle's informers, when she was working in Clichy. *Commissaire Adjoint* Dominique LaSalle."

Bonnetain looks interested, for the first time.

"Tell me about him. Lindholm."

René Mercard takes a sip of horrible coffee and begins to lay out Lindholm's background as far as they know it.

"He's originally from Minnesota, America, and is a minister of Protestants. He's worked in France for about ten years and feels, *pardon*, felt, that he had a mission to fight against Islam. We suspected he was behind that Islamic terrorist attack that wasn't, last September. I know Pucelle heavily suspected him."

"It was a worrying case at the time," says Fleur, "although it turned out to be different from what we had thought. But we could not prove anything. And with Pucelle leaving ..." She looks disgusted.

"It has been *mis en veilleuse*, put on hold in favour of other things," says Patrice.

"I see." The aged *commissaire* begins to pace, much as Patrice does when he's in charge. "And what, exactly, did Madame Pucelle suspect him of?" He regards each of the team in turn. Clémence is too new to have known Pucelle, although she has heard tales.

"She suspected him of setting up the fake *attaque terroriste* in order to implicate Muslims in more incidents than those for which they are actually responsible," says Fleur. She taps on her desk. She is not allowed to smoke now, in their public building. She hasn't been out to catch up on nicotine for an hour and a half and is beginning to feel desperate.

"She felt it might be him because it had to be a fanatical Christian, *n'est-ce pas*, and Pucelle thought he might be one. We didn't have much else to go on."

"*D'accord*," says Bonnetain, producing a handkerchief and blowing his nose. "Next step. Anyone?"

"We have not got the full report of forensic science yet," says Fleur, "but they have said that the window had been opened. He had not been pushed through it when it was closed."

"And what does that mean, Detective Olivier?"

"It often means that he jumped rather than he was pushed, although I am not thinking that applies in this case."

"What's that, then? A personal feeling, women's intuition?" humphs Bonnetain.

When no one has spoken for several seconds, Patrice picks up a blue folder from his desk. He looks at Bonnetain a while before speaking.

"Search Lindholm's *appartement*. Ask his neighbours if there has been anything funny lately. Visit his church; does he have one? Talk to his congregation, if any. Find his superior, if any. Keep on Rousseau's back in case there's anything odd about the autopsy findings. In addition to what we know. *D'accord*? Who is looking at the TV film?"

"*Moi*," says Clémence. "It is my task."

"*Bon*, let me know about that," says Bonnetain. "Tell me more about the terrorist threat," he adds, probably because it will pass some time and will avoid his having to do any work.

Fleur recalls every nuance of that excruciating thirty-six hours; she had been very afraid – for her family, for friends, for France. She recites what everyone knows, including Bonnetain. Although he is not from Paris, it was on the national news, indeed, on the international news.

"We had a warning," she says, "that there were two hundred and fifty terrorists going to blow up Paris, and worked out that they were going to cause an explosion in the Notre-Dame."

***

Back then, after the big terrorist scare, Fleur Olivier, perched on her own desk, looking as if she was about to do something even though she wasn't, asked:

"Who dressed them up then?"

Everyone was back at work, except Pucelle, who was on leave of absence following her ordeal in the Paris drug scene.

"Some over-the-top Christian," Mercard stated firmly, confident that he knew. Patrice, back at his own desk, laced his fingers together and steepled his thumbs. He placed his joined hands on the desk.

"Who do we know?" he asked.

"Some priest?" suggested Fleur, shaking her head at the same time. "Probably not. Something so extreme has a bit of the taste of the convert about it, *quoi*?"

"Do we have anything at all, on the record, about Christian extremists?"

No one knew the answer to this. Christian terrorists had not been a thing.

Olivier picked up the telephone and called the *PJ* archivist, Clare, a young woman of fifty-one, with whom she trained at police academy. Head custodian of all the books of pictures, and a dedicated computer geek, she could locate information faster than Alain Prost could drive. She agreed to send up the relevant book.

When they had gazed intensely at all seven photographs, Olivier and Mercard left to visit those portrayed. Patrice stayed in the office, staring into space, wondering about finding another avenue of approach.

2

"What exactly do you want me to do?" asks Patrice, sitting opposite the team leader of the Interpol art theft detail, who is visiting *le Trente-Six*. The only thing he knows is that they have asked especially for him – he cannot think why. He knows nothing about art. He only knows what he likes. His wife, Colette, who has an opinion on everything, says that is all that is necessary.

Commissaire Duchamps, a short, slight man in his thirties, is wearing a tawny summer suit, despite it being January. His shirt is cream, and he has chunky gold cufflinks. His sandy hair has been gelled with what Patrice is learning (from his son) to call "product". The younger man clucks a little as if the question is boring.

"Monsieur Lanier," he says, "are you aware that art theft is the fourth most common type of crime in the entire world?"

Patrice says that he is not. Which is true.

"*Oui*, after illicit drugs, arms smuggling, and money laundering. That's stealing, copying and reselling of works of art – anything from old master paintings to modern works of art, to sculpture, to furniture."

Patrice is surprised at this and indicates that the Interpol man should carry on explaining.

"It is more complicated," Duchamps says, "much more complicated than investigating ordinary thefts, where one may track stolen goods through ordinary fences, through bars, through confidential informers. Sometimes, the works of art never reappear ... that's usually when they have been stolen to order, for someone who wants the painting – if it is a painting – just to adore in private. Although that is not nearly as common as most people think.

"There are some who do, of course ... usually very rich obsessives. Art lovers, I suppose. But who don't care about the citizens having the chance to look at it. Selfishness." Duchamps, sitting with both forearms on his borrowed desk, fusses with his hands. Patrice notices they are long-fingered and pale, with manicured nails. Delicate hands. Artistic, *quoi?*

"Of course, we in France believe in the right of the people to see the works; it is égalité.[1] Sometimes, of course, they are hidden until they can be sold, or until the artist dies – they can increase hugely in value. Sometimes they are terribly damaged by being buried in the ground without proper protection.

"They are often stolen by criminals who have no idea how to protect them and, really, have no idea how to sell them on either. They see that such-and-such a Van Gogh sold for four billion euros, and they think it's a good idea to get hold of one. Selling these things is a specialist job, though, and holding them can be very risky, as well as a huge embarrassment."

"Interesting," says Patrice. "I believe that, sometimes, works of art can be held until the company which insured them offers a reward – and then they are returned for whatever sum that happens to be."

"*Oui*," says Duchamps, "that is true, but it needs a level of managing which is difficult to arrange. As well as a lot of confidence, which robbers don't always have. Insurers suspect people who spontaneously 'find' things. Of course, not all works of art, especially ones of potential great worth, are actually insured. The premium would be far higher than anyone could possibly afford."

Patrice does not react to this string of surprising facts, saving them up for future cogitation.

"And then, of course, there are fakes, although it can be hard to tell in some cases. And most criminals don't know whether they have the real thing. Then there are the works stolen during the war – they turn up reasonably often. Stolen from the Jews, stolen again from the Germans;

---

1   From the French motto "*Liberté, égalité, fraternité*". *Égalité* is equality

maybe stolen from the Russians after that. It's a circus which is actually circular!"

"I am wondering," says Patrice, "exactly why you have asked for me to be part of this circus? And why you aren't talking to the BRB? You do want me, don't you?" He regards M Duchamps quizzically.

"I do," says the younger man. "I most assuredly do. Of course!"

"Why?"

"Because you have something I haven't got in my team. And neither has the *Brigade de répression du banditisme*."

"Which is?"

"You are a phenomenologist. You can analyse what is the truth from original conversation and written texts. Or can you not?" He sits back, setting his expression as if he has just done something very clever.

Patrice, realising what this is all about, says he can. He frequently tells police officers and witnesses that there is always something they know that no one else does. And that better questions must be formulated.

"*Alors*, that is exactly what I want. This particular work is one the *l'histoire contestée*[2] of which is in the writings, some from the seventeenth century, bills of sale, books of business, manifests of transportation, establishing the provenance.

"There will be deep research into the artist, or supposed artist. Of course, there is some doubt whether the picture mentioned in some texts exists, or ever existed. And if the one which has turned up is that one, or another. Of course, we could put a big team on it but, as I said before, it is a different thing."

Patrice is thinking that if Duchamps says "of course" again, he will hit him with a piece of furniture. Instead, he

---

2   the disputed history

nods and asks what they think this painting is, who they think it may be by. Duchamps looks him straight in the eye and doesn't punctuate his reply with "of course"s.

"It is a painting of Judith and the Head of Holofernes," he says. "It might be by Artemisia Gentileschi."

***

"*D'accord*," says Colette, "what is it all about then?"

They are sitting in their *salon*; the children have gone to their rooms to do their homework. The parents are finishing their coffee. Sartre, the blue Bedlington terrier, is dozing on his cushion, waiting for one or both of the Laniers to take him for his evening walk, before jumping onto Amélie's bed for a cuddle, and his much-deserved night's sleep.

"It's art," says Patrice, positioning his half-empty cup on its saucer. "Interpol's art theft division has asked for me because I am reputed to be able to do miraculous things with texts and conversations to find out the truth – whatever that is."

"Truth?" says Colette. "We're always being told that we live in a post-truth world."

"*Les fadaises*[3], though, isn't it? Propaganda trying to make us not value what is true."

Colette says of course it is and asks whether Interpol expects him to become an art expert overnight.

"*Non*," he says, "I don't think so. They have plenty of experts – and it is a very complicated business, taking a long time to learn. Duchamps explained a bit about it to me, but I am to go on a rookies' course next week and a special seminar on *le weekend* so they can give me the basics of how everything works.

---

3   piffle

"It seems that there are paintings that have been recovered, after being stolen and lost for many years, which may or may not be genuine; which may actually have been 'sleepers'. This weekend thing is specifically about 'sleepers'."

"I know what sleepers are in spy novels," says Colette, "but what are they in art?"

"Apparently, it's all to do with deception," says Patrice. "I've been given a book to read – although I am not sure I should read anything at this stage; it could spoil my *epoché,* my bracketing of what I already know."

"Ah. You don't know much, though, do you?"

***

Fleur and René are on the scene at the Hôtel des Jardins at 08.30 Their plan is to interview each of the reception staff – Mademoiselle Szonja Horváth, who is on day duty, and Monsieur Jean-Didier Desmond, who is the night manager – separately. M Desmond has been asked to stay on after his shift to see them. They take him first, into the office, leaving Mlle Horváth on duty.

"Name and address, please, for the record," says René, starting the recording machine. The night manager has around *35 ans,* he thinks, about average height and perhaps a little underweight, but not much. He is fair-haired and comes from Amiens. He is intelligent and articulate, and very clear that he knows nothing about anything.

"You had never seen, or heard of, Monsieur Cedric Lindholm before you saw him lying on the snowbank outside, having fallen from one of your upstairs windows?" asks Fleur, who is in charge of asking important questions.

"I have not seen him or heard of him," repeats the night manager. "I do not know him. He is not registered at the hotel. I did not see him come in or go out at any time in

13

the last five and a half years during which I have worked here. *Non,* madame."

"Can I ask," says René, "about the owner of the hotel? Does he or she live here?"

"The owner is Madame Yvette Sanday," says the man. "*Elle habite à Nice*, for the weather, you know; she suffers."

"Her telephone number, *je vous en prie*[4]," says Fleur. "We shall be in contact."

"She has not lived in Paris for many years," says Jean-Didier. "She is very old."

"Notwithstanding."

***

"What the art world calls 'sleepers'," says the man from Sotheby's in London, "are works of art that have been kept out of circulation for some time – possibly a long time, but not necessarily. There are, however, other conditions which must be met for a work to be called a 'sleeper' – and these are to do with my profession rather than yours."

His audience, of around fifty Interpol agents from many countries, in a conference room at the Lyon headquarters, shuffles and gets itself ready to dismiss anything he has to say which does not, in their opinion, apply to them.

"I," he starts again, mumbling over much, "am an art appraiser, specialising in Dutch and Flemish old masters." He smiles smugly, and everyone turns to his or her neighbour. Those who are from France execute the Gallic shrug in unison.

"There are three conditions which must be met: first, the sleeper must be an artwork or antique; second, it is to be sold by auction; and third, an auction house is responsible for the incorrect and undervalued attribution.

---

4   please

"For the official definition of 'sleeper' all these conditions must be met. So, for most of your purposes, objects at which you are taking aim will not comply." He wrings his workmanlike hands and looks as though he has just said "Told you so".

The appraiser is a tall, lean Englishman, with pepper-and-salt hair and a grey, elegantly trimmed beard. His name is Nigel Hansbury.

"Naturally, we are all looking at artworks of whatever kind. But most of your objects will not be being sold at auction …" He stops, chortles, waits for the laugh which doesn't come. "And no auction house is involved in incorrect or undervalued attribution."

The room sighs in the hope that is the end of his lecture. It isn't.

"What is of most interest to you is not what is currently happening – that is, in the present time frame. The interest is in past attributions or undervaluing from many years ago."

A young woman at the other side of the room is standing, waiting to ask a question. Hansbury ignores her for a while as he straightens his cuffs. Eventually, he focuses on her, saying "Yes?"

The young woman is a pale redhead, junior and reluctant to speak. She has, however, avoided the rookie mistake of raising her hand, as in school. Her new colleagues would not have easily forgiven that.

"But an auction house could, er, undervalue a work, *n'est-ce pas*?" she stutters. "There may be reasons why …" She leaves those reasons to be guessed at and the question is bounced back at the appraiser.

"Um, well," he says, "unfortunately, auction houses are not always averse to the manipulating of values, for various reasons."

An older man, mouth tight under a glowering moustache, stands up and says, in an Eastern European accent, that it's anything to increase the money value, isn't it? Paintings don't really have any value intrinsically, do they?

The appraiser looks shocked; the room takes a deep breath.

"That very much depends on your point of view," says M Hansbury. "And we sometimes talk of quality – and that is a difficult subject. Why is a Van Gogh worth more than a daub by my auntie Madge? Even if she uses the exact same colours and other materials?"

"Because," says someone French, standing up to answer the question which does not expect an answer, "Van Gogh could paint and your *tante* cannot?"

Another detective is standing up and asking whether Van Gogh could actually paint? And what's more, could Picasso?

The Eastern European delivers himself of the opinion that it's definite that Picasso couldn't. It is all a huge confidence trick. The red-haired young woman says she cannot let that pass – Picasso could not only paint, but he could also draw: "hence the *Garçon à la pipe* and *Reading the Letter, quoi?*[5]"

Someone else says to look at *Guernica* if paintings are supposed to move people. "And what about *Massacre in Korea* from 1951?"

The woman says that that owes a lot to Goya. Someone else says that *c'est extrêmement* émouvant[6] in any event. Someone mentions propaganda. Someone else tuts loudly.

A stocky man in a loud suit says that quality has to be considered. And that can be very difficult. Does it actually

---

5   what? For emphasis – French
6   it is extremely moving

exist, or does it just turn on what the buyer will pay? Patrice notes his American accent, although not where he comes from specifically.

Lots of people begin to shout, and Hansbury has clearly lost control of the room. A middle-aged woman shouts that talent, skill, must count for something. Someone else says, "But who is to judge?"

Patrice folds his arms and closes his eyes. He is only a beginner at this and does not feel that he himself should stand and restore order; there must be other high-ranking police officers in the room. The middle-aged woman looks like she may be one of them. He is intrigued to have something approximating a riot in an Interpol conference room. This is not going to be as boring as he thought.

***

The young woman who staffs the reception desk at the Hôtel des Jardins is a very different prospect from the night manager. She is from Hungary and has lived in France for two years, but only been employed at this hotel for three months. Her papers, which the *PJ* check, are entirely in order.

Mlle Horváth is twenty-three, with light-brown hair, beautifully styled up on top of her head. She has excellent skin, and dark eyes which smile at you. René, almost smitten, pulls himself up and decides not to be.

Like M Desmond, she lives at the hotel when not on duty.

"*C'est très pratique*," she says, happy that it is so practical.

"Had you seen Monsieur Lindholm before he landed on the snowbank outside?" asks Fleur. "Around the hotel, or anywhere else?"

17

"*Non*," says the woman. Her French is not at all bad; presumably a prerequisite for working the reception desk. "I had never seen him before. And I did not know his name until it was in the newspaper."

"Has there been anything strange at the hotel during the time you have worked here?" asks Fleur, trying for something, anything.

"*Non.*"

"Nothing odd about the guests?" asks René, taking confidence from his partner.

"*Rien*," she says, "*rien du tout.*[7]"

3

The audience present for the beginners' course, starting on Monday, is very different from the Saturday and Sunday one about sleepers. This is a much younger audience, although Patrice does recognise a few who had been also present at the weekend.

The teacher is different too. This is an older woman with a great deal of grey hair, wound into a complicated thing on top of her head, and the spare face of an aesthete. She introduces herself as *Commissaria Professoressa* Francesca Bartolini, Interpol's head controller of art theft.

She is wearing an elderly grey cardigan and a rusty long black skirt, and pushes up her sleeves before beginning to speak in very slightly Italian-accented French. Patrice is somehow reminded of pictures of Marie Curie, heaving all

---

7   Nothing, nothing at all

that pitchblende, in pursuit of her genius. She says she will be here this morning to introduce the subject, and on Friday afternoon to give them a summary.

"I am here to tell you," she begins, "that art theft is the most difficult and complicated of all types of police work. It is also, by far, the most fascinating. If I could find something more interesting, I would do that instead. But I cannot." She stops and looks at her audience. There are thirty of them and only seven are French. How would she know? Because they look French.

Patrice has already identified the red-haired woman, and he suspects that two more, youngish men, sitting together in the back row, are probably French detectives who are mates, and who probably come from the south. He has a list of course participants and has noticed "Marseilles" against two male names. The redhead is Chloë Valéry from Toulouse, and there are three other men from Boulogne, Lille and Le Mans. The usual French paucity of females. Not that the other countries are much better. Patrice scans the sheet of paper and identifies only one other woman, who is from Beijing. So, twenty-eight to two. Umph.

Commissaria Bartolini is getting into her stride, talking about why the investigation of art theft is important. Not just because it's the fourth biggest crime division in the world, nor because individual pieces are worth a huge amount of money. It's important because of art's history, its beauty, its culture; because of the way great art lifts the spirit, speaks to the soul. Art theft is a crime against civilisation.

"But yes," she says, "the money also." She sighs as if this is the least important factor. "A Mark Rothko, the *No. 6 (Violet, Green and Red)*, oil on canvas from 1951, was sold in August 2014 for 186 million US dollars. *Oui*," she goes on, "all those details are important. You need to know the medium, the materials, the date the work was made, and where it has been since then. I know. It's a lot. Stolen jewellery, in its aspect as art, can also be fascinating. But not quite this fascinating!"

Bartolini turns and faces the whiteboard on a stand at the side of the lectern. It is still completely white; she hasn't even written her name on it as Patrice remembers his own university lecturers doing before addressing a new class. Now she takes a black marker pen from a deep pocket and writes, in large, beautiful letters:

APPROACHING A PAINTING

TITLE? – what is it called? Are there others with similar names?

WHO? – who was the artist? (are you sure?) – check any attribution

WHEN? – what dates was it painted between?

WHERE? – was it painted in Italy, France, America, Holland, etc.

WHAT? – is it oil on canvas, oil on board, linen, paper, pastel, watercolour or other? Or a fresco, on a wall?

PROVENANCE? – where has it been since painted? Is the provenance genuine?

"We shall take these in order: first, the title. It is usual to call a painting by the name the artist, or his *mécène* or person who gave him the commission, gave it. Although if that *artista* made several of similar or the same subject, they are often referred to as the Metropolitan something or the London *David*, of whatever artist. You will find that there are many paintings, sometimes with similar titles, of the same subject. This is because of fashion."

She talks of Dutch paintings, of prosperous merchants and of seascapes with authentic marine rigging – trade topics, akin to advertising, often commissioned by traders. Religious paintings come next, and she exemplifies many commissioned by popes and princes of the church. She speaks fluently of all these, before returning to the desk and perching on the front edge of it, long skirt draping like a curtain, gazing out across the group of police, and begins on attribution, referring momentarily to the weekend course they have all just taken.

"Attribution, avoiding all the auction house *merda*,[8] may be a mistake or wish fulfilment, as well as the desire to deceive. Some art may be specifically made by the master – whoever he is – but some may be by his apprentices or journeymen in his studio. Some may be copies – the making of which is a learning tool for apprentices; some may be partly by the *maestro*, with less important bits by his underlings. They may even be by great masters, painting less important parts of other people's paintings when they themselves were apprentices.

"Do you know of the angel, now thought to have been painted by Leonardo da Vinci in *The Baptism of Christ* by Andrea del Verrocchio?" She presses a button on the desk panel and the picture comes up on the screen.

"Oil and tempera on a poplar panel. The angel to the far left is Leonardo's, although most authorities think he did a lot of the background too, as well as Christ's torso. It is in the Uffizi in Florence. We shall not be covering technique in this course – we are not trying to train art appraisers, and there are people you can ask if the course

____

8   shit – in Italian

of your work runs in that direction."

A middle-aged man stands and gruffly asks what about signatures, then?

"A word about signing the work here, then," says Bartolini. "You should look for signatures, but don't necessarily expect to find them. Especially in Renaissance works, many are not signed. It wasn't widely done in those days – so, if some are signed, that may be an indication that they are not authentic. If you find, for example, a signed Leonardo da Vinci, it is not authentic. Leonardo did not sign any of his works. Of course, some artists didn't sign the work with their accepted name. Van Gogh signed 'Vincent' – I daresay you all know that?"

A few people around the room, including Patrice, nod their heads wisely – at least they know something about "this very complicated subject".

"And he only signed those paintings which he felt were ready to be sold. He regularly didn't sign at the bottom right-hand corner, which is an established area to place a signature – sometimes it is on a piece of furniture or on the vase of sunflowers. He prints 'Vincent' too – not that hard to forge, you wouldn't think."

She goes on to the second part of the morning after they have poured themselves coffee from the thermos jugs at the rear of the room. She gives them pictorial examples of fresco (the Leonardo *Last Supper*, deteriorating away in its monastery in Milan); oil on canvas (Rembrandt, Leonid Afremov, *Alley by the Lake* – palette knife and oils); David Hockney's *The Bigger Splash* – acrylic on white duck canvas; Henri Matisse's cut-outs.

She talks briefly about Rembrandt van Rijn's palette of pigments, which have been scientifically established by the analysis of thirty paintings as bone black, charcoal black and lamp black, lead white, azurite and ultramarine, yellow lake, lead-tin yellow, various ochres, Vandyke brown, vermillion, and madder lake.

They break for lunch at *13 heures* and adjourn to the very busy dining room. Patrice finds himself on the same table as Chloë, the art expert, and a Sikh man wearing a blue turban.

They crowd onto the bench behind a yellow melamine table, opposite what looks like a married couple. The Sikh introduces himself as Govinder Singh Makkar, a police sergeant from Kolkata. The diminutive Chloë also introduces herself. She is both painter and art history scholar. When it is Patrice's turn, he realises that he holds the highest rank. The food is abominable, and neither Govinder nor Patrice is willing to eat it. Chloë, who has recently been a doctoral candidate, manages all of hers, and a little of theirs. They talk a while about Toulouse, where Patrice spent his first year as a policeman.

***

On Monday night, when Patrice returns to the Interpol Lyon accommodation, where he has been given a bleak single room for the week, he telephones Colette, who is just in from work, with reading to do. She asks him how he is and whether he is enjoying being back at school.

"Oh, *oui*," he says, "it's most interesting. I'm learning a lot about art and, what's his name, Duchamps, was right. It's very complex. I am hoping, though, to be able to simplify it somewhat."

"What did you learn today?" she asks as she would *les enfants*.

"A lot about the headings, where we need to apply consideration. The titles and provenances, and whether certain works come from the *maestro* or from his workshop—"

"Or from the *maestra*. Or her workshop!"

"*D'accord*. Especially in my case. My *maestra* turns out to be Artemisia Gentileschi."

"Oh, *superbe*. How are the teachers?" asks Colette, hoping they are good because he is picky.

"Okay so far," he says. "We just had two today. The morning was *Commissaria Professoressa* Bartolini, the head controller of art theft, who was terrific and is coming back to do the summing-up on Friday."

"So, the afternoon wasn't so good?"

"Um. It was an American special agent from the FBI. He is … er, well, his accent is hard for me. He has a very good reputation, though, and we can learn a lot from him. He has caught a great many art thieves and recovered many millions of dollars' worth of art."

"But you weren't keen?"

"*Non*. Not so much."

***

René Mercard has gone out because *le Trente-Six* is *le bordel*.[9] He has decided that he dislikes Bonnetain and thinks he is *paresseux*.[10] He also wants to have a look around the hotel from which M Lindholm descended on his own, without necessarily talking to anyone. He does not think the instructions given to the original searchers were very good. He is concerned that some of the people he would like to talk to may already have left.

He arrives in the rue Mondoré as it starts snowing again. He leaves the unmarked car at the *trottoir*[11] with its police

---

9   literally "a bordello", but in slang, "a mess"
10   lazy, idle, slothful
11   kerb

identification and enters the Hôtel des Jardins. The day receptionist is still on duty although it is *19 heures*. She is looking tired and bored. He flashes his ID and says he must look around the hotel again, in search of evidence regarding M Lindholm. She says "*D'accord*," and he takes the creaky *ascenseur* to the top floor.

There are no occupied rooms on the top (seventh, attic) floor; they are drab and smell abandoned. Mercard looks quickly and discounts all. He leaves it for now and proceeds to the floor below, which has 607, with, still, police tape over the door. He tries 601, without result, but hears shuffling behind the door of 603.

A man in *un pantalon et un gilet*[12] answers on the second knock. He has bits of shaving cream on his chin and is clearly in a bad temper. Also from the north; the accent is industrial. He wants to know what the hell is the matter. René increases the temper by flashing his ID.

"Can I ask you your name, monsieur?" asks René, "and whether you slept here last night?"

"*Non*," he says, "I only got to Paris at lunchtime today. Registered at *14 heures* before I went out to see clients, as you will see. I have a company, in Blois, selling office equipment and furniture."

"*Mais*, your name, sir?"

"Cloche. Bernard Cloche. From Blois." He raises his voice on the last two words, as if he thinks René too deaf or stupid to have noticed them. René makes a mental note of this.

"You could not have heard or seen anything of the incident which happened during the night, then. You were not here."

"*Non*. I was not here."

---

12   trousers and a vest

René has a sense that something is wrong here and makes a further mental note to check again later, before establishing that M Cloche is leaving on Wednesday the sixteenth. He gives him a *PJ* card, which will go in the wastepaper basket, and continues his knocking on doors.

René arrives back at the reception after he has spoken briefly to six of the seven people resident in the rooms above. There are four more doors open for cleaning *au matin* and he has Fleur's list of Thursday night's occupants from the night manager, who has now come on duty. The addresses must be on the list also. He asks whether the basement is used for anything?

"Just storage. There is nothing there." The night manager indicates a door to the left of the reception desk, saying that it is, anyway, locked. René asks him to unlock it.

There is very little light in the cellar. It is chilled and damp. The floor is wet, the parts which may be seen; not much. The idea that there is nothing there is untrue. There are many things. He must have meant that there is nothing which is useable or worth anything. That is true, certainly. René struggles to walk around the vast, undivided room, recognising broken old furniture, deceased insects, and packaging. Everything is on the floor; there are no shelves, only old-fashioned packing cases.

He finds the whimpering girl huddled against the far wall.

***

Clémence, at her desk in *le Trente-Six*, is spooling through the CCTV footage, which isn't at all clear. It is on old-fashioned videotape. She wishes that people who think they need security would move it into the digital age and invest in better equipment and film stock which works. There are two cameras which point in the vague direction of the Hôtel des Jardins; one captures the snowbank, one the entrance to the reception area.

Nothing at all happens as the film runs until she sees Monsieur Lindholm emerge from above the snowbank, gracefully descend, splay out on its top; arms and legs assuming the positions in which he was found. The second camera shows people entering and leaving the hotel since *8 heures* on 10 January. With a lot of perseverance, she manages to capture the backs of the heads of several people going in, and the blurred faces of many fewer coming out. The hotel is not busy. She does not think that the people will be recognisable – although, when they identify suspects, they will need to look again.

***

The second day in Lyon is much like the first, although the information in the lectures proves rather different. Another Englishman talks about fakes, copies and pastiches, and is followed by a Frenchman, whose specialist subject is homages by artists to their predecessors, such as that of Edward Manet's *Olympia* to Titian's *Venus of Urbino*, and symbolism. They learn that palm leaves indicate holy martyrs, and that there are differences between homages, plagiarism and fraud.

"The Roman philosopher Seneca said three thousand years ago that all art copies nature – and, of course, all portraiture copies people; unless you count Francis Bacon's Screaming Popes series, about which I am somewhat doubtful ..." He clicks a picture on the screen and everyone in the room makes some kind of noise, a whistle, an "*ouf*", a verbal shudder. The picture is stunning. Patrice and a few others appreciate the horror portrayed within and how it may well represent some people. This is depressing.

"Some, many, painters copy their own works so they can double or triple up on their income from one idea. Sometimes this is good for art because increasing maturity can produce better, more thoughtful work. Or not. Some painters, Leonardo da Vinci comes immediately to mind, were very loath to finish anything. As we all know, Leonardo had a mind which was always jumping to another topic, not necessarily a subject for painting. A helicopter, a war machine, a child in the womb. Many of his customers got very angry.

"Semiotics, or symbolism, is a huge subject, and you may discount anything you have read in Monsieur Dan Brown." Monsieur Devereaux pauses and puts up a slide on the PowerPoint display. It is a list, and he talks them through it, first saying that this is only a tiny fraction of the most common symbols they will see.

Books – learning, study, the transmission of knowledge

Birds (especially a pair) – the transmission of the soul at death

Bees and butterflies – hope & reminders of fragility of life

Clocks – refer to passage of time

Cats – refer to prostitution & lust in mediaeval paintings, but later just signify enjoyable company

Feathers – stand for Faith, Hope & Charity, as well as freedom

Fruit & flowers – can hold many meanings in paintings other than still life

Monsieur Devereaux goes on to talk about fruitfulness, love, wisdom.

"In religious works, the apple often represents original

sin; not to mention woman's anatomy and sexuality" – which he does not wish to discuss in depth. He mentions, briefly, the language of flowers, before discussing the many meanings of the presence of candles.

"Candles can convey a wide range of meanings, from time passing to light in darkness, or the Light of Christ. It can be purification of sin, or the corruption of matter. When it is snuffed out, it can mean the loss of virginity, or even death." He puts a painting up on the screen and lets them look at it for a time.

"What," he asks his audience, "does it mean here? And how does it unite the two subjects I have been discussing this morning?" He looks around, waiting.

After a few minutes, Chloë Valéry stands and makes a confident declaration.

"Here," she says, "it is an homage to Caravaggio, who was the master of chiaroscuro. It is also symbolic of Judith bringing light into darkness – saving the Jewish people from the Assyrians. The painting is *Judith and her Maidservant*, known as the Detroit *Judith*. It was painted by Artemisia Gentileschi, around 1625." She sits down, with a breath from deep in her being.

Patrice sighs. Wow! The first mention of Judith and *Maestra* Gentileschi.

***

It takes René Mercard quite some time to persuade the girl to come out from where she is cowering behind some tatty old boxes. She seems to be very frightened of him, even though he speaks in a low voice, putting as much friendliness into it as he can. He folds his shoulders into himself and bends down to her level, making himself smaller and less threatening. He avoids gesturing with his arms and keeps his face as neutral as possible. He does not reach out towards her.

"Hello," he says, making eye contact. "My name is René, and I am from just around the corner." No questions, not yet. "I wonder whether you would like a little drink of water or something to eat …"

A hopeful, hungry look comes into her dark eyes, but she doesn't speak. René wants to ask her if she is all right, but that will be for later. He says that she could come with him to the café upstairs, but she shies dramatically away from him, her eyes racing with fear, her face turning away.

"*D'accord*," he says, "not that, then. I am going to walk down to the park, it is very close. We can go together and get some soup from the stall if you like. They have all kinds of soup, and their *soupe aux oignons* is famous. You have it with *croûtons au fromage; c'est magnifique!*"

She has turned back to him and is again looking hungry. She tries to rise from the nest she has made behind the boxes; it is difficult, she is not steady on her feet. René, who wants to put out his hand to help her, resists the impulse. He knows he must not touch her, even out of sympathy. He waits patiently, keeping a friendly, but not too friendly, look on his face. Eventually, she manages to get out and stand up. She is well below one metre fifty. He thinks she may have *9 ans*.

René moves away from her, just a little bit, and half turns to see whether she is coming with him. Happily, she is, and continues as he moves slowly across the filthy floor of the cellar. They ascend to the door behind the reception desk and René whispers to the night manager, asking him to go outside and lock the car, keeping the keys for him. René and the child exit into the street.

The park is only about a minute's normal walking time from the front of the hotel, but the odd couple get there slowly, and the girl stops a little short of the *stand de soupe,* hiding in the shadows, avoiding the yellow light.

René buys two plastic bowls of onion soup, with a large, deep, cheesy crouton floating on the top of each. He picks up two plastic spoons and moves to the girl, stretching his arm to give her the bowl. She doesn't look at him as she takes it, and attacks it immediately. She must be extremely hungry. He wonders what on earth he is going to do next.

4

"*Eh, bien,* still interesting, eh?" asks Colette on the telephone that night.

He has told her about the artist and about Rembrandt, about chiaroscuro and impasto. He is fancying going to Holland to look at the Rembrandts. Colette, who would prefer going to Italy, reminds him that he is interested in Artemisia Gentileschi.

"*Mais certainement,*" he says, "but you know what I am like. I must look all around it. Painting technique and materials are important!"

"*D'accord,*" says Colette, "but you will have experts for those, *quoi?*"

"True," says Patrice, reluctantly, "but I need to be able to tell if they know what they're talking about, don't I?"

"*D'accord,*" again. "René Mercard telephoned earlier, *à propos.*[13] He wanted to know your contact in Lyon. I told

---

13   by the way

him you are on your cell phone. Did he ring?"

"Not yet," says Patrice. "What did he want? Did he say?"

"*Non*," says Colette. "It must have been important for him to disturb you, though."

"I'd better hang up, in case he's trying to ring now," says Patrice. "What on earth is that horrendous noise?"

Colette tells him it is Sartre, with his new toy. "I'm not being cruel to him, *en toute sincérité*.[14] It is unseasonable. It is a rubber English Christmas pudding. He found it in the street. I scrubbed it."

***

Mercard telephones just after *20 heures* to say that he has found a young girl in the basement of the Hôtel des Jardins, and she has absolutely nothing to say.

"I have a feeling, though," he says. Patrice is always telling him to trust his gut. "She may have seen something, but she won't talk at all. I am treating her very carefully and gently and avoiding asking questions. She is not looking great; she has scratches on her arms, but I don't want to take her to the hospital in case it stops her talking to me – if she ever does."

"I'm assuming you don't intend to arrest her?" asks Patrice.

"*Non*," says Mercard. "I don't suppose she's done anything. But I could do with a safe place to put her until I can get a female officer to talk to her. Fleur has *la grippe*[15] but it may be political; I am considering contracting a cold myself."

"Monsieur Bonnetain not suiting, then?"

---

14   honestly
15   the flu

"*Non*, he is *un bâtard paresseux*.[16] We need you back, *patron*."

"*Désolé*," says Patrice. "Not until the end of the week, anyway. I must be in Lyon for this course; there isn't another until July, and I need the information now. When this is finished, I shall be moving between Lyon and Paris – and probably other places in Europe – so I can be with you a certain amount."

"*Oui?*" says Mercard. "That's reassuring. I expect Monsieur Bonnetain to go down with the *Trente-Six grippe* any time now, he's sniffing a lot … I truly wish you could get Pucelle back, *patron*." Patrice does not respond, although he totally agrees.

"*Écoute*,[17] René," says Patrice. "Why don't you take the little girl to the house of Madame Paston? We have stowed people there on occasion. She would be safe and could have her cuts and bruises attended to …"

"Of course, *patron*," says Mercard. "That would work. And then you can see her when you come home."

"I don't suppose," says Patrice, "that you managed to get someone to draw blood from your girl?"

"I didn't," says René. "It isn't that I didn't think. I felt that she would be less likely to trust me if she saw that as another assault. And I remembered that many date-rape-type drugs disappear too quickly anyway. I hope …" He wonders if he has judged correctly.

"Of course," says Patrice. "Well done. You did the right thing."

***

René telephones Monsieur and Madame Juliane, who live in one of the Paris suburbs and had been staying at the

---

16 a lazy bastard
17 listen

Hôtel des Jardins because their upstairs neighbours had somehow managed to flood their flat. It had been unliveable for twelve nights, from New Year's Eve to 11 January, placing the couple in residence at the hotel when Monsieur Lindholm flew from the window. They checked out at *11 heures* that day.

"I am wondering," René says, when connected to Madame Juliane, "whether you heard anything strange during the nights of your stay? Especially, of course, on your last night at the hotel? That would be the eleventh."

"*Non*," says madame, "*nous n'avons rien entendu à aucun moment.*[18]"

René, thinking that most people would have heard something, anything, even if there was nothing happening, finds this hard to believe.

"*Rien?*" he says. "Nothing at all?"

"*Oui.*"

"Not even loud noises? Or music? Or people passing your room door in the middle of the night?"

"Oh. There might have been a few people in the corridor."

"You were in residence on New Year's Eve," he says. "Was there no noise then? No one drunk? No one passing? No one falling down?"

"*Mais certainement!*" she says, catching on, speeding her delivery. "There was noise on New Year, music and such. But not otherwise."

"Is Monsieur Juliane at home?" he asks in moderate desperation.

"*Non.*"

"When may I come around to interview him?"

"He will be in this evening from *21 heures.*"

"I will come then."

---

18   we heard nothing at any time

***

On Friday morning in Lyon, they learn about fashion, about customers' requirements, and about paintings being stolen to order, from a US street cop who pronounces "Medici" as "Medissey". Odd, as he has an Italian name.

"The Medisseys," says Sergeant Umberto Corelucci, "were big patrons of art in medi-evil Italia. Probably only after the Pope and other bigwig church folks. Although the Rennysonce was well underway when they came to power, Lorenzo de Medissey, who became Grand Duke in 1449, *patron*ised an awful lot of art and encouraged lots of other people to do so, too. They included big names such as Leonardo da Vinci, Botticelli and Michelangelo.

"After him, there were two grand dukes called Cosimo, the First and the Second. And they were whacko patrons too. With the Gonzagas in Mantua, and the Sforzas in Milan, they pretty well ran the Rennysonce in Italia in the fourteenths and fifteenths."

Corelucci steps to the side and writes on the board the names Giovanni di Bicci de' Medici, Lorenzo d' Medici, Cosimo I, Ferdinando, and Cosimo II, with plenty of blank space between them. He speaks as he fills in the names of prominent artists under the *patron* for whom they worked:

GIOVANNI di BICCI de' MEDICI
Masaccio, Brunelleschi

LORENZO
Leonardo da Vinci, Sandro Botticelli, Michelangelo

COSIMO I
Donatello, Fra Angelico, Vasari, Michelangelo

POPE LEO X (de Medici)
Raphael

FERDINANDO
Caravaggio?

COSIMO II
Galileo

"Cosimo the First Medissey, Grand Duke of Florence (or Firenze, as we pronounce it) was *patron* to loads of big-noise artists like Michelangelo and Donatello, whereas Cosimo the Second was less into art and was a great supporter of Galileo Galilei, who was a scientist and astronomer."

For the last hour, they are again addressed by *Professoressa* Bartolini, who sums up all they have learned. The small party which seems to have formed around Patrice (or is it Mlle Valéry?), and now also features an Irishman, Michael Joseph McTurk, decides to go for a beer afterwards, to talk over the course and decide how much use it will be to them. They decide it will be quite helpful.

***

René calls back at the Hôtel des Jardins on his way home to talk to M Desmond about the girl in the basement.

"Were you not aware," he asks, "that there was a young girl in the hotel cellar? You seemed surprised the other night when I found her."

"I was very surprised," says Desmond. "I had no idea she was there. Or who she is either."

"That surprised?" says René. "And yet it's your basement? You never saw her go in or come out? You have no idea how long she's been there? Or why?"

"Non."

***

"What we have to do," says Duchamps, "is to keep our focus on the painting we are looking for, and not get distracted by the stories around the artist."

Patrice, sitting opposite the younger Interpol man in his office on the Friday evening, hoping that he will not miss his train home for the weekend, has been expecting an interim briefing on his secondment before now. This represents the last minute, and he really doesn't want to have to come back on Monday – he needs to get back to *le Trente-Six* and see what is going on with the Lindholm inquiry. And what, anyway, are the stories around the artist?

"You know the story?" asks Duchamps, proceeding to assume he doesn't and giving him the outline. "Artemisia's dates are 1593–1652 or 1653, born and worked in Rome, as her father's apprentice. He was Orazio Gentileschi, a fairly well-known painter, a friend and follower of Caravaggio."

"Of course. But what are the stories around the artist that you do not wish me to be distracted by?"

"Stories of her life, in Rome and Florence, and Naples and Rome again," says Duchamps. "She was raped by one of her teachers, and many art historians have argued that it determined her life and art. There is an article, which I shall email to you in Paris. It is by the feminist art historian Griselda Pollock, and she has very much another reading."

Duchamps makes a note and goes on to say that his advice to Patrice is not to get too involved in the feminist issues either; he is supposed to be working out whether a certain painting exists, and whether it might be the one Interpol thinks it is. If it does.

"As you know, or you will if you have read the book I left with you last week in Paris, the most famous painting by Artemisia Gentileschi is of *Judith slaying Holofernes*, although the one being referred to at any time could be any of at least four main canvases."

"Why was the subject so popular?" asks Patrice. "She, Artemisia, obviously wasn't copying her own painting. Or was she?"

"Not entirely. She may have painted each for a different reason. Bible scenes were popular, as well as pictures of heroes and heroines. Those who accepted commissions tended to do whatever was required of them. Don't forget that there were many artists. It was a big trade in Baroque times, lots of competition too, plenty of money flying about from the nobility and the Church. Lots of building in Rome, and in Florence, everywhere really.

"And it all needed pictures, holy pictures. And so, money could be made – even from repetition of the same subject. It was the beginning of the modern age. It was also a religious thing – the Counter-Reformation. The Catholic Church was trying to remake ground that the Protestants had cut out from under it." He stops and stares at Patrice, assessing him.

"Please don't get involved in the Council of Trent," he says, as if daring the *commissaire*.

"So, what other *Judiths* did Artemisia paint?" asks Patrice, preparing to make a note of the names. Duchamps turns a page backwards in his pad and says that she painted the two already mentioned, the *Judith Slaying Holofernes* of 1612–13, and a picture of the same name but painted around 1620, now respectively in the Capodimonte in Naples, and the Uffizi in Florence;

plus *Judith and her Maidservant with the Head of Holofernes*, now in the Pitti Palace, Florence, from 1618 or 1619.

"Then, there is what's usually referred to as the Detroit *Judith* – because it's in the Detroit Institute of Arts in America – probably painted in 1625, when Artemisia returned to Rome from Florence. It's not a painting of the beheading, it's Judith and the maidservant (who is putting the head in a basket and covering it) after the killing, listening for noises as they worry about being caught."

Patrice keeps silence on the Detroit *Judith*, which was introduced to the art class earlier.

"So, five in all," says Patrice. "You said that other people had painted Judith too. Who were you thinking of?"

"Of course, Artemisia's father painted a *Judith and her Maidservant* in 1608 or 9, but the most famous one is Caravaggio's *Judith Beheading Holofernes* of 1599, which is in the Arte Antica in Rome. There are many differences from the Artemisia canvases, and a significant one may be that the maidservant, not mentioned in the title, is a skinny old woman, rather than the youngish person Artemisia paints.

"Some other versions come from Michelangelo, 1512; Cristofano Allori, 1616; Lavinia Fontana, 1600; Felice Fichcrelli, 1665; Lucas Cranach the Elder, about 1545, as well as many other times; Valentin de Boulogne, about 1626; Johann Liss, 1622; Botticelli, 1470, Giorgione, 1504; Titian, 1515; Rembrandt, a drawing in 1635; Peter Paul Rubens, 1616 ..."

"So, there are at least five Artemisia *Judiths*, and many by other people ..."

"*Oui*," says Duchamps, "probably a lot. Now, to our own, or may I say your problem?"

5

René imagines that the Ascher couple will probably speak French or even English, even if their names are *suisse allemand*. He decides to call them now.

"*Allo! Je suis* Sergeant René Mercard, *de la Police Judiciaire à Paris*. May I speak with Herr Friedrich Ascher, please?"

"This is Doktor Friedrich Ascher. How may I help you, Sergeant Mercard?"

"Can you confirm," asks René, "that you were resident at the Hôtel des Jardins, in Paris, from 27 December 2018 until 11 January 2019? And that you and Frau Ascher stayed in Room 607?"

"*Ja*," says Herr Doktor Ascher. "All that you have said is correct."

"Could you tell me what was your purpose for being in Paris on that occasion?"

"Of course. We were having a little holiday over the New Year. My wife and I have had a very trying time lately. Our daughter has been very ill, and now she is well, we do not have to visit her all the time in the hospital. So we decided that we should travel to Paris, where we went when we were first married, a long time ago."

"And," says René, "were you aware that a Monsieur Lindholm, an American preacher, fell out of your room – 607 – during the night of the tenth to eleventh of January? You must have been there at the time, must you not?"

"*Non*," says Doktor Ascher, "of course we were not there. There must be some confusion about the room numbers – our room cannot have been 607. Perhaps it was 307? *Oui*, I think that is it. It was 307, on the third floor.

"I did not know the details of the incident. I did hear the shouting, and the police coming, but my wife was sleeping. She had taken a sedative and heard nothing. So, I kept the room door closed until it became quieter, and then I slipped out of the room to see what had happened. I came down to the foyer and the night manager told me someone had fallen from the window. He did not mention the room number."

"Did you not read the details in the newspaper?" asks René.

"I did not. I was keeping the details of the accident from my wife. You have to understand, Sergeant Mercard, that Heidi is a very nervous person, and has been even more so since our daughter has been so ill. Knowing that someone had died would not have been a good thing for her; she would have wanted to leave immediately. And the trip to Paris was doing her much good."

"But you did leave immediately, did you not?" asks René.

"We did. I decided that it would be best not to have the police question my wife. As there was nothing she could tell you ..."

"I see," says René, "and do you now know that Monsieur Lindholm was murdered by being hit in the back of the head with a brass lamp?"

"You mean it wasn't an accident?" asks Doktor Ascher.

"*Non*," says René, "it could not have been." He pauses for a few moments and then asks Doktor Ascher if he can talk to Frau Ascher now.

"There is really no point," says the man. "She was asleep all the time. We never even saw the man on the stairs."

"On the stairs?"

"Or anything," says Doktor Ascher. "On the stairs or anything ..."

***

René also must interview, by telephone, Monsieur Michael Denthwaite, who lives in Auckland, New Zealand. This is because Fleur is embarrassed that her English is *vache espagnole*.[19] René's is not much better, but he has much more confidence.

First, though, René needs to do a sum to ascertain what time it might be in New Zealand. To avoid this, he consults the internet to find out and discovers that Auckland is ten hours ahead of Paris. So, in New Zealand it will now be midnight. Too late, he thinks, I shall try on Monday.

***

Saturday afternoon is dedicated to a consideration of the *Judith* paintings of Artemisia Gentileschi. The children are both in their own room, confined to working at home (both when they have to) and sleeping (Jean-Pascal when he can get away with it). They are both, simultaneously, texting their friends, whom they saw every single day last week.

The Laniers have set up the *salon* as an office, the dining table furnished with a laptop computer, a desktop computer, a printer (for important but portable notes), paper (for rough notes), and Patrice's notebook (for penguins). Also, coffee.

Patrice has obtained, through Faye Benoît, their civilian assistant who can find anything, good colour reproductions of all four of Artemisia's main *Judith* paintings. They are laid out on the surface of the table, in line of sight always.

---

19   a Spanish cow – i.e. not so good

42

"This is the one in the Museum Capodimonte in Naples, probably painted in about 1612, where Judith is wearing a dark blue dress and her maidservant a red one. Judith is actually severing his head from his body – at the moment of the painting," says Colette, pointing to it.

"This is the other, in the Uffizi in Florence, painted around seven years later and featuring Judith in a gold dress – which the Florentines were so fond of (so that's probably condescending to fashion) that the colour became known as 'Artemisia gold' – and the maidservant in blue. And you can see Holofernes's knee in this later one. So, he's more of a complete figure. The layout of the figures is geometrically similar in both paintings."

"And the other two," says Patrice, "the one with the neck" – he lays a finger on it – "and the Detroit Judith. I think I like that the best – although I am tempted by the neck!"

"That is four, and they are all fine," says Colette. "She was extraordinary, wasn't she? I wonder whether we need all the stuff about her life and conditions appertaining in mediaeval Italy. Just look at the work!"

"Someone told me that she said that," says Patrice. "The works speak for themselves. There's something important there."

"There's a fair amount of information about Artemisia being a Caravaggio follower, too. And she was, in realistic style, but she was only thirteen when he left Rome after murdering a man, and he died in exile in 1610. She was still, probably, grinding and mixing her father's colours then. She did use Orazio's techniques, and he followed Caravaggio. You'll have discussed chiaroscuro and tenebrism during your recent studies …"

"*Oui*," says Patrice, "and those make everything more dramatic and realistic – as well as conveying something of the seriousness of the subject."

"Something else," says Colette. "It's sometimes pointed out that this is a scene of female solidarity: 'we can't do things on our own, but we can do them together'. It's a modern thought that I'm not entirely sure of, but it's a possibility, I suppose ... There are three others, though, the minor ones – two similar to the Detroit one and the early copy of her father's painting."

***

"What else do you know about Artemisia?" asks Patrice when they are lunching, alone, on Sunday. *Les enfants* and the Bedlington have gone out with the little dog's poodle girlfriend, Chantal, and Madame Herceaux in her new, heavily resisted wheelchair. Acquisition of the wheelchair, and its reluctant acceptance, have seriously impacted madame's life for the better.

"Artemisia? It's a plant," says Colette, indicating the winter veranda, which also has a layer of slushy snow, "isn't it?"

"Is it?" asks Patrice in surprise. Colette rises from the table and walks to the desk containing her laptop.

"Um," she says. "*Oui*, it's mugwort, tarragon, wormwood."

"Absinthe?" he says.

"*Oui*. The plant has over twelve million hits on Google. And between two hundred and four hundred species. Belongs to *Asteraceae,* daisies. Their selective advantage is to be too bitter to be eaten too much. Some butterflies do, though. The chemicals are terpenoides and sesquiterpene lactones."

"Of course they are!" says Patrice. "*Non*, not plants. Painter, as you know."

"Ah," says Colette, "I do know about her being something of a feminist icon. Her work? There's one in London, at Hampton Court Palace. We saw it when we were there, *n'est-ce pas?*"

"Did we? What was it of?"

"A self-portrait – as *the Allegory of Painting*. Woman painting in green dress. You admired the arms."

"Oh. Can't remember. Can you get it up on the internet for me? I should like to look at it."

Colette and Patrice finish their lunch, and she settles in front of her laptop to search for Gentileschi's *Self-Portrait as the Allegory of Painting*. She reads to him the description of the picture, which is in the Royal Collection of Great Britain. He studies the photograph closely and declares it interesting. He remembers it a little.

He has not thought of pictures from the Baroque period looking quite like that – the brown apron over her shapeless green dress and her sleeves pushed up out of her way. Strong arms. The impression is one of strength and determination, workmanlike. Workwomanlike. He can understand why he liked the arms.

"Her early life was quite sad," says Colette, accessing further information, "although one wonders if that made her stronger. Her mother died when she had *12 ans. Certainement*, she had to be very tough to make it in Renaissance Rome and Florence. She started to be a feminist icon only in the nineteen seventies, after having been ignored for all those years. We could make a highly topical point here: in 1612, Artemisia was tortured, with the Sybille (a sort of string wound around the individual fingers and tightened – terrible for a painter, whose hands could be maimed), to assure that she was telling the truth about being raped."

"Still not too different," says Patrice. "Rape trials punish the victim as a matter of course, even now."

"Precisely," says Colette. "Although we have hopes it's getting better. We'd like to think, wouldn't we, that it's a thing of the past, *quoi?*"

"In some places, women who have been raped are still blamed, stoned, et cetera," agrees Patrice. "It's part of the religious blaming of women for the weakness of men. It seems to me that people who think like that don't think much of men either. That they can't control themselves."

"Or they can't be expected to control themselves, more like," says Colette. It gives men an out, doesn't it? The scorpion thing ..."

They begin to clear the table, still talking about this. They usually read, sitting together on the sofa, if the children are out on Sunday afternoons, and they sit down to do that, ready to return to the subject of Artemisia Gentileschi and her life and work in seventeenth-century Rome and Florence.

"Thing is," says Colette, "torture, in the seventeenth century, was routinely used to establish that witnesses were telling the truth. There's an article somewhere – I'll see if I can find it."

"That would be great," says Patrice. "I need to get a feel for the time and other points of context – without going too far off-piste."

"I suppose," says Colette, "that you have some headings of things you will have to study?" Patrice tends to be obsessive about these things and do a great deal of reading. Colette doesn't really think he needs to work so hard – although he has had a lot of success as a policeman, based on his phenomenological method. This includes the quest for better questions; the more these can be refined, the more useful answers they obtain.

"*Oui*," Patrice agrees, "painting in seventeenth-century Italy, for a start. But it may be that I have much of what I need from the course last week, as well as some learning from my new colleagues about how the specialised thieving and fencing works.

"But I shall have to study Gentileschi's work quite closely,

as well as that of some of her contemporary artists.
Caravaggio is important, and they painted some of the same
subjects too. But I hadn't realised that most of the art
around that period is situated in the Counter-Reformation,
so there's more than one religious aspect. By the way, did
you know that the Book of Judith isn't in the bible?"

"Is it not?"

"*Non*. It's in the Apocrypha. And there seems to be no
historical record of either Judith or Holofernes, the Assyrian.
Or Bethulia, where Judith is supposed to have come from,
for that matter."

"Ah. That's a surprise."

"It's a hero story. Of a beautiful widow who saved her
people."

"Does it matter that it's not historical?" says Colette.

"Probably not."

"Ah. Then there's the Council of Trent, *n'est-ce pas?*"
says Colette, with more than a hint of a superior sniff.
"Well, there are lots of religious paintings. But some of the
famous ones are from bible stories. You'll have to read the
Book of Judith in the Apocrypha."

"*Oui*," says Patrice, wondering whether they have a
bible, and if they do, whether it has an Apocrypha.

"A lot of Artemisia's paintings are in Italy, by the way.
Any chance of a working holiday to have a look?"

6

Monday morning, at *le Trente-Six*, Patrice tasks his team
with the usual things in the absence of M Bonnetain, who

has telephoned in with *la grippe*. Fleur has returned from her political illness and gone out again to interview Lindholm's church people. Mercard and Clémence Godard are sitting, waiting for proper instruction.

First, *le patron* asks René about the girl he found in the basement of the Hôtel des Jardins.

"I took her to Madame Paston," says the detective. "She is still there and is reasonably well, although still will not, or cannot, speak. I thought I'd bring her in and let you speak with her, *patron*. Maybe you can manage it?"

"Has Fleur tried yet?" Patrice asks. René says not. Patrice is wondering how long he will have until Interpol starts getting on his back about the secondment, and decides he'd better try to get the girl to speak as soon as he can. It is at times like this he really misses Pucelle.

He gives out other assignments:

"Get the young woman – have we given her a temporary name? *C'est une douleur*[20] to keep saying that – to come in, and I'll have a go in a fatherly way. If not, Fleur can try. In the meantime, Fleur can chase up the church of Monsieur Lindholm and find out what he was doing, what he was like, et cetera, as well as what he might have been doing in the Hôtel des Jardins in the middle of a nasty night in January.

"If Fleur is not back, and Clémence and I have not managed to get anything out of our Jane Doe (let's not call her that, *je vous en prie*), you can take over and get her to speak? At least her name and where she lives? Before that, and after that, I want you to check missing persons, nationally. We have no real reason to assume she's from Paris – or France, even. Leave Interpol for the moment, but *certainement*, see whether there are any likely matches nearer

---

20   it is a pain

home. I know that Fleur's friend, Madame Clare, will be able to help, but I know you can do all the database stuff."

Clémence, who, Patrice suddenly notices, is not unlike the Mademoiselle Valéry he met in Lyon, looks quite excited. Data is her speciality, and she is known to be very quick. She is always pleased, too, to be deployed outside her own subject, in real police work. Perhaps she was right to come to the Quai des Orfèvres after all; where her talents are used, not just her difficulties pronounced.

***

He is very disturbed by the look of her, by the *restes jaunes d'ecchymoses*[21] on her arms and legs (she has damage to her chest and abdomen too, according to Mme Paston, who has given her nightclothes and a jumper and skirt, and helped her put them on), but he is disturbed mainly by the deeply bruised look around her eyes, where there are no bruises. She looks hunted, fragile, despairing.

There are men out there who find this look attractive.

She is wiping her face with a very wet handkerchief. She is sniffling to control the procession of snot. He hasn't got her name yet. He is the second person at *le Trente-Six* to have tried; she won't say. Perhaps she is just looking for protection.

She is sitting in a metal chair screwed to a floor smelling strongly of disinfectant, in an unpleasant interview room, with René Mercard standing by the door, avoiding putting his hands on the grimy wall. Patrice asks Mercard to try and fetch Olivier; *peut-être*[22] she can get something useful from the young woman. Before he leaves, René asks what his *patron* wants to call her.

---

21   yellow remains of bruises
22   perhaps, maybe

"What would you like to be called?" Patrice asks, trying to think of a horrible name to which she might vocally object. She does not react, answer, or even turn her head. He tries her with "Lucille", "Germaine". No reaction. He finally decides on "Gertrude" as a default, and presents it to her without any response.

Patrice remains while René hurries to see if Fleur is back yet. She isn't. Instead, he pushes Clémence's wheelchair into the *ascenseur* and delivers her through the open door of the interview room. Patrice, watching closely, thinks that, just maybe, Gertrude reacted when she saw Clémence's wheelchair. Very slightly, obviously, just wondering, perhaps, who this person is; another interviewee, not a policeperson, surely? He goes out of the room, leaving the three of them together – the vulnerable Gertrude, the man who rescued her, and another young woman, vulnerable, in a wheelchair. Maybe it would even work.

***

Fleur Olivier is a hugely experienced detective, as well as a woman of considerable life-experience. She has interviewed murderers and monsters, child molesters, thieves, rapists, assorted human fiends who hang around big, busy cities like Paris. She has also talked to many, many victims of as many kinds of crime as she can think of. *Également*, engaged refugees from, she thinks, every country in the world.

Today, she has arrived at the Paris headquarters of the Holiness Church of the Olive Branch, which is housed in a building of concrete with eight floors and all the lights on in defiance of the miserable day and global warming. Standing outside, and looking up to take it all in, she had thought "the light shining in the darkness", but perhaps it was only because it is *février* and quite dark at *16 heures*.

Inside, a receptionist, in her middle years, who has clearly had work done on her smooth, very, face, sits behind a large mahogany desk and asks the weary French detective how she can help? She tries for a smile but cannot achieve it as her facial skin is gathered up behind her ears.

Fleur asks to see the *patron*, the person in charge. Asked about her business, she says openly that it is about Monsieur Lindholm's demise. The other woman's French is clearly learned from a non-native speaker. It is correct, but stilted and non-colloquial. She says she will telephone to the office of the Reverend Doctor Gard Baker, the director for France.

Olivier, not impressed, sits down to wait. They leave her there for twenty minutes, until the lift door opens and the clone of M Lindholm comes into the atrium.

He welcomes her with (almost) open arms, and she is slightly concerned he is going to touch her. If so, he will soon be writhing on the floor. He says she is very welcome and asks the tight-faced receptionist to request some coffee for his visitor and have it brought to his office. He steps, without checking it is still there, back into the lift, begging Fleur to accompany him.

She looks at him, trying to weigh him up as they ascend. He is speaking but she is not really listening. He is not that much like M Lindholm. They have the same clean but grating look, with no *délicatesse*, a certain pallor, a certain surface friendliness, thin over what may be a ruthless core.

But M Baker is probably taller (Fleur has only seen Lindholm lying down) and thinner. Their suits, too summery for winter Paris (what is wrong with non-natives?), could have been cut from the identical cloth, a *lin écru*.[23] Their hair seems by the same *coiffeur*. Monsieur Baker's shoes look brand new and are of a pale violet-coloured patent

---

23   ecru linen

leather Fleur has never seen before. She recalls Pucelle mentioning Monsieur Lindholm's pale green shoes, after he had come to see her in the Paon matter. How interesting.

They arrive at *le dernier étage* and turn down the corridor to the corner office; windows on both faces of the building, carved antique desk with a pristine blotter and a writing set centred, and no visible paperwork. M Baker indicates an armchair, in a conversation group with a view of slushy Paris streets, and himself plops down in the centre of the sofa, establishing it as his throne and denying his visitor access. The decorations of the office are tasteful but soulless. *Le révérend docteur* does not ask her what she wants to know but tells her what he wishes her to know.

"Cedric Lindholm was a good friend of mine," he says, in American-accented English. He doesn't seem to have expected to have to use French. Fleur, who can manage, is fine with that. "I shall miss him. He did great work; he was a terrific person. He was from Minnesota, as I am myself, and had good, solid Minnesota values. He was a great Christian man, who had a mission from God to convert the Islamics. We have some in our congregations around Paris now, very penitent, very guilty for what they've done. It's highly successful.

"He's been here about five years, coming straight from the US, where he worked with other valued members of our church in the Midwest. He made many conversions there too, as well as curing many sodomites of their perversion and preventing many godless abortions."

When he pauses, Fleur finds it difficult to get her own breath back. He speaks very rapidly indeed, as if he is catching a train and is late. She manages to ask him if M Lindholm had left a widow.

"No," says Baker. "His wife died some years ago, when he was about thirty-five, I think. He has dedicated himself to Almighty God and the Church ever since. There were no children; unhappily, because Cedric loved children very much. He would do all he could to save their souls. You know, madame, that there is none so poor as those who have never heard the Word of God." He turns his body so that he is facing Fleur directly, and asks, in a sympathetic voice, head on one side, "Are you a believer?"

He looks at her, with a flexible face, ready to contort into a mask of satisfaction at her belief, or misery at the blackness of her soul. She says that she is not here to talk about herself and asks him if M Lindholm had had anything particularly on his mind recently. The answer is "no". M Lindholm is not only a paragon of all Christian virtues but also a strong resistor of the Sin Against the Holy Spirit, i.e. despair.

"He would have no truck with depression, or people who thought they had it. He was cheerful and vigorous, and knew that God would protect him against those who sought to foil him." He stops short, gazing at Fleur, who is thinking that God hadn't done a very good job last Thursday night.

"*Tiens,*" says Fleur. "What, exactly, was his current job? Where did he work from? Who did he work with?"

Without consulting any documents – there are no *classeurs*[24] in the room – Monsieur Baker says that Lindholm had been heading the Church's Islamic conversion team out of this very building. He will introduce the detective to his assistant and his secretary, who work on the fourth floor.

"Fourth floor?" says Fleur. "I'm sure I can find it. No need to interrupt your important work, *n'est-ce pas?*" She leaves his office, thanking him for all the useful information he has given her, and goes down to the fourth floor to seek

---

24   filing cabinets

an office advertising itself as something like "Islamic Conversion Team". She finds that written on a beige door, exactly like all the others. She knocks.

She has knocked three times before the door is opened, and a smiling male face, topped by a blond crewcut, asks her how he can help. She says she understands that this is where the late Monsieur Lindholm used to work, and she wishes to ask his comrades a few questions. The crewcut bristles slightly at her deliberate use of the term "comrades".

"Um," he says, opening the door slightly wider, "please come in. I think it is I, and Mrs Derek you want." They show her to an upright chair; no comfortable furniture here, penance for their sins. The crewcut says he is Linden Fraser, and the woman opposite is Kristen Derek.

Fleur checks Madame Derek out. She is middle-aged, a clean, Scandinavian type of look, with no sign of the results of a gathering of tucked flesh at the back of her head. She had been fair once but is now pepper-and-salt grey. Kristen does not have nearly so many wrinkles as Fleur herself, but then Fleur is considerably older. Both the Christians are dressed in American suits, and their ethnic whiteness is very prominent. They are waiting, obediently, for Fleur to begin.

"You both worked with Monsieur Lindholm, *oui?*"

"We did, yes," replies Mme Derek. "We have all been working together for over a year now." She appears to be the team spokesperson.

"I wonder, can you tell me what sort of a person was he? I expect the two of you know better than the director; you worked with him every day ..."

"Not every day," says Monsieur Fraser. "He did a lot of work outside the office, on the street and in meeting places for Islamics."

"But you are mainly in the office?"

"Of course," says Derek. "We wrote up his reports and did his admin."

"So you were not on the streets with him?"

"Not so much," says Derek. "He preferred to work alone, so as not to overwhelm the Islamic people. He went out a lot by himself. Sometimes he asked one of us to go – especially if he was going to be in a meeting, or in someplace known to be dangerous. And he sometimes took me with him if he was going to speak to groups of women."

"But he was very courageous," says Fraser. "He really had no fear in any of these terrifying places. He never needed a bodyguard or anything."

Fleur does a double take around the suggestion that he might need a bodyguard, and asks the tired old question: whether Lindholm had any enemies.

"No, no, of course not," blusters Mme Derek. "Everyone loved him. Everyone knew he was there representing Our Lord Jesus Christ. He was respected by everyone. Everyone loved him."

The repetition at the end would have had *le patron* doing loop the loop. She asks where Lindholm was expected to be on Friday, and why would he have been around at that time of night? They tell her that Friday is his day off as he was accustomed to respecting the Islamic Sabbath, and it's hard to talk to them then anyway. He usually, as far as they know, stayed at his flat on Fridays, reading and praying. It was his quiet day.

"Did he carry a mobile phone?" asks Fleur, sure that he would. "We didn't find one on the body."

Madame Derek shudders with her own when Fleur pronounces the word "body", before saying that he did have a mobile. He must have left it in his apartment.

A team from *le Trente-Six* has already been through the deceased's flat and found neither computer nor mobile phone. Nothing in any way interesting at all, just a slightly down-at-heel set of rooms, with theology books and an acetic single bedroom with a plain wooden cross on the wall above the bed.

Fleur asks if there is any chance Lindholm's mobile is here, in the office. They say not but promise to look for it. Fleur says that now would be a good time. The staff indicate Lindholm's desk, which looks pristine, with a blotter like that of his boss upstairs. There is, however, a computer on an adjacent shelf, giving an L-shaped arrangement.

"This," says Fleur, "is the computer he used?" She sits down at his desk and starts booting it up before they even agree. Everything looks fine, nothing odd at all. She asks young M Fraser to carry the vital parts of the machine down to her car.

When she gets back to *le Trente-Six*, Fleur learns that there are no possible matches for Gertrude in missing persons records anywhere in the north-west of France. René telephones New Zealand at 11 a.m. Paris time (9 p.m. Auckland time) and asks the man who answers whether he is Michael Denthwaite.

"Yes," says the voice, in English, with what René concludes must be a New Zealand accent, which he has never heard before. "What can I do for you?"

"My name is René Mercard, and I am a sergeant in the judicial police in Paris. I would like to speak to you about your recent stay at the Hôtel des Jardins. It was, I believe, from the fifth to the thirteenth of January of this year?"

"Yes," says Monsieur Denthwaite. "I was there when the man jumped out of the window."

"You must know," says René, "that is what I am
calling about. We are checking whether anyone heard or
saw anything during the night of the tenth to eleventh
January?"

"Well, no," he says. "I didn't wake up until I heard all
the noise outside in the street. People were shouting and
there were police sirens. The sirens were around a quarter
past midnight; it was Friday by then. I looked out of the
window and people were gathering below. I put my
dressing gown on and went down to see what was
happening. There was a lot of rushing about, and a few
police asking questions of the guests who had already
come down."

"Did anyone question you?" asks René.

"A uniformed policeman asked me if I heard anything,
and I told him I didn't. He wrote down my name and
telephone number and the duration of my stay – when I
would leave and that ... oh, and my room number, which
was 303. That was about all. It was nothing to do with
me!"

"Did you happen to know Monsieur Lindholm?" asks
René.

"Who? Oh, was that his name? The man who fell? No,
no, I didn't. I haven't been to France before. Look, I need
to go, if you have no more questions ..."

"*D'accord*," says René. "And no one told you not to
leave the country until you had been properly questioned?"

"No, no, they didn't. But why would they? I'm not
suspected, am I? I was just in the wrong place at the wrong
time!"

"Perhaps," says René, knowing that this is not the
last time Monsieur Denthwaite will be interviewed, but
sure he is far away enough not to run yet somewhere
further.

7

Patrice is late home on the Monday evening, Colette has been in since *17 heures*, and she and *les enfants* have already consumed most of the cassoulet. His portion is in the oven, guarded by Sartre, who is allowing his Christmas pudding a short respite.

"What do you have to study *ce soir, mon amour?*" asks Colette, negotiating her way around the Bedlington and serving Patrice some rather overcooked potatoes as well as the bean, duck and sausage casserole.

"Need to have *un petit coup d'oeil*[25] at the Medici family and their patronage of art," he says. "There are more of them than I expected. I hadn't heard of Giuliano or Ferdinando before. Thought there were just two Cosimos, and one Lorenzo the Magnificent …"

"Ah. Probably many more. It takes generations to dominate if you start from commerce."

"From textiles, which I think they did start from, before the banking. I don't need too much detail, but an appropriate list would be good. With which artists they patronised. I have only a few."

"Can't help tonight," says Colette. "*Soirée carrières*[26] avec Amélie. We are going to tell them, for the first time, that she will study medicine." She looks fiercely at her daughter across the table, and Amélie stares back *avec insolence.*

Patrice wonders what is this? There is obviously more to it than he knows. Jean-Pascal is also going out, to something at the university, and Patrice is soon alone. He

---

25   a little look
26   careers Evening with Amélie

takes a glass of wine and his coffee into the *salon*, and settles by the computer, with Sartre draped over his feet. He types in "Medici" and mentally staggers under the number of hits.

***

Inspecteur Olivier delivers the confiscated computer of Monsieur Lindholm to the *salle squad* at Quai des Orfèvres, wondering where Clémence has gone. She pours herself a cup of coffee *horrible*, and drinks it, longing for a cigarette despite just having had one outside before she came upstairs. Somehow, to her, smoking and detective work go together. She misses it hugely where it is not allowed. It has been there all her working life.

Although Fleur knows her way around a computer, she has not the skill of Clémence; she can only work with what she sees. Clémence, seemingly like all young people, can get inside and find things deeply hidden. The tech part will have to wait until she returns. René isn't here either; she wonders what he can be doing. And whether the revolting Bonnetain is going to come back, now Patrice is home to help.

About five minutes later, René and Clémence return to say that "Gertrude", in the interview room, still hasn't spoken. They will put out photographs of her tomorrow if still nothing results from their records search.

***

René leaves home for the house of Monsieur and Madame Juliane at *21 heures* to speak with Monsieur, who turns out to be rather older than his wife, around *50 ans*, and a sweaty jewellery manufacturer, with a luxuriant moustache, giving the aspect of a silent-film villain.

He is obviously in a bad temper and reluctant to talk to the police. René, discounting the inconvenience, wonders why this should be so. The interview produces precisely the same result as that of his wife. That is, nothing.

René returns to his own flat and goes to bed with a *bouteille d'eau chaude*[27] and hides under the duvet, hoping for dreamless oblivion.

***

Patrice has not gone to bed when Colette and Amélie arrive home. The daughter says immediately goodnight, as Colette makes chocolate. Sartre is excited. When he has checked the parents out, reunited with his Christmas pudding, and joined Amélie on her bed, Colette brings in the chocolate, and Patrice asks her what has been going on with the girl.

"Ach, it's career-choice time," Colette says. "I did not expect this. We had so little with Jean-Pascal."

"Of course, but it isn't time for Amélie to start to be revolting, *quoi*?"

"It starts sooner than we think. She suddenly said, the day before yesterday, that she wants to be a nurse!"

"A nurse? And there is something wrong with that?" Patrice looks puzzled.

"Because she has the brain to be a doctor, *quoi*!" his wife pronounces loudly. "It would be a terrible waste to have her holding hands and cleaning up *le vomi et la merde*!"[28]

"What about what she wants?" asks Patrice.

Colette snorts and shrugs her shoulders, turns away from him in disgust. She had counted on full and immediate support.

"I bought you a book in *le marché* today," says Colette.

---

27 hot-water bottle
28 vomit and shit

"It's about one of the big art thefts in America." She hands him the second-hand paperback which she has taken from her briefcase. It is used, but in good condition; otherwise, she couldn't have brought herself to touch it.

***

Monsieur and Madame Albert Sansone live in Bordeaux, and came to Paris for the New Year shopping. Fleur, whose job it is to telephone them, deliberates on what the monsieur would have been doing whilst his wife was hitting the shops. It is standard practice at the *PJ* to telephone married couples during the day, in the hope of getting one partner on her or his own – and then ringing the other in the evening.

It is Brigitte Sansone who answers, and makes it immediately clear she's a talker. She confirms the facts as Fleur knows them, that what she has is their Bordeaux address, that she has *45 ans* and her husband, Albert, has 48, that she keeps the house, and he manages a highly successful boat-building business, although it is not his own, he is the *directeur* général.

"Albert has been the director general for *15 ans*, he supervises many workers: carpenters, engineers, salespeople, office people. Our son, Michel, went to work there, when he graduated from the University of Bordeaux with a master's degree in Marine Engineering. Michel is married now and has two children, Wolf and Erika, who have *4 ans et 10 ans*. His wife is Swiss. Her name is Angelika. They have been married almost twelve years. Their anniversary is on twenty-ninth May this year.

"We also have a daughter who studies at Montpellier University. She is reading French Literature. She hopes to be a teacher, although she has met a boy, called Gaston. I am hoping they wait to get married until they have both graduated. He is a scientist, a chemist, I think, or a physicist, something like that. Liliane will bring Gaston to meet us at the Easter holidays."

"That is interesting," says Fleur. "But I am mainly interested in your visit to Paris in January. You arrived on the sixth of January, *n'est-ce pas?*"

"*Oui,*" says Mme Sansone. "We arrived at *15 heures* and went for coffee in the lounge before checking into our room. The room was quite nice although a little, um, small. There was an even smaller bathroom. But we were only there for six nights. I wanted to visit the sales.

"I needed some clothes for the summer. I don't really care if they were fashionable, more last year. We don't live in Paris, and Bordeaux is a little bit behind the times. I purchased a beautiful duster coat in ecru, which I shall wear all the season, with many silk scarves in the very most beautiful colours, they will all go with it, because it is so neutral. And five cotton dresses in beautiful prints. They are colourful. And the *lingerie* – it is *fantastique!* I got everything in ecru, silk and lace – and for next to nothing!"

"Eh," says Fleur, "all to match the duster!"

At last, madame shuts up for a second. Then she begins to laugh, with a little embarrassment.

"Ah, officer," she says, "you are making the joke?"

"*Oui,*" says Fleur. "You are aware, are you not, that someone fell from an upper window of the hotel in which you were staying, just before midnight on Thursday night, Friday morning, the tenth and eleventh of January?"

"Oh, *oui,*" says Mme Sansone, "but we weren't aware at the time. We retire early, we are country people really. We didn't even wake up! We only found out in the morning when we were eating *petit déjeuner*. It was a great shock. We had passed the man on the stairs when we were coming down to dinner. We did not know his name. We recognised his shoes. They were patent leather, and they were almost the colour of my new coat!"

"So, you did not hear anything at all?" says Fleur. "Is Monsieur Sansone going to be home this evening? I can get my assistant to telephone him at, say, *20 heures*?"

"Oh, *oui*," she says. "But he didn't hear anything either. Neither of us did."

"I know," says Fleur, "but we must get that directly from your husband. It is the law."

***

Clémence telephones Monsieur Sansone from her home at *20 heures*. He tells her he saw and heard nothing, until he is reminded that the couple saw M Lindholm on the staircase at around 20.30. He admits this. Reluctantly.

***

Patrice has been in the flat for two hours or so, trying to make up the time to his Interpol job, having been using, possibly, too much on the homicide of Monsieur Lindholm. M Bonnetain is still not back at *le Trente-Six*. And they are getting nowhere with Gertrude. Patrice has decided that they should give the girl a few more days at the house of Mme Paston, which is halfway between a women's refuge and a hostel, although it will be charged to their *PJ* budget. He expects to hear growling from the financial sector.

He has been trying to think of their next strategy to get Gertrude to talk. Fleur is spending time with the girl this afternoon, but he hasn't heard anything yet. His *inspecteur* is almost convinced that Gertrude cannot actually speak and is going to try to persuade her to write something down, if she can. He wonders if Pucelle might get her to speak.

Patrice resolves to visit the ex-nun tomorrow, maybe try to entice her back into regular service. He is now feeling the need for her wise counsel and solid steadiness growing with every day.

Colette has gone into the kitchen to make coffee, something she always does when she arrives home, whether or not her *mari* is here. Patrice looks at the modern clock on the creamy marble chimney piece, noting the time is just after *17 heures*. Still early, he thinks. Colette may have bought pastries.

She brings in the coffee tray but, *hélas*, no sign of sweet things. He is disappointed.

"Are you interested in the Gardner heist?" she asks as she pours two cups of coffee. "Do you know about it?"

"Um, I know a bit now," says Patrice, fingering the book. "It was in 1990 in Boston. The Isabella Stewart Gardner Museum. I think about fifteen paintings stolen, and none ever recovered. The only other thing I have read on my skim through was that it must have all been stolen to order because they took only certain things from amongst a whole lot more. If they had gone upstairs, they would have got a Titian that they missed.

"Oh, and there was an odd thing. They took a bronze finial from *le drapeau de l'empereur*,[29] which wasn't really in the same class, as to monetary value, as the paintings; although to some military historians ..."

"Different sort of customer?" says Colette.

"*D'accord.*"

Both children arrive as they decide that Colette will read to Patrice from the Gardner thing this evening. This is a technique they often employ to discuss something written

---

29 Napoleon's flag

down, rather than reading it separately and having to refer to it. This way, it is immediate, even phenomenological. Sometimes one reads, sometimes the other.

***

It is Clémence Godard who gets to interview Mlle Barnier, who is a permanent resident at the Hôtel des Jardins. She has arranged for the lady to be in the lounge of the hotel at *10 heures* in the morning. She is there when Clémence arrives, about two minutes late because she had not allowed quite enough time for parking and extracting her chair from the car.

Mlle Barnier is just as Clémence expected: tiny, thin, grey, papery. She is wearing an old-fashioned print dress, dull brown with almost indecipherable flowers all over it, topped by a cardigan of whose colour Clémence cannot be sure. Thick beige stockings and brown brogues complete the outfit.

She welcomes Clémence in an accent from the east, like Clémence's own. She must be from the Jura. Clémence is unutterably delighted. They exchange names and birthplaces. They would have been almost neighbours had Mlle Barnier not left when her parents died within three months of one another. The *PJ* officer says she is sorry. Mademoiselle says it was a long time ago, nearly thirty years.

Clémence is interested in why she lives in an hotel, and Mlle Barnier says that, although she has sufficient money, from her parents and a part-time job sewing in one of the lesser *ateliers*,[30] she could not afford an *appartement* in Paris, they are too expensive. And she took care of her parents in her early life, so only knows how to sew and clean, not even to cook, only invalid food. It is best to have

---

30   fashion houses

65

all these done for her. She is happy in her hotel suite.

"Do you remember the night between Thursday the tenth of January and Friday the eleventh of January?" asks Clémence.

The woman looks mystified, then seems to realise what the younger woman is talking about.

"When that man fell from the window?" she says. "I only heard the police sirens and the shouting afterwards. It was very loud, but my rooms are mostly at the back, so I don't hear what happens at the front so much."

"Had you, by any chance, seen the man – his picture was in all the newspapers – around the hotel? On the street or in the lobby? Or anything?"

"I didn't."

"Did you happen to know his name? Before he fell? Had you ever heard of him?"

"*Non.*"

Clémence brings her questioning of Mlle Barnier to an end, mentioning that she may need to speak with the older woman again. Before she leaves, she wheels by the reception desk to have a quick chat with Mademoiselle Horváth.

The receptionist, called from the back office, is surprised to see a detective in a wheelchair. She pushes her hand through her loose hair, which is, seemingly, different from what other police officers have described, and asks how she can help.

"I understand," says Clémence, "that Detective Mercard has spoken to Monsieur Desmond, who was on duty when the young girl was found in the hotel basement. I am wondering whether you were aware that she was there?"

"*Non*," says Horváth. Her reaction is sudden, as if shot in the back. The look on her face reflects that position also. Seeming to get herself together a touch, she looks down, trying, without success, to avoid Clémence's eyes (which are on a lower level than her own). She repeats no, and says it a third time, just to make sure no one is in any doubt.

"You didn't see her come in or go out? You couldn't know how long she has been there, of course?"

"I don't know anything about her," says the woman. This is not true.

She cannot hold Clémence's gaze.

***

Colette, sitting on the sofa, next to Patrice, close enough to cuddle, has begun reading the Gardner heist book. Her husband has a clipboard and is making a few notes. He hasn't stopped her yet, but then she has only got to page ten, the end of the opening chapter. She stops before the page is turned. She realises that there are things in the chapter he will want to talk about. Like what was actually stolen.

"It seems remarkable," says Patrice, "for what they didn't take, as much as for what they did."

"I think that too. You'd imagine that a Michelangelo and a Titian, not to say a Raphael, would have been too tempting to leave."

Patrice looks thoughtful before saying that will depend on their motivation for the theft in the first place. And the Titian *Rape of Europa,* or any Michelangelo, would have been impossible to sell.

"Good, though, to have a list of what was taken. Thirteen in all, not counting the Rembrandt they abandoned on the floor. Rembrandt does appear to have been popular with them, though. One, two, three. Is the Vermeer the prize?" he asks.

"Well, it's rare," she says, looking a few pages back. "One of only thirty-six surviving Vermeers. The book says probably worth about three hundred million dollars – and this book was published in 2009, so …"

"If the Vermeer reappeared now," says Patrice, "it would fetch considerably more than that – notoriety, they tell me, increases price. A stolen masterpiece recovered, thanks to months of sensationalised publicity, can triple in value overnight. Its story can titillate the market, and the monetary value can break the roof!'"

"Of course, it may have been destroyed," says Colette. "Unless it, they, were stolen to order and are inside a volcano with *un Bond méchant.*[31]"

"I have been told that is not a big thing – not as important as we think. Among the artworks, there are four oddities. The Napoleonic finial being one – we mentioned that before – but also the Shang era 'Ku' beaker, which was dated 1200 BCE, one of the oldest artefacts in the museum. Then there's the odd collection of Degas's drawings. The other is the painting of Govaert Flinck, whatever it's called …"

"*Landscape with an Obelisk,*" says Colette, referring to the text. "Never heard of him, *toi?*"

"*Non,*" says Patrice, extricating himself from his comfortable place at her side and stumbling; his leg is still a little *rigide* when having not moved much, from the old shooting. He stumps over to Colette's laptop, which is switched on, and googles the Dutch artist.

"Ah, so," he says, "*nous sommes ignorants.* He was a Dutch painter of the Golden Age and a pupil of Rembrandt. Apparently, this picture was mistakenly attributed to Rembrandt himself. I wonder when it changed?" He taps a few more keys, seems to be having trouble finding the information. "Not many want to tell me. Although I would

---

31   a Bond villain

have to say that it doesn't look like a Rembrandt. Do you see?"

He carries the laptop over to Colette, and carefully sits down so that she can see the photograph of the work he has zoomed in on. She agrees that it does not seem to her like other Rembrandts.

"It doesn't say here," she says, "what the Rembrandt that they left was. Let's find out, shall we?"

She takes the laptop from Patrice and googles something which tells her it was a Rembrandt self-portrait – but painted on a wooden panel, not canvas.

"Won't roll up," she says, "so not easy to transport."

"But," says Patrice, "if they were stealing to order ..."

"*Oui*, the customer would have known when she or he asked for it, *n'est-ce pas*? That it would be more *difficile*, and that person would have wanted it. Isn't the board more relevant if they were just taking stuff they fancied?"

"We should look at the Degases," says Patrice. "The book thinks they were worthless – within the context of the Vermeer et cetera, of course. Does it say what they were?"

"Not in the book we are reading, yet, but I can cheat by internet."

She quickly gets a list and photographs of all the works stolen.

"They are," she says, "two drawings called *Programme for an Artistic Soirée*, of which one is a more finished version of the other. But both look quite unfinished and crude to me. They look like advertising – the right lower corner of each has a blank square for the details. One of Florence, antiqued with a sepia wash, is called *Cortège aux Environs de Florence*. One, which does look finished, *La Sortie du Pesage*, in watercolours, with horses, and this other jockey one. Oh, I like that, that's the one I'd have stolen!"

Patrice has a quick look and comments that she likes it because it's pink.

"Rose," she says, "a rose wash. Don't you think it's lovely? It's not just the colour, although I do like that. It's the drawing too. I really like the way it is set on the paper. According to the internet, the Degases were not displayed on the walls or anything. They were stored in drawers – cabinets designed by Isabella Stewart Gardner herself. So in their case the thieves couldn't have chosen from what was on display. They must have known where to look."

"I am wondering," says Patrice, "whether all these are in your Bond volcano or the Freeport in Genève, standing as collateral for something big."

"Maybe so," says Colette, "but perhaps we are casting our nets too wide, *mon chéri*. Are we trying to solve this case, rather than preparing you for what you must do?"

Patrice humphs, as he does when he is caught out, and then asks her about the Artemisia novel, which Colette has by their bed to read at night. It was given to him by Duchamps, but he has not had a run at it yet. Reading novels in bed is one of Colette's favourite things, and she wrested it from him as soon as she saw it.

Colette struggles to rise from the sofa to go and fetch the novel, *Artemisia* by Alexandra Lapierre, crisply instructing her husband to make some fresh coffee.

Settled back on the sofa, Colette finds the passage marked with a scholar's bookmark, a piece of scrap paper, and reads him the passage as he brings in the coffee:

"'From now on, the clerk would write down his answers and note his physical reactions: his complexion, his movements, the tone of his voice. The truth would emerge from the combination of these elements. But the judge could not give a verdict unless the accused actually confessed to his offence. Guilt or innocence had to appear as a divine revelation. In order to seek this truth and reach the soul, it might be necessary to torture the body. The law had faith in trial by ordeal. And torture was applied to witnesses and defendants alike without distinction. In neither case was it a punishment; its purpose was to prove and confirm what was said. If the witness repeated his testimony under torture, it meant he spoke the truth.'

"This is about witnesses, not an accused," she says, "but it shows how they were thinking."

"It's an excellent way of persuading no one to come forward," says her husband. "I need to trouble you, also, for a bit of a feminist reading. Duchamps is very keen on keeping me away from any of that. Makes me wonder why ..."

"Naturally," says Colette. "I was going to give you a 2016 thesis from the University of North Carolina. It centres around Artemisia's *Judiths* and takes a social-psychological perspective. I think it might be of interest."

"Bring it on," says Patrice. "How much can it damage my thinking?"

"Maybe a lot," says Colette. "But never mind."

8

Fleur Olivier and Clémence Godard talk, almost in turn, to Gertrude – horrible name; what was the *patron* thinking? Now there are no male persons in the room, maybe she will come through? But no, she still will not speak. Or she cannot. Both women are being as genuinely kind as they can – and they are both *tout à fait naturellement sympathique* to vulnerable females.

"She seems to hear quite well," says Godard, "but maybe she is mute. We need to try to get her to write something down." She tears off a sheet from her pad and places it in front of the girl, with the ballpoint pen she has been using. Gertrude looks as if she has never seen anything like them before and doesn't care if she ever sees them again.

"Doesn't look good," says Olivier. "We may have to think of something else."

The sergeant rests her chin on her hand and gazes at the girl, making sure to retain her non-threatening look. Without turning to Godard, she says, gently, that she thinks they need a conference. She stands and walks out of the room. Clémence wheels herself behind.

They stare through the glass, a mirror from the other side, at Gertrude, who sits motionless, and Fleur asks if her younger colleague knows whether she has been immobile as long as she has been here. Clémence doesn't know because she hasn't been there every minute herself. She offers to ask René when she sees him.

"*Je ne sais pas*," says Fleur. "Maybe it's worth a try. I was just thinking of shock, and how they say there's a third option. Not just fight and flight, but also freeze."

"I didn't know that," says Clémence, "but it sounds sensible – if you can't fight or run, what's best to do? Play dead, *quoi*?"

"It would mean she was helpless," says Fleur. "Do we know what her injuries were? I know René didn't take her to *le service d'urgence* because he didn't want to scare her."

"Madame Paston, at the women's refuge, said she had some cigarette burns and some lacerations, but she did not think enough to be called torture. She would have said it was 'play' had the girl not been so young. Although René thought she was about nine years, and Madame Paston thinks probably twelve. Still too young for any consent, of course."

"Do you think that a freeze reaction would have been strong enough to have saved anyone the trouble of tying her up?"

"*Le bon dieu!* Do you think it could have been?"

"Maybe," Fleur sighs and then looks suddenly interested. "Look what she's doing! Be quick!"

Clémence, who has placed her wheelchair close to the rear wall, wheels herself very fast to the pane of glass overlooking the interview room. She looks in and sees Gertrude has picked up the pen and is making some kind of marks on the paper.

"She's writing something?" Clémence almost shrieks.

***

Thursday morning, Patrice stays home from *le Trente-Six*, studying a selection of art books he has borrowed from the library of the University of Paris. They all have plates of Renaissance paintings. He has checked that each contains something about Artemisia Gentileschi which he can use to flesh out his understanding. This is basic work which needs to be assimilated before he returns to Lyon on Monday to see Duchamps and discover the details of the actual case. He has been longing to focus in on it since he was given the secondment.

He reads a little of the first book he has chosen and makes a note on his pad that there are probably seven *Judiths* that might be attributed to Artemisia; so, that seems to indicate that another would be one too many. Or does it? He thinks, why would anyone want to paint so many on the same subject? Not identical, of course. *Non,* there seem, up to now, to be only two versions of Judith beheading Holofernes; the others are separate in time – after the act. Still, only four main paintings in total that he is aware of.

He makes a quick note that there are two separate aspects of time to keep in mind. One concerns the time which has historically passed in the painting; the other, the time between them being painted. They are by no means the same thing.

The next book he selects has pictures of the Judith story by other artists.

Patrice looks at the painting by her father, Orazio, now in the museum of Oslo. It is very different from the Artemisia ones he has already looked at. He recalls that Orazio was a follower of Caravaggio, and he appreciates the chiaroscuro, which is obviously good (he thinks "painterly", a word he has adopted from Chloë Valéry).

The figures of Judith and her maidservant, dressed in wonderfully decorative fabrics, are lit from the front of the picture, but the background is not. There are objects present but they are darkened, reduced in presence.

The positioning of the figures in the work is sophisticated too, with the maidservant's arm making a triangular frame around the head of Holofernes, sitting in her basket. Orazio's painting is one of stillness, both women listening in case they have been discovered. It seems likely that what is said in the book's notes is true – that Artemisia probably took her idea to paint her first *Judith* from her father's painting.

Patrice will have to decide about how many pictures of Judith not by Artemisia he is prepared to look at – although he will, naturally, examine all those painted by her, or attributed to her, in detail. Should he really go as far as Rubens, Botticelli, and Lucas Cranach the Elder? *Probablement pas.* He is aware that he will have to have a good look at both Orazio Gentileschi's and Caravaggio's portrayal of *Judith*, but he doesn't feel a viable connection with any of the other works. He does not want to have to survey the entirety of mediaeval painting.

Sitting at his desk, in the *salon*, he brings Caravaggio's *Judith* up on his laptop, followed by *Judiths* by Cristofano Allori and Valentin de Boulogne. He will make do with these, in the hope that they will show him what to look for in a similarly dramatic painting which is not attributed to Artemisia.

He turns pages for a moment, to check that he should not be looking too much at Cranach or Botticelli. *Non,* they are both very decorative. In the Cranach, he cannot believe that Holofernes is dead – his body could be hiding under the veined white marble surface, with just his head sticking out and a smear of stage blood. He laughs shortly. The Botticelli seems like a pastoral stroll, with a countryside background and no drama at all – unless you count the bodyless head in the basket atop that of the maidservant. The head appears to be asleep.

There could be something relevant to learn from Johann Liss, he realises, and, perhaps, Valentin de Boulogne, so he makes a note of these two, plus Caravaggio and Allori. Patrice turns to the first of these.

The Liss, probably painted around 1622 by the German-born artist, who was based in Venice, is very dramatic and provides a still of the violence. Much closer to Artemisia's vision than Botticelli's country walk, it has Holofernes's head already in the basket held by the maidservant, and his headless corpse reclining next to the back view of Judith. The viewer can see the bloody neck, even the top of the spinal column, and the focus of the lighting is between the victim and his killer. There is no fancy drapery here; just the immediacy of struggle, amplifying the crucial nature of the act which has taken place.

He turns to French artist de Boulogne, and notes the similarity of its composition to those of Artemisia and Caravaggio's Judiths. Like the Liss, it may be an homage to Caravaggio, and perhaps even to Artemisia. Like those, there is the play of light and the sumptuous textiles. The action, however, is nearer to Artemisia than to Liss, Judith's sword at Holofernes's throat.

Judith is younger than in other renderings, and concentrating on what she is doing, both slicing his neck and holding his hair; the subtle threads of blood almost hidden in the dark. Abra, the maid, is a very dark shadow (although not as dark as Johann Liss would have her) and her face is wild. Maybe she carries the emotion of her mistress who shows none?

The very theatrical Allori is next and there is no darkness, not even blood, in the focus, which is gorgeous. The three characters are there, unless you count the sword as a character – handle in Judith's hand with no blade showing – and Abra is nurse-like, in a white headdress, showing no hair. Holofernes's head is suspended, with no sign of his body, in Judith's hand.

But the fabrics are the stars of the show; the Florence gold (or Artemisia's) of Judith's dress, damask, shining, her widow's virtue. Her cloak, lined with scarlet, a peacock-coloured tasselled cushion and matching velvet curtain, ruched behind. It is said that the head of Holofernes is Allori's self-portrait, with Judith representing his mistress, and Abra, her mother. The artist is also reputed to have been close to Artemisia. Um.

He will leave Caravaggio until another day.

***

Colette comes home late, after Patrice has taken a break to roast a chicken and place a home-frozen gratin of potatoes in a slow oven. He has prepared *artichauts* and *carottes* for steaming when the family arrives. His wife has had a tough day, and he gives her a big hug and offers to read to her this evening – anything she wants. She collapses onto the sofa and asks for a glass of wine, before telling him how much she is missing Antoine LeBrun. Her new(ish) assistant, Lucie, just doesn't know everything that he knew.

"It'll take a while," says Patrice. "It always does. It's nearly a year since Pucelle took her sabbatical, and I still miss her, *quoi?*"

"Of course," says Colette, taking a sip of dark red fruitiness, "I know. And I know Lucie's going to be great. It's just me. I'm a *femme horrible.*[32]"

"I disagree. Sometimes you are so good it makes me worry!" They discontinue their conversation when the front door bangs into the wall, signalling that Amélie is in the building.

"Hey, *ramps!*[33]" she yells at high volume. "*Teuf*[34] tonight and I have to take *mon reuf!*[35]"

Patrice stands up from where he had perched on the sofa after hugging Colette and does his best to loom over his daughter. Neither of the Lanier parents completely approve of Verlan – it is often used to separate falsely classified desirables from falsely classified undesirables; although young people will always find some kind of slang to perform this function and to discuss taboo subjects.

Patrice is probably about *dix centimetres* taller than his

---

32   horrible woman
33   parents – Verlan (a type of French slang that involves inverting syllables in words to create new words)
34   party – Verlan
35   my brother – Verlan

daughter but never feels there is that much in it. She gets her colouring from her mother's side of the family and her stocky shape from his.

"Oh, *Papa!*" says Amélie. "*Papa, ne te fâche pas, s'il te plaît*[36]."

Patrice sits down next to Colette, delighted that she hasn't used the Verlan verb *véner*, from *énerver* – to be angry. He usually understands when the children insist on speaking Verlan because he hears criminals, and policepersons, speak it all the time at *le Trente-Six* and in the street. Colette doesn't hear it or, really, know it, except the odd things she picks up from *les enfants*. She is well placed to despise it.

Colette is asking Amélie where is this party, and why does Jean-Pascal have to go? Amélie says that it's actually a party at the university; it's Jean-Pascal's department, and he telephoned her earlier to ask if she could go. The engineering department is *un morceau* short of women for the newly popular *danse de salon*. Colette asks if she is sure that is where she's going? Amélie says it is, and does *Mama* think she is lying?

Papa, meanwhile, telephones Jean-Pascal and establishes that his sister's story is correct. Colette insists that she have her dinner first, there is plenty of time. Although Amélie wants all the time to get into her finery, as well as persuading one of her parents to drive her, she eventually concedes that she can spare *quinze minutes* for several vegetables, but no pudding, *merci*.

Patrice drives the child whirlwind to the venue and returns to his exhausted wife and irritated dog. He has made sure that Amélie and Jean-Pascal have a taxi booked, which will bring them home at *23 heures*.

---

36 Daddy, please don't be angry

Sartre is cross. He is sitting facing the front door with his stiff back to the room. Amélie and Jean-Pascal have gone to *le dancing* and left him with the Lanier parents. He wants to go too. It isn't fair. His resentment illuminates the outline of his small woolly self. Both Colette and Patrice have tried to tempt him with his Christmas pudding, and with actual dog biscuits. But he isn't interested. *Bof!* He is now into the second hour of his filibuster; he refuses to lie down and wait quietly.

"Do you think he's all right?" asks Colette worriedly.

"*Mais certainement*," says Patrice, "he is just in a mood. Because *les enfants ont vamoosed*. He will be fine when they are returned."

"I don't like it when he does this," says Colette. She knows he is a dog and not a third child, but holds a theory, which she is sure is not widely shared, about dogs being equal too. Emotionally anyway. She wonders how long Sartre will resist the call of his dinner dish, and whether the demands of his stomach will triumph before the children are returned.

The small blue dog resists his stomach's rumblings until Amélie and Jean-Pascal arrive, at which point he throws himself at them and bounces off their united front, before transmuting into Christophe Lemaitre for the dash to the dish.

***

Fleur and Clémence are trying to see what Gertrude is doing in the interview room behind the glass window and decide that she is trying to fill the whole sheet of paper with shading.

"*Qu'est-ce que c'est?*" Fleur asks. "Is she trying to communicate or just, *je ne sais pas* ..."

"Don't know," says Clémence, "but I think she may need more suitable drawing materials. Shall I go to the art place and buy some?"

"*Oui*," says Fleur, almost shouting, as Clémence overhands her chair towards the door. "We need to do something, maybe this is it. Get some money from *la petite caisse*[37]. Not paint, too messy; things like coloured pencils and markers, and a sketch book – how big should it be? Big enough but not *intimidant* ... Get a receipt!"

***

The Laniers spend a long night considering what M Duchamps had not wished Patrice to know about. Both have already read the feminist perspective of Mary Garrard, and Colette has produced the thesis by American undergraduate Hannah Criswell. They are ready to dissect and disseminate it.

"We need to keep in mind," starts Colette, "that this is an undergraduate thesis – although none the worse for that. It makes some very interesting points."

"Such as?" asks Patrice. "I have never really understood what 'social psychology' means."

"Ah. It's just mumbo jumbo, you would think; considering things in terms of other things – in this case, the mind and the environment, in place of her life and work. Feminist perspectives and the psychoanalysis of rape concepts don't much take into consideration how life was lived in the seventeenth century."

"Well, *oui*. Sounds interesting – different, anyway. Give me the gist."

"*D'accord*. Mademoiselle Criswell says that one must establish what it was like being a woman and an artist in

---

37   petty cash

the times we are talking about."

"*Oui*," says Patrice, "a bit obvious I should have thought."

"It might be about certain things being more acceptable then than now. Doesn't make them all right, though, does it?"

"*Quoi?* Rape, you mean?"

"Probably. Although I also seem to recall Ms Lapierre saying that Artemisia lived more or less as a single woman, as a single mother even, for most of her life."

"She didn't marry, then?"

"Oh. She did. But it wasn't very successful, and I think she must have thrown him out at some stage. His name was Pierantonio Stiattesi, a Florentine artist, although it's reputed that her second daughter (she had two) was likely fathered by the Spanish ambassador. She also had three sons. Looks like she had the odd affair – although with her work rate I don't know how she had time!"

"So, what's the first point?" Patrice asks.

"The death of her mother," answers Colette, "when she was *12 ans* and had three younger brothers, who she seems to have brought up. My sense is that her father wasn't a bad provider, he was a well-known artist and in demand, but a bit helpless around the house. There was also a woman called Tuzia, who was a kind of guardian, companion, but not really a mother figure, when Artemisia was a bit older."

"Not known to be the mistress of her father?" asks Patrice, who has a suspicious mind.

"No one says that," says Colette, "although anything is possible. But, as Orazio was a widower, why would he not have married her? She might have already been married, I suppose – the mediaeval era is a bit spotty in that area."

"Um. So, Artemisia learned from her father and continued following Caravaggio – and became a professional painter in her own right, in a time when women's duties were to do with home and family."

"*Oui*. It was quite odd, I gather, for a man to have an unmarried daughter, independently earning her own living in his house. So already Artemisia was peculiar. No suitor, no babies."

"And how long did that carry on?" asks Patrice.

"Until after Orazio arranged for Agostino Tassi, an acquaintance of his, and an extremely proficient painter of detail, to come to the studio and tutor her. She was, though, well integrated into the local artistic community, not just as Orazio's daughter but as a female artist who was rather different. Women artists, there were a few, mostly painted still life and portraits – some holy pictures. Artemisia attempted huge, dramatic subjects – subjects usually painted by men."

"And that's when the trouble started, after her father brought the serpent into the garden?"

"*Oui*. Although he might not, at that time, have been a serpent. It was somehow acceptable that 'forcible deflowering' happened, and the participants often went on with a sexual relationship until their marriage – and she had *17 ans*, quite an old virgin for those days. This happened with Tassi and Artemisia – he had promised her he would marry her. He could not have done so, however, because he was already married to someone else – although he may have killed her …"

"Nasty Tassi," says Patrice. "Does Mademoiselle Criswell say a lot about the rape?"

"She does. A lot about how rape myths develop in certain ways due to the cultural. You might almost think it was acceptable. And when you read some of the trial stuff – which, of course, came later – it is very clear that the victim was blamed."

"Not much different nowadays," says Patrice. "Although that isn't true. It is better, much better. It's just still not good enough."

Colette gives him a big smile. She approves of his thoughts on this.

"We do need to look at what Mademoiselle Criswell says about the *Judith* paintings," says Colette. "You will want to make a reduction of them."

Patrice locates Mlle Criswell's description of the First *Judith*, the one which was, seemingly, painted around 1612, now hanging in the Capodimonte in Naples. He reads the whole section to Colette, before beginning his phenomenological reduction.

It takes him some time to produce the 465 words he needs to understand it as much as possible:

Phenomenological Reduction of Criswell's Description of *Judith and her Maidservant with the Head of Holofernes*, 1610

The picture referred to as the First *Judith* is that supposed to have been painted by Artemisia Gentileschi in 1610, when she was working in her father's studio in Rome. The artist, then, had 17 years.

There is much speculation around her rape by Agostino Tassi in 1611, and a conclusion that this determined the remainder of her life and work.

The description contains the following statements about the physicality of the work:

> The painting is intended to be viewed vertically (the modern portrait orientation)

> There are abrasions on the surface and the painting has been subject to harsh cleaning

Shadowed areas have deteriorating dark tones

Part of the painting has been excised on the left side – may have contained other elements

The description contains the following comments on the moment of action:

The action depicted is the moment of beheading

The beheading is not yet complete at time of painting

The technique is described as:

Chiaroscuro is used, where the main elements are light and dark – these are used to light, brightly, the focus, whilst pushing back the dark background

There is a soft highlight from the left – further illuminating the main focus

The three figures are entwined while remaining individual

The skill of the artist is described within the following terms:

Technique shows masterly rendering of flesh and fabric

Figures of both women are rendered fuller than many other examples in the genre – showing undeniable strength and power

Their sleeves are pushed up in a workmanlike fashion

The top margin of Judith's breasts is rendered in a way which underlines her ability to seduce.

She is calm and determined, holding the sword in her right hand while her left holds Holofernes's hair tightly. This appears realistic

Holofernes's face attracts the gaze after Judith – his eyes are rolled back, mouth slightly open. He is probably in shock but still able to fight (but not enough to get out of the situation)

Holofernes's body is mostly concealed, keeping focus on the beheading

The maidservant, often called Abra (which just means a maid and is not a name), in this work, is of an equivalent age to Judith – there is a definite equality to them

In the Apocrypha story, Abra is not in the room at all, she is left outside the tent

In this painting, Abra supports Judith by holding Holofernes down on the bed – Judith could not do the deed without her

Description of what the action looks like:

Most of the bottom half of the painting shows the bed, more than one mattress, sheets, blood

The rendering of the blood is rusty, providing a grittiness, and there is little sign of an arc of blood – the flow being straight on to soak the sheet

The sword enters the neck in a darkened section

Colette, who has been shuffling through various piles of paper on the table, asks whether there are things in all this with which he does not agree. Of course, there are.

"It's a workable description," he says, "but still manages not to comment on some things I would not do."

"Like?"

"The blood," he answers, starting from the end. "A plain description would have described it without hinting at the lack of an arc. And I am drawn to the odd rendering of the sword. It strikes me as floppy, not realistic. Criswell's description is quite a good starting point, though. I shall have to have a complete set for the four main paintings, plus our own *Judith*. Then I can make a plausible comparison – maybe even see whether ours could possibly a part of the set."

***

On Monday morning, Colette is delighted to receive a phone call from Antoine LeBrun, inviting her to meet for lunch at a rather pleasant restaurant just around the corner from her office. She wonders what he might want, although Antoine is enough of a friend and confidant to meet just for *un bavardage*[38].

He is already at the table when she arrives, a couple of minutes late, and stands for a friendly hug and to allow the waiter to seat her. The table looks, nicely, over a small garden at the back. It is too cold to eat outside, but it is fine to look at.

Antoine is looking well and is dressed in a suit more decent than the ones he used to wear to work. The tie is new, in shades of rust and yellow – nothing like the conservative neckwear he alternated for six years in the office. He asks Colette how she goes, and she says that she goes well. Antoine goes well too and passes the menu.

When they have ordered the soup, followed by *poisson*

---

38   a chat

et salades[39], he says he is wanting to ask how she does with Lucie.

"Oh, it's fine," she replies. "I found it difficult to accustom myself to not having you there, Antoine, but you trained Lucie well and she is a clever woman."

"That is why I chose her," he says. "That, and I thought you and she would get on together. She is different from me – not just because she is female, but she is younger and quicker, also funnier. I have been losing my sharpness over the last year or so, and you really need someone to be able to jump ahead rather than trail behind."

"I never saw any sign of that with you," says Colette. "You were ideal for me right up until you left!"

"I did my best," he says gravely. The soup arrives and they are quiet as they eat it. As they wait for the fish, Antoine asks about the monsieur.

"Seconded to Interpol," says Colette, "and spending some time in Lyon. He's learning about painting now, before he starts an investigation into a forgery, or a misattribution, or a stolen or lost masterpiece. Or some such thing."

"I did not know he had expertise in that area," says Antoine. "Although I have always felt it could be very interesting. I enjoy looking at art myself."

"He doesn't actually have any expertise in that," says Colette. "He's trying to acquire a certain amount because that's what he does – you know – but they don't want him as an expert, they have plenty. They want him to analyse texts and various written forms to give them clues to what went on in the seventeenth century and since. You know, his phenomenology."

Antoine ducks his head to acknowledge that he not

---

39   fish and salads

only understands this, he recalls Patrice's tendency to over-research the background. He realises, which Colette really doesn't, that this is because her husband has a need to not be caught on the wrong foot. His usual serene aspect balances on it.

"I hope he doesn't develop Stendhal's syndrome," says Antoine.

"*Qu'est-ce que c'est?*" asks Colette.

"Oh, it was something I read somewhere," replies Antoine. He has frequently said this to Colette, broadening her focus to help with situations at which they were looking. He reads widely, has a broad approach to everything. This is why he understands Patrice's approach to knowing things.

"It's a thing which hasn't made the DSM[40] yet but might in the future. Said to be triggered by looking at a lot of art, painting, sculpture, even things like the city of Florence as a whole. An alternative name is 'Florence syndrome'. Maybe it might bring back past or early trauma or something ..."

"Well, if whether it's in DSM or not, it's thought to be a mental illness rather than physical."

"*Oui.*"

"What might the symptoms be?" she asks.

"Fainting," says Antoine. "Feeling overwhelmed. Hallucinations. Tachycardia. Chest pains. Anxiety."

"What do you think? Sounds a bit hey-ho to me. DSM, therefore, psychiatry, not taking it up? Where did it come from?"

"A psychiatrist working in Florence," says Antoine, "Dr Graziella Margherini. She wrote a book in Italian, which doesn't appear to have been translated into any other language – which can't be a good sign. I don't think I

---

40   The Diagnostic and Statistical Manual of Mental Disorders

believe in it for the moment, although I'm willing to be persuaded if there is any actual research I have overlooked. Couldn't find any."

"So, it's just a vague possibility at present?" says Colette as the fish arrives, looking and smelling wonderful. "Funny, *n'est-ce pas*, how the existence of some psychiatric conditions so often requires faith?"

"*Je suis d'accord.*"

9

Mercard is showing photographs of Gertrude in the extended area surrounding the Hôtel des Jardins, accompanied by a couple of uniformed *PJ* officers. He is aware that he is, perhaps mistakenly, involving Gertrude in the Lindholm case when there is no necessity to do so; it could be completely separate. It's just that he has a feeling, and he has already constructed a scenario which would fit. This is a bad idea, and he has not mentioned it to *le patron* because he can predict what would happen. Patrice has frequently explained the phenomenological *epoché*,[41] and although René doesn't fully understand how policepersons can do it, he tries his best.

As far as René knows to date, no one had either seen anything of the Lindholm defenestration of a week ago or can recognise Gertrude from the photograph. None of the uniformed *PJ* officers has been in contact either. He presumes no one has found anything; there seems to be

---

41 bracketing of previous knowledge and opinions to try to start from "the things themselves"

absolutely no evidence. Apart from the dead body of Monsieur Lindholm. He sighs and knocks the door of the next house in the street. It is divided into flats, and he rings the top entry bell first.

René rings the top entry buzzer first as the house is divided into flats, and persuades the timid-sounding woman who answers to let him in. He pants his way up the stairs, arriving breathless on the *dernier étage*. René is approaching *30 ans* and has been neglecting his *adhésion au gymnase*[42] in the traditional French way. He makes a promise to the exquisite Greek Gods that he will attend this week. He knows, in the back of his mind, that he will find himself far too busy.

The young woman who opens the *appartement* door is extremely thin and dressed in a very short scarlet mini dress, partnered with long, dangling red and gold plastic earrings. She has a tattoo of a rose on her left bicep, also red. René has a deep phobia about needles and cannot bear tattoos of any kind (nor piercings, naturally). He stops himself from turning away from her, as well as suspending the assumption that she is a *poule*.[43] He asks her if she was at home on the night in question or, if not, she was where? She says she was out with a friend. They had visited *une discothèque*.

He asks her where, and what it is called. She tells him, first, that she is not sure as she doesn't speak French all that well. Although he has noticed a foreign accent, it is by no means strong. Her French seems serviceable. He tells her this and asks from where she comes.

"Latvia," she says, "from Riga."

René asks his question again, and she tells him she thinks the disco is called something like "Varavīksne".[44] The club

---

42   gym membership
43   tart, prostitute
44   The Rainbow – Latvian

is called l'Arc-en-Ciel,[45] and it is in the next street from the Hôtel des Jardins.

"Did you go at all into the street next to that of the discothèque? That would be rue Mondoré?"

"*Oui*," she says, having reverted to her original well-learned French. "We came home that way, it is a straight line."

"There was an incident," says René, "that night, around midnight, so into the Friday morning. Did you happen to be in the street at that time?"

"*Non*," she says, "but we heard police sirens as we were just turning the corner. We didn't know what had happened until we saw in the newspaper that someone had jumped."

René, disappointed, writes the details of her name and address, along with those of her friend, on his tablet. The friend is a neighbour from further down on the other side of the street. He fishes in his pocket for the photograph of Gertrude and shows it to her, asking if she knows this person. She lets out a slight gasp and says:

"*Oui, c'est* Mollie!"

René leaves the Latvian woman, who has told him that Mollie is British, to cross the street and talk to her friend, a Chinese woman who is called Chang Su-Ming. Ms Chang is a little older than the Latvian *meuf*.[46]

***

Patrice arrives at the Lyon headquarters just before *12 heures* on Monday, and reports to Duchamps's office. The *commissaire* is today wearing a dark blue suit with white shirt and silver cufflinks. The hair is gelled as before. He manages to summon a slight smile for Patrice as they shake hands.

---

45   The Rainbow – French
46   girl, woman – Verlan (from *femme*)

They get straight down to business, as if there is no time to lose.

"*Allons*," says Duchamps, indicating a chair by the side of his own, where Patrice can sit and look, with him, at the large picture book, which is open at two coloured illustrations. One Patrice recognises as Artemisia Gentileschi's *Self-Portrait as the Allegory of Painting*, and the other, clearly on the same subject, not by the *maestra*. "Tell me what you see."

Patrice, feeling partly like a schoolboy, partly like a half-trained art person, looks for longer than he needs, just to make the point that he is really looking, not skimming.

"This is the picture my wife and I saw in London," he says, "at the Hampton Court. It is the *Self-portrait as the Allegory of Painting* by Artemisia Gentileschi. She painted it while she was in England, around 1638."

"And what about the other one?"

"That isn't."

"Why not?"

"It's a copy."

Duchamps flexes his fingers and repeats: "Tell me what you see."

"I see a female painter, painting on a surface the head of a man with a beard and moustache. The artist is holding a palette rather uncomfortably in her left hand, with red and yellow pigments and some others suggested but not specified. She is dressed quite finely, with an expensive-looking brooch and an embroidered or laced sleeve. She has a nice gold-coloured wrap around her, over what may be a green dress – not workmanlike. She has an earring in her left ear—"

"Er," says Duchamps, "why not say 'she's wearing earrings'?"

"I can only see one ear," replies Patrice. "I have no idea

whether she has another earring or not. Or even another ear."

"Excellent!" says Duchamps. "This is what I want. Please go on."

"The artist's pose is facing the viewer in a kind of three-quarter view, but she is looking out straight at the viewer."

"*D'accord.* Now tell me the differences you see from the painting on the other page."

"Okay. The whole painting is less subtle than the Artemisia. It looks superficially similar, but it really is not. It isn't supposed to be about the artist painting Jean Dupont or whoever he is. It's meant to be an allegory of painting. So, there should really be no subject in the painting. There is less impression of a working painter – dress and wrap too fancy, brooch and earring too.

"This" – he touches the painting he is sure is not from the brush of Gentileschi – "does not have the necklace which is in the other painting. The jewellery might not be important if it were not for the mask on the chain. But it's an iconographic representation signifying an allegory of painting, so very important.

"The anatomy of the painting hand in the real Artemisia is superior; it looks like a working person's hand, a hand which can do, is doing, great work. The main thing, I think, is that the architecture of the work is so different. In the real Artemisia, she leans into a position which is authentic, kind of triangular, but innovative; she is working, not posing for her portrait."

"Would you be surprised to learn that this picture" – Duchamps taps the coloured photograph on the right-hand side of the open book – "was attributed to Artemisia for a long time?"

"I don't know," says Patrice. "Before I started to divide it into its constituent parts, I thought it was quite like the real one. But now I don't – it simply reminds me of it. The architecture of my mind on this subject has changed; I can no longer see it as anything other than a not-too-great copy." He screws his face up trying to get back to his previous attitude (intentionality) and finding it impossible.

"Just so," says Duchamps. "That is what I want. I want you to look. I want you to use your analytical capability, so that we have new eyes on this."

"Not on this subject, specifically, though, is it?" says Patrice. "I thought it was something to do with a religious painting, possibly another *Judith*?"

"*Oui*. It's about a possible Gentileschi *Judith* which has turned up in Helsinki of all places. We have been asked to, almost, arbitrate between two sets of experts, most from Italy, who disagree whether it's by Artemisia or not. One group says definitely (because of provenance), the other one says not (because of brushwork and pentimenti). Neither will allow the other to win. So, they are at an impasse.

"If we, or the Finns, got in another expert to side with either of them, it could get very bloody. There are also political implications – and, of course, the whole Italian fine art crowd is weighing in as well – they want it back if it's real, but want to despise it if it's not. Our director felt that we needed to do it in a different way.

"Because there are original documents, bills of sale and personal letters available, it may be possible to find some evidence, or at least something which is plausible, that might give us a nudge one way or another. There are several Artemisia paintings which are thought to be lost, and which are mentioned in texts. So ..."

"And that's where I come in?" says Patrice.

"*Mais certainement.*"

***

"She's drawing a car!" says Fleur Olivier. "Is she trying to tell us something? She's been in someone's car – been taken somewhere?"

"Or maybe she just likes cars?" says Clémence.

Olivier groans and agrees that may be true.

"I'm not sure that bringing her here is getting the best out of her," says Fleur. "Would we be better to talk to her at Madame Paston's? At least she might see it as a safe place."

"*Je ne sais pas*," says Clémence. "Is it, does she see it, as safer than here, where her shining knight, René, brought her out of whatever was happening to her where she was?"

"Have you seen him today?"

"I haven't. I think he was going out to show her photograph around a wider area, as well as ask about whether anyone had anything to say about Monsieur Lindholm."

"We need to watch this," says Olivier. "We are joining these cases together and we shouldn't yet. And the possible murder or suicide of Monsieur Lindholm is perhaps more important."

"Is it?" asks Clémence. "I am not so sure. *Les vivants ne sont-ils pas plus importants que les morts?*[47]"

***

"The painting I am considering is possibly one of the 'lost' Artemisias from her Florentine period," says Patrice. "It is presently in Finland, but no one seems to know how it got there. It was found on a landfill site in the north of the country."

The Laniers are having dinner in a restaurant on the Île-St-Louis; they make sure to go out for dinner at least

---

47   aren't the living more important than the dead?

95

once every week to ward off the staying in all the time, reading, which is a danger. Amélie is out with friends and indulging in that strange modern habit of a sleepover. Jean-Pascal is writing an essay, Sartre draped over his feet between him and the *radiateur*.

Colette wears a cream Merino-wool dress, the skirt cut on the cross to give a little flare below the waist. The neckline reveals a fine gold chain with a rose-pink stone set in a minimal gold diamond shape. The necklace was given to Colette by her parents on her twenty-first birthday. The earrings are the tiny golden roses Patrice gave her last year in Languedoc-Roussillon.

"Will you need to investigate the provenance?" asks Colette.

"Need? Probably not. It may well be relevant, though, and I should like to know where the painting has been. But whether it's genuine or not is the most important. Although" – he looks thoughtful – "it's hard to attribute something to someone without closely examining the provenance. It needs 'connoisseurship'. I must go to Helsinki next week to have a look at the actual painting. Photographs, of course, are insufficient."

"*Zut!*" says Colette. "I can't come next week. There is a conference in Tours which I must attend."

"It will be very cold," says Patrice, mentally assessing his winter wardrobe. His wife is looking *vénère*.[48] She has clearly been hoping for foreign travel – they have never been to Scandinavia. Colette takes a deep breath and changes the subject, a bit, not much.

"How will you use the phenomenology to investigate this, then?" she asks. "What they want you for ..."

Patrice is grateful for the slight change; he does not want

---

48   angry – Verlan (from *énervé* – it creeps in!)

to discuss travel with Colette over the duckling *á la Niçoise.*
He is saving the other thing for the walk home.

"What Duchamps thinks is that I shall examine the bills
of sale and letters and diaries, and follow up, if possible,
that such-and-such a painting was made and sold, or given
away, or copied, or whatever. Which is fine."

"Sounds tedious. You are going to do other things,
though, aren't you?"

"*Oui,*" says Patrice. "I must take a wider view than
that. I must look at paintings, not just other people's
descriptions of them, in a phenomenological way too, as
if they are documents. Thinking about perception and
intention as well as materials and colours and technique –
what is given, or beginning to be given. A way to identify
the thing itself."

"Aha. So, you are looking at what is there and what is
not. And what might have been meant by the artist. You
start, don't you, with an actual painting, seeing the frame,
the canvas, the paint ..."

"*D'accord,* followed by the brushstrokes, the palette,
the structure, the symbols or props, and then who
commissioned it, if anyone, what it depicts, is there politics
around it?"

Colette interrupts him with a muttered mention of the
Council of Trent and the Counter-Reformation.

"*Absolutement!*" says Patrice. "It could be important."

"How long have you got to do this?" asks his sceptical
wife. "Five years?"

***

"So," says Colette, "you are taking some young woman
whom you met in Lyon with you to Helsinki." They are
walking over the bridge to the Île-St-Louis, and he has just

97

told her he has asked for Chloë Valéry, the art historian, to assist him. His wife is not pleased.

"I need a bit of help," he says, trying not to look like a pleading worm by not reminding her that she can't come anyway. "Our first sight of the painting is very important – and I want an extra pair of eyes."

Colette humphs at the triviality of that before she decides *c'est teub*.[49] She decides, in a flash, on a different plan. It will, anyway, be extremely cold in Finland.

They arrive home shortly and Patrice, in cowardly reparation, makes the hot chocolate for them and Jean-Pascal, who is still in the *salon*, asleep on the sofa, absorbing information from a heavy book of electronic engineering through his stomach wall.

Colette leans over to plant a kiss on her son's forehead, waking him suddenly. He pretends to have been reading as she asks him how far he got.

"Oh," he says, sounding like he's breathing marshmallows, "I read a lot, but some of it I don't quite understand – although my piece for tomorrow is finished."

"Good!" says Colette. "Could you do it earlier next time? You are always at the last minute."

Jean-Pascal sits up to take his cup of chocolate from Patrice and rubs his eyes.

"I know," he says. "I find it easier to work when there is *une date limite*.[50]"

Neither parent replies to this – all Laniers are cut from the same cloth.

---

49   this is stupid – Verlan
50   a deadline

10

René Mercard arrives back at *le Trente-Six salle squad*, still holding the secret that he has got a real name for Gertrude. It is around *16 heures* and the lights have all come on, banishing the darkness beyond grimy windows. Fleur and Clémence are huddled at the desk of the former, pouring over something.

"*Bonsoir, mesdames*," he says, and asks what they are doing. Clémence wheels back a little to let him see the drawing of a car. It is now coloured lime green but has no number plate. It is recognisable as a Renault Clio. He looks puzzled.

"*Qu'est-ce que c'est?*" he asks.

"*Un auto*," says Fleur.

"Gertrude has drawn it," says Clémence. "We think she may have been driven in it from somewhere. We thought she might write the answers to questions, but she has drawn instead. And it is not the answer to anything we ask. She still hasn't spoken, not even said her name."

René's face takes on a triumphant smile, and he tells them she doesn't need to tell them her name any more.

"It's Mollie," he says, "it's Mollie Cartwright. And she's from England."

***

Patrice turns up at avenue des Magnolias, to visit Pucelle, in the hope that his friend and *commissaire adjoint* is in. He has decided to use his need to go to Helsinki to tempt Pucelle to help him out of his difficulty in leaving *le*

Trente-Six in the care of Fleur and René. It is not that he does not trust them. Not precisely. He is more concerned that they will rend one another.

Pucelle is in. She answers the door, bids him to enter, and they go into the kitchen to make drinks. Pucelle is looking well, much better, obviously, than when she returned from her trip into the drug culture, although still tired and thin. He suspects her of working too hard for the refugee charity – which she is still sampling, and from which Patrice wishes to extract her. Somehow, it doesn't take much time to achieve his aim. She will attend at *le Trente-Six* when she has freedom to do so.

***

Mademoiselle Valéry meets Patrice at Charles de Gaulle airport for the joint Air France–Finnish Airlines lunchtime service to Helsinki. This is the fastest service on the route. Chloë has two bags: one cabin, one check-in. She says she is travelling light; nothing which doesn't go in the two bags goes with her. She seems quite flustered, and Patrice asks her if she is afraid of flying.

"*Non*," she says, "not at all. I love it. I love the split second when the plane begins to get airborne – the take-off point. It's fresh every time because I never think it is possible."

"Are you thinking of René Thom's 'catastrophe theory'?" asks Patrice. "When something happens, and smooth change becomes discontinuous?"

Chloë looks at him as if he is *fou*, and asks him what on earth is that?

"Oh, nothing," says Patrice, shamefaced. "It's mathematical. We can discuss it more if we need it."

"Ah," says Chloë. She checks in her larger bag and asks

the *commissaire* where is his. He says he has just his shoulder bag, and repeats back to her what she said about nothing going if it won't go in. They both laugh, still *un petit peu* unsure of one another.

Chloë is wearing dark jeans, and a padded jacket in a coral colour, with black, workmanlike ankle boots. Her red hair is tied up in a high ponytail, and she wears little make-up. Patrice notices, though, that the fingernails are manicured and polished in a near perfect match for the jacket.

They go through security with no problems and board the aeroplane. The flight takes less than three hours.

***

Helsinki is a beautiful city and Finland an exquisite country. When Patrice and Chloë arrive at Helsinki-Vantaa airport, their host, a Finnish policeman called Jaakkima Kyllo (call me Jak), is waiting for them. He is exactly what they have been expecting: tall, slim, and blonde, with striking light blue eyes.

He is lightly bronzed, and the French police are unsure whether this is suntan or sunbed. He wears a beautiful silver-grey fine-wool suit, with a pale blue shirt and a bright blue silk tie. His hand is warm as he shakes, first with Chloë, second with Patrice. He turns and introduces them to his assistant, a long-haired Finnish blonde called Lumi Salonen.

"*Hyvää iltapäivää, kuinka voit?*[51]" she says, giving them a bright smile.

Both *PJ* are bothered that the Finnish detectives are going to speak to them in Finnish (known to be one of the most difficult languages to learn) but are immediately

---

51   Good afternoon, how are you? – Finnish

reassured to hear Jak's straightforward French with little accent. It turns out that he can speak English, if they prefer, as well as Swedish and German.

"We are taking you to the Hotel Seurahuone," says Jak. "It's good, and in the middle of the city. We can let you have a car if you want to drive, although Helsinki is quite compact and it is easy to get around on foot. And, naturally, we can arrange for you to be driven if that is better; you are our honoured guests. If you want to see the sights, we can arrange that too."

He takes Chloë's suitcase and hefts it into the boot of a Finnish police car, navy blue and white smart BMW Series 7, whilst Lumi looks, in vain, for Patrice's luggage. On the way to Kaivokatu 12, where the traditional 180-year-old hotel is situated, both Finns give them the tourist chat. They learn that Helsinki is a seaside city with parks and over three hundred offshore islands. It has many restaurants and nightclubs. Its population is almost 621,000 people, and the temperature from December to March is between zero degrees and minus thirty degrees centigrade.

"It doesn't feel as cold as that!" says Chloë, and they all agree that it doesn't.

"Cold enough for winter sports," says Lumi, "which we have quite close to the city. Skiing, snowboarding ..."

They stop the car, driven fast by Jak, outside the hotel and, leaving it in what appears to be a loading bay, escort the visiting detectives into reception, registering on their behalf, telling them that they should rest and have a good meal. They will be collected at 08.30 tomorrow to go to the auction house and gallery, which is in the country.

With that, Chloë and Patrice are efficiently left to themselves. Patrice suggests that they settle in and then meet in the restaurant for something to eat.

"I know it's early," he says, "but I'm starving!"

Chloë's still-student stomach is always starving.

***

"Mademoiselle Cartwright?" says *Inspecteur* Olivier. The girl does not look up; she does not seem to recognise her name. Noticing someone is there, she smiles happily at Fleur and René as if she has known them for years. But still does not speak.

Both policepersons sit down opposite her, and René talks in his softest voice, asking her if it is her car. She shakes her head. Although it is a ludicrous question, she readily forgives him. She puts aside the drawing she has been working on and begins another. She draws a person, a human being, a man. The *PJ* wait.

Mollie's ability to draw cars seems far in excess of her ability to draw people. It is true that the man has two legs, two arms and a head, but the facial features are rudimentary, as is the wild hair. She has coloured the hair in bright blue and is now adding in a car at the side. She really likes lime green.

"You aren't able to speak, are you, Mollie?" asks René gently, in English. Amazingly, because she has previously been almost totally innocent of body language, she shakes her head once. "Can you write down the answers to my questions?"

The young girl looks baffled and returns to her drawing of the man with few features, standing by the lime-green car.

"I think we need to find the car," says Clémence.

***

The *PJ* plan to retire early to their beds and so decide to have a light meal in the hotel coffee shop. The snack proves to be quite hearty: *grillimakkarat,* large Finnish sausages in a bun for Chloë, *leipäjuusto,* fried cow's milk cheese with lingonberry jam and rye bread for Patrice. Lapin Kulta local beer for both.

They talk over their meal. Patrice takes the opportunity to give Chloë the instructions he wants her to observe tomorrow when they look for the first time at the painting.

"I know," he says, "that you have professional ways of doing this sort of thing; special ways of looking at paintings. This time, though, just at the start, I wonder if you can suspend all that? Is it possible that you can hold back all the knowledge in your conscious mind and just use your subconscious?"

Chloë, again, gives him a look as if he has asked her to eat a live duck.

"It's difficult," says Patrice, "I know. But sometimes it gives us something that we can't get any other way. It does come from your expertise, accumulated over years of hard work and close attention, but it works extremely quickly, without you necessarily being aware of it. And, more often than not, it is rather useful.

"The painting will be covered; I have asked for that. And they will unveil it in front of us. I want you to say the first word which comes into your head."

"How does it work?" asks Chloë. "I am wondering if, perhaps, I have heard something about it before."

"Well, there is a fairly well-known example in the art world," Patrice says. "There was a kouros, you know, the Greek sculptures of young men? This one was about to be purchased by the Getty Museum of America. It was well documented and guaranteed genuine, but some curators or other high-flying experts thought it was a fake – even though they couldn't say why they thought that."

"I remember," she says. "And it turned out that it was a fake, wasn't it?"

"It was," says Patrice. "This is the same. This is what I want you to do: disconnect your conscious knowledge, hard-won though it is. Do you think you can do that? And see what happens?"

"I'll give it a try," says Chloë. "I can only do my best."

"*D'accord*. I'm happy I managed to remember the kouros story," he says. "I didn't really want to give you the other anecdotal case I know …"

"What's that?"

"My own first reaction when I saw the *Judith*, the first one, with Judith in the blue dress – the one now at the Capodimonte in Naples."

"Why?" asks Chloë. "Whatever did you see?"

"A new beginning, a new birth," he says. "Judith and her maid delivering Holofernes's head in blood and pain."

"*Oh, mon dieu!*" says Chloë, in shock.

***

Lucie places the morning's mail on the desk before Colette, who appears to have finished looking at her email, flagging up anything which she needs to deal with later. There isn't a lot of snail mail, unless it's specifically required; most people use the internet.

"How are the preparations going for our conference with the American pharma people next week?" asks Colette. She has tried to leave Lucie alone as much as possible to do the work – as Antoine would have done it – but she is still too worried that the new assistant will do something wrong. Antoine has said that Lucie can be trusted to bring anything she isn't sure about to her *patronne*, but Colette has been working with Antoine for so long ... It is *difficile*.

"It's fine," says Lucie. "There will be five of them. Don't know why so many, but that is what they said. I have booked them in to the Hôtel Miraisent, just down the road, so we will not need a car, we can walk. And I have sent them a sort of itinerary or programme, which is what they asked."

"They are only coming to see me and Docteur Bowers," says Colette. "What kind of programme are they expecting?"

"Oh, I think they want to know what they are doing every minute. It is an American thing ... they like to use all their time well."

"And should we be encouraging it, do you think?" asks Colette imperiously, looking over her reading glasses at Lucie.

"We do not know them," says her assistant, "so I thought we might be careful just this time. I have only scheduled the three meetings you asked for; they did not ask for anything else from you, so I did not bother too much. I put in the evening dinner you said you could probably stand, and Blanche Bowers said she would take them for lunch on Wednesday. Tuesday, I said I would take them to the palace. They can either do an official tour (which might be best) or wander around on their own. I said they can ring me when they want to come back – so I can get on with some work. I expect that to last all day.

"I have booked all their meals, as well as a bit of a tour around our own offices; you can join if you like, but you do not have to – you must admit that is the most exciting part!"

Colette rolls her eyes and agrees. Offices, very small laboratories, a couple of conference rooms. All super exciting.

Colette thanks Antoine under her breath. Everything is fine.

***

There are still several persons who were staying at the Hôtel des Jardins on the tenth to eleventh of January who need to be reinterviewed. René has the list, and is going to work through them, whilst Fleur and Clémence try to work with Mollie Cartwright, who is taking up a lot of their time.

René realises that Bernard Cloche lives in Blois, not that far away. Perhaps he and Fleur could take a drive to talk to him again? Face-to-face interviewing, he feels, still works better than the telephone.

The next two on the list, Albert and Brigitte Sansone, Fleur has done. He has himself talked to M Denthwaite – although he didn't believe what the New Zealander said – and the Julianes in Paris. Clémence interviewed Mlle Barnier at the hotel. So, who is left? Mme Magda Simon, and M André Melzer and M Pierre Renault. The last two both live out of the capital, one in Nantes and one in Nancy.

11

Colette arrives home after a very long day and finds Amélie already there, on the sofa in the *salon*, with Sartre on her lap. The Bedlington yips at Colette's entrance and gives her the biggest smile of which Bedlingtons are capable. She asks Amélie if she would like a drink of something.

"*Non*," says the girl, stroking Sartre's head, putting him into a trance, "I am not thirsty."

"I can pour you lemonade if you don't want coffee or tea?"

"*Cimer – rien, Maman.*[52]"

Colette makes herself tea, brings it back into the *salon,* sits down opposite the daughter and dog. Amélie is folding her shoulders into a shrug, expecting a scolding, preparing. They have not talked about Amélie's career choices since the meeting at the school.

"I've been wanting to talk to you about what happened at *ton soirée carrières*[53] the other day ..."

"*Oh, reum, ché aps!*[54]"

"And, *s'il te plaît*, stop speaking that vulgar language!"

"It's only Verlan. *C'est chanmé.*[55]"

"*Non*, it is not," says her mother, trying to close that part of their conversation.

"Please yourself then."

Colette swallows the rebuke which springs to her lips, and reminds herself that she loves this daughter of hers to distraction. She will not alienate her if she can avoid it.

"I wanted to talk with you about what you said to Madame Forestier. You had already told her you wanted to study nursing, hadn't you? She was not prepared for what I had to say at all?"

"*Oui*," says Amélie, "we had watched *un film* about it. All my friends want to be nurses."

"What, clever girls like you?"

"*Certainement!*"

"If they wanted to boil their heads, would you want to do it too? Do you always do what the other girls do, Amélie?"

"*Non*, of course not! But it is *tigen*.[56] I can care for people."

---

52   thank you – nothing, Mum – Verlan (from *merci*)
53   careers evening
54   Oh, Mother, I don't know – Verlan
55   It's wicked (i.e. great!) – Verlan
56   nice, gentle – Verlan (from *gentil*)

"But you will be wasting your brain!" says Colette.

Amélie has had enough. She stands, tipping the little dog from her lap. He stands and shakes himself on the sofa, leaping down to follow as she makes off towards her bedroom.

"Oh, *laisse beton!*[57]" she shouts at her mother.

***

In the morning, Patrice meets Chloë in the restaurant of the Hotel Seurahuone, and they broach the subject of Finnish breakfast. There is a buffet containing *charcuterie, fromages, bœuf, saumon fumé et hareng, salade.*[58] There is a large black porridge pot, with a ladle through a slot in its lid, for customers to help themselves, plus butter and sugar and rye bread, cinnamon rolls, and many kinds of berries.

The *PJ* are standing, slightly overwhelmed by their choices, when Lumi Salonen, dressed in cold-weather gear, including a furry hood (looks like wolf), arrives, coming over to them, yelling "Hi."

She says, in poor French, that she thought they might like some help in selecting their breakfast, "which is very important in Finland," and proceeds to choose for them.

Chloë is helped to a bowl of hot porridge into which Lumi drops a large lump of butter and covers the whole surface with pearls of white sugar. She instructs the Frenchwoman, adding sign language, to let the butter melt, and gives her permission to add yoghurt if she likes.

Patrice, she says, must try something different, which Finns love. He looks a little nervous as she goes through

---

57   forget it! – Verlan
58   cooked meats, cheeses, beef, smoked salmon and herring, also salad

109

the swing door into the hotel kitchen. A few moments later, she returns bearing a dish covered in a linen teacloth, and crosses to the table at which her French colleagues have settled.

"*Pour* Monsieur *le Commissaire*," she announces in better French, placing it in front of him, before revealing an oval-shaped pastry. "A Karelian pie!" She goes to fetch coffee for them – it is "soft", milky Finnish coffee – and then plates of cold cuts, salami, ham, *fromage*, with tomato and onion and green leaves.

Patrice stares at the Karelian pie, which is made of pastry, dark enough to be made with rye flour, filled with a thick rice porridge, egg mashed with butter on top. When he tries it, it is quite delicious. Chloë has already finished her porridge and declared it filling (her major requirement), and is tucking into her own-made rye bread sandwiches with ham, green leaves, tomatoes and mayonnaise.

Lumi has joined them, bringing herself a bowl of porridge with lingonberries and raspberries piled in the centre, as well as large pinwheel-shaped warm cinnamon rolls for all of them.

She speaks now in English, saying that her French is not so good, but they can understand her, can't they? Patrice says that he can, although Chloë's Dutch and Italian are better than her English. Lumi says she has never learned Dutch or Italian and continues in a hybrid of English and French as best she can, which serves – with goodwill.

"We are going to see your painting," she says in this curious mixture, "after we have had breakfast. We shall meet Jak at the place. I will drive you; it is the country, and you would not find it alone. In any case, there will be blizzards today and the temperature will be very low."

She looks at Chloë and Patrice, and asks if they think they are dressed warmly enough? They are not, of course, wearing outdoor clothes. Does this Finnish policeperson think Patrice's perfectly ordinary winter suit and Chloë's jumper and jeans are unsuitable?

"Do you just have what you were wearing yesterday?" she asks.

"*Oui*," says Patrice, "my wool overcoat. Mademoiselle Valéry has a padded jacket."

"Not good enough," says Lumi firmly. "For Finland you need at least a hat. Usually of fur, with pieces for your ears" – she indicates her own grey wolf hat, which is sitting, smartly, on its own seat at the table – "and scarves, wool or fur, and earmuffs. We shall go to a shop." She rises from the table, leads them out of the restaurant. They obtain hats, scarves and earmuffs at considerable cost from a nearby shop, and set off for the countryside with Mlle Salonen in charge.

***

No one has been detailed to take charge of Patrice's unit while both he and M Bonnetain are away. There is no sign of Bonnetain, and Olivier has ventured that he will have *le Trente-Six peste* until he retires. *Le patron*, of course, is in Finland, *de tous les lieux*[59] – about what, they don't really know.

Fleur Olivier is, therefore, in technical charge, and she gets the others together in the *salle squad*. Bonnetain has taken possession of, and locked, Patrice's office.

Both René and Clémence have brought coffee.

"*D'accord*," Fleur begins. "Did you make a file for Mollie, René?"

"I did. Shall I tell you what there is?"

"*Oui*. Although I think we know."

---

59   of all places

111

"We have a girl, who seems about nine or ten years old, who appears to have been, at least, physically abused – she has bruises and cigarette burns, and she is, or was, frightened. She was hiding in the basement of the Hôtel des Jardins. We have moved her to a place of safety, where she has been bathed and dressed in clean clothes.

"She has slept, we think peacefully. She has not been able to speak. We do not know whether she has a physical problem which causes this, or a mental problem. Or whether she is faking. She has not yet been examined by a doctor, although Madame Paston, who is a nurse, feels she has no danger of serious physical injury; about mental injury, she is not so sure.

"We have discovered that the girl is named Mollie Cartwright and is known to some other girls and young women in the nineteenth *arrondissement*. I have requested that the young woman, a Latvian who told me Mollie's name, come in to see us. There is also another woman; her name is Chang Su-Ming, originally from Hong Kong, speaks good French and English as well as Cantonese. She, too, recognises Mollie from a photograph."

"What will you say when they ask you why you didn't take her straight to the hospital so that a rape test could be done?" asks Fleur, although she already knows.

"Because I took a risk," says René, staring at her without shame. "I felt that we could get more out of her if we didn't upset her by insisting on the correct procedure."

"Quite right too," says Fleur. "But we shall have to be ready to field that question when asked."

René blusters a little and says that the *patron* would have done the same. Olivier does not reply.

"As you know," he resumes, "someone spotted Mollie scribbling on some paper and decided to give her paper and *les crayons de couleur*, and she has drawn a car, and a man and a car."

"But the car has no number, and the man has no face," Clémence interrupts.

Fleur looks at her in reproof; although she herself has already interrupted once, it is not done by junior officers. Clémence is desolated.

"What are we going to do next?" says René. "We cannot keep Mollie at Madame Paston's much longer, they are quite full, and we cannot return her to where we found her."

"Or know whether it's safe to return her anywhere," says Clémence before putting her hand over her smart mouth. No one appears to mind this time.

"I am minded to continue encouraging her to draw," says Fleur. "There is probably stuff she could tell us like that. But I expect that Mademoiselle Chang will have useful information. When do you expect her?"

"Tomorrow," says René. "I have ordered a car to go for her. She seemed to be quite confident and I don't think she is easily frightened. I am not bothered about close questioning with her."

"*D'accord*," says Fleur. "The next thing to do, now we know Mollie is English, is to contact the British embassy and get them to take some responsibility. They need to find out if she is a missing person from England; she does not seem to have gone missing *en France*. Now, we must speak about our murder case. Do you wish to present that, Clémence?"

"*Oui, cimer,*[60]" says Clémence. "Monsieur Cedric P. Lindholm arrived on a snowbank outside the Hôtel des Jardins just after midnight on the eleventh of January. We

---

60   yes, thank you – Verlan

have yet no post-mortem results, but the *legiste medicale*[61] has said that he was not killed by the fall from the sixth floor but from blunt object trauma. *L'identité judiciaire*[62] says that the object was a lamp found in the room he seems to have fallen from, because its base has blood and brain tissue.

"Monsieur Lindholm is known to the *PJ* because he may have been involved, last year, in the *terrorisme de* Notre-Dame."

"Let's not call it that," says Fleur. "It wasn't terrorism at all. It was a set-up."

"Sorry. Monsieur Lindholm is American – was American, and a preacher who worked for his church, trying to convert Muslims to Christianity. We have talked to his boss, Docteur Gardiner Baker, and there seem no problems at his employment. We have talked to his colleagues, and they concur. He is said not to have enemies.

"We have brought in Monsieur Lindholm's hard drive, and I have looked at it. At least on the surface, there is nothing much *étonnant*.[63] I need to perform deeper scans to see what has been erased. We have not found his cell phone, although he is said to have had one. We do not know what he was doing in the Hôtel des Jardins when he was on his day off. Especially why he was there during the night.

"We have not yet been able to talk to everyone who was present in the Hôtel des Jardins. It seems that no one, so far, saw anything – but Monsieur Lindholm was not registered at the hotel, and neither the night manager nor the receptionist had seen him before."

***

---

61   forensic pathologist
62   forensic investigator
63   remarkable

Apparently, all Finns are fast drivers and accustomed to driving on ice and snow. Lumi is a faster driver than Jak Kyllo. Patrice ruminates on this as they proceed, at the speed of light, to a small town, the name of which he cannot begin to pronounce, set in the Finnish countryside.

At least they do not have to deal with Paris traffic. Their journey takes about one and a half hours, and Lumi insists that they must stop at a café for early lunch. Finns seem obsessed with food.

The café is very traditional and dark. There are reindeer heads around the walls, and hanging rugs which Lumi says are Sami, from Lapland. There is much dark wood. Lumi says she will get them a treat, traditional Finnish food. Chloë accepts this with insouciance; Patrice is more wary. It could be anything.

They lunch well on salmon soup and mushroom omelette roll, rye bread with everything. And more berries. They arrive at the art auction house gallery at *14 heures*.

Jak is there, talking, simultaneously, to around a dozen people. All male, and tall, except one who is very short, dark and looks like a stereotypical Italian. Jak turns as they enter and introduces the *PJ*, generally, to the men.

"I have been telling our friends here," says the Finnish inspector, "that all you are doing today is having a first look, not trying to determine anything in particular – what is it that you call it? A pre-reflective examination?" Jak looks pleased with himself; he has obviously read something phenomenological. Patrice is happy with this – at least the man has tried – but many people trying to get a handle on the philosophy get it all wrong.

"Thank you," says Patrice. "I am the phenomenologist, and Mademoiselle Valéry is the art historian. We are both police officers."

The men mumble among themselves in a reasonably friendly way. Jak has not attempted to introduce them individually to the *PJ*. Perhaps he thinks there are too many; perhaps he can't recall their names.

To phenomenologist Patrice, the group is a statement, an element of his investigation. He is interested in them.

The detectives are shown into the next room, where an easel in the middle of the large gallery holds a shape covered with a white cloth. There are paintings from varying schools around the walls, some classical and some primitive. Patrice does not try to identify any, although Chloë thinks she may have spotted a landscape of the Norwegian master Hans Dahl.

Everyone, all twelve, groups in front of the covered painting in tense silence. The *PJ* have no idea what to expect. Even so, what they get surprises them.

Chloë Valéry, pale and excited, starts to say:

"*Bon dieu!* It is very remarkable—"

"*Arrête! S'il te plaît, ne dites rien!*[64]"

Patrice's voice is harsh, clipped, irresistible. Chloë does as she is told, and says the single word "*vesce*[65]".

12

Patrice asks all the others please to back away from the painting, leaving him and Mlle Valéry to walk slowly from side to side without speaking, either to one another or the crowd. They take a considerable time about it. One of the

---

64   Stop! Please don't say anything
65   Vetch – possibly wood vetch or similar small roadside plant

assorted admirers suddenly asks, in English, if he should take "the photographs". Patrice turns to him quickly and gives his orders:

"Please do. But do it according to Mademoiselle Valéry's instruction."

He makes a small gesture to Chloë, and returns to his performance, stroking his chin and pacing. She quietly tells the photographer which angles to use – getting the best impressions of the rather small painting.

The police officers continue their silent examinations as the assembled art experts traipse into an adjoining room, where they can be overheard shouting at one another. The evening has already begun when Patrice and Chloë are satisfied for the present.

"All finished?" asks Jak, as the conflict in the next room clearly comes to an end. "Our hosts, the curators of the collection, have invited us all to dinner. I'm sure you will enjoy it."

Chloë demurs because she is not dressed nicely for dinner, but everyone agrees that there is no need for concern. Finnish dining is not always formal, and the visitors will be welcome as they are. Patrice looks around at the group and sees that the men are all respectably dressed in suits that would, mostly, serve them for dinner in Lyon, although perhaps not in Paris. Lumi Salonen is wearing a sage green shirt with embroidery on the yoke and sleeves, and a dark green midi skirt, ending halfway down the length of her moderately-heeled, soft leather boots. She would be welcome in any Paris restaurant.

They take three cars to a restaurant which is about half a mile away, along a road through deep forest, and find their large table reserved and waiting.

***

Monsieur Melzer lives in Nantes, and it is Clémence's duty to telephone him. It so happens that there is a business number for him on the file, and she rings around the middle of the afternoon. They will have to try and clear up all these people from the Hôtel des Jardins today, because there is a team meeting soon, which will include Monsieur Zabi, the *juge d'instruction*.

It is a young-sounding voice which answers:

"*Bonjour*, Maison et Foloff, *comment puis-je vous aider?*"

"May I speak with Monsieur André Melzer, please? It is the *Police Judiciaire* in Paris."

"André Melzer speaking. What may I do for you, madame?"

"I believe," says Clémence, "that you stayed at the Hôtel des Jardins in Paris on the nights of the ninth of January until the fourteenth of January, this year. Is that correct?"

"*Oui*," says a youngish voice. "I was meeting my old friend Pierre. We went to some nightclubs and things."

"Is that Monsieur Renault from Nancy?"

"*Oui*, it is. We have known each other since we began school, but his family moved away when we were about twelve."

She asks him whether he heard anything on the tenth or eleventh of January. They hadn't been in their room. Both he and Monsieur Renault had been out clubbing and didn't get back until *3 heures*. They had been told about the accident by others in the hotel lobby. It is terrible.

Clémence asks him whether he knew Monsieur Lindholm. He didn't. Had he seen the preacher around the hotel at any time? He hadn't. Answering for his friend, M Renault hadn't either.

The *PJ* officer rings Monsieur Renault to check his story agrees. It does. In fact, apart from each man naming the other, his story contains exactly the same words, no more, no less. Funny, thinks Clémence.

***

Over dinner, the policepersons and art experts attempt to be civil to one another, although there is a tense atmosphere in the dining room, as well as half of the art experts seemingly refraining from taking part in any conversation whatever, while the other half never stop talking over one another, sometimes vehemently.

Patrice, Chloë, Jak and Lumi all appear to feel this is rude and concentrate heavily on their food, making the occasional remark to the policeperson next to them. The seating could have been optimised for conversation between them and the art experts – but had not been.

The serious discussions are reserved for the next day.

***

"We have still not managed to interview Madame Magda Simon," says Fleur, sitting sucking her ballpoint pen as if it were a cigarette. "Who has tried telephoning her?"

Both René and Clémence say they have tried, but the number they have is defunct. Mme Simon's name is also missing from voting records in Reims where she is said to live. Fleur says that Reims is, by car, about one hour and forty minutes on A4, does someone want to go?

Neither René nor Clémence is electrified by the idea, and Clémence offers to telephone the local police and, maybe, Hôtel de Ville, and see if they will have a go.

At Fleur's nod, she does this and hands it off to them.

***

Colette and Amélie are having a row. The *fille* has come home from school with her uniform skirt tucked up, short, under a cinched leather belt she has got from somewhere, and her top buttons are undone.

"*Qu'est-ce que tu as fait à tes cheveux?*[66]" asks Colette, surveying the unruly mop of hair, which was blonde and pony-tailed this morning and is now short and black, verging on navy blue. She is shocked because she had thought that her daughter was entirely satisfied with her hair.

"I changed it," says Amélie. "*C'était zarbi!*[67]"

"*Non*, it was not!" says Colette. "And I've told you about using Verlan. I really wish you wouldn't."

"*Laisse béton!*[68]" says Amélie, moving towards the hall door and the route to her bedroom.

"*Non*, I shall not forget it," says Colette, enunciating her Parisian French very precisely. "And sit down while I'm talking to you!"

"Oh, *Maman*," says Amélie, her eyes migrating to look heavenwards. She sits and looks stonily at her mother who is being *guedin*.[69]

"You look terrible, Amélie. You look like a street child!"

"Everyone is looking like this," says Amélie.

"So why would you want to?"

"Because it is *chanmé!*[70]"

Colette does not reply but rapidly sucks in her breath in frustration. She wonders if there is any point in challenging her daughter about the Verlan – would she be better, and more successful, in weighing in just on Amélie's future career? Would there be a greater chance? More important,

---

66   what on earth have you done to your hair?
67   it was bizarre – Verlan (from *bizarre*)
68   forget it! – Verlan
69   crazy, mad – Verlan (from *dingue*)
70   terrific, mean, bad – Verlan (from *méchant*)

anyway. Pick your battles?

"You can't go to medical school interviews looking like that …"

"I'm not going to medical school interviews at all!"

She gets up and stamps out. Again.

*****

Monsieur Nicholas Redfearn, the third secretary of Her Majesty's embassy to the Elysée Palace, arrives from the Faubourg Saint-Honoré, half a day after they have been alerted that one of their citizens is at *le Trente-Six*. He asks at the desk for the *commissaire de police* and says he is here to see a British Citizen named Mollie Cartwright. He speaks in clipped public school English, guaranteed to make any French *PJ* want to slap him soundly around the head.

The desk sergeant picks up the telephone, without speaking to the diplomat, and talks to Fleur Olivier. He has decided that he does not speak English; his view is that diplomats posted to France should speak French. He tells the man:

"Madame Olivier *est en train de descendre.*[71]" He does not ask him to take a seat. It takes Fleur about eight minutes to *descendre*. She welcomes the Englishman, and conducts him to the room, where Mollie is drawing a picture of a horse. She is slightly shocked. Could there possibly be a horse involved?

Mollie looks up and considers the new man carefully. She doesn't smile and returns to the horse after checking out M Redfearn's charcoal suit and striped tie. Getting the harness exactly right is a challenge, and she needs peace and quiet to do it.

Monsieur Redfearn introduces himself and puts out his

---

71   is coming down

hand to shake hers. She does not even look up.

"What is wrong with her?" he asks sourly. "Is she deaf?"

"*Non*," says René, from behind the door. "She can hear, but she doesn't speak."

"How do you know who she is?" asks the diplomat. "And how do you know she is British? Where is her identification?"

"She has no identification," says René, "nothing at all. But we have intelligence that she is British, and that is her name."

"Intelligence? From whom?"

"From someone who knows her," says Fleur. "A friend, neighbour. She recognised a photo."

M Redfearn looks extremely cross.

"So, you don't really know?" he says. "Tell you what. Call me back when you know for sure she's British!" He storms out.

"*Bon dieu!*" says Fleur. "*Relou!*[72]"

Mercard agrees, but ventures that they only have the Latvian girl's word for it.

"We can't be absolutely sure," he says, "because she herself hasn't said. To us."

"Have you any reason to doubt what the Latvian girl said?" asks Fleur. He tells her that he hasn't, but that Chang Su-Ming will be here later and they can hear what she has to say.

***

Neither Patrice nor Chloë can face even biscuits this evening; the lunch and dinner were huge. They have done hardly anything but eat since they arrived in Finland. The reindeer steaks, cloudberry sauce and mashed potatoes were heavy

---

72   oaf – Verlan

even for winter, and followed by Finnish rice pudding with more berries, and reindeer milk cheese with rye bread and crackers … and beer, rather more than any French person could want.

Back in Helsinki, each hotel room has an alcove with seating, and they decide to avail themselves of Patrice's light-blue tweed chairs and rosewood table, trying to get French-style coffee from room service but receiving only the "soft" milky Finnish stuff.

"*D'accord.* Chloë, do you want to explain to me your first impression of the painting, as I asked? You said the word '*vesce*'. What was that about?"

"I did exactly as you said, *patron*," she says. "And it struck me, immediately, that there was one thing in this painting which is not at all in the other *Judiths*. Easy to miss – it is quite small. There is a basket ready to catch Holofernes's head at the front. And it has a tiny stalk of flowers in it – they are a small wayside-type, a weed really. Bright yellow. I thought they looked like an orchid at first, but then said 'vetch' because I don't know what is their actual name." She pauses, screwing up her face. "It seems a bit strange. Is that really what you wanted?"

"*Absolutement!*" says Patrice. "Exactly that. My own impression is not as vivid as yours because I have not had your experience, either in breadth or depth. The word I produced was 'conclusion'. Somehow that everything had been said. I don't yet know what that could possibly mean."

"What do you take from it?" asks Chloë.

"I don't know yet," answers Patrice. "*D'accord,* for now, I don't want your usual impressions. I don't want, at this first stage, you to tell me that it's a Renaissance painting of – whatever it is of – in the style of – whatever it's in the style of – or even what the colours are – you'd say 'palette', wouldn't you?"

"What on earth do you want me to say?" asks Chloë, puzzled. "You've just assassinated my vocabulary!"

A surprised expression crosses Patrice's face but is followed by a more benign one. How can she understand when he hasn't explained yet?

"It's like this," he says, covering his mouth momentarily with his balled fist. "When I was recruited for this job, I wanted to know what the picture looked like but without specific detail.

"I know how difficult that is to arrange. I try to look at things pre-reflectively, getting back to the things themselves. I don't want to know who painted it, with what or on what, in what tradition, the artist's life history, what it's supposed to represent, what palette it uses, to whom, if anyone, it is an homage. Definitely not whether it's a fake or not.

"What do I want? I want to know how big it is. I want to know how it makes you feel – straight off the bat, knowing nothing about it; how it makes me feel, ditto. This is hard. We'll come back to it. The second thing I want to think about is the composition, perhaps even in respect to the way into it, the way the eye is led, the journey around it. What may be hiding behind the tree if there is one."

Chloë sips her coffee, considering what he has said. She tells him that the photographs which were taken at the auction house will arrive soon, so they can have a good look. There will be many photos. Not like having the painting to refer to, when they are not in its vicinity – but she has done her best to get as much detail and clarity as possible.

"Perhaps it will help us to remember how we have seen it?"

"Part of me didn't want to see it yet," says Patrice, "and I shall need to see it again. But for now, the photographs will be fine. Along with your expertise. I have dipped into a couple of books," he says, "and I should not have done that. Extra knowledge, at this stage, doesn't help the method. But I was curious – needed to try to get a handle on what it was about. I shall be more resistant another time. Monsieur Duchamps, who is in charge of us, thinks he has a good idea of the method I shall use for this, and I want to encourage him. But he really doesn't know enough. Maybe he will learn when we wrap this up, *quoi?*"

"How will we wrap it up?" asks Chloë. "You have told me nothing yet. All we have talked about in our time together has been our flight, Finland, our hosts, the food. We haven't even talked about art until now."

"I'm so sorry," says Patrice. "You should have said."

"But you don't want to talk about it!"

"*Non.*"

"What are we going to do then? I think I need some idea of the procedure and running order, the steps ..."

"Tell me what you felt. *Non*, I'll tell you." Patrice drinks the last of his cup of milky, and steeples hands in front of face. "I saw a space, about sixty centimetres by about forty centimetres. It is an interior, and it has three human figures, two standing and one recumbent, on a pallet of some kind – perhaps a bed, with multiple mattresses and rumpled sheets. You felt, I think, that this was an intimate scene, maybe even a brothel scene. You feel a sense of sex having taken place before the viewer arrived ... you wonder what the third figure is doing here ... interrupting whatever has been going on in the room. Until you see what is present, what is revealing itself to your senses. The pattern your brain is putting together ..."

"*Un moment*," says Chloë. "You are, then, making me a sudden observer, someone who is puzzling through the narrative behind the work?"

"*Precisement!*" replies Patrice. "I am trying to slow down your perception, to separate it into manageable sections. We normally do this very fast, missing some parts of the process as we go along." He takes a breath before continuing. "So, at this stage, you do not know who the figures are meant to represent, or where they are, or their relationship to one another. I know that is difficult because you actually know all these things, and more. You have to bracket them – what Edmund Husserl called the *epoché*, the suspension of previous knowledge."

"*D'accord*," says Chloë, beginning to understand, just a little, what he is talking about. "I see, it's a fresh eye, a necessarily uneducated brain. It feels very different from what I saw before."

Patrice smiles joyfully; he enjoys it when someone catches onto what he is talking about. It is not a particularly easy concept. The young artist asks him what the picture means for him, what it reveals to him. The last part of the sentence is tentative, as if she is still not quite sure and is trying the concept out.

"It affects me similarly," says Patrice. "Although I do not, of course, have as much to bracket as you, not having anywhere close to the same level of knowledge. That is why I am here. So that I can, we can, break the argument between the art experts who are tied."

"And we shall proceed with that tomorrow," says Chloë.

He pours more milky and sits back, seeing the picture in his mind.

***

Patrice doesn't telephone Colette until after *23 heures*. She has not been expecting it; if he is away, he usually rings when he gets back to his hotel room after a day's work.

"Sorry to be so late," he says. "I had to have a long discussion with Chloë. Needed to explain the method I want to use. Don't think she was all that impressed."

"Oh, really?" says his wife, who is already in bed, curled up under duvet with telephone. *Les enfants sont au lit, le chien aussi.*[73] "Well, if she's used to something else, what do you expect?"

"*D'accord*," he says. "I think she got it, though. She's very bright, an art historian. We'll make a detective of her yet."

"How did it go today?"

"Not too bad," he says. "Finns eat more than French persons!"

"Surely not," says Colette, convinced that French people eat more than anyone in the world.

"Oh, they do," replies Patrice. "You have no idea what we had for lunch today. Chloë and I couldn't eat any supper, we were so stuffed with reindeer ..."

"*Bon dieu.* Not Rudolph?"

"*Oui,* the same!"

"How could you?" asks Colette. "And what happened to calling her Mademoiselle Valéry?"

13

Chang Su-Ming is not tall, but she is slim and elegant. Nothing like Mollie. Her black hair is smartly bobbed, and she wears a dark blue silk shift dress under her dark winter

---

73   the children are in bed, also the dog

coat. Her earrings are sapphire-like but fake; the simple gold settings climb her shell-like ears.

René, who of course has met her before, welcomes her to *le Trente-Six* and seats her in the interview room.

"Mademoiselle Chang," he says, "this is Madame Olivier, my boss, and Mademoiselle Godard, our computer expert." Both women nod in greeting.

"I wonder, Mademoiselle Chang, if you could tell us what you know about Mollie Cartwright? Where and when you met her, what she is like and, perhaps most important, where she came from?"

The Chinese woman's voice is pitched at a pleasant level. She tells them that she believes that Mollie is from England, and that she has known of her for about one year. She appeared one early evening when Ms Chang was setting up the bar, where she works, for the night's business.

"I am in charge of the bar at l'Arc-en-Ciel in rue Palmier. I serve drinks often, but also do the necessary paperwork and manage the staff. Mollie wanted a job, but she was clearly too young."

"*Attendez!*[74]" says Clémence. "How did you know she was English or that she wanted a job? She cannot speak."

Ms Chang looks mystified and denies this. She says that Mollie said she was English, and that she had asked for a job as a waitress.

"Why do you think she cannot speak? What you mean is that she will not speak to you."

René admits that the *PJ* have not been able to get her to speak so far.

"But you are sure that she can?"

"Of course. We have had many conversations. But I am still not sure about her age. On the third night she arrived,

---

74   hang on!

I asked her if she had anywhere to stay and she said no. So I took her home with me that night, and I found her a bed at one of my friends after that. As far as I know, she still lives there."

Clémence asks for the name and address of this friend and makes a note.

"Did you notice," asks René, "when she stayed with you, whether she had any injuries or, well, things like cigarette burns or anything like that? On her arms or back?"

"*Non!*" says Mlle Chang. "Nothing of the kind. I helped her undress for the shower and saw nothing like that. She was fine. I think she may have recently, at that time, have arrived from England. I think she said she came from Birmingham? Could that be right?"

"We have no idea," says Fleur Olivier. "As Sergeant Mercard said, we have not got her to speak."

"What have you done with her?" asks Chang. "My friend says she has not returned for several days."

"When we found her," says René, "she was in distress, and had bruises and burn marks on her skin. We have put her in a safe place. That we are keeping confidential." "But I am her friend," blurts Mlle Chang. "You can tell me! If you let her return to my flat, I can take care of her. She will speak to me!"

"I'm afraid not," says Fleur, assuming the senior position. "We need to know a great deal more before that can happen."

"Like?"

"Who are her parents and where are they?" says Fleur.

"How long has she been in France? In Paris?" says René.

"What has she been doing while she has been here?" asks Clémence.

"I do not know any of those things," says Chang Su-Ming.

The serious meeting with the art experts takes place in the auction house gallery, with the painting itself dominating them despite its small size, daring them to judge it.

There are two clearly marked cabals of experts, plus one or two loose cannons, distributed around the room. The Finnish police, or whoever is really running the show (of which Patrice is unsure) have obviously assembled everyone they can think of to solve their problem.

Jak Kyllo is in the chair, at the head of a large boardroom table. The table is in itself a fine antique, polished to a glassy shine. The Finnish policeman welcomes them all again and asks for individual introductions. Chloë, still in student mode, dutifully writes down all the names. Patrice begins a new page of penguins.

Jak gives the story so far, in French and English – which must cover everyone present, Patrice supposes. He keeps his intro short and businesslike.

When it comes, it comes from the eldest of the experts, a *Professore* Guglielmo Denovo, a native Florentine, and so confident he is falling over backwards. All present must lean forward to hear his sharply whispered words.

"This picture is clearly not by the hand of Gentileschi," he says. "Why would she paint yet another *Judith*, eh? Tell me that!" It is a spurious argument, simple in the extreme – as well as something Patrice has already considered. Why would she not?

"But she painted at least three other main *Judiths*." Another Italian explodes into the mixture. "The Uffizi, the Detroit *Judith*, as well as the *Judith and her Maidservant with the Head of Holofernes* ... And Lucas Cranach the Elder painted twelve!" The second Italian is much younger, a dark, serious aesthete, probably a walking encyclopedia.

"*Professore* Gambino says that as if she painted this one," says *Professore* Denovo at full whisper, "and she did not!"

"She did!" shouts Gambino. "It is clear she did. This is the last one. The culmination!"

"But Gentileschi never painted so small," whispers Denovo loudly. "Why would she suddenly do that?"

To that, *Professore* Gambino has no response. He simply does not know.

Patrice hears this and stores it under his mental heading of "conclusion", although the younger professor seems unable or unwilling to elaborate on why he thinks this. Denovo subsides in a splutter.

Patrice, still digesting Gambino's interesting point, almost misses the loud contribution from another man – middle-aged this time, a grey man in a tweed suit, who says, simply, that the picture is really too small to be by Gentileschi.

"Calm, calm!" shouts Jak Kyllo above the furious chattering which has broken out. "I shall not proceed unless everyone waits to speak until his predecessor has finished. Do not make me get the conch shell." The Finn turns half to Patrice, who is sitting next to him, and says, in English, this is what always happens.

"They just argue and argue and never get anywhere!"

Lumi, from the foot of the table, rises and leaves to arrange for coffee with the director, a stout individual in a hairy brown suit, who has been hanging around outside the main group, with nothing to contribute, on both visits of the French police officers, as well as at last night's dinner. The group, completely ignoring Jak, is still muttering furiously among itself, when Chloë rockets to her feet and shouts "*Basta!*[75]" in a very loud voice. Everyone is so

---

75 enough!

surprised that they immediately stop talking, and Lumi and the hairy-suited man bring coffee trays into the room.

Reconvening the meeting, Jak decides to try something different, deferring to Patrice to speak about why he has been asked to come to Finland to take part in this investigation.

"My speciality is phenomenology," he says. "The method of Edmund Husserl, Martin Heidegger and others. In different words, I look at 'the things themselves', and attempt to bring a certain objectivity to the table." He looks down at the actual table for a few seconds, as if reflecting metaphorically as well as in actuality. Looking up at them again, he says:

"I am not an art expert of any kind. I am looking at what is there, not at beauty or form or history. I am searching for the essence, independent of any feelings or emotions the form of the work induces in me."

"*Impossibile!*" whisper-shouts *Professore* Denovo, the exploding man. "You cannot avoid having an emotional response. It is the function of great art!" The whole group begins mumbling dangerously again, although both Chloë and Lumi Salonen stare at them as if trying to put them under a spell.

"I had been hoping," says Jak to Patrice, under cover of the babble, "that we could have a sensible conversation and come to some conclusion. I suppose that was crazy of me, really."

"It may well have been," says Patrice. "I think I shall have to do some research around the contemporary records to get a sense of what the situation of the time was and determine why the artist may have painted this work. And, of course, why she may not. I am afraid, Jak, that this will not be today. Nor in Finland."

"I know," sighs Jak. "I thought maybe it was too good

to be true. There will be more to it; there always is." He looks harassed as he says this, looking older, perhaps his real age. He claps his hands like a schoolmaster and the assembly stops yelling at itself and turns towards him:

"I'm afraid we cannot do anything more today," he says. "I will advise you all when I am convening another meeting. Goodbye for now. And have a good lunch." He does not tell them how to obtain their lunch, nor bother to translate this into English.

***

It has been almost a year since Pucelle left the *PJ* and began working for the refugee group in the *banlieues défavourisées*. She is beginning to feel she has done as much as she can. It is a difficult matter for her – she felt called to do the work at the time, but the call is becoming fainter as she sees how it all fits into a much bigger picture.

It becomes clearer by the day that France has space and work for refugees, which its citizens do not especially wish to do, but that the same citizens feel overwhelmed and intimidated by non-French persons coming into the country to escape from where they are endangered. They doubt their government can treat them appropriately without disempowering them in favour of the new people.

Pucelle even has a query in her head about the problems she sees everywhere only being solvable through politics. And she instinctively does not wish to go there.

She knows she could be switching from job to job forever and never find one that will fulfil her need to change the world.

Maybe she should just give in and go back to *le Trente-Six*?

***

"There are, then," says Patrice, sampling coffee in the lounge with Kyllo, Lumi and Chloë (it is just the same milky), "two main views of this painting – speaking for the 'experts', one represented by *Professore* Denovo, and one represented by *Professore* Gambino."

"*Oui*," says Jak Kyllo, "but there are at least two other opinions – that we have – which may be considered variations of the two themes. One feels that the painting is an homage, one that it is a copy. There is really nothing that we need to consider as outlying. Which is quite disappointing."

He does, indeed, look faintly disappointed, as though he thinks having two established opinions opposite one another is tedious.

"Am I, so, the random element?" asks Patrice.

"In a way," answers Jak. "But I see you more as a method of breaking the deadlock."

"*D'accord*. It will not be easy. And it is not as if you have obtained the consent of all parties to abide by our decision."

"No," says Lumi, in halting English, "but we do think they will have to. Jak and I have made it clear that the Finnish police and Interpol will together decide. They will, of course, take us to court if they do not like it."

"But they will not win," says Jak, "unless they perform some gymnastics in Italian politics and cause an international incident."

"Do you think that is likely?" asks Chloë, reverting to French. She looks horrified, being unused to being involved in court proceedings.

"Don't think so," says Jak Kyllo. "They have plenty of things they wish to conceal, these art folk. They will have to be very determined to take things too much further. I do not think they will."

"Tell me a bit more about that," says Patrice. "Exactly what are the risks and benefits?"

"As an example," says Jak, "many of them, as well as their academic appointments, have connections to the great galleries – who have definite interests in maintaining the value of the paintings they are showing. Some of these may not themselves be genuine. It does not pay them to look too closely."

Chloë inclines her head slightly at Patrice. She obviously already knows this.

"You are saying," says Patrice, "that these experts are complicit in maintaining the face of fakes?"

"I am," replies Jak. "If you talk to the Italian police, they will tell you that there are several well-known fakes even in the best galleries. And it does not do to even question the very famous ones!"

"Some of them are very famous?" asks Patrice incredulously. "*Mona Lisa* and that?"

"Not that," says Jak, "specifically not that. I think that has been too much examined. But some lesser ones, which are still very well known. And that isn't even considering the actual copies that galleries can sometimes pass off as the real thing, while the real thing – or is it? – is being 'cleaned' … I could introduce you to an artist in Finland who swears that the most famous painting in the Finnish National Gallery, hung in 1750, is not by the artist who signed it."

"It is difficult," contributes Lumi Salonen, "to maintain absolute truth when you must depend entirely upon 'experts' to tell you what it is. And money plays a big part."

***

Jak and Lumi arrive to drive them to the airport at *08.45 heures* the following morning, and hand some painting photographs, in a buff folder, to Chloë, who opens it to look. She catches Patrice's eye, and he moves his head slowly from side to side; he doesn't want her to look yet.

They say *au revoir* to their Finnish colleagues, with the promise of a return visit, and thank them for all they have done. The Finns say that they have only provided transport, and perhaps next time they can give more police help?

The aircraft is in the air on its way back to Paris CDG when Patrice asks Chloë to give him a general rundown on art forgery.

"I realise," he says, "that it will be a very big subject – so you will need to summarise as best you can without missing anything important. But I need to rule the forgery aspect out, I think. My sense is that we do not need to worry about it for this picture. What do you think?"

"I don't know yet," she answers. "I'm trying to keep all options open. But *non*, I think I agree with you. Probably not a genuine fake. More probably, if it isn't by Artemisia, it's by one of her studio. Although the size of the picture makes it seem an unlikely project for a joint enterprise. Trying not to think too far ahead!"

"*D'accord*," says Patrice. "So, to *falsification d'art*!"

"Art forgeries are described in a number of ways," says Chloë, "but, for most purposes, we can disregard homages, known copies, and pastiches; they imitate, often without the intention to cause harm. Having said that, I wonder if it's completely right. It probably isn't! Never mind for now."

"There are," says Patrice, "so I now understand, quite a lot of forgeries pretending to be real in the collections of both private buyers and galleries?"

"*C'est tellement réputé*,[76] but it's certainly difficult to be sure when some private buyers keep their collections to themselves. They have a vested interest in not furnishing evidence of how stupid they were to think that painting was a Picasso ..."

"There is no remedy for that, then," says Patrice.

"Alas, no, but I am not deeply harrowed by it," says Chloë. "They are asking for it, aren't they?"

"Well, maybe. *Mais le contrefaçon est toujours un crime.*[77]"

Chloë looks doubtful but quickly moves on to her next point.

"Because it can be hard to fence stolen art – because the real value can be so discounted, because of the scarcity of buyers, and the scarcity of thieves with sufficient knowledge of what they have got – obtaining forgeries can be seen as a way to profit from art. It depends on who you talk to as to whether forgeries are worth it or not."

"It looks a good idea from the outside – but may not be from the inside?"

"*Précisément.* Would you like a worked example of forgery detection?"

"I would," says Patrice. "I do like a worked example, *quoi.*"

"I'm sure you know the Munch painting, *The Scream*, which was stolen from the National Gallery of Norway in 1994?"

"*Oui.*"

"*Alors*, there are several ways of detecting whether a painting turning up purporting to be that one could be detected. There are, in that case, certain things which are

---

76   it is so reputed
77   but forgery is still a crime

known to experts about the painting, which have little to do with the technique, correct pigments, et cetera. A person trying to pass off a fake, or trying to sell on the original, would have to know what they are – and most wouldn't."

Patrice gazes at her, taking in all the pure expertise.

"Firstly, it is known that, unlike the remainder of Munch's Frieze of Life paintings, of which *The Scream* is a part, it is a work of tempera, pastel and chalk, on cardboard (which actually shows through a bit on the face of the main character of *The Scream*). The others are oil on canvas."

"So, different media. Wouldn't that look like a forgery?"

"Of course. But a painting of *The Scream* in oil on canvas would *be* the forgery!"

"Ah."

"There are other things. There is, for instance, some writing on one of the red bands in the sky. It says, 'This must have been painted by a madman'. The handwriting is not Munch's and must have been acquired after he painted it – but without the graffiti, the painting is not genuine.

"Munch himself tried to alter his painting by slicing off the red stripe down the right-hand side, and then changed his mind. So, there is a stripe of dark green paint trying to cover the knife marks. You can also see white spatters of wax at the bottom right-hand corner where Munch, tired and emotional, blew out his candle and spattered the painting. Without the wax, the painting is a fake."

"That's better than a signature then?" says Patrice.

"It is."

14

"So, where are we now?" asks Fleur Olivier, hoping that somebody knows. The others are sitting around the *salle squad*; Mlle Chang has recently left.

"We're nowhere," says Clémence.

"Don't be a quitter," says René. "We are making progress. We've discovered that Gertrude's name is Mollie and that she's English, from Birmingham. And that she can speak but doesn't want to. That the bruises and burns were inflicted after she arrived in Paris, not long before we found her."

"Do you think by Monsieur Lindholm?" asks Fleur.

"*Oui*," ventures René. "*Mais*, I am guessing, *n'est-ce pas?*"

"Alone or in company?" asks Fleur.

René admits he has no idea. It's just that it seems to fit together.

"But," says Clémence, "she could not have thrown him out of the window. She would not have been strong enough."

"She wouldn't have done that," says René. "She's just a little girl."

Both women look at him sceptically; is he protector, romantic White Knight, or detective?

"We need to reinterview anyone who was in the Hôtel des Jardins that night," says Fleur, "or a few nights previously, come to that. Also, someone needs to speak again to the religious people. We should change around. René, you go and talk to Monsieur Lindholm's workplace people, and see if you can turn up his *téléphone portatif*.[78]

---

78 mobile telephone

Are you finished with his computer, Clémence? *Non,* all right. I shall go to the hotel and have a go at anyone left, and obtain addresses for those not."

"And *le patron* will be back tomorrow," says René.

***

"*Chérie,* how have you been?" asks Patrice as soon as he comes through the door.

"I'm okay," says Colette. "But Amélie and I are having some unpleasantness."

"Fighting while I was away?" he says. "Still about her choice of career?"

"Mais *oui,* of course, but other things too." Colette cringes *parce que l'idée lui est anathème,*[79] as well as having a reluctance to watch Patrice going ballistic.

"Like what?" he asks.

"She got a tattoo."

"Of what? Where?"

"Of a tarantula. At the *salon de tatouage.*[80]"

Patrice realises that he should have spoken more precisely. It is the kind of stupid misunderstanding that causes friction in a detective team as well as a happy marriage. He repeats to himself the mantra that he must remember to ask better questions.

"I meant where on her body?" he says.

"On her wrist," says Colette, indicating the back of her own. "It's huge. A monster! She will have to wear evening gloves!"

"*Bon dieu!*" says the subject's father.

***

---

79   because the idea is an anathema to her
80   tattoo parlour

Fleur Olivier arrives at the Hôtel des Jardins, thinking it is misnamed. She sees no flowers anywhere, but it is still only February. They might have tried some dried ones. Although, on the reception desk, in a glass vase thick with dust, the flowers are indeed dried. The receptionist is not obvious but as the detective announces herself in a loud voice, she scurries out of the back room.

"*Oui*, madame?" she says. "How can I help you?"

Fleur cannot quite place the accent but thinks that asking will show a prejudice she keeps under control. She flaunts her *PJ* identification but does not take the opportunity of folding back the front of her jacket to display the shoulder holster.

"I want to ask you about guests at the hotel on the night that Monsieur Lindholm fell out of your window," she says. "I assume you have a guest list which is complete?"

"What day was it?" asks the woman. "I have only been here for three months, but I was here during that time, I remember. Although I was not on duty, it being the night-time."

Fleur tells her it was the very early morning of Friday 11 January, but she would like to see the records for every day since *Réveillon de Noël*.[81]

"Up to when? Ah, the tenth day of February, *s'il vous plaît*."

"I will have to get the papers from the office," says the receptionist. "I don't think they have gone to the *gendarmerie* yet ..."

She leaves Fleur in the foyer and returns to the back room. Fleur looks around for somewhere to sit. There are chairs and sofas in the lobby. Once, they would have been acceptable, but are no longer. They look down-at-heel and,

---

81 Christmas Eve

mostly, broken. She can see some of the support straps from under the seats hanging loose. There is a straight dining-room chair standing by a small writing table, and she decides to classify it as germ-free and settle her ample *derrière* on it.

It is some time before the receptionist comes back, although Fleur can hear her pounding around in the office. Eventually, the woman emerges with a sheaf of papers and lays them on the desk.

"These are the ones," she says, out of breath. "All the people who stayed here between *Réveillon de Noël* and the tenth of February. It is not too many. You can make comparison with the register, here."

She hands the register to Fleur and moves to re-enter the office.

"*Non*," says Fleur. "Please carry all these for me to the table where I sit. I will examine them here."

The woman looks sullen but does as she demands, and Fleur asks her for a coffee, pays for it (*très importante*), and opens the *Registre d'Hôtel* 2018–19.

***

René Mercard enters the offices of Lindholm's church and follows the route previously taken by Olivier, being received by the Rev Dr Gard Baker, complete with more fancy shoes. What Dr Baker says seems suspiciously congruent with what Fleur has reported. Unsure whether the director can tell him anything else, he asks to talk to Madame Derek and Monsieur Fraser.

Both remaining members of the Islamic conversion team also say much of what they said to Fleur, and René decides to throw a metaphorical bomb at them.

"Why," he asks, "did you conceal the fact that you have located Monsieur Lindholm's cell phone?"

He almost shouts this, and both react guiltily. Mrs Derek starts to say they were going to ring Detective Olivier, and Mr Fraser opens a drawer in his desk and produces a smartphone. He hands it to René shamefacedly.

"*Merci*," says the *PJ*. "I wondered when you were going to tell me." He hadn't, of course, he had not known they had it; he was just pushing his luck. "Have you examined it?"

"No," says Fraser, "I only found it a day or so ago."

"Where was it?" asks René.

"In his car," says Madame Derek.

"And where, exactly, was that?"

"In a car park in the fourteenth *arrondissement*."

"Still there, is it?" asks René.

"Yes."

***

Chloë Valéry arrives early at *le Trente-Six*. It is her first day, when she will meet the remainder of Patrice's team. There is no one in yet, which was how she hoped it would be. She is very nervous as she signs in and shows her Interpol ID at the front security door. She is directed to the *salle squad* of *Commissaire* Lanier's team.

It is a large office, with several metal desks and chairs of various sorts. Most of the desks are untidily piled with paperwork, but she spies one which is clear, and close to the window, with a view of Notre-Dame. Funny, she thinks, the best view and no one using it. She puts her shoulder bag on the free desk and removes her dark blue coat. She has just hung it up and returned to the desk when the door crashes open, and a woman in a wheelchair barrels through.

"Who are you?" asks Clémence Godard.

She wheels in and approaches one of the crowded desks – the one with two computer monitors sitting on it as well as a personal printer. She tucks herself into the space and boots up the computer. She does not appear to be waiting for an answer.

"Um," says Chloë, "I'm Chloë Valéry from the Interpol art squad. I'm working with *Commissaire* Lanier."

"Humph," says Clémence, as she types faster than the speed of light. She sends something to the printer and continues typing until it's ready to collect, when she whips it off and puts it on her desk, joining all the other stuff already there.

"Do you know when *Commissaire* Lanier will be in?" asks Chloë.

"Madame Olivier and Monsieur Mercard will arrive soon," says Clémence.

"Is it all right for me to use this desk?" asks Chloë.

"*Non*, it is not."

Clémence does not look up from whatever she is doing and ignores the newcomer. Chloë gazes around the room, waiting for something else to be said. There is nothing. She drops down into a different chair and looks at Notre-Dame, long distance, for a while.

She has taken in the appearance of the other – presumably – detective, and reflects upon it whilst being ignored. Whoever she is, she seems confident, pugnacious even, despite or because of the wheelchair. Chloë is curious as to why she can't walk – an accident, a birth defect? She is rather delicate-looking, with pale skin and rosy cheeks, which could indicate health or tuberculosis – *non,* thinking about her as if she is a character in a painting. Stupid, must be health.

Both young women have red hair: Chloë's is gingery, that of the other woman darker, closer to titian. Both wear spectacles, Chloë's artistic pink and purple frames contrasting with Clémence's businesslike gold wire rims.

Looking at the way she is sitting in the chair, Chloë takes in the fact that the detective has legs, although they look thin and not shapely. Can't see her chasing a suspect, she thinks.

Clémence is wearing a white sweater and a red tartan wool skirt. A green raincoat has been thrown onto a chair, placed by the door, perhaps, in order that she can do this. A sidelight on the relationships in the office ... The door suddenly opens to admit a much older woman, in a taupe raincoat, with a silk scarf tied over her grizzled hair. She has a black shoulder bag and is wearing rubber rainboots. She is swearing under her breath.

"*Bonjour*, Clémence, *ça va?*" says the woman, dripping on the floor.

"*Ça va*, Fleur?" says the younger detective cheerfully, this time politely stopping work and looking up.

"And who are you?" asks the woman, coming over to shake her hand. "*Non*, you must be Chloë, Patrice's art history expert. From Interpol? Welcome, mademoiselle!"

Chloë stands up to shake her hand, and confirms her name and that she works with Patrice, for Interpol.

Fleur asks Clémence to get coffee and, as the woman in the wheelchair exits, tells Chloë that that desk belongs to someone called Pucelle, and that this other one will be all right for her to use. Chloë moves her shoulder bag to the new desk, and sits down on the chair, ahead, by a split second, of the arrival of *Commissaire* Lanier.

Patrice's briefcase *écorné*[82] is clutched under the arm of his trench coat, and he almost throws it to land on the nearest desk, which is piled with someone else's *accoutrements*.

---

82   tatty, dog-eared

He hangs the coat on the stand in the corner, which everyone else has ignored, and leans his collapsed umbrella against it. He turns to Fleur and Chloë and asks how it goes.

Fleur says that Clémence has gone for coffee and asks him how was Finland?

"Hasn't Chloë told you?" he asks. "It was very cold, very beautiful, very blue and white!"

"What about the painting?" she asks. "Did you make your mind up?"

The patron and Chloë laugh in a conspiratorial way.

"No chance," says Patrice. "It will be a long, long time before that happens, won't it, Chloë?"

Chloë, relieved that she and Patrice appear to still have common cause, says that it will indeed. Patrice says that he and Chloë will get together after the morning briefing, to talk about their next steps.

René Mercard and Clémence arrive together; he with a backpack, she with a tray of four cups of coffee from the shop, not the detectives' supply *horrible*.

When all the greetings have been exchanged, Patrice convenes the briefing.

Chloë explores what kind of coffee Clémence has brought without having asked what she wanted. It is latte made with semi-skimmed milk. It is awful. Chloë, thirsty, drinks it anyway.

"We are back, as you see, from Finland," says Patrice. "We have seen the painting about which Interpol is concerned but have little yet to report. Now, how is the Lindholm homicide, if indeed it was one?"

Fleur leans back in her chair and says that she has been to the Hôtel des Jardins once again, and examined their police forms, comparing them with the register. Everyone has moved on, of course; it is late now. She has addresses, though, and some are not too far away. There is one in

New Zealand. Would Patrice like her to go there?

"*Je ne le pense pas*,[83]" says Patrice. "And you, René? What have you been doing?"

"I have been to Monsieur Lindholm's office," says René, "and have recovered his cell phone."

He puts the cell phone on Clémence's desk and she picks it up immediately, fingering buttons to bring up the late M Lindholm's call list as they talk.

"And," says René, "it was found in Monsieur Lindholm's car, a lime-green Renault Clio, in a car park in the fourteenth arrondissement. And ...", suddenly recalling that Patrice did not yet know about Gertrude, "I have identified Gertrude as Mollie Cartwright from Birmingham, England!"

"Excellent," says Patrice. "And how do we know all this?"

"I guessed that the staff at Lindholm's office might have found the phone," says René, "and I tried it on. They had. And they said it had been in his car. I had the car towed; it's in our garage. We haven't had the report from forensics yet.

"I interviewed two girls from the area around the hotel and found a Latvian girl who identified Gertrude from the photograph – Mollie Cartwright. The Latvian also gave me the name of a bartender, Chang Su-Ming, who would know more – we interviewed her but didn't get much."

"Except that she can speak," says Clémence. "Mollie. She just won't speak to us."

"And you, Clémence?" asks Patrice.

Clémence looks up from Lindholm's telephone and says that she has little to report, yet, but is on it.

Patrice asks Fleur and René for transcripts of their latest work by lunchtime and signals for Chloë to join him in his office.

---

83   I don't think so

"There are video recordings of the interviews with Mollie and with Mademoiselle Chang," says Fleur, in her last act as *patronne*.

***

Fleur's Transcript

15/01/2019
09.05

Arrived at the Hôtel des Jardins and disturbed the day receptionist, who was in the back room, leaving the desk unstaffed. Identified myself as *Police Judiciaire* and showed warrant card. She asked, in French, how she could help me. She is not French, she is Hungarian.

I asked for the guest list from the night M Lindholm fell out of the window. Receptionist said she has only been in post 3 months but recalled the night in question, although she was not on duty. I asked for all guest lists from Christmas Eve until February 10. She went back to the office, and I waited until 10.15 until she produced the forms. She also brought the hotel register and gave it to me. I ordered a coffee and paid for it in cash (receipt attached).

The Hôtel des Jardins has 7 floors, the ground being reception, a bar, lounge, breakfast room and office, with the main entrance and access to the one main staircase and adjacent elevator. There is no separate dining room. Above this are 6 floors of bedrooms, each having a mixture of singles, doubles and one suite on each floor. All rooms whose number ends in 7 are suites. There are housekeeping storerooms on each floor. At the top of the house, there are several small attic rooms which are now thought too small to be used regularly. There is a fire escape at the back of the building. There is a large undivided basement storing only packaging and broken furniture.

The normal complement of the hotel is 72 guests, not counting the attic which is, allegedly, never let these days. The guest complement on the night of 10–11 January 2019 was 12 persons, although the number varied over the period 24 December 2018–10 February 2019.

There were 10 persons who had signed the register for the night of 10–11 January 2019, there being one permanent resident, and Herr Doktor Ascher signing on behalf of his wife and himself. The period in question consists of 32 nights. List and analysis is attached.

This produces the names of 12 persons in whom we are primarily interested as follows:

Ascher, Friedrich
Ascher, Heidi
Barnier, Cécile
Cloche, Bernard
Denthwaite, Michael
Juliane, Agnès
Juliane, Max
Melzer, André
Renault, Pierre
Sansone, Albert
Sansone, Brigitte
Simon, Magda

"I also have a note, *patron,* of our interviews so far: the Sansones were interviewed by Fleur; the Herr Doktor Ascher by René; Monsieur Renault and Monsieur Melzer, on the telephone, by Clémence; Monsieur et Madame Juliane by René; Mademoiselle Barnier by Clémence; and Monsieur Denthwaite, in New Zealand, by René. There are three left over: we have not, so far, traced Madame Simon; the Herr Doktor Ascher was reluctant to allow his wife to be interviewed; and René and I are planning to drive to Blois to reinterview Monsieur Cloche in person."

"*D'accord*," says Patrice. "You have followed up on Madame Simon? I suppose you are not proposing to drive to Switzerland for Madame Ascher? Please find a way to speak to her which reflects that, or get the Swiss police to do it, whatever you think best. We shall be going to the *juge d'instruction sous peu*.[84]"

***

René's Transcript 1

15/01/2019
14.23

René Mercard asked the occupants of 7 flats in rue Palmier, which is the continuation of rue Mondoré (where is the Hôtel des Jardins), who were at home, whether they recognise the photograph of the person known as Gertrude. None did, with the exception of Signe Zvenieks, who is from Riga, Latvia. She says that her French is not good but it seems excellent to me.

Det Mercard: Do you recognise this person?

Mlle Zvenieks: Yes. It is Mollie.

Det Mercard: Mollie?

---

84   shortly

Mlle Zvenieks: Yes. Mollie, from England.

Det Mercard: Where in England? Do you know?

Mlle Zvenieks: No, I do not know. But my friend Mlle Chang Su-Ming will know.

René's Transcript 2

16/01/2019
09.30

René Mercard meets Rev Dr Gardiner Baker at the headquarters of his church, the Holiness Church of the Olive Branch. Dr Baker repeats, almost verbatim, what he is reported to have said in the transcript of *Inspector* Olivier's interview with him.

Mme Derek and M Fraser are then spoken to in their dedicated Islamic conversion team office. They also appear to be repeating what they had already said to Insp Olivier, so I decided to take a chance on something they were not telling him.

Det Mercard: Why have you not told me that you have located M Lindholm's cell phone?

Mrs Derek: We were going to ring Detective Olivier …

(M Fraser opens a drawer in his desk and produces a smartphone and hands it to me without speaking.)

Det Mercard: *Merci.* I wondered when you were going to tell me. Have you examined it?

M Fraser: No, I only found it a day or so ago.

Det Mercard: Where was it?

Mme Derek: In his car.

Det Mercard: And where, exactly, was that?

M Fraser: In a car park in the fourteenth *arrondissement.*

Det Mercard: Is it still there?

Mme Derek: Yes.

Det Mercard: How did you know it was there?

(Mme Derek looks sheepish and flustered.)

M Fraser: He sometimes leaves it there.

Det Mercard: Why?

M Fraser: Er … I don't know.

Mme Derek: It is easier to park and walk from there.

M Fraser: We Americans don't park just anywhere like you French!

(I instruct headquarters to collect the Renault Clio from where it was parked and deliver to the *PJ* garage for forensic examination. When it arrives, I note that it is lime green, the same as Gertrude has drawn.)

15

When Patrice and Chloë have reviewed their work on the painting so far, the *commissaire* asks for a little seminar on colour. He has seriously taken in what Chloë said her first impression word had been, *vesce*, and the colour had been yellow. Now he wants to pick the young woman's brain on colour in mediaeval paintings.

"There are many different physical ways of determining whether a painting is genuine these days; many ways of looking through the varnish and pigments and restorations: X-rays, infrared, ultraviolet, et cetera – we'll talk about that later, when we have copies of what the scientists have already found to be insufficient for attribution."

Patrice looks at her with pretended alarm – to warn her not to be too scientific at him; although Colette never pulls her punches in this respect. The young woman resumes:

"We can tell, very quickly, if pigments used in a painting were not available at the time the work was supposed to have been made. There has, over many years, been much advancement in the making of paint. But we must realise that this progress has not been entirely modern – it has been going on for a long time. There are databases of pigments, but people like me frequently make guesses without consulting them, confirming later. Pigments do have well-documented histories."

She goes on to talk about how samples are obtained – trying to damage the works as little as possible – from under a frame, perhaps, or somewhere not obvious.

"There are lots of examples," says Chloë, "but I don't want to overload you. We have other things to talk about." She looks thoughtful, sifting through her database. "I think just one more thing. There is a wide variety of blues to consider: azurite was a relatively cheap blue pigment in the fifteenth and sixteenth centuries, and then there were different mineral blues. But ultramarine was derived from lapis lazuli from Afghanistan – I'm sure you realise how difficult and expensive that must have been to get. Prussian

Blue was only invented between 1704 and 1710, and only in widespread use from around 1720."

"So, no Prussian Blue in our painting if it's really painted by Artemisia?" says Patrice.

"*Absolument*," says Chloë.

***

When Patrice arrives at the Île-St-L*ouis* after work, he finds Colette is, again, in a fluster about Amélie.

"She's almost *une Apache*![85] She wears her skirts up to her, um, even the school uniform, and the *tatou*, and now she tells me she has *un keum*[86] – she means *un petit ami*[87]… She has only *16 ans*. She's still too young for a serious relationship, and we must remember her dalliance in Romania, which tore her apart and could have ruined her life … And there is her career to think of also." Patrice escapes into the kitchen and puts water on to boil. He is making *tisane* for his wife in the hope it will calm her. He will have some himself, even though he does not like it and it is not likely to calm him. He is thinking of Apache dancers as he pours the water on the herbs in the glass pot. He's never seen any; they were out of style by the time he arrived in Paris to live. He would like to see some – but probably not his daughter. He goes back in to see Colette, fuming on the sofa.

"And she's making up her eyes, like Celeste last year. Do you remember? Apparently, it's the latest thing on the streets – dark grey and black cat's eyes. With her cropped black hair. Which she never combs. It's just cropped in rags

---

85   one of the extreme tango dancers, popular in 1920/30s Paris – say it A-pash.

86   a guy – Verlan

87   A boyfriend – Verlan (from *mec*)

and logs! She looks *indescriptible.* Do you think we should send her to Avignon? To get her away from *le keum?* And let her grandparents impose some discipline?"

Patrice hands her a glass of the herb tea and takes one for himself. He had not, for some reason, expected a row about Amélie this evening. He really wants a time of quiet to think about his work. Thinking about delivering his daughter, kicking and screaming, to Provence makes his eyes sweat with the heat and dust – not usual for the end of February in Paris. He doesn't think Colette has realised she herself is assuming the Verlan.

"*Non,*" he says, "I don't really think so. Do you?"

"*Mais, je ne sais pas quoi faire!*[88]" says Colette, with exasperation.

"Drink your tea," says Patrice.

***

They watch the *PJ* interview films starring Mollie Cartwright and Chang Su-Ming, and Patrice asks about the forensics on the lime-green Renault Clio. It happens that the primary report has arrived and has found evidence that Mollie travelled in the car.

"Objects or DNA?" asks Fleur, momentarily forgetting that Patrice is back.

"DNA, from hairs," says René, "and fingerprints on the front door handles, inside and out. I got her to let me take a cheek sample. She wasn't too worried about it."

"A little odd," says Patrice, "that there should be prints on the outside. Suggests she got in voluntarily."

"*Patron,*" says Fleur, "what are we going to do with Mollie? We can't keep her here or at Madame Paston's

---

88   but I don't know what to do!

155

much longer; ça *fait deux mois*.[89] But where shall we let her go to?"

"There's no way to tell," says Patrice. "Perhaps I should have a long talk with Mademoiselle Chang. Shall I go to see her or bring her in again? What do you think?"

René thinks he should bring her in, onto their own ground. Fleur thinks he might have better luck if he goes onto her own ground. Clémence just wants to go with him, wherever. Chloë, who is listening with her mouth shut, just sits there. He asks Clémence to telephone Mlle Chang and ask if he can see her at *13 heures*.

He asks her to check with Chang if the *ascenseur* is working in her building as one of the team uses a wheelchair.

He asks René and Fleur to ask around among journalists and in the British community – find out if anyone knows or has heard of Mollie Cartwright or anyone with that surname. Picture in paper, et cetera.

***

Antoine LeBrun is waiting for Colette in the coffee shop they often used when he worked with her in the laboratory *scientifique et* éthique[90] at Versailles. It is pleasant at *10 heures* before people have their mid-morning coffee and pastries. And there is a wider choice of pastries also.

He has been there, having *café complet*,[91] for about ten minutes when she blows in through the door, sporting a pink *parapluie*[92] and a deeper rose winter coat.

She collects a coffee as she passes through, promising to return for pastry, making her way through almost empty

---

89   it has been two months
90   scientific and ethical
91   a French breakfast
92   umbrella

tables to get to Antoine. He rises to attend to her chair.

"*Hou la-la!*" she says. "*Quelle histoire! Il fait du vent.*[93]" She tries to recover her breath, snatched away by the gusty wind.

He asks how she is; she says she's fine, although he can tell that she isn't. He tells her he is all right, although Marianne, his wife, has a nasty cold. She sniffs all the time. It is *abominable.* Colette sympathises.

Antoine is always interested in how are *les enfants*; he and Marianne have none of their own. Colette bores on about Jean-Pascal and his work at university, he is clever, he is working hard, *il se porte bien.*[94] After a while, Antoine asks about *la petite.*

"Ah," says Colette, "another story."

"Oh, is she not well?" asks Antoine with concern.

"Her health is well enough," says Colette, "but I am worried about her."

Antoine sees that she is close to tears and says, "Tell me," gently. She does.

"*Nous nous disputons beaucoup,*[95]" says Colette, "about her future ... and her present." She purses her lips in frustration.

"She is at that age," says Antoine, who, having no children, nor any experience, has no idea whatever.

"You should see her," says her mother. "Black nail polish. Dyed black hair. Skirts up to her bottom. Big clodding black boots. A horrible *tatou.* A new boyfriend. And after that awful business in Romania too ... And she's using Verlan just to bait me!"

When she appears to have finished speaking, Antoine asks if he should get her a pastry. She says she couldn't eat

---

93   What a palaver! It's windy!
94   he is doing well
95   we are arguing a lot

a thing. He goes anyway, bringing back a slice of Austrian Sachertorte, of which he knows she is extremely fond. He has also ordered more coffee. Colette calms down as she waits for the coffee and looks sideways at the cake.

"She has *16 ans* now," says Antoine. "She is a young woman. Do you not think she's going to want to have *un petit ami*? And make her own fashion decisions?"

"They are not fashion decisions! She looks *horrible*! Like an Apache!"

"Do you think that you are objecting because you don't like what she has chosen?"

"Of course," says Colette. "Her taste is *abominable*! And the Verlan is so vulgar!"

"Of course." Antoine repeats her phrase. "But the young like to separate themselves," he says. "Verlan, or other 'in' languages, have been around for hundreds of years. You could always start speaking it yourself. And wear black nail polish. And see if she likes it on you?"

"I could do that," says Colette, "although I'd hate the nails being black. It's not hard to pick up the Verlan. I'm doing it already. It's *zarbi*!"

***

Alone in the *salle squad*, René makes a quiet call to Mme Paston at the refuge.

She says she doesn't mind how long Mollie stays; she is delightful and loves to help around the house. She can even cook, although Mme Paston hadn't expected an Englishwoman to be able to; she herself has been to England.

"Are you sure," she asks, "that she is English? She doesn't seem it."

16

Fleur and René look up those journalists they know well, whom they have used before for finding people. They go, separately, to meet Karin Allard and Thierry Fontane.

René's meeting with Karin is saturated with flirting. She is considerably older than he, and a member of the sisterhood of experience, women young Frenchmen traditionally idolise and lust after. She is a bleached blonde with dark eyes and a much-admired *décolletage*. She and René are old acquaintances, if not friends.

He tells her that a girl of about *10 ans* has been found and is reputed to be English, from Birmingham, but does not speak so cannot tell them anything. They have found out that her name is Mollie Cartwright. He shows Karin the photo, and she examines it carefully.

"Where was she found?" asks Karin. "And who found her?"

René tells her the story of his discovery in the basement of the Hôtel des Jardins following the January night when M Cedric P Lindholm of America had fallen out of the window of the hotel.

"They may or may not be linked," he says. "We do not yet know."

"Anything else you want to tell me?" asks Karin. "Was she naked or anything?"

"*Non*," says René, "but poorly dressed for winter, and she had bruises and cigarette burns."

"Ah. But you don't know how she got them?"

"Obviously. We removed her to a safe place. Where she remains. Can you help me find out where she came from? I need to send her back – if it is safe, of course."

***

The *PJ* contacts in the British expat community, which is large in Paris, are diplomats, businesspeople, or retired businesspeople. One is a dowager countess, widow of an earl.

They will begin with those who own businesses around the area of the Arc-en-Ciel nightclub. There are several who own cafés, and one who is a *couturier*. None of the café people have ever seen or heard of Mollie. The *couturier* takes his time but, essentially, says that neither has he. All of them accept a copy of her photograph to circulate among their employees. None holds out any hope.

René goes to interview the penultimate of the British community, who lives a little out of the city, while Fleur talks to Thierry Fontane, whom she has known for many years. He has been a journalist most of his life, has had four wives and two boyfriends, and several rounds of rehab for alcohol and substance abuse. He was Fleur's first arrest, for possession, when she was a rookie detective in the Stone Age.

Fleur is unsure whether Thierry can see the features of Mollie's photo; he is looking at it with his usual bleary eyes. She wonders what time he got to bed this morning. He tells her he has been covering a fire in the city and has not yet been to bed at all.

He offers her coffee, and they each drink a large cup; he pours a slug of vodka into his, offering her some as she says he's off the wagon then.

"*Oui*," he says. "It's too hard with all this *merde* going on, America, Brexit, Venezuela, *gilets jaunes*,[96] fire and flood. I want to stay at home and drink! What will be next? Plagues of *grenouilles*?[97]"

96   yellow jackets protests in Paris
97   frogs

160

"Could be," says the detective. "Can you help me?"

"I can get this in tomorrow's paper," he says. "Any background at all you can give me?"

"Almost not," she replies. "They say she is English, and that her name is Mollie Cartwright. She may come from Birmingham. It is said she can talk but we can't get her to do so. She is not deaf. She seems to have been in Paris for a year, and we found her in the cellar of the Hôtel des Jardins in the early morning of the eleventh of January. It was, incidentally, the morning when Monsieur Lindholm, the American preacher, fell from an upper window at the same hotel. There may be no connection."

"*D'accord*," says Thierry, "I'll do what I can."

***

When Patrice and Clémence arrive at Mlle Chang Su-Ming's flat, it turns out that she is not only at home but has three other young women with her. They are smoking, drinking tea and eating snacks as the *PJ* introduce themselves.

Mademoiselle Chang introduces her friends: they are the Latvian woman, Signe Zvenieks, whom René has already met, a very young Frenchwoman called Marie Lagrange, and an Australian, Julie Dorrity. They all seem to speak excellent French.

"How many of you," asks Clémence, "know the girl, Mollie Cartwright?"

They look at one another as if wanting someone else to speak.

"We all know her," says Chang at last. "We have all had drinks with her, and she has slept at some of our houses."

"How long do you think she has been in Paris? In France?"

"A while," says the Australian, who is tall and strong-looking, like an athlete, a swimmer, perhaps, with long fair hair tied in a high ponytail and jeans and sweater. "I think she may have been in the south before she got to Paris. Nice or Cannes, perhaps?"

"But in Paris, definitely, from the autumn," says Chang. "That is when she came to the bar to ask for a job."

"How is her French?" asks Clémence. "Is it good? I have never heard her speak."

"Her French is very good," says Signe. "Much better than mine!"

"What about the English?" asks Clémence.

"Good," says Su-Ming. "She is a native, so it is naturally good."

Clémence turns her wheelchair to confront the Australian head-on.

"What do you think, Julie? You're an English speaker. What sort of accent did you notice?"

Julie Dorrity looks baffled for a moment and then shakes her head, her ponytail.

"Sorry," she says, in English, "I didn't notice an accent. I don't think she had one. Just ordinary British, I guess."

Patrice addresses her in English.

"Not a Midlands accent then?" he says. "Not Black Country? Not Birmingham?"

"No. But lots of people in the UK don't have an accent to speak of," says Julie. "They talk just like I do."

"*D'accord*," says Patrice. "So we can say that Mollie arrived in France sometime in the late summer of 2018, and in Paris a little later. That no one knew her before that?" He looks around at the women, noting their reactions. "That she told you she was from Birmingham in England, and that she spoke as an English-born person would. Do we know her age at all? Or whether she has family in France or in England?"

"*Non*," says Chang, "we don't know that; she never said she had family – anywhere – and we don't know how old she is. I made an estimate that she was too young for bar work, that is all. I expect she has around *10* or *11 ans*. Everything you have said is true. We do not know anything else."

The other women agree with the estimate of age among themselves, expressing the idea that Mollie is small for her age. And that that is all they know.

Outside, by her disability-adapted car, watching Clémence woman-handle the chair into the back unaided, Patrice tells her he is not happy that these women did not know Mollie before, he is not happy that they don't know, or won't tell, any more, he is not happy that her name is Mollie Cartwright nor that she is English.

"*Non*," he says, "*elles mentent*[98] about everything. It is all wrong. We must begin again."

***

Patrice has returned home early to take the opportunity of talking to his daughter. Colette is going to be late as there is a big meeting at her place of work, to determine their organisational goals for 2020. She may even be so late that she will stay in Versailles, at Antoine and Marianne's house. Jean-Pascal is out too; father and daughter will be on their own. Except, *naturellement*, for Sartre, who has already been out with the concierge, been fed by Patrice, and, having scoured the flat in case Amélie or Colette are hiding, settled on the end of the sofa *avec Papa*.

"*Papa!*" says Amélie as she drops herself on a sofa in the *salon* and pets Sartre. "*Ça va?*"

---

98   they are lying

"*Ça va?*" returns Patrice. "I really want to chat with you about the arguments you and your mother are having."

"Oh," says Amélie. "*Laisse béton,*[99] they are nothing!"

"*Oh, je pense que ça l'est!*[100]" says her father. He spots that she is starting to move, probably preparatory to flouncing to her bedroom. He asks her please to sit where she is. She sits with a stubborn look on her face. Not best pleased.

"Amélie," he says, "may we talk civilly? I don't want to fight with you."

"You'll be on her side, though, won't you?"

"There are no sides," says Patrice. "I am not your enemy; nor is your mother!"

"*Teubé,*[101]" says Amélie. "You are *ramps,*[102] therefore against me!"

"Don't make the mistake of thinking I don't know what you're talking about, child. *N'oublie pas que je suis un feuk!*[103]"

Amélie is surprised by the double verlanised term used by her father; paradoxically, the obliviousness of youth has never noticed that times have moved on. The fast-changing language developed to separate youth, gang and cool from the police has readily been adopted by the police – in order to keep pace with youth, gang and cool. Verlan holds no anxiety for Patrice; he is not held in the unchangeable civilised establishment as Colette tends to be.

"*Maman* is concerned, mostly, about how you are looking," says Patrice. "The hair and short clothes particularly. As well as the *keum.* Who is this boy? Surely,

---

99   forget it! – Verlan (from *laisser tomber*)
100 Oh, I think it is!
101 stupid – Verlan (from *bête*)
102 parents – Verlan
103 Don't forget I am a cop – double Verlan (from *flic – keuf*)

you don't really need to be told how *dangereux* it can be for young women on their own in Paris?"

"*Papa*, I am not *toute seule*,[104] I have Luc!" says Amélie. "He will take care of me."

"*Eh bien*," says Patrice, "tell me about Luc. Who is he? Where did you meet him?" He stops before asking the question most on his mind. "How old is he?"

"He is very nice," replies Amélie. "*Il est Parisien*[105] and he sails on the Seine. *Nous nous sommes rencontrés à une rave.*[106]"

"And he has how many years?" asks Patrice. Cringing. It's going to be thirty.

Amélie is looking shifty. Patrice braces himself.

"He has *19 ans*," lies Amélie, blushing fetchingly.

"Do you think I don't know when you are telling a lie, *quoi*?"

She looks down, ashamed. Is it because she has lied or because she has been caught?

"*Il a vingt-et-un*,[107]" Amélie says in defiance.

"Aha," says Patrice, wondering why two years is sufficient for lying about.

"Can we meet him?" he asks, to her utter horror.

"*Non!*" she says.

***

Samedi,[108] it is Colette's frequent job to assume her dark green mechanic overalls and become servant to her car. The Goddess needs a little maintenance occasionally; she is, after

---

104 all alone
105 he's from Paris
106 we met at a Rave
107 he is 21
108 Saturday

all, forty-one years old, but is remarkably trouble-free most of the time.

Colette treats her extremely well. They have been together for so many years.

The tur*quoise* bodywork of the Citroën DS glows in the shaft of sunlight through the high back window of the garage. The window requires cleaning. She will do it before she leaves for dinner; she has not been home since *vendredi sept heures.*[109]

She switches on her CD player, plays the Beethoven "Spring Sonata" – which seems to suit the weather – and begins to do a full service and safety check. She will get this done by the middle of the afternoon and, finally, assess what larger jobs may need to be done. She hums along with Ludwig and then plays a bit of Bach. With difficulty, she has put Amélie out of her mind for the moment.

***

Chloë and Patrice are talking serious art, again, over their early lunch. His team has asked him to interview the dowager countess later this afternoon, and has made an appointment for him in the rue Montférrer, where her apartment is situated. They have asked him because he knows the countess slightly, has met her several times. His eminence will not incur her wrath at being interviewed by inferior ranks. She is standard English *snob.*

***

"Where were we?" asks Patrice.

"Last time," says Chloë, "we talked about faces and how they are manufactured when you can't see the Virgin Mary in life."

---

109 7 a.m. Friday

"*Oui*," says Patrice. "I think it's time to raid my brain and talk a little *phenomenologie, quoi?*"

"Um," says Chloë, less alarmed now she has got to know him better.

"*Regarde*," says Patrice, "I don't want to convert you into a phenomenologist, nor take too much time – so I thought I'd just take you through a few things about the phenomenology of art and see if we can manage with that. Is that all right?"

"Of course," says Chloë, who is enjoying being a grown-up detective rather than a student.

"A quote first, then. I saw it somewhere and put it in the notebook I use for such things. It is from Steven Crowell:

"'... of all the philosophical approaches to aesthetics, it is phenomenology that best accounts for why art matters to us. Phenomenology uncovers the "meaning" of art.'"

"I have studied some philosophy of art," says Chloë, "but not phenomenology. I think people were saying that it wasn't very useful ..."

"*D'accord*," says Patrice, "some say that. It will come back, I think. It is already beginning. I find it useful, anyway."

"We looked at Cézanne," she says, "at some of his *natures mortes*[110] and some Mont Sainte-Victoire ..."

"*Oui*," says Patrice, "he is often used as an example. I like what he said, his aim; that's in my little book too: 'to astonish Paris with an apple'. That immediately brings to the mind the biggest, shiniest, greenest, most juicy apple which can ever be imagined. It vibrates, it oscillates in my consciousness."

"But how does that relate to phenomenology?" asks Chloë.

---

110 Cezanne painted a number of 'nature mortes' i.e. still lifes

"It is, simply, the use of our own, each individual's, perception. You know that, you are an art expert, a connoisseur; that the appreciation of objects, of art, is a partnership between the object itself and the viewer's consciousness. That is why everyone brings something to the work. And why some say they don't understand it – especially modern art, say Rothko."

"*Certainement*,[111]" says Chloë, "one can get a lot from Rothko. But one has to put a lot into it."

"Precisely," says Patrice. "And we shall be doing that with our painting eventually. But for now, we have to start at the beginning, at the thing itself. Do you see?"

Chloë decides to tease him with a quote of her own.

"Virginia Woolf wrote," she says sweetly, "that human nature changed on or about December tenth, 1910 … the date of the first post-impressionist exhibition. People thought Paul Cézanne was literally insane!"

"Um. But his apples are experienced as real, not just as representations of reality. But that isn't what we think of as realism in painting, is it?"

"*Non*. The idea of realism in painting is Caravaggio and company in the Renaissance. They tried to get back to reality from the more decorative style."

"We need to talk about the development of perspective in the Italian Renaissance," says Patrice. "And I want to discuss Medusa."

---

111 of course, certainly

17

"*Qu'est-ce que tu portes?*[112]" asks Amélie, in real French, as she comes through the sitting-room doorway. Her mother is, unusually, doing petit point on her knee on the sofa. It is too cold to do this on the veranda, where she would prefer.

"*Pardon?*" says Colette. "I don't know what you mean."

Amélie can see her mother's right hand very clearly, on top of the embroidery frame; it has black polished fingernails. It is *horrible.* Colette is wearing a dress which Amélie has never seen before. She cannot see much of it but it is certainly red, a bright scarlet colour. Not the sort of colour her *maman* ever wears. Colette usually wears neutrals, spiked with bright colour, or blues or rose; she prefers to be elegant and stylish. When she stands up, Amélie can see *le froc* is way too short also.

"You don't usually wear that sort of colour," says Amélie. "And the black nails are *horrible.*"

Colette lifts the right spaghetti strap of the awful dress and displays her collarbone, upon which has appeared a large screaming bat in black ink. Amélie looks as if she is going to faint, and rushes off to her room, followed by a Bedlington terrier barking with excitement.

***

A maid in a dark green afternoon dress and sparkling white apron opens the door to the *commissaire* and tells him that the countess is ready for him immediately. He will have to

---

112 Whatever are you wearing?

fit into the space she has, before she needs to get ready for a reception this evening. Time is not much.

Patrice looks around the entrance hall, which is dark and cluttered, with both walls crowded with what he perceives as English Victorian paintings – oils, country subjects. He expects *The Monarch of the Glen* but does not see it. There is hunting, though, lots of it. And his embryonic knowledge of art nods to him and says that it is likely genuine.

The countess is to be found in her *salon*, presiding over a table set for afternoon tea.

Caroline Harrice, Dowager Countess of Merramdale, has an English *appartement*, imported from an English stately home, on the fourth floor of a block of luxury flats (in no way resembling her own) in one of the exclusive *avenues de Paris*. It is decorated in plum velvet and lavender silk, old and expensive materials, deteriorated by ingress of rainwater in some places. This is not English; neglect like this normally belongs to the French aristocracy. Or French domestic staff, as here. There is clearly a shortfall of euros. Patrice revises his pre-reflective opinion of the wall art in the entrance. Perhaps it is not genuine after all? Otherwise, why would she not sell some?

***

The next day, tips begin to come in, in response to the articles in the newspapers of Karin and Thierry, as well as the news channels, who are catching up under their own curiosity.

There are five hundred and fifty-three tips. They will be mostly bogus or useless. Nevertheless, they have to be taken seriously, the perpetrators spoken to on the telephone, fielded if they have come to *le Trente-Six* in person, their emails or letters read. Everyone, including Patrice and Chloë, is taking part in this. Chloë is sorting emails into categories.

Fourteen people have turned up so far at *le Trente-Six*, and Fleur, René, Clémence and Chloë have to talk to three each. A *commissaire adjoint* borrowed from another unit is taking the other two. Patrice is writing up his notes from the countess, and thinking, in his office. M Bonnetain has sent in his resignation this morning, to the chief. The chief has had a note left in Patrice's pigeonhole.

The latter has important implications for Patrice's work for Interpol. He can begin his examination of the texts, Artemisia's letters and surrounding written materials because he can do this at home and at weekends; but Bonnetain's resignation will mean he has to manage his team in Paris more directly – not that Bonnetain has actually been much there; he is largely notional.

The other thing which Patrice has begun to think of is that he will have to make another three trips abroad. He needs to go back to Helsinki, to re-examine the painting in question (but not for a while yet); he needs to study the Gentileschi paintings in London, Rome, Naples and Florence.

He telephones the *PJ* office of administration and asks them to block out the whole of May. He will just have to hope that Colette can come with him to London and Rome, maybe to Helsinki. Chloë will have to come to Finland too. He hopes that will work seamlessly. But he is not happy about leaving the team in Paris. He longs for Pucelle to appear as if by magic.

He opens the notebook, filled with his neat handwriting in black ballpoint, adorned with downtime penguins, and turns to the countess's answers, placing the book at the left side of his office desktop computer. He opens a new document.

P. Lanier: This is a photograph of a young woman who was found hiding in the basement of the Hôtel des Jardins, rue Mondoré, on the morning of 11 January of this year. I wonder if you have seen her before?

C. Harrice: No, I don't believe I have ever seen her. Who is she? Has she been beaten up?

P. Lanier: You are sure that you have not seen her?

C. Harrice: I said so, didn't I? I have never seen her.

P. Lanier: I beg your pardon, I am just making certain. We have been told that her name is Mollie Cartwright and that it is believed that she is from Birmingham.

C. Harrice: Ah. That is why you are asking me. You think I know everyone from England who is in Paris!

P. Lanier: I really don't think that. But I do think you are aware of anything which is going on in the British community ...

C. Harrice: English community. I don't have any responsibility for the mad Welsh or Barbarian Scots!

P. Lanier: Thank you. But Birmingham is in England, is it not?

C. Harrice: Of course. I still haven't seen her. Had she been beaten up?

P. Lanier: She had some bruises and such, and we do not know where from they came. Thank you. It happens that, on that night, early morning, a certain Reverend Cedric Lindholm, an American preacher, fell out of a window in the Hôtel des Jardins – that is the same hotel – and died. Did you happen to know him, or have seen him?

(She regards the photograph, taken at post-mortem, and pales very slightly – English aristocracy is hard to shock.)

C. Harrice: Yes. I knew him a little. I think I have been to his church or something. He seemed quite nice for an American. Suicide, then, was it?

P. Lanier: We think not. I cannot say anything more at this point. When did you last see him?

C. Harrice: Could it have been Christmas Eve? I always go to midnight Mass at the Notre-Dame, but that wouldn't be it … no, it would have been …

(Reaches for appointments book on a small table and shuffles through pages.)

C. Harrice: … at the Christmas market. I needed some last-minute bits and bobs. I saw him there.

P. Lanier: Did you speak to him? How did he seem? Was he nervous? Happy? Upset? Was he in good spirits?

C. Harrice: One question at a time, *Commissaire*. As far as I can recall, he was in good spirits. He was always talking about saving souls or something. It was usually Muslims – he didn't like them, or their religion. But this time it was some other people. Now what was it? Oh, I know. It was sex trafficking; saving young girls. He had a theory about someone, but he didn't say who.

P. Lanier: Are you absolutely sure, madame?

C. Harrice: Of course I am! Do I seem the sort of person who would be doubtful? Or unsure? Yes. That is what he said. Definitely.

P. Lanier: Did he say anything else? Amplify it in any way?

C. Harrice: No. He just said what I told you.

P. Lanier: If you think of anything else, will you ring me at *le Trente-Six*?

C. Harrice: I'm sure I won't think of anything else. In the unlikely event that I do have some sort of brainwave, I'll get Marie to telephone you and you can come back when it is mutually convenient.

P. Lanier: Thank you, madame.

***

René is in an interview room on the ground floor of *le Trente-Six*, fingering the minuscule bald patch he has found this morning on the top of his head, about which he did not previously know. The sergeant on the front desk is sending him visitors wishing to speak about Mollie's picture in the paper, accompanied by a young female uniformed officer. René spares a thought about whether the girl has spotted his bald area but must quickly dismiss the idea and get on with work.

The first person, no doubt having arrived early and pushed his way up in front of the desk, is Jean Landal, well-known professional confessee. He shoulders his way in and throws himself down on the relevant chair, his thin beige hair glinting with oil, his skinny shoulder bones sticking up under his not-very-clean sweater.

"*Ça va*, Jean?" says René, making a note on his pad before the man begins to speak: *Jean Landal confessed to abducting and murdering Mollie last Wednesday night?*

"*Ça va*, René," says the non-suspect. "It's me you want. I did it. I abducted her from near the Arc de Triomphe, took her to my garage and hung her up. Then I cut her till she died."

"*Non*, you did not," says René. "You never saw her. Go on, get out! Get a coffee in the mess before you go."

"*Non*, it's me you want, I swear on my mother's grave!"

"Your mother is alive, and turning tricks in Montmartre, and you don't have a garage," says René. "*Laisse-moi tranquille!*[113]" He telephones the front desk and asks the sergeant to come and throw Jean out. The sergeant sends his female assistant, who does so, via the coffee room.

The next person with information doesn't have any either; she is lonely, and René takes her name and address, and her description of who she thinks Mollie is – a shop assistant from Dusseldorf. The next, Emil Chavez, may have some information though. René invites him to sit, writes his name and address, and records what he has to say.

"I have seen her," he says, "around about the city centre. And I have particularly seen her in rue Mondoré and avenue Palmier. I saw her there a lot, early in the year. I suppose it was about January. I remember thinking that she had not enough clothes on for the weather. Do you remember? It was very cold at that time."

"*Oui*, I do," replies René. "What exactly was she doing? When you saw her?"

"Just wandering around. She was often alone. But sometimes she was with a man. I thought perhaps he was

---

113 Give me a break!

her father. They seemed to be talking quite closely. And they went into cafés sometimes."

"Did she seem comfortable?" asks René.

"Oh, I think so. She took his hand and held it. He did not initiate it. And she was smiling. Was he not her father?"

"I can't say," says René. "This is under investigation. Can you tell me what the man looked like, please?"

"*Mais certainement.* He was of a bit over medium height, and a little plump. He was quite pale and had thin fair hair, going bald but not too bad yet. He, too, looked as if he could use some more warm clothing. That's the reason I thought he might be an American – they never put on suitable clothes for the winter in Paris.

"Oh, and he had some really fancy shoes on. I've never seen anything like them before. They were shiny, you know, like dance shoes. And they were a sort of bright blue colour! Not something I myself would wear."

"Can I ask you if you have seen the girl more recently, monsieur? Say, within the last month or so?"

"*Non,*" he says, "I haven't. Not a sign. It was only around January, I'm sure."

René picks up the telephone and dials the *salle squad*, asking Chloë, the only one there, to please bring down the photograph of M Lindholm. When she arrives, Monsieur Chavez identifies him as the man whom he had seen with Mollie.

***

Patrice has brought Chloë Valéry home to the Île-St-Louis for dinner, having telephoned Colette previously to warn her. It is time, maybe past time, for the two to meet, and he feels that, maybe, it will be helpful for all three to be present when he talks about his plans for trips abroad during May.

Unhappily, it is clear when they enter that Colette and Amélie have had another row. Colette is speaking as if she were at a diplomatic function – perfectly polite to everyone but suppressing fury close beneath the surface. There is a white patch on either side of her nose, not covered by make-up. Amélie is not speaking at all, muttering under her breath, and *ressemblant à un toxicomane.*[114] Jean-Pascal has already retired to his room "to do some work" but promised he will emerge when called for dinner.

Patrice joins Colette, briefly, in the kitchen, asking if he can help whilst knowing that she will shuffle him back to his guest. "*Non,*" she bites, "I am organised. You can take the salad. Amélie is being *chelou et vénère!*[115]"

Patrice gazes at her, wondering whether she realises she has used Verlan. She lays a floury hand on her forehead and, flustering, says that now *she* is doing it.

"*Le saumon est prêt,*[116]" she says as she produces it from the oven. It is *en croûte,* and steam is coming out of the holes. The pastry is crisp, golden and beautifully decorated with roses and leaves. There is broccoli, too, as well as a salad.

They return to the *salon,* where the table has been prepared, to find Chloë and Amélie chatting pleasantly about a bestselling novel they have both read. The atmosphere has changed beyond recognition.

***

Fleur is talking to the last of her three allocated members of the Parisian public, well past hometime, when she realises that, perhaps, out of all the pointless tip-offs she has heard today, this might actually be something.

---

114 looking like a drug addict
115 strange, weird, and angry – Verlan
116 the salmon is ready

Janine, not admitting to a last name, is one of the 3,641 people, according to the second ever census of the homeless, conducted in February 2019, who is sleeping on the streets of Paris. She looks around forty years or so, but is probably much younger but ground down by poverty, stress and hunger. She is white and speaks with a homegrown Paris accent.

Fleur, along with a surprising number of her *PJ* colleagues, has closely studied the report of *Nuit de la Solidarité*[117] because of the need to reduce crimes against them, as well as crimes committed by them. Fleur is especially interested in the statistics about the increasing numbers of women on the street, although she has also noted that the general numbers have increased by 21 per cent between February 2018 and February 2019.

Janine is appreciating a mug of *chocolat* as she talks to Fleur. The steam is warming her face, changing it from grey and scabby to pink and scabby. She says that she has seen Mollie several times. Sometimes she has been with a young Chinese woman, sometimes with a couple of older men.

"How old?" asks Fleur. "Did you see her with them more than once?" She ruffles through the copied file in pursuit of a photograph of Chang Su-Ming and finds one tucked into a flap after the final page. She waits to show it to Janine until the woman has answered her questions about the men.

"*Non*," says Janine, "I saw them only once. Although ..." She pauses, indicating that her mug is empty. Can she have another? The uniformed officer guarding the door moves forward with his arm extended. Fleur would have been pressed to distinguish whether he was offering more hot chocolate or defending Fleur from a violent prisoner. It

---

117 the "Night of Solidarity" project

turns out that it is the chocolate, and he departs to fetch it.

"I think I may have seen her with men another time. But it was different men. And I'm not sure it was her. I only saw her back. But it looked like her. My friend Barney said it was, but she was wasted, so I don't know. She said something funny about one time she had seen the girl with a man in a café. Barney was on her own that time."

"Funny?"

"*Oui*. She said that he had weird shoes – they were pink!"

"Did Barney not want to come in?" asks Fleur.

"She's in the *hôpital*,[118]" says Janine. "She has *das*.[119] She is very ill."

"Oh, I'm so sorry," says Fleur. "Are you close?"

"*Oui*."

"Tell me about the first set of men," says Fleur. "What sort of ages? How dressed?"

Janine wipes her eyes and mouth with a dirty handkerchief and tells Fleur that the men she saw the first time were old, about forty or fifty, then says she is sorry, she didn't mean any insult. Fleur takes none and makes a note as the uniform returns with *chocolat* for Janine and coffee for her.

"They were both grey-haired," says the younger woman, "and well dressed, you know, suits, good but not new. Shirts and ties. They looked like they might be flush enough to hand out a few euros. So, we tried, me and Barney. The taller one – one was a bit taller than the other, but neither were very – he pushed Barney over, and she fell and banged her face. He laughed and said she'd never get him to fuck her looking like that."

---

118 hospital

119 AIDS – Verlan (from "sida")

"Not very nice," says Fleur. "Did the other do anything? Or say anything?"

"He laughed too," says Janine. "It was a nasty laugh, like a bray. *Non,* not a donkey. Donkeys are nice. It was like a horrible man, making fun of a woman with her face streaming with blood."

"Did Mollie seem to be with them voluntarily?" she asks.

"I don't know," says Janine, sipping chocolate slowly to lengthen the experience. "The other one, the one who pushed Barney over, he wasn't holding Mollie. But the one who laughed, he was. He was holding her arm in his. Folded, you know, hard, I think. He wasn't pulling her along though. I don't think so. But he was forcing her to stay with him."

"Do you remember what direction they went in?"

"Oh, *oui,*" she says, "to the left down the street. I can show you on the map. There is one in your office, isn't there?"

"What about the other men? The ones you saw when you weren't quite sure whether the girl was Mollie, but Barney was?"

"They were the same kind of men," she says, "older, perhaps, nearly *60 ans, peut-être.* One was bald but had a beard, as if *sa tête était à l'envers,*[120] you know?"

It is Fleur's turn to laugh. She gives the girl full credit for being able to find humour in adversity.

"And the other?"

"Grey hair, not much of it. Suits but not good, older, grubbier. One had a bright orange tie, the other no tie. The bald one had a bag – or maybe a briefcase or something …"

"And Mollie?" says Fleur. "If it was Mollie. What was she doing? How was she reacting to them?"

---

120 as if his head were on upside down

"She wasn't," says Janine, "not really. She looked stiff, and her shoulders were hard. But I didn't see her face."

"Did Barney say anything about it; like if she thought Mollie was being forced or anything?"

"*Non*. She just said it was that girl again. She said she was too young for that sort of thing."

"What did she mean by that?" asks Fleur.

"I don't know," says Janine. "I suppose *la prostitution*."

Fleur turns over the photograph of Chang Su-Ming, which she had placed face-down on the table between them, asking Janine if she recognises the Chinese woman. Janine does. She confirms that it is the bartender, Su-Ming, who sometimes gives her and Barney leftover food and a part-bottle of Coke, left half-drunk by a customer.

18

It is when they are tasting Colette's chocolate honeycomb mousse and whipped cream that Patrice tells them he must return to Finland during the spring, as well as at least one visit each to London, Rome, and Florence and Naples. He hopes that Colette will be able to come to both England and Italy; even to Helsinki if she can. But he will definitely need Chloë in Helsinki, for the work; although Colette will find that he will be very busy then. He is sure, though, that she can find lots to do, if she wishes to come with them.

"What are the dates?" asks Colette. "And why do you have to go to London? I can see why to Florence and Helsinki ... and, of course, Rome."

"I need," he says, "to look at Artemisia's work in London. To get the feel for her. The one we saw before, you recall? *Self-Portrait as the Allegory of Painting* in the Hampton Court? And there is the newly restored *Self-Portrait as St Catherine of Alexandria*, rediscovered in France in 2017 and now in the London National Gallery."

"Ah," says Colette, "I see. I would certainly like to come to London again. And I have never been to Helsinki. I think I couldn't do Italy if it's too near the end of the children's vacation …"

She looks across at Amélie, who looks snarly, and Jean-Pascal, who couldn't care less. Chloë offers that she may be able to take a little time in Helsinki, while Patrice is writing, to show Colette the city and countryside.

"It is very picturesque," she says, "and Lumi Salonen, the woman police officer we worked with, is very keen to show off her country and culture. When I am there, I need to buy some chocolate too!" She looks greedy as she describes the "Fazerina" bar, which consists of orange truffle filling covered in thick milk chocolate, and "Marianne", which is sweet peppermint shells, also filled with milk chocolate.

"They like their milk chocolate," says Patrice, to his wife. "You won't like their coffee. It also is milky."

***

"Looks like a break to me," says René when Fleur has related the story of her interview with Janine.

"If we find any men of interest," says Fleur, "we can maybe get Janine to identify them. And Barney too. If she ever comes out of hospital."

"You think she won't?" asks Clémence.

Fleur's shrug says "not a chance", and they leave it at that.

Patrice, having laid aside his interest in mediaeval art for the moment, agrees that the young Janine's testimony could well break the case, but they would have to find some likely looking men first.

"And now," he says, "we have a connection to Monsieur Lindholm."

***

"It's interesting to think about the power of images," says Patrice, "as opposed to the things they represent."

He and Chloë are sitting on the bench by the river, which he has often shared with Pucelle in the past. It is almost the first fine day; the first day with sun. Chloë is wearing large blue sunglasses, covering a great deal of her face. Patrice abhors sunglasses, and never wears them in France.

"Are you referring to Aristotle?" asks Chloë. "The bit about the essentiality of realism, and that a painting is an imitation of the form of a thing?"

"Hadn't really thought of Aristotle," says Patrice, "but I do recognise the point. The Greeks were interested in the imitation or reflection of reality, *quoi*? Narcissus fell in love with his reflection, but it doesn't mean that the reflection was superior to the reality – it was a divine punishment."

"What about the story of Perseus and Medusa – you wanted to discuss that?" says Chloë. "Obviously, I'm thinking about Caravaggio's *Medusa*, do you know it?"

He nods that he does. He has also seen the painting by Peter Paul Rubens on the same subject. He doesn't want to think about that but he must.

"Images do have power," says Chloë, "But the power is not necessarily the same as that of the real thing." She stops and then adds, "Maybe a different power? Side turn to the *Mona Lisa*. Do we think that the model, whoever it was,

183

had the power, in life, of the Leonardo painting? I seriously doubt it. The *Mona Lisa* has its own power, and it is of a different order from the living woman … is it not?"

Patrice closes his eyes and thinks about that a moment. He is not keen to bring either *Medusa* into the front of his mind, although the Rubens is, in his opinion, much, much worse. He replaces them, momentarily, with the *Mona Lisa*'s serenity.

"*Tiens*," Chloë says, "you could not look directly at the Gorgon because she would turn you to stone. In some versions, the other two Gorgons were horrific but Medusa was beautiful – though she could still literally petrify you. And although the others were immortal, Medusa could be killed. So Athene gave Perseus a mirrored shield, and he cut off the Gorgon's head by looking at her reflection rather than her real face. The reflection did not have the power of the monster.

"See now the Caravaggio *Medusa*. It has power, *n'est-ce pas*?"

Patrice, against his better judgement, brings up the painting on his laptop, concentrates on how the Medusa reveals itself. It is even more horrible than he remembered.

"*Oui*," he says, "it certainly has its own power. I am trying, though, to except the snakes, which are a bit of a problem with me. Perseus mounted the Gorgon's head on his shield, didn't he, and thereby could turn other people to stone while being safe himself?"

"*Certainement*," says Chloë, "and Caravaggio used that concept to indicate that he himself was immune to her – he gave her his own face – picturing her at the moment of the severing but still conscious."

Patrice brings up Caravaggio's painting.

"*Dieu! Horrible.*"

"*Oui*, but it's a fine work. It was commissioned by

Cardinal Del Monte, who was a Medici agent, from an earlier painting of the same subject which has since been lost. The known one is in the Uffizi; you can go and see it when you go to Florence."

"I would rather not," says Patrice, "but I may have to force myself."

"You should look at the effect of the painting, looking as if concave and the actual head projecting outwards. He's painted it as if it is really on the surface of the shield. It's a wonderful technical achievement. Notice the blood dripping down in straight lines too.

"I want to talk about that in connection with Artemisia's *Judiths*, by the way. Medusa is screaming too, as though she's caught a glancing reflection of her own face in the mirror. There isn't quite that effect on the viewer, though. She's not looking at us!

"Michael Fried, the art historian, says that the definitive realist painting would be one that the viewer literally could not look at, because it causes the same neurocognitive effect as the original model. Another *Medusa*, of course."

"The Reubens?" asks Patrice, with some dread.

"*Oui. C'est vraiment terrible.*[121] Its original owners, in Holland, kept it covered for quite some time because people could not bear to look at it. I'm not so sure myself, and I don't have a problem with the snakes. I think she does look frightened, though, Medusa."

"What about the blood?" asks Patrice, keen to move on and get something else in his head. "Artemisia?"

"The *Judiths*," says Chloë, "the one in Naples, and the one in the Uffizi. It's about the arc of blood. And I want to say that they, too, made the viewer uncomfortable. The *Judiths*. I'll have to check the reference because I can't quite

---

121 it's truly terrible

remember. I think one of the Medici women kept the Uffizi *Judith* covered up ..."

***

Fleur and René are driving to Blois to interview, again, Monsieur Bernard Cloche, the sales representative in office equipment, who stayed in Room 603 of the Hôtel des Jardins from Thursday 10 January to Wednesday 16 January. M Cloche will be the latest person they have reinterviewed of those staying at the hotel.

The countryside on the periphery of the A10 is that of the Loire Valley and very lovely, despite the time of year. It is still cold but crisp, and it is good to get out of the city. The drive lasts just over two hours, Fleur driving fast and René hanging on *craignant pour sa vie*.[122] He has taken to checking the bald patch when he has nothing better to do – especially when someone else pronounces the word and reminds him. Today, on their journey, he is wearing an unaccustomed tweed cap in the English style. Fleur has regarded it without saying anything so far.

The *PJ* officers gaze briefly through the windscreen of the police pool Peugeot at the Gothic architecture all around them, the traffic plan avoiding the cobblestoned centre of Blois. There is no time for sightseeing. The office address of M Cloche leads them to a two-storey modern office building on a piece of ground looking like it had been left over from the invasion of France.

There is a young woman on the desk who does not appear to speak French.

Fleur tries English; René tries shouting. Neither receives any helpful response. The shouting, however, brings M Cloche from an inner room. He looks taken aback, for a

---

122 in fear for his life

second, when he recognises the detectives, and takes little time to shuffle them into his office. This is well equipped with the sort of stuff they think he might be selling. They are surprised it is so high-end, and that he is here. Why is he here if he is a travelling salesman? They have sacrificed the possibility he would not be here for a chance to surprise him.

"What is it that you want now?" asks the man in a gruff voice.

He has not asked them to sit, nor offered any refreshment. They sit anyway, and ask him why he was in Paris between the tenth and sixteenth of January. René prepares to write the names and addresses he visited in his notebook. M Cloche rasps that he didn't know anything then and he doesn't know anything now. He was not there. He arrived on Friday.

"Monsieur," says Fleur, "we should also like to know why the hotel records indicate that you arrived on Thursday the tenth?"

Cloche looks flustered for a moment, turns pages in his large desk diary back to January. He says *non,* that he did not arrive Thursday afternoon; he arrived at the hotel on Friday evening, after he had spent much of the day in the commercial district.

"Monsieur Eli Benoît, at Ergan and Benoît Office Furnishers, will confirm that we went out for lunch and a discussion of a big contract he is giving us. I was with him discussing the best colours for the furniture and carpets. It is a very important government office which they are refurbishing. There are computers and photocopiers and laminators and *classeurs.*[123] And a new communications system."

---

123 filing cabinets

"Your police registration form and the hotel register both say you checked in on Thursday. Is that a mistake?"

"It must be," he says. "My diary says Friday, see?" He turns it so they can read. Incontrovertible proof then, Fleur thinks. Not.

"Perhaps you can give us a list of all the people you visited, with their addresses and what was the result of the call? What you sold them, et cetera?"

"Please account for all the time, and give the telephone number of anyone who can substantiate your being there," says Fleur. "We shall wait outside for your list."

"I don't get any time?" says the man miserably. "I shall email you the details …"

"*Non*, we shall wait," returns René. That would give him way too much time to think. He himself would have stood over the man while he compiled the list, but Fleur was occasionally, in his opinion, far too kind to suspects.

M Cloche makes them wait for two hours. The list may or may not be useful. There are seventeen people to follow up, not including M Benoît.

***

"*Ecoute*,[124]" says Patrice, "what is it you wanted to say about the blood thing? In which *Judith*?"

"It's both of the Judiths slaying Holofernes, the Naples and the Uffizi," says Chloë. "It's possibly the most striking comparison. In the first one – the Naples one, 1612 to 13, we think – the blood from Holofernes's neck is dribbling onto the sheets in a passive way, but in the Uffizi, the later one, the blood from Holofernes's neck is shown spurting in arcs, as it would in real life. She has clearly cut the carotid artery and it spurts because of the pressure from

---

124 listen

188

the heart. I think in the Naples one, Judith has cut the jugular vein – so, no pressure from the heart."

"It's interesting," says Patrice, "but she takes the head off, so she would cut both in almost the same time frame."

"Almost is right, and it probably isn't significant for our investigation," says Chloë, "but it's one of those small points you are particularly interested in, *quoi*? It is a measure of time, isn't it? Judith is cutting the neck, moving the sword away from her body; so, the carotid is cut first and spurts, the jugular, second, and drips."

She continues. "The scientific theory in 1610-ish was that projectiles followed an almost straight path, at the angle of launch (it applies to all projectiles, although Galileo was probably thinking about cannonballs); then, when it had lost its momentum, it declined and made a short arc, then fell to earth in a straight line."

"But Aristotle knew about projectiles following a symmetrical arc; Euclid said so, a long time ago!"

"They seem to have forgotten," says Chloë, "and only rediscovered it later. I know, it's *zarbi*!"

"I was looking at Artemisia's letter to Galileo," says Patrice, "and I think I have extracted the essence." He gives Chloë a sheet of paper on which he has typed his phenomenological reduction. "It is quite fascinating. It seems to illustrate an interesting and delightful relationship between them. Although I don't think they met very often, I am sure there would have been more letters; I think they kept in touch. If they hadn't, her letter that we have would have come out of the blue and seemed quite impudent."

"They possibly didn't see one another too much when he was being investigated by the papal authorities," says Chloë. "He wouldn't have wanted her implicated; it was far too dangerous."

"*D'accord*. And she definitely met him at the Florence *Accademia del Disegno* in 1613. Significant, because it was in between her painting the Naples *Judith* – with the blue dress, which was painted around 1612 to 13 – and the Uffizi one, with the gold dress, painted around 1620."

"The second version of the *arc de sang*[125] is greatly more dynamic, and I imagine that's what appealed to Artemisia. It's more horrific as well, more disturbing to those she may have wanted to disturb."

"Has anyone measured whether the blood spatter on the Uffizi *Judith* is actually parabolic?" asks Patrice.

"*Oui*," Chloë says, "Monsieur Topper and Monsieur Gillis, of Canada, in 1996." She flourishes a piece of paper and throws it down on top of his typed reduction of the letter to Galileo.

"What, then," asks Patrice, "is the trajectory of the blood of Holofernes in our *Judith*? And what about the thing you noticed when you first saw it – the funny yellow flower thing?"

Chloë takes a deep breath, ready to deliver herself of something big:

"The trajectory of the blood is definitely parabolic," she says, "and there is more of it – so, my sense is that it had to have been painted after the Uffizi work. And I have been looking at the language of the flowers – you will remember that was quite popular then – to convey a message, secret or not so secret? The 'funny yellow flowers', as you call them, I have identified as bird's-foot trefoil, a fairly common wildflower."

"Ah," says Patrice, as if he understands – which he does not. Yet.

"It's the flower which signifies revenge," says Chloë. "I

---

125 the arc of blood

think that it may also signify Artemisia's final revenge on Agostino Tassi."

"Why is the painting so small, though?" asks Patrice. "And why does it not appear in bills of sale and other documents?"

"Because she didn't sell it," says Chloë. "She never meant to. It was devotional size – although one doesn't pray to Judith of Bethulia, does one? It was so she could keep it and look at it. At her final revenge on Agostino Tassi!"

***

"We are considering," says Patrice, "each of the five paintings, in order to compare and contrast. It seems to me that it is a better way to decide if our *Judith* is one of a series or not. Then we can be clearer why she might have painted it."

"Not the provenance or letters or anything?" asks Chloë.

"I think we are confident that the technique and materials are fine, *n'est-ce pas?*"

"*Oui*. If it were only those, we should be fine."

"So, we need something else."

"We do."

"This is what has occurred to me," he says, regarding the prints laid out on his desk. They are in order: the First, Second, Third and Fourth, then their *Judith*. He moves his head slowly from side to side.

"*Non*," he says, "it is not correct."

"It is," says Chloë, "the exact order of painting – and although we are not sure of our *Judith*'s date – we are sure it would have been later … because it is so accomplished."

"*Non*," says Patrice, picking the prints up and laying them down in a different order. The Naples one, the First, remains first, with the fourth one next, followed by their *Judith*, then the Second and Third.

Chloë looks down at the prints, trying to work out the rationale of new order. She shifts her questioning glance to Patrice, unable to see it.

"A different concept of the timeline," he says in excitement, "The time of the deed, not of the painting. Natural order!"

Chloë smiles as she gets the point.

"Ah. I see. The two at the beginning are of Judith actually engaged in doing the deed, our own one is in the split second she completes it, and the other two are afterwards. I see."

"*Oui*," says Patrice. "So, our one is the central one, the most important for Artemisia's revenge. She has killed her rapist. The deed is frozen in time. She kept the canvas."

19

Clémence Godard, police officer and computer expert, is sitting in the *salle squad* at *le Trente-Six*, gazing at the screen of one of her computers, displaying M Lindholm's mobile telephone records, formerly deleted. They cover the time from the end of the previous September to the day he fell out of the window, 10–11 January of this year. There are only eighteen calls. He must have made other calls, surely. He'd have had another phone.

She wonders why he obtained a new one, if he did. Not necessarily suspicious, he could have lost one or broken one. He could simply have updated; everyone does. Nearly everyone. Patrice doesn't, but then he is *réactionnaire*.[126]

There are two calls on the day Lindholm likely bought the phone: one to a number in Lille, one to a number in America. She has already traced both of these. The Lille call was to a landline, lasted three minutes and proved to be to the Hôtel de Ville.[127] Clémence had rung the number and asked to whom M Lindholm could have spoken. They did not know and could not find out.

The American call was to the headquarters of M Lindholm's church in St Paul, Minnesota. She has decided that she will ask *le patron* to follow it up. Her English is insufficient.

All eighteen entries are in front of her and she has classified them into the different numbers. Three calls – one, the third call listed; one on 3 January; and one on 10 January (the night M Lindholm ceased to be) – are to the Hôtel des Jardins; the remainder are to unregistered mobile phones, which could be anywhere in the European Economic Community. Arghh. Not much help there.

She telephones the Hôtel des Jardins, asking their operator who would have answered the calls on these dates. The operator does not know – it wasn't her; she has only been in employment for three days. Clémence says a rude word and bangs the receiver down. *Inspecteur* Olivier at least has a rudimentary relationship with a different receptionist; she can call when she gets back from Blois.

***

Patrice is staring at Chloë in amazement. They have made a strange joint leap of intuition and although he is somewhat stunned, he is minded to ride it further.

126 reactionary, Luddite
127 town hall

"So," he says, "does that mean she was finished? That she had closure with her past? Does that mean, *quoi*, that her revenge is over?"

Chloë, perhaps regretting her outburst, mutters that she thinks so, that this may be the last *Judith*.

"She would, you see, have no more need to paint it again. If she has done all she can to revenge herself ..."

"It would be a late painting, then. Maybe her last painting. When did she die, by the way?"

"In Naples, 1653," says Chloë. "She had *60 ans*."

***

Detective René Mercard is extremely worried. The almost completely circular, hairless patch on the top of his head looks bigger. He has investigated this by positioning several mirrors and examining what they reflect. He himself reflects that rain has become more wet on his head, sometimes almost sharply drilling into his normally thick hair. He will have to buy more hats.

***

Patrice has arranged for two days off work; avoiding going in to the office, anyway, and he is at home, with copies of Artemisia's correspondence. Chloë, he has sent to her temporary *PJ* accommodation with the file regarding the patchy provenance of their *Judith*. It is a lot to study; she needs to be as comfortable as possible.

Before he addresses the correspondence, to which he is greatly looking forward, he muses on the construction of a timeline. This is often of much assistance in the clearing of his thinking – seeing what it looks like. He can sometimes make connections which hide from him during his extensive reading.

At *le Trente-Six*, Patrice has access to whiteboards and other facilities, but at home he uses an old-fashioned flip chart stand and pads – retired from the *salle squad* in favour of successive technology.

He writes "Artemisia Gentileschi – Timeline" at the top; divides the large sheet of paper into three columns: Month/Year, Incident and Note. He begins to pencil in a few years he can remember. He will alter them in marker pen later, perhaps with meaningful colours. Artemisia's birth and death dates are easy: 1593 *julliet*, Rome, and 1653 (no month), Naples. He does not require many notes. He fills in the big events of her life: the rape, the trial. The dates of her most important works. Checking with the list of the artist's letters, he adds their dates in between.

It will need more work but it is fine for now.

The entire Artemisia correspondence consists of twenty-eight letters written by the artist, two letters from one of her *patron*s, and an exchange of notes with a different *patron*. They cover a thirty-two-year period from 1619 until 1651.

He is starting to do phenomenological reductions of these texts in order to determine their essences. He is examining the evidence, if any, in Gentileschi's correspondence, of her having had a commission for their *Judith*, painted it, sold it, shipped it, or anything else.

The remainder of the family Lanier is about its own business, although there was another Colette versus Amélie face-off last night. Patrice puts it out of his mind for the present; it will, doubtless, return this evening.

Patrice reads the text of Artemisia's letter to Galileo with some awe. After all, this is the polymath scientist, physicist, engineer, called the father of modern physics, the scientific method, even modern science. A leviathan.

Somehow, it seems amazing that someone he is getting to know, Artemisia Gentileschi, should have known the great scientist – to have spoken to him in person, to have written him letters. He looks at the notes he has in Mary Garrard's book about this letter. He has copied it, not because he thinks it may be useful in his task, but because it is to – well – Galileo.

After five months being held in Siena by the papal authorities on charges of heresy, Galileo had been allowed to return to house arrest in his villa at Arcetri in 1633. He had offended church and state by stating that the earth moved around the sun.

In this letter, Artemisia is imploring Galileo to help her obtain the money she is owed by Ferdinando II de' Medici, son of her former *patron* Cosimo. Galileo has already helped her obtain her payment from Cosimo I for what is now known as the Uffizi *Judith*. There is no note of what the two paintings were that she had sent to Ferdinando this time.

Ah, to work! Patrice, putting aside his amazement at being somehow involved in the life of Galileo, bundles his notes up and lays them aside. It is time to examine the text. He sits for ten minutes, clearing his mind, reminds himself that epoché is never perfect, and starts the task.

20

Jean-Pascal is the first of the family to arrive home. He has left the university early because he is feeling unwell. Patrice lays a hand on his son's forehead and it is true, he is burning up. He tells Jean-Pascal to get into bed while his father makes him some hot milk and looks for the painkillers. It is probably *la grippe*,[128] which is currently laying waste to Paris. No doubt they will all get it. Patrice himself is feeling slightly less than well – and Amélie was disinclined to go to school this morning (not unusual). As far as he knows, Colette is fine. Germs shun her; they are afraid of big-gun pharmacologists.

Jean-Pascal does not want to eat anything, even though Patrice has made lasagne, which he loves, with broccoli, which he hates. Even offering him the pasta without the broccoli does not tempt him. Patrice has just come back into the kitchen to check the oven setting is low enough not to burn the food, when Colette arrives. She slings her bulging briefcase onto the desk and flops down into an armchair. Sartre, who has been anxiously waiting for Amélie on the veranda, comes in to check what is going on.

"*Quelle journée de merde!*[129]" says Colette. The pleading expression on her face begs for a gin and tonic with ice and lemon. Her husband makes her one.

"You look very tired," he says, putting the glass into her hand. She sips and sighs, before asking whether Amélie is home yet. She isn't.

Amélie is still not present when it reaches 6.30 p.m. This is late, even for Amélie. Colette rises and telephones the school. She left at 5.15 p.m., as usual, following her drama class. She should have been home at 5.30 p.m.

"*Oh, bon dieu!*" says Colette. "What shall we do now? And where is Jean-Pascal?"

"In bed," says Patrice. "He has the *grippe*. He came in early, feeling rotten. I'm not well myself!"

---

128 the flu
129 What a rubbish day!

His wife waves her hand in dismissal, trying to think where her younger fledgling can be. There are telephone numbers in their list, of Amélie's friends at the *lycée*. Perhaps she has gone to one of them, and stayed over her time unwittingly?

Patrice has already located the list and placed it by the telephone. He dials the first number, Lucy, possibly Amélie's best friend. Amélie is not there. Lucy's *maman* says that they have not been best friends for ages.

Colette, taking the chair, makes the next call. Brigitte says that Amélie is not there; they said goodbye at school. Colette asks whether Brigitte has any idea where Amélie might be. She hasn't.

Patrice rings Laure, an older girl, once a friend. Laure hasn't even seen Amélie for a couple of weeks. Solange, Liliane and Marci don't have any bright ideas either. All saw her at school, none was aware of any reason she wouldn't have come home. *Non,* there was no after-school club or class running that late – or anything, really. The next school colleague freaks out. Lise is hysterical. Patrice makes soothing noises but she won't be calmed. Her mother takes the phone and shouts at him for upsetting her daughter. He asks why her daughter should be so upset at the news that his hasn't arrived home from school.

Madame Vollender, who is Swedish not French, says she hopes it isn't that man, that boyfriend. Patrice asks for the details and Mme Vollender says that he is older than the girls, and she reckons that it is a mistake, on the part of Amélie's parents, to let her go out with him.

She is stiff and short with Patrice, clearly not approving of them or the upbringing they are giving their daughter. Colette wrestles Patrice for the handset, but gets no further, or nicer, information. She looks baffled and deeply worried as she hangs up.

"She hung up on me!" she says. She sinks back into her chair; there are no further recorded numbers for Amélie's friends. "What if she is with this *keum*? This *petit ami*?"

"Do you think she is in danger?" asks Patrice.

"*Oui. Non.* Could be. Don't know." Colette is panicking. She gets up and begins pacing. "I don't know what to do …" She wrings her hands as if doing washing.

Patrice picks up the telephone again and calls *le Trente-Six*. He gives his daughter's details to the desk sergeant, and says that he will be in shortly to commandeer a car. Of course, it is far too early for Amélie to be considered a missing person – and she has *16 ans* anyway, so over the official age to think for herself. The desk at *le Trente-Six* will just keep an eye out. Patrice will check a few places he knows. He telephones René, who will come with him.

Colette wants to come too, but he stations her by the phone with the instruction to call his mobile when Amélie turns up.

"She will," he says.

His wife looks *distrait* as she goes to sit by the phone. Sartre positions himself over her feet, drops down, anxious.

***

Patrice and René are both exhausted when they arrive in the *salle squad* after a night bouncing around the city in one of the Crappy Little Peugeots. They have visited hospitals, nightclubs and *pensions*, although not all, obviously. They have even been to l'Arc-en-Ciel and spoken to Chang Su-Ming behind the busy bar. She asked them where Mollie is, and they had to refuse to tell her again. She is not best pleased by this and claims, again, that she is quite capable of taking care of the lost girl.

She knows nothing about the *commissaire*'s daughter. *Oui*, she will telephone him if she sees her. She does not know anyone called Luc. The policemen think it is highly unlikely that the Chinese girl does not know anyone called Luc – it is a common name.

Patrice, sitting at the desk he uses in the detectives' space, rather than his personal office, runs his hands through his hair and lets out a frustrated moan. The middle-of-the-night panic has produced nothing. René takes it upon himself to ring the front desk and ask Officer Zondé whether he has any news. He hasn't. René goes for coffee to fuel further exploration.

"I am telephoning to ask if my daughter has arrived at school today," says Patrice, on the phone to the *lycée*, having introduced himself as *Commissaire* Lanier of the *Police Judiciaire*.

"*Non*, Monsieur *le Commissaire*," says the school administrator, "she has not come in. Is she unwell?"

"*Non*," snaps Patrice, "*elle a disparu*![130] Let me know on this number immediately you see her."

René places the carrying tray from the coffee shop on Patrice's desk. He has bought capuccino for both of them and a couple of pastries in a paper bag. Patrice drinks gratefully, and tells the younger man that Amélie had not turned up at school this morning.

While he drinks his coffee, Patrice rings Colette, who has stayed at home, supervising her eldest. He tells her the bad news and spends some time comforting her. This is hard; she is in deep distress. Jean-Pascal is still in bed and coughing loudly every three seconds. She is keeping him hydrated and refusing to allow him to get up and go looking for Amélie. She has, however, interrogated him and he has

---

130 She is missing, she has disappeared!

come up with a couple of places they can check. He has also come up with a family name for Luc. It is Havéne.

Patrice tells Colette that he and René have already checked out both places which Jean-Pascal has suggested, to no avail, while René looks up the name Havéne in the telephone directory. There is only one. It is Monsieur et Madame Claude Havéne, in the boulevard Rémarque.

Patrice and René reclaim the Peugeot and go to look. They are arriving at the front door of the opulent house when Colette phones to say that Amélie has returned. There is a great noise of Bedlington barking in the background as Sartre welcomes his best girl home.

***

Chloë has read all the provenance documents which could possibly refer to their *Judith*. There is not that much of it, and it has substantive gaps.

There seems a possibility it may have been sold, after Artemisia's death, to someone from the Spanish court and exported to Madrid, where it may have spent forty years before going to Barcelona for one hundred and sixty years and, eventually, travelling via Paris (there is a coach receipt for its fare) to somewhere in France. It appears to have been in a private collection in France from 1838 until 1942. Then it predictably disappeared, possibly to Germany.

Coming forward to modern times, an anonymous painting is accounted for in the collection of a Monsieur Harper in London from 1961 to 1967. He bought it from a gallery in Berlin and, in turn, sold it on to an anonymous collector in France. There are bills of sale from Berlin to M Harper; and from M Harper to Anon in France. It was sold again in 1980, to a Mme Hersey, in Colorado, America, who donated it to a museum in California in 1982. The museum, probably because it was in financial difficulties, sold the painting to a firm of corporate lawyers in New York, for their new headquarters. There is paperwork for all these transactions, and it all looks real. Chloë reminds herself that it may still not be the right painting.

Only the disappearance from 1942 to 1961 is unaccounted for in this timeline, as one would expect.

Chloë is sure the spotty provenance is in itself suspicious. She still feels that Artemisia did not sell her revenge painting – that there must have been two of them.

***

When Patrice arrives home, having raced from *le Trente-Six*, Amélie and Colette are both in tears, Sartre is bouncing around, barking his head off, and Jean-Pascal, looking like a wraith at a birthday party, is trying to console all of them. He is not making much ground.

Papa sends his son back to the sick bed and tells the dog to shut up, leaving him with the two females, clutching one another for dear life on the sofa.

"*D'accord*," he says, trying for a comforting tone. He can hardly believe his daughter is back and alive. He has been making up ever increasing stories of the macabre since teatime yesterday. He wants to hug Amélie and shake her, and yell at her, and confine her to the house until she has thirty years – all at once. He is shaking with fury and delight.

They don't seem to be hearing him so he goes into the kitchen and makes tea. It will be calming.

"*Bien, mesdames, obtenons quelques informations, s'il vous plaît,*[131]" says Patrice loudly. He has frightened the dog and, while waiting for the girls to declench, he reaches

---

131 Right, ladies, let's get some information, please

down and rubs Sartre's little woolly head, fondling his ears. The Bedlington is very forgiving.

Patrice looks at the wet, white faces of his wife and daughter, waiting for some kind of explanation. From someone. It is quiet for a few moments, then Amélie says:

"*Oh, Papa, je suis vraiment désolée!*[132]"

"Where have you been?" he asks.

It is Colette who replies.

"She has been with Luc," she says, "at his house. She overstayed her time, and was afraid to come home."

Patrice cannot believe this; how could his daughter ever have been afraid to come home? They are not harsh parents, they try to be understanding. Colette says she has told their daughter this already; she must have got the idea somewhere else.

Amélie gets up from the sofa and rushes to her father with enough speed to knock him down. He takes a step back to recover his stance, and almost succeeds in raising her above the ground, as he used to do when she was *petite*. The only thing she seems to be able to say is "*Papa, Papa*" or "*Mama, Mama*". Eventually, even this dries, and all they do is hug each other in silence. Further information about what actually happened will be reserved for tomorrow.

***

Patrice asks Fleur and René to call around to the house of M and Mme Claude Havéne, in the boulevard Rémarque, and enquire into their son Luc. For some unadmitted reason, he does not wish to go himself.

They arrive at the front door, and find it answered by an elderly woman in an old-fashioned dark blue dress. Her

---

132 Oh, Daddy, I am so sorry!

grey hair is strained back in a bun, with a hairnet. She seems reluctant to answer the door.

"*Oui?*" she says.

Fleur asks if monsieur and madame are at home, and receives the reply that madame is, but monsieur is at the factory. She advises them to return in the evening, but Fleur says they will speak with Mme Havéne now. The woman ushers them in with a reluctance hard to beat, and seats them in a small library to the left of the front door. They sit and wait. René takes a look at the books when he becomes bored, after about five minutes. There is no self-help guide to maintaining a good head of hair.

It is half an hour later when the housekeeper, or whoever she is, comes back to conduct them up the curving staircase to a small drawing room, nicely appointed in French country style. Mme Havéne is reclining on a blush velvet *chaise longue* and has a largely blush complexion. Her hair is prematurely white, and she wears a beige maxi dress with its hem tucked in over her feet. She extends a weary hand in greeting, and a frail voice welcomes them in.

As they take seats, Mme Havéne asks the housekeeper to bring coffee "and some of those little cakes baked yesterday". When she leaves, madame asks for their names, and introduces herself as Lavinia Havéne.

Fleur quickly tells her why they are here; the boulevard Rémarque is quite close to the Hôtel des Jardins. Mme Havéne, of course, knows nothing about the dive to the pavement of M Lindholm, and has never laid eyes on anyone looking remotely like Mollie (when René shows her the photograph). Neither detective, naturally, had expected that she would have. Then René gets to why they are really here, and asks whether her husband, or anyone else in the house might have any information for them?

"My husband works very hard," she says, as if he neglects

her, "and retires early when he has had dinner. We rarely go out, and certainly not at late hours. I suppose our son, Luc, may have been out that night; I am unable to remember. He has *21 ans* after all, I don't monitor him as if he were a child."

"Is he in the house now?" asks Fleur.

"*Non*," says madame, "just myself and Georgiane. She was Luc's nurse and is now my carer. I have a bad heart."

"Perhaps we can talk to Georgiane," ventures René, "and call back to talk to Luc later?"

"*D'accord*," says the invalid, "I am sure you can do that. Please telephone to make an appointment with my son, later this evening. Georgiane will talk on your way out."

They are processed efficiently through the front door by the nanny-slash-carer, who knows not a thing. They don't get any coffee or cake.

***

"*Oui*," says Chloë, "I have looked at the provenance, and found it to be way too gappy; but, after all, it's more than five hundred years to account for. I doubt we have enough time to do all that work."

"Um," says Patrice, "I think I am with you on that. What does the experts' report say?"

"As we found in Finland. Gambino thinks that everything's fine," she says, "although it can't be, if he is being honest. The other one thinks it is all spurious."

"Perhaps they think the same as we do – that there are better, less arduous ways of finding what we need to know? What's our next step, *quoi*?"

"Putting aside our going back to Finland, and you going to Florence and London, and maybe Naples and Rome, we should maybe talk about our *Judith* – you have not, yet, prepared a description, have you? You are not thinking of

205

going to America to view the Detroit *Judith* in person, are you …?"

"*Non*, I don't think so."

It is the afternoon in the *salle squad* and everyone is out following up various leads. Patrice settles to contrive a plain description of what they have called their *Judith*, although perhaps now it is the middle *Judith*.

He notes the dimensions first, from the notes Chloë took when they first saw the work. Then he continues to describe it, following Mlle Criswell's template:

> The work is oil paint on canvas and is a vertically composed scene containing three figures: Judith, her maidservant and Holofernes, the Assyrian general.
>
> The eye is drawn immediately to the actual moment of decapitation. The sword edge, rendered to look extremely sharp, is approximately halfway through the neck of the victim; his blood is both dripping down, under no pressure, and spurting in an arc under pressure of the heart. It is coloured, respectively, rusty and bright reds.
>
> The scene is, again, lit from the left side, with the central figure of Holofernes greatly illuminated. The women are still in strong focus as central players, but the lighting directs us to the victim, who has now given up fighting and lies passively under the edge.
>
> Judith is dressed in a golden robe and decorated with finely detailed jewellery. The maidservant is approximately Judith's age and is clearly an equal collaborator rather than an accessory. Her robe is not as fine as Judith's but is better than serviceable and coloured blue/purple and white. She wears modest jewellery.

The women are posed as if killing a pig – there is something of the slaughterhouse present. The sleeves, again, are pushed up above the elbows of muscular arms, and the design of the dresses suggests the wearing of aprons. The bloodstains on Judith's dress front are heavier than in any of the other paintings.

Holofernes is covered by the sheet and fringed blanket from halfway down his torso, giving the feeling that it will be pulled to cover the remainder of his decapitated body very soon.

At the very bottom of the painting, at the foot of the bed, is a basket (similar to the one shown in the Detroit *Judith* into which the head is placed). In the back edge of the basket, a sprig of flowers may be seen. They are bright yellow and have been identified as the common wildflower bird's-foot trefoil. In the language of flowers, this plant signifies revenge.

"The essence of it, then," says Chloë, returning to the room, "is the blood and the flower."

"Showing what, exactly?" asks the *patron*.

"What she'd learned from Galileo – about the trajectories of objects – and that this painting, more than any other, is her revenge on Agostino Tassi."

21

It is Sunday, and Colette and Patrice are having a quiet day at home. She has been in heavy meetings all week and is exhausted (especially with the emotional toll of thinking Amélie had been abducted). He desperately wants to read something which has nothing to do with Renaissance art. He needs a break.

Colette, who does not believe in mortal sin, has missed Sunday Mass for the second time in a row, and stayed in bed this morning for a long sleep. She doesn't really enjoy it – it is a fantasy that it will somehow help her to feel not tired. She comes into the *salon* around *10 heures*, fresher from a long, hot shower.

Patrice is lying on a sofa opposite the half-open *porte-fenêtres*;[133] it is sunny, although still cold. He appears to be halfway through an English spy novel. She asks what it is and he tells her. It doesn't seem to be her sort of thing. He sits up and offers to get her breakfast.

As they drink coffee and eat the croissants for which Patrice has already been to the bakery, they talk about the news from England and the big human-trafficking case which is presently being decided in court. Neither of them has a clue about English law, but they know enough about modern crime to be scandalised. Neither of them is inclined to say that this could never happen in France. They know it does; it has.

"Might it not be a part of your current case?" asks Colette.

"It might be a part of both my current cases," replies Patrice. "The finding of Mollie, the girl in the basement of the hotel when Lindholm took a dive from the window, may be part of something like that, although we don't know yet. And I think there are many indications of that kind of thing in my art appreciation task too."

"Oh," says Colette, "trafficking in fifteenth-century Italy?"

---

133 French windows, opening onto balcony

"Not original, I'm afraid. Lots of feminist articles on how it might have seemed for young, vulnerable women then – when they were objects owned by their fathers and husbands … even brothers sometimes."

"Ah, I see. What sort of line does your Chloë take?"

"I don't yet know," says Patrice. "We are scheduled to talk about that tomorrow. There are various accounts by different art critics, although I think I probably shall favour the feminists. I have a couple of books Chloë has loaned me to read relevant parts of before tomorrow. That is why I need this distraction now." He waves towards his spy novel.

Colette says she wants to talk a little about Amélie today, later.

"Ah," he says. "How is that going, by the way?"

"I'm trying a tactic involving using Verlan myself, as well as dressing like a whore and having black nails and *tatoux*."

Patrice acts stunned, although he had seen the horrible thing last night in bed.

He had held his tongue then and turned over.

"*Tatoux*?" he asks. "Surely not! I know the nail polish can be expunged, but a tattoo?"

She pulls aside the short sleeve of her taupe wool dress to show him her shoulder close up. He starts away in revulsion from the screaming bat. It is horrible. Can she have it removed? Thank God it isn't a spitting cobra. He could not cope with that. But she would not do that to him.

"Don't worry, my love," she says in a soft voice. "It's only a transfer, not permanent! I will take it off tomorrow."

"*Merci dieu!*" he says, with a certain amount of devotion. "Please keep the T-shirt on in bed, *s'il te plaît*."

She agrees; she doesn't much want to catch sight of it either.

***

Monsieur Micah Zabi, who will be the *juge d'instruction* should the *PJ* ever arrest anyone for the crime of killing M Lindholm, is tall and rangy and has a shiny black bald head, high Masaai cheekbones which could cut vegetables, deep brown eyes which make you feel that you are the most interesting person in the entire world, and a beautifully tailored winter wool suit in medium grey.

His forebears must have wandered from East Africa, through the central area of the continent to République Démocratique du Congo, because that is where his parents immigrated from in the nineteen sixties. The *juge d'instruction* himself was born and bred in Paris, attended law school in Paris, married his lawyer wife, Juno, in Paris, and practised as an *avocat* for a while in Paris. Now, he is a *juge* with whom the *PJ brigade criminelle*[134] frequently works. He is very well educated and fiercely intelligent. Also very strict.

Patrice's team has arrived in Zabi's office in order to summarise the case so far, and to receive Zabi's input, from a useful distance. The *juge* has seated them all in the very untidy room, filled with piles of papers and files, including those on the windowsill, which is at least one half obscured by the stacks of stuff. Mlle Roxanne has provided good coffee to oil the wheels.

The team has already provided its paperwork, although whether Monsieur *le Juge* will be able to find it may be another thing. He will have gone through it and noted items he wishes to ask about in bright yellow highlighter. It will

---

134 criminal division, detectives investigating serious crimes

210

be his job to convene a pre-trial hearing when asked to do so by the *procureur de la Republique.*

"*D'accord*," he begins, "I have your witness list, and Roxanne has inscribed it on my wall." He indicates his own whiteboards with a wave. He leaves them to gaze at it for a while.

"*Maintenant*," he says," there are some interesting blanks on this, *quoi?*"

"There are," says Patrice. "The blank for Madame Magda Simon and the blank for Madame Heidi Ascher."

"We have been unable to find any trace of Madame Simon," says Fleur. "She is not on the electoral roll in Reims, from where she is supposed to come, and the telephone number she gave the original police interviewer is disconnected. I have telephoned the local *PJ* and asked them to see if they can find her. They have not yet done so but not given up so far."

"Madame Heidi Ascher, according to her husband," says René, "knows nothing about the incident in the hotel; she had taken a sleeping pill and slept through everything. Monsieur Ascher does not wish us to question her, as he kept the information about the murder from her because she is nervous and it would have upset her. Although I'm not sure we are suspicious enough to take a trip to Switzerland, I am not satisfied – and won't be until I can talk to her."

"Ah," says Zabi, "you do need to talk with her, don't you? And push on to try and find Madame Simon also. *Alors*, on to other things.

"I have read over your interview reports, and although I haven't given them a thorough study yet, there are a few things I'd like to check with you. First, Sergeant Mercard: you seemed quite definite that you did not believe Monsieur Michael Denthwaite of New Zealand?"

"I did not," says René. "Although some of it is not really logical, more a matter of instinct. He said he didn't know Lindholm and seemed to think an excuse for not knowing him was that he had never been to France before. He said, 'Was that his name?' and that he had not been asked not to leave the country, although I am sure he would have been.

"He was rushing to get away from me, even on the telephone. And then he asked if he was suspected and said that he'd just been in the wrong place at the wrong time. Which I always find dubious."

"I think René is right to feel that," says Patrice, and the team members nod. "It is something which often happens."

"The second thing," says the *juge d'instruction*, "is those who saw Monsieur Lindholm on the stairs and those who did not …"

"*Certainement*," says Fleur. "Madame Brigitte Sansone, who is a great talker, who told me all about her husband, and daughter, and daughter's boyfriend, and what she bought on her shopping trip to Paris, said that they saw him on the stairs. She mentioned his bizarre footwear, even though I hadn't mentioned it."

"And what my Herr Doktor Ascher said was most peculiar," says René. "He said that they hadn't even seen Lindholm on the stairs, and when I questioned that, he added, 'or anywhere else'."

"*Passer à autre chose*,[135]" says Zabi. "There are the two sightings you managed to obtain from – whom? Ah, *oui*, from a Monsieur Emil Chavez, and two people you call Janine and Barney: no family names?"

"*Oui*," says René, "Monsieur Chavez mentioned seeing Mollie Cartwright with Lindholm – which is our possible

---

135 Moving on

connection between the cases. But he said he wondered if Lindholm was her father; there didn't seem to be any coercion, and the man may have bought her something to eat and drink. And he mentioned the footwear spontaneously."

"You didn't have any suspicions that what he said might not be true?" asks Zabi.

"I did not, Monsieur *le Juge*."

It is now Fleur's turn to talk about Janine and Barney, and to confess that she has not seen or questioned Barney.

"She is dying of AIDS in the hospital," says the inspector, softly. "But I thought that I had a good view of the information just from Janine. She said that they had seen Mollie with two different pairs of men – their descriptions are in my report. This time, it does sound like she was being coerced, and one man pushed Barney over too. Janine reported that Barney had said Mollie was too young 'for that sort of thing'."

"She meant prostitution?" asks the *juge d'instruction*.

"*Oui*, we all thought so."

"*D'accord*," says Zabi, "I think that will do for now. Please keep me informed about where you are, and who you are liking for a suspect or, perhaps, suspects."

***

"So, the feminist reading," says Patrice, sitting in the *salon* with Colette and Sartre, "if you please. I want to talk a bit about the concept of trafficking in young women too, and I know you will have much to say about that. This is not only relevant to my art case; it's relevant to our Lindholm–Mollie case, do you see?"

"*Mais certainement!*" says Colette, who has already heard a rundown of the cases so far. "Interesting that they are coming together, *quoi*?"

"From the reading Chloë gave me to do," he says, "I have noticed that there are different opinions, even controversy."

"*Oui*," she says. "I have updated myself on your Artemisia too. And it seems that many critics base a reflection on Artemisia's art on the circumstances of her life. Perhaps too many."

"Of course, most critics are men?"

"*D'accord*. There used to be quite a lot of fuming among women critics, and artists, about Artemisia's painting – not to forget her reputation – being in the control of men who could not possibly understand what she was on about ..."

"But has that all gone now?" asks Patrice.

"*Non*," she says, "but the world has changed, *n'est-ce pas?*"

"It has, but I'm not one of those people who thinks that just because things were different in past times, they can be excused. I suspect, in fact, that things don't change all that much; rather, they change their form. And we don't always recognise the relationship. I suppose what I think is that what is wrong is wrong, *quoi?*"

Colette looks slightly impressed, although it is not in accord with her feminist principles to be too impressed by any man, even Patrice.

"In mediaeval times," she says, "women were certainly a means of exchange between men. One's father provided a dowery, if he was of the class which could afford to do so, and tried to make 'good' marriages for daughters. The word 'good' usually meant financially good, although there were many power marriages too – and aristocracy and royalty almost always brokered power by that means, only secondary to conquest."

"Of course. But there were women, powerful women, who engaged in financial and power-broking too?"

"*Certainement*. But I think you'd find that the power of women to do that was mostly derived from men, possibly by widowhood or minority of a son. Something like that anyway. In the case of Artemisia, the rape trial was mostly about her father losing the 'goods': the reputation and various capacities of his daughter. Have you studied the trial transcript? You have it, do you not?"

"I have not read it yet," says Patrice. "I have resisted so far because I doubt that it's relevant. I do feel that I ought to do a phenomenological reduction of it, so that I can see the essential parts. As a policeman, I don't want to let too much of it into my head because it will certainly muddy the waters."

Colette says um, she wonders if that is correct. Can he get a proper idea of Artemisia's character without reading the transcript of this very important event in her life? Patrice says he will reserve judgement on that for now, return to it later.

"I am thinking," he says, "about the fact – it is a fact, *quoi* – that women and girls were trafficked in mediaeval times; their value being either in a dowery, or their father's power, or some other 'good'."

"*Oui*," says Colette, rubbing the woolly head of Sartre, who has briefly woken up, "of course they were. In those days. I noticed that it has been put forward that Artemisia's rape was nothing unusual, because things like that happened often – well, not personally to her, but to others. Are they saying that she should have been accustomed to it? Are they saying it wasn't traumatic enough to have had an effect on her art? Are they saying it didn't hurt? Are they saying it didn't have the potential to ruin her life?"

"You are angry about this," says Patrice, "and I don't blame you. They are also saying that either 'men can't help it' or it's all right if a man does it – because he's a man, it's his nature. Like the scorpion and the frog. You mentioned that before."

"Do you think that it doesn't happen any more? I'm not talking about what we call specifically 'trafficking'. I'm talking about now, trafficking in women's bodies, and even more so in the recent past. I am convinced that aristos still rarely marry for love, and many bourgeois marriages are legalised prostitution!"

"*Non,* I don't think it doesn't happen any more, but I do wonder whether at least some of it has changed into sexual abuse of the people who are most vulnerable. It is interesting, though reprehensible, that the abuse rings we hear of prey on girls and young women who are either homeless or living in terrible circumstances; they only need to offer somewhere warm to stay, food, company. It often employs the drugs later to keep them in thrall. The only measure is how desperate the victims are."

"And you are thinking, now, of your Mollie?" asks Colette.

"I am. There may be more to this than we have thought."

***

"What about the other *Judiths*?" asks Patrice, back in the *salle squad* with Chloë Valéry. "We haven't really talked about those two. We probably should, *n'est-ce pas*? – the Detroit one and the one in the Pitti Palace. With the neck." He is uncomfortable in describing it like this – referring to a woman by a part of her body. He reorients himself with a deep breath. He is really impressed by the neck.

"Ah, *oui,*" says Chloë, "they're both extremely interesting 'after the event' pictures, so not so threatening ..."

"So, the Pitti one first, I think," says Patrice. "Painted between the Naples and Florence pictures. I rather like this one – it's got real women in it!"

"Don't you think all the Artemisia *Judiths* are real women?"

"Need to reflect on that, although I tend towards it," he says.

"The action's over in this one," says Chloë. "They're listening in case someone has been alerted and is coming to catch them. But they're still resolute, concerned but not necessarily alarmed."

"I like Judith's neck," says Patrice, confessing. "It isn't pretty but it's real! And she has the sword over her shoulder, like the tool it is. There's plenty of suspense, *quoi*?"

"Another moment in time," says Patrice, "a cinematic still. I wonder how Artemisia would have done had she had access to film? Magnificent work, I shouldn't wonder."

"Other things said about the Pitti *Judith*," says Chloë, "is that the palette is narrower, reflecting the fact that the deal is done."

"Ah, I wouldn't have thought of that. Good point."

"And the composition is tighter, more intimate. The women are even more co-conspirators than in the Naples and Uffizi versions. It's subtle."

"*Oui*," says Patrice, who has brought up the picture on his laptop, "I can see that. Is the placing of the sword referring to Judith as 'Justice'?"

"It has been said. Maybe. Do you see the resemblance to a cross, too? But there is tenderness there. Elena Ciletti thought so. Others have referred to its proximity to the tender flesh of Judith's neck. 'The executioner who exposes her own neck to the blade.' It draws the glance upwards too, to her wispy hair, and downwards to her beautifully rendered hand holding the sword. And we see my favourite bit – the inner wrist of Abra, delicate and sensitive. It's exquisite!"

"Ah. I see, you are right. And Judith is gently placing her hand on the maidservant's shoulder. I hadn't seen that before."

"You see, *patron*," says Chloë, "art scholarship is helpful after all."

"I never doubted it for a minute," says Patrice, the scholar. "But the Detroit one is the superior one, is it not?"

"Do you think so? Why?"

He looks thoughtful before answering, to gain time. "I don't quite know … it's somehow more accomplished, *n'est-ce pas?*"

"*Oui*, I think it is. But it's very strong on sisterhood, and, dare I say, equality? There is no trace, is there, of privilege? It feels like 'we are together in this enterprise and we are unassailable'."

"A great deal to read into it," says Patrice, "but I am wondering how it may take us forward – perhaps wrongly. I wanted to look at the two *Judiths* showing what happened after the actual beheading as a start to constructing a timeline. Unhappily, though, we do not have any paintings of the minutes before the beheading – we only have the apocryphal text."

"Ah," breathes Chloë, "that would be Judith trying to seduce Holofernes, presumably?"

"I expect so. I shall have to read it – but only if I decide to pursue that path. And I am not yet sure I shall. I am hoping that the construction of the timeline of Artemisia's career, though, may clear my mind a bit. And I feel that I need to examine the Caravaggio version in the flesh, so to speak, and that can only happen when I go to Rome."

"We may have a problem there," says Chloë, wincing slightly. "It's on loan to a gallery in Minnesota until the summer of 2023."

22

This morning's tasks in the *Police Judiciaire* team are for Patrice to telephone Lindholm's church headquarters in St Paul, Minnesota, and for the whole team, probably including Patrice, when he has finished with the religious people, to follow up the seventeen sales calls M Bernard Cloche made during the period he was in Paris.

Patrice goes into his own office to ring America. He will have to concentrate hard on the conversations he has, because the accents may be confusing. What he imagines to be the switchboard answers, and he asks to speak to the Reverend Professor Milton D. Hafflinger, whom an examination of the church's website has identified as the "Reverend Executive Director" of the church in the United States.

He cannot, of course, speak to him. He is either not in, or too eminent to talk directly to a miscellaneous police officer in France. Patrice asks for his assistant, name unknown. They connect him to Monsieur Hafflinger's executive secretary.

"Good morning, this is Mrs Greta Smith, Dr Hafflinger's executive secretary. What may I do for you today?"

Patrice introduces himself as *Commissaire* Lanier and tells her that it is equivalent to the American chief of police of a city force.

"I am investigating," he says, "the murder of one of your ministers in Paris. A Reverend Doctor Cedric Philip Lindholm. You are aware that he has been killed?"

"Yes," she says, without any sign of emotion. Well, it has been a while, and Monsieur Lindholm has, presumably gone to his reward.

"I have a list here of calls he made on the mobile telephone he purchased last September, and there is one to your number. I am wondering who he spoke to, and whether they can tell me of what the call consisted?"

"Of course. Doctor Lindholm is part of the team of Reverend Doctor Gardiner Baker, in Paris, but it would be normal for him to telephone Dr Hafflinger on occasion. Many missionaries do. What you have to understand is that Dr Hafflinger is not only our executive director, he is our prophet; he has a direct connection to the Holy Spirit. He is always available to speak to people about spiritual matters."

But not to me, thinks Patrice.

"Would he have spoken to Dr Hafflinger on that occasion? Let me see, it was the twenty-ninth of September 2018. Do you have a telephone logbook to check?"

"No," she says, "not for calls like that. Only for the more mundane sort of call. Spiritual direction is always confidential."

"So, there is nothing you can tell me?"

"No. But every blessing to you and have a blessed day now."

***

The detectives, who can easily see the cathedral from their windows, have been looking away from the building, whose fire is not yet out; pretending that it is not there, still smoking.

There is a knock on the door of the detectives' room as Fleur, René and Clémence gather around Fleur's desk to talk more about Mollie Cartwright and Cedric Lindholm, still not quite sure whether they are two cases or one. It seems odd that they should not be connected when they both involve the rather strange Hôtel des Jardins.

Pucelle, returning especially to look at the damaged cathedral, does not wait to be admitted but enters, asking them how are they?

René and Fleur jump up and rush over to her. Clémence turns the wheelchair from desk-facing to door-facing and waits.

Pucelle walks over to the desk which used to be hers, the one which Clémence still sternly forbids Chloë to use and looks out at the burned Notre-Dame with a deep sigh. It had always been the view from her personal window; the solidity of her life in Paris. She has come, this morning, just to look at it, to see if she can bear to do so. She sighs again and turns away.

"*Ainsi sont les* œuvres *des hommes disposés.*[136]"

Pucelle grabs her old chair by the back rail, and turns it around to face the officers, sits on it and asks where is *le patron?*

"He has gone out with his new girl," says Clémence shortly, receiving a sharp look from them all in response. Clémence makes a show of muttering "sorry" as if she is – which she isn't. They have gone out for early lunch, to talk about the case.

Pucelle asks if she may have coffee and, at the direction of harsh looks from them all, Clémence goes to fetch it.

"How is everything?" Pucelle asks, when Clémence has wheeled herself out of the *salle squad.* "Work, children, grandchildren?"

This is clearly directed at Fleur, as René has only one of these things. Fleur tells her that her husband is well, although a bit arthritic, better now he has retired, and is

---

136 so are the works of men disposed

learning to cook; her daughter and three grandchildren are very well. Work is, well …"

René, pausing only for a little genuflection to confidentiality, mentions Monsieur Lindholm and Mollie Cartwright. Pucelle is interested in M Lindholm, as it was she who took the lead role in relation to him last year.

"Any suspects?" she asks. "Or did he actually fall?"

"*Non*," says René. "His head was bashed in and he was quite dead before he hit the snow."

"Obviously, you've interviewed everyone from the hotel?"

"*Certainement*," says Fleur, "and René discovered this girl, who turned out to be Mollie, in the hotel basement. She doesn't speak, although her friends say that she can. We haven't managed to persuade her to speak to us."

"And we don't yet know whether they are two cases or one," says René.

"Ah," says Pucelle, realising she should stop as she is not, momentarily, a police officer.

They discuss domestic issues over the nice coffee Clémence has brought back from the café on the corner. Fleur says there might be some troubles between *la jeune* Amélie and her mother.

"She is sixteen," says Fleur, "*toujours un* âge *difficile*.[137]"

"What were you like when you were sixteen?" asks Clémence of Pucelle.

"*Moi?* I was taking my preliminary vows," says the *commissaire adjoint*, ending that section of the conversation. "I understand that *le patron* is to do some of the research on his art case by travelling to Italy and returning to Finland. I believe in May?"

---

137 always a difficult age

Everyone stares at her as she concludes with the statement that she will be returning to *le Trente-Six* for the entire month of May – while the *patron* is away.

"He feels we need supervision?" asks Clémence, clearly *outragé*.[138]

"He feels you may need a bit of help," says Pucelle, not actually helping with anything.

*****

As April marches on, the team begins to pull its evidence in the Lindholm case together, and as the month approaches its end, Pucelle begins to arrive most lunchtimes, staying for much of the afternoon. She cannot be required to begin in the mornings; she is not being paid at all. She mostly sits listening, not speaking. Trying to get up to date.

"We shall need to marshall our witness list and evidence for the *juge d'instruction*, in the case of Monsieur Lindholm," says Patrice, when the whole team has assembled in the *salle squad*. "Let us send the witness list, in advance, to Monsieur Zabi, *je vous en prie*."

Each of them produces a file from her or his desk and starts shuffling the information between them. Fleur has the witness file for Monsieur Cloche, but she needs René's comments on their visit to Blois, plus the information Cloche has given them. The others are similarly bereft of some of the components of their file.

When they have finished the shuffle, Patrice calls them to order, and asks for a list of hotel residents and witnesses to be put up on the whiteboard, so he can see it.

---

138 put out, offended

Residents of Hôtel des Jardins

Ascher, Heidi	607 (suite)	Not interviewed	Basle	
Ascher, Friedrich	607 (suite)	**René Mercard**	Basle	
Barnier, Cécile	507 (suite)	**Clémence Godard**	Permanent resident	
Cloche, Bernard	603	**Fleur Olivier/René Mercard**	Blois	
Denthwaite, Michael	303	**René Mercard** (tel)	Auckland NZ	
Juliane, Agnès	406	**René Mercard**	Paris	
Juliane, Max	406	**René Mercard**	Paris	
Melzer, André	403	**Clémence Godard**	Nantes	
Renault, Pierre	403	**Clémence Godard**	Nancy	
Sansone, Albert	503	**Fleur Olivier**	Bordeaux	
Sansone, Brigitte	503	**Fleur Olivier**	Bordeaux	
Simon, Magda	407 (suite)	Not interviewed	Reims	?

Hotel staff

Szonja Horváth, day receptionist
Jean-Didier Desmond, night manager
NOTE: The Rev Dr Cedric P. Lindholm exited from window
of Room 607

Church staff

Rev Dr Gardiner Baker
Kristen Derek
Linden Fraser
Mary-Anne McCready, receptionist

Persons who may be witnesses

Mollie Cartwright
Chang Su-Ming
Signe Zvenieks
Marie Lagrange
Julie Dorrity

Tips from public (553)

Of these most were useless or spurious – list maintained
for future use
Jean Landal, professional confessee
The following may be useful:
Emil Chavez
Janine & Barney (no family names)

"It is not long now until I must disappear to London,
and the other places on my schedule," says Patrice. "Are
you coming up to speed, Pucelle?"

The *commissaire adjoint* nods silently. Of course she is;
she will take what he has told her, add the extras that the
remainder of the team has not told him yet, and put it

through her own filters. Then she will have it all. Surprisingly, though, Patrice has a special question for her – one only she can answer.

"Stepping aside from the Hôtel des Jardins matter for a moment," says the *patron*, "I want to ask you what we might call a religious question."

Pucelle makes a face as if she cannot be bothered with such references to a life she left behind long ago.

"Remind me," he says, "what reasons there were for artists in the Renaissance and Baroque producing so many religious paintings and sculptures."

Pucelle thinks for a moment, ordering her lecture, deleting details he does not need.

"For money and fashion, to start with," she says. "Many of them were unlike what we consider artists today – although we often get it wrong and think modern artists do what they do because of their, *quoi*, calling. And don't need money to do it. It isn't even like that today, let alone all those years ago. Artists, then, tried for commissions from patrons – often churchmen and noble families (our equivalent is probably grants from the Academie Française) – and, of course, fashion came into it."

"What about religious devotion, though?" asks Patrice, trying to keep his natural disbelief out of his voice.

"Oh, there was certainly that," says Pucelle, "some of it no doubt real. Although some for show, naturally. Art consumers were human, even in those days!"

"I am told," says Patrice, casting a glance at Chloë, at the other side of the table, "that some smaller pictures were made for personal devotion." He stops as Pucelle nods in time with the art historian.

"*Oui*," says Pucelle. "Usually they were quite small. A picture of a martyr or saint might be used to focus the mind during private prayer. Much as does a crucifix."

"*Mais*" – Chloë bursts in to the conversation – "our *Judith* isn't devotional. No one could use it for personal prayer, could they?"

"*Non*," answers Patrice, drawing his lips together in disdain at that idea, "but the artist might keep it herself, to focus her mind on something private. Something in which she was particularly interested. An event in which she had an investment."

***

The *PJ* is not worried, now, about Mollie being tucked away with Mme Paston, and this helps to open out the investigation. Pucelle, who has worked for the longest time with *le patron,* is not convinced he would have allowed this new aspect; he'd have called it slack and considered it a negative influence towards solving the case. How are they going to move it on? The *commissaire adjoint* is concerned that Patrice will leave and return to see they are still in the same place as before he left. This, she thinks, will not do. She calls the meeting to order.

"*D'accord,*" she begins. "Where are we in the case of Monsieur Lindholm?"

René and Clémence look at her without speaking. Yves Mercier, a junior detective, seconded from another section while the *patron* and Chloë are away, shrugs his shoulders.

He is a bright young man with a law degree but little police experience; he is there simply for the numbers. He does look thoughtful, though, which gives Pucelle a pale ray of sunshine which she knows she will have to nurture carefully.

"Perhaps," she says, "new eyes would help. Yves. Outline the case of Monsieur Lindholm for us, *s'il vous plaît.*"

The young man, dark-complexioned, with lots of dark brown, shaggy hair, gelled, deteriorated blue jeans, black T-shirt, gives them a straightforward rundown of M Lindholm, indicating the whiteboards as he does so. Pucelle's half-formed plan that he might turn up something out of the ordinary doesn't work. The young man's thinking is banal.

Clémence suggests that they look, again, at the CCTV footage, which has so far been ignored as *ripou*.[139] And have a look at the *dossiers de police* they have formed for all the witnesses. Fleur wonders whether Pucelle has lost her touch, and if they should work through all this with the *juge d'instruction*. She puts in a call to Monsieur Zabi. He will call in to the *salle squad* at 13.30. He will bring cakes.

***

When Patrice emerges from his office, not in the best of tempers, Fleur has made three phone calls to Monsieur Cloche's customers, and René has made two. Clémence has got a good talker on the line in her first call. It is her natural inclination to let those who wish to talk, talk, and she has been instructed by Patrice that it is often a way to get interesting information available in no other. None of Fleur's calls has produced anything useful; all the sales calls were made and resulted in small sales. None of them seems to have lasted very long.

The first of René's calls is with a very angry man who confirms, reluctantly, that M Cloche had visited him on the afternoon of 13 January but they had not made any kind of deal. He had done a lot of talking, Cloche, but had been unwilling to shift on price. The angry man had told him

---

139 rotten, corrupted – Verlan

not to come again. René's second call is a photocopy of Fleur's three – calls made, small deals done, Cloche left after about ten minutes.

After fifteen minutes, Clémence is still talking to the proprietor-slash-bookkeeper at the shop of M et Mme Clery. Mme Clery is obviously lonely, isolated in a male-orientated plumbing and kitchen-fitting business. Clémence seems to be specialising in talking to lonely women.

"I am seeking information," explains Clémence, "about a sales call made to you by Monsieur Bernard Cloche on the fourteenth of January. I wonder if you yourself were present that day?"

"Oh, my dear," says Mme Clery, "I hardly remember, but I can look at our day book. We keep a record of all visits and telephone calls, as well as what staff were in the shop. It is incredibly useful, I can't tell you how many times it has saved arguments and other kinds of problems! Do you keep one yourself? You must, of course, being the police.

"*Oui*, my dear, Monsieur Cloche visited us on January the fourteenth, at nine forty-five in the morning. My husband and I were both here, and André, the apprentice. My husband, Charles, has known Bernard for years and they went out for coffee. He was sparing me. He knows I do not like the man. André went to do some stocktaking in the warehouse. I could have easily made the coffee here, and we could have had a pastry. I get them most mornings from the *pâtisserie*, which is next door to our showroom. They are very good. Madame Mélande makes them herself, she is the main baker. The one I like best is the one with pineapple sauce in the middle with the custard – oh, it is so good! But you don't want to know about that, of course ..."

"Tell me," says Clémence, "did Monsieur Cloche make a sale to your husband that day?"

"There is no note," says madame, "so I don't think so. I suppose my husband may have made a contract but it is not likely. He always tells me afterwards, so I can write it down. And I can't think of anything we would need that Bernard could supply. That time of year is quiet for kitchen- and bathroom-fitting work. We mainly mend burst pipes and swab floodwater out of ground floors and basements!"

"I see," says Clémence. "Madame, have you any idea how long Monsieur Cloche was with you, or with your husband? What time did he leave?"

"Oh, I really don't know," she says. "He did not return back with Charles. I know Charles had a call to make, with André, at *10.40 heures*, so they could not have been long. I think Charles came back to pick up the boy at *10.25 heures*, the job was quite close. They got in the van and went off. It was a complicated job, though. They did not get back until almost *17 heures*. I closed up as soon as they came in; there was no trade anyway, it is always quiet at this time of year."

"So, we can imagine that Monsieur Cloche was with your husband about forty or forty-five minutes, then?"

"*Oui, je le pense.*[140]"

***

Fleur's next three calls produce a total of one hour's work for M Cloche between them, including the time it would have taken to walk from each place to the next. None of the proprietors admitted to him making any sales. They all said that it was a quiet time of year.

The tenth call of the overall seventeen, made by Fleur, produced a tiny bit of information. Monsieur Cloche had not turned up at all, even though he had made an

---

140 Yes, I think so

appointment to see Monsieur Dubois. M Dubois *avait* été *très en colère*.[141] His order had gone elsewhere.

Both of Clémence's next two calls had not wanted to talk much; one man who was shy, one who was *bourru*.[142] She learns that M Cloche had stayed only minutes before leaving *avec une puce dans l'oreille*.[143] He had been told not to come again.

René got a conversationalist on his own next call, but it still turned out that Cloche had not been exactly welcome at the premises of most of his customers. Only Monsieur Jaques, in addition to Clémence's Madame Clery, wished to talk. And this time, the customer took the opportunity to tell René that his Monsieur Cloche is *un fils de pute*[144] and can go to hell.

"Not exactly popular with his customers," says René, looking around the *salle squad*, and wondering what Monsieur Mercier is doing. He hasn't taken one of the scraps of paper on which the relevant telephone numbers are jotted. René will make one more call then kick him up the backside.

René's next call produces another no-show for Monsieur Cloche, although the customer sounds complacent, as if it has happened before. René stands up and shouts:

"*Zyva!*[145] Where is Mercier? How many calls has he made?"

It appears or, rather doesn't, that he is not present.

Fleur tries one last time, and rings a company called Tellier Plomberie et Chauffage,[146] asking for Monsieur

---

141 had been very angry
142 gruff, grumpy
143 with a flea in his ear
144 a son of a bitch
145 Let's go – Verlan
146 Tellier Plumbing and Heating

Tellier. Unhappily, Monsieur Tellier has not been alive for seventeen years, and a Monsieur Etienne Pichot is now in charge. He denies all knowledge of M Cloche.

Clémence and René take telephone calls sixteen and seventeen, and find that Monsieur Cloche hasn't attended on either customer.

23

On the second day of the Interpol art course in Lyon, Chloë had referred to the Artemisia painting known as the Detroit *Judith* as hosting an example of homage from one artist to another. In this case, homage by Artemisia Gentileschi to Caravaggio.

Today, when they have been through a huge amount of art history over several weeks, connoisseurship and attribution, she and Patrice begin to consider the 1625 work as a prime example of Artemisia's oeuvre.

Patrice is pleased, when he learns of M Bonnetain's resignation, that his travelling has been scheduled for May. The children will be still at school and university, Colette can manage all the dates – although she will, doubtless, telephone Lucie in Versailles daily – and they can meet Chloë, who will be having her early summer holiday in Helsinki, with which city she has fallen deeply in love. And Pucelle is coming home to *le Trente-Six*.

"We can't go away for the whole of May without coming home at some point," says Colette. "Just from the perspective of luggage – I don't think that one set of clothes will accommodate Florence, Rome, Naples, London and

Helsinki. We shall need different things!"

"*D'accord*. Are you going to make the reservations today, *chérie*? We need to work out when we shall pop back to Paris. We did think that a quick trip across *La Manche*,[147] perhaps Eurostar, would do. Have you gone off that idea? Won't be much difference in price, and Charles de Gaulle to Heathrow is quicker."

"And more damaging to the environment," says Colette. "But I think we have to if we're only going for a couple of days. How long will we need?"

"One night to sleep, one trip to the Hampton Court, one night to sleep, one day at the National Gallery, one night to sleep, back next day. So, three nights. May begins on a Wednesday. Therefore, fly on Wednesday the first – we should manage a nice day flight – Hampton Court on Thursday second, National Gallery on Friday third. Fly back Saturday fourth. Sunday *chez nous*."

"*Eh bien*," says Colette, "then to Florence. Rome. We'll need the whole week. There are some things I want to see. We've only been once, and we hardly did any art!"

"We had an excuse," says Patrice. "There were several things … That'll be all right, though, we can manage a week."

"Excellent," says Colette, "I'll make a list of what I want to see. Then we need to go to Helsinki. How long will you need, do you think?"

"I already have a note from Chloë about what she's booked. She'll stay in a *pension*, not the hotel like last time." He sees Colette making a displeased face at him and says, "It's her choice. The department will pay for her return travel, of course, but she'll only get a week's hotel. So, she's having two weeks, as her holiday, and staying somewhere less expensive.

---

147 English Channel

"She doesn't want to cramp our style anyway – I don't know what she thinks we're going to get up to, but I do see her point. When you arrange to go out together, one of you can go to the other. Apparently her *pension* is close by."

"If we are arriving in Helsinki on Saturday eighteenth May," says Colette, "what are we doing from the sixteenth?"

"Ah. I need to talk to someone about this painting we're looking at. He lives in Stockholm. The flights between are easy, so I thought three nights in Sweden might be quite nice. I can tidy up what I need from Monsieur Larsson quickly, so we'll have a bit of time to see the city. We have never been to Sweden."

"*D'accord*," says Colette, "I'll make the reservations then, shall I? Or do you want the department to do it?"

"I'd rather you did," he says. "Then I shall know it will be correct."

***

In his office, having given out a "do not disturb or else" notice to the rest of the team, Patrice brings up the Detroit *Judith* on his desktop monitor. Both he and Chloë look at it in silence, digesting what it looks like, what it is. Both consider it a sublime example of Artemisia's work.

"It's interestingly different from the others, don't you think?" says Patrice.

"Um. To a certain extent," Chloë says. "It kind of makes a pair with the Pitti Palace one though, doesn't it?"

"As opposed to the Uffizi and Naples *Judiths*? Also a pair?"

"*Oui*, well, both are later in time, of course; I mean in the time of the narrative – because they weren't both painted in the middle between the Naples and Uffizi; only one was – the Pitti. What I mean is that both are situated after the beheading; the women are still in danger because they haven't yet got away."

Patrice gazes at the painting, wishing it were here and not just on his screen. The resolution isn't bad, it just isn't as it would be "live". He makes a little sigh of frustration.

Chloë says that the composition is a complete wonder; how the artist has assembled her figures in a broad stripe of light – purporting to be lit by the candle (the homage to Caravaggio), although it isn't … and the shadow over much of Judith's face.

"Did you read about the idea that the shadow makes a crescent moon of Judith's face?" asks Chloë. "That it could be a reference to Galileo's work after he looked at the moon through a telescope? And/or could be a reference to Artemis – goddess of the moon and Artemisia's namesake?"

"*Non*," says Patrice, "I haven't read that. Where is it, do you think?"

Chloë scans his desk and lifts the paper with the Galileo parabola article, which she lays over Patrice's phenomenological reduction.

"It's here!" she says triumphantly. She hands it to the *patron*, and he reads through the article slowly.

"*D'accord*," he says, "I see what you mean. Do you think it's a real thing, though? Or just fanciful? I can see that because there's so little actual documentation, that people might want to make it up. To elaborate what we have?"

"*Je suppose*," says Chloë, "sometimes you think that people make stuff up, things that the artist or writer never put there …"

"But to our painting?" says Patrice.

"*Oui*," says Chloë. "Christiansen and Mann, in the catalogue of the Metropolitan exhibition of 2001, say that the conflict between drama and formal elegance is resolved in this picture as it isn't as violent or threatening as her Uffizi and Naples canvases. They think it's her most accomplished, her finest work."

"They'll get no argument from me on that," says Patrice. "Although I have to say that I don't necessarily agree with their reasons. It isn't that it isn't violent, or threatening men by having a woman kill one; it's because there are so many things in it which are superlative."

"Aha," says Chloë. "You are beginning to sound like an art historian – or even a connoisseur! What are the things? What have you seen?"

Patrice keeps silence for a minute and then begins with the foot.

"The foot isn't in a glamorous sandal, it's in a workmanlike shoe, just peeping out under her dress. And Abra's toes show horny, hard-working feet. You mainly get those on shop assistants and waitresses these days. Holofernes's head is coming towards being hidden, it's being wrapped up, literally. It even takes a bit of a brain twitch to see it's there at all. Of course, the women would try to hide the evidence, at least temporarily, that they had killed the general. And of course, it wouldn't have worked for long because the decapitated body was in plain sight.

"And I like, very much, the table, covered with green velvet, holding the light for Judith to bring as well as Holofernes's gauntlet, empty now, never to be filled, and the scabbard of his sword, which is in the heroine's hand.

"I like the sword better, too. It's a scimitar now, which it would have been if Holofernes had been an Assyrian general. It would not have been a European broadsword or any kind of straight sword. And a sabre has a very sharp edge, as well as a point. And she would have needed a sharp edge to have hacked off his head in the two strokes the apocryphal account says it took!"

"*Attends!*" says Chloë. "You said 'holding the light for Judith'."

"I did."

"Could she be reclaiming the light of righteousness when she has finished with the murder? Or is that way too fanciful?"

"Don't know," says Patrice. "When we are doing this, anything could happen."

"The critics say," says Chloë, "that the Detroit *Judith* is her masterwork, because it shows maturity, subtle palette, lighting and composition. It is thought to have been painted when Artemisia was about thirty – hence maturity. What about the suspense, though?"

"On account of the chiaroscuro?" asks Patrice. "*Oui*, I think its enhanced, and the velvet hanging is pure Artemisia, *quoi*?"

"It is. Her profile is underlined too. As well as her beautiful hand, stretched to quiet any sound."

"Have you noticed, Chloë," he says, "speaking of fanciful things, that the sword cuts off the two women? It literally comes between them. The first thought I had was that Judith intended to kill Abra – which is silly, isn't it?"

Chloë looks at the picture again for a moment and then at Patrice.

"I never noticed that," she says, "and it's never been pointed out to me before. Don't think it's in any of the literature." She ponders awhile and then says:

"Maybe it's to make Abra look blameless? Making Judith the murderess, and her maidservant just someone who has been drawn in? Is she saving Abra in case they get caught?"

"Or is she claiming the hero's role?" asks Patrice.

***

237

Fleur, René, Clémence and the elusive Yves Mercier are all present in the *salle squad* when Monsieur *le Juge*, Micah Zabi, arrives with Roxanne, who is carrying a large box of cakes whilst the *juge* himself wrestles with a big shoulder bag, a briefcase, and a medium-sized cardboard box with a top which keeps flapping loose. He greets them and says that he should rather have scheduled their meeting in his office – then everything would have been at hand. This is his idea of a lightweight joke; he makes it his business to come out to the *PJ* workplace regularly. He believes in *égalité*.

Monsieur *le Juge* asks if they have all the dossiers to compare to the CCTV footage. He addresses Fleur as if she is in charge, which she technically is at this moment. *Le juge* is exquisitely good at understanding the hierarchy and how it modifies itself when someone is missing.

Clémence is the technophile running the film, which is projected on the wall screen. She runs through the two films, back-to-back, with no commentary.

Fleur says that there are some possible identifications they have tentatively made but there is no sign of anyone who could be Cedric Lindholm.

"So, Monsieur Lindholm may already have been in the hotel?" says Zabi. "And we have no film from an earlier time?"

"*Non*," says Fleur, "just from *08.00 heures* on tenth January. It would have meant him arriving early or the day before, because his flight from the window was on the date of the tenth. And we have that on film, of course. The films both conclude at *07.59 heures* on the eleventh of January."

"Um. Let us look at who is coming out of the hotel," says Zabi. "I think that is fewer people all together, *n'est-ce pas?*"

Clémence rapidly finds the section. There are nine people leaving the Hôtel des Jardins, although one is clearly a woman, and two of the men have their faces turned to the side, as if trying to conceal their identity.

"*Hélas!*[148]" says M Zabi. "Let's look at those in particular."

Everyone stares at the halted film. The men are not together. One comes out at 14.30 on January tenth, and one comes out at 06.07 on the eleventh. Just before Lindholm is declared dead at 06.15.

"Presumably," says Yves Mercier, "we can exclude the first one; he had left the hotel before Monsieur Lindholm fell?"

"That is probably true," says René, "unless he came back in. Is there any sign that he did?"

"*Non,*" says Clémence, "although I have allowed for him to have changed his clothes. I do think I have identified Monsieur Renault and Monsieur Melzer. Both told us they were out most of the night, coming in in the early hours. And the woman on this piece of footage is Mademoiselle Barnier, whom I talked to myself. She leaves just after 07.30 to go to work in the sewing room of the *atélier*[149] Maison Diane. We shall see her coming in from work at about 17.30, but on the tenth of January, of course."

"The remaining four?" asks Monsieur *le Juge.*

"I think that may be Herr Ascher," says René, indicating, "although without his wife. He probably went for a walk, or a newspaper, and we shall see him coming back later. I don't know about the other three."

"One, the tall man with blonde hair, is the night manager, Monsieur Desmond. He is leaving at a minute before eight

---

148 Alas and alack
149 fashion house (not quite *haute couture*!)

because Mademoiselle Horváth will have taken over. She works from 08.00 to 20.00. They both live in the hotel, but he will be going out to his gym, which he does every day."

Roxanne has made additions to the *PJ*'s whiteboards, in red marker, and the *juge* decides to let them have coffee and pastries while they discuss the dossiers of all the possible witnesses. Fleur and René have produced what American law enforcement officers call "the jackets" of any who have previous criminal activity, or even mentions in police records.

"None of the following are known to any French police force," says René. "I have checked with the *brigade criminelle* and the *gendarmerie*, as well as the *police financière*. No one has any records for Monsieur Lindholm, for Monsieur Baker, Monsieur Fraser or Madame Derek. Both witnesses with no family name, Janine and Barney, have been picked up for soliciting a couple of times, for begging and for possession of illegal substances. But no violence. Monsieur Emil Chavez has a totally clean record.

"Mademoiselle Barnier is not known to the authorities, and neither is Madame Magda Simon, of whom there is still no trace – we have not yet received any further information about her from the *PJ* in Reims."

"We have word from the police in Auckland, New Zealand," says Fleur, "that Monsieur Denthwaite was arrested for defrauding his agricultural company three years ago, but they were unable to make their case stick, and he was released. He has also sealed juvenile offences, some of which were reputed to be for violence – but that is many years ago."

"Monsieur Cloche has a record," says Clémence, "and it isn't very pretty."

"Ah," says Zabi. "Tell us, *s'il vous plaît ...*"

"Nasty stuff," she says. "He's a registered sex offender. He likes little girls …" She chokes slightly, not liking this. "Likes to beat them up too if they are small and weak. He was convicted of this in relation to four foreign children aged between eight and eleven, and served twenty years. He got out five years ago and used his late father's estate to set up in business in Blois. He's stayed out of trouble since then, but he is frequently visited by the *PJ* and cannot leave home without them being advised."

"You have talked to him in person, haven't you?" asks the *juge*.

"We have," says Fleur. "He did not, of course, tell us about his record."

"Is he then the prime suspect?" asks Zabi.

"Not sure," says Fleur. "He may, obviously, have something to do with Mollie Cartwright, the girl whom René found in the hotel basement, but he has no record of killing anyone."

"What about any records on the other people?" Zabi looks over at the whiteboards. "They appear to be three married couples: the Sansones, the Julianes and the Aschers. You have spoken to them all?"

"We have," says Fleur, "with the exception of Frau Ascher, who is said to have been asleep throughout. Herr Ascher said he did not tell her about the murder. We spoke to the Swiss police, and they say that Frau Ascher died several years ago."

"Ow!" says Monsieur *le Juge*. "There's an unexpected development."

"*Non*," says René. "I am beginning to think there are several people implicated in this case who don't actually exist."

Clémence is looking at the dossier labelled "Caroline Harrice, Dowager Countess of Merramdale". She mutters that both M Sansone and M Juliane have motoring offences over a long period of time. Sign of general lawlessness and accrued privilege maybe, and they don't seem to think that traffic regulations apply to them. She adds, incidentally, that the countess also has motoring offences, and there is an ancient note from the English police, from before she came to live in France, saying that she has been a thorn in their flesh and a menace on the roads for several years. Clémence adds that there is no record of Mme Harrice having driven in France and she certainly does not, now, own a car.

"*Alors*," says Zabi, "Madame Sansone, I think, mentioned the shoes, *quoi*? That seems like it might have significance … it is a positive identification of Cedric Lindholm anyway. We have him ascending the hotel stairs around *20 heures* on Thursday tenth January in his shoes of nougat patent."

"And Monsieur Ascher," says René, "definitely did not see him on the stairs, or anywhere else, meaning that he did. I don't think he mentioned the shoes though … Monsieur Chavez, on the other hand, did mention the shoes. He said he had seen Mollie Cartwright in the area near the hotel around January, just wandering, but then he had seen her with someone he thought might have been her father but who can be identified as Monsieur Lindholm by his shoes." He shuffles through papers in his lap. "Ah, *oui,* here it is:

"'Oh, and he had some really fancy shoes on. I've never seen anything like them before. They were shiny, you know, like dance shoes. And they were a sort of bright blue colour! Not something I myself would wear.'

"So, we know there is a connection between Monsieur Lindholm and Mollie Cartwright," says the *juge*.

"Um," says Fleur, "there's something *un peu* wrong with that, Monsieur *le Juge*."

"*Quoi?*"

"Monsieur Gardiner Baker, the head of Monsieur Lindholm's church, also wears such shoes. They were pale lavender patent when I spoke to him. What about when you interviewed him, René?"

René looks shamefaced. He hadn't noticed.

***

The meeting in the office of the *juge d'instruction* is turning into a bloodbath.

René has already been sharply told off for not noticing M Baker's shoes. He has restrained his reaction and swallowed the comment "How was I supposed to know his shoes were important?". He is aware that *le patron* would have said "Everything means something" – for him it does.

Zabi is now being short with Fleur for not including the "girls", friends of Mollie Cartwright, in their survey of previous records for witnesses. Clémence tries to say that they did not know whether the cases were connected but is steamrollered by Zabi, who is fighting not to lose his temper.

"*Je suggère*," says Zabi, "check the records of Mademoiselles Chang, Dorrity, Lagrange and Zvenieks with alacrity. There is something here about which we do not know."

24

The Air France afternoon flight from CDG to London takes off as predicted, and the Laniers land and go easily through European Union immigration – making a few comments about being in good time before the United Kingdom is, now, scheduled to leave.

Their hotel is a small one in which they have stayed before, which is owned and run by an expat from Normandy. It is also reasonably central. They go out for dinner, returning for an early night and to telephone the children. Both children seem to be happy enough under the supervision – which will be periodic during the whole month – of their maternal grandparents. Jean-Pascal reports, responsibly, that *grand-mère* Agnès is happily cleaning the flat.

On Wednesday morning, Colette and Patrice take the bus to Hampton Court Palace.

Artemisia Gentileschi's painting *Self-Portrait as the Allegory of Painting* is hanging in the Cumberland Bedchamber. They stand in front of it in amazement. Having seen many photographs of the work, the real thing still stuns. Neither can find any words, and the palace is quiet. There is the silence of deep appreciation. Eventually, Patrice finds his voice:

"Interesting, at least to me, is that its provenance consists of exactly two lines of type in the guide:

> "'Reported by the Trustees of the Sales of Charles I in October 1649, at Hampton Court; sold to Jackson and others on 23 October 1651; recovered at the Restoration.'

"It's a delight not to have a complicated provenance to study!"

"I expect it is," says Colette. "I remember looking at it before – knowing little about Artemisia – and finding it peculiarly satisfying. I didn't know why. It's something about the structure, *n'est-ce pas?* The way she's arranged herself at work?"

"Ah, *oui*," says Patrice. "It's not gorgeous or beautiful or anything like that, but it's real and strong. You're right. It's satisfying. Let's go and get coffee and come back?"

"*D'accord.*"

***

Pucelle arrives at the *salle squad*, at 09.00 promptly, on the first day of May. Neither Fleur nor René are yet present, and Clémence and Chloë, looking like twins separated at birth, are glaring at one another from opposite sides of the room.

Clémence wheels herself towards the *commissaire adjoint*, greeting her and asking if she should go for coffee. Pucelle, who sees signs of a regular ritual, agrees, and asks that she cater for all six of those expected. She, Pucelle, wants to hold a discussion on the two Hôtel des Jardins cases.

"We have," says the *commissaire adjoint*, "the killing of Monsieur Lindholm, by being crowned with a blunt object and thrown out of a high window, and the mystery of *la petite* Mollie Cartwright being found in the basement storeroom. Are they one case, or are they not? Mademoiselle Valéry, which do you favour?"

"They must be one case," says Chloë, "must they not? It is unlikely that the two things in one location should not be related."

"Why should they be related?" asks Pucelle. "Is it your opinion that there are no coincidences?"

Chloë looks a little confused. Of course, she recognises coincidence; not to do so would be a betrayal of the *patron*'s method. The senior officer goes on to read her a lecture on the relevance of chance in police work. When she has finished, Chloë feels thoroughly chastised. Clémence, returned from getting coffee, is aware she should not be enjoying this. Pucelle, however, has not finished. She checks with Chloë, asking whether she is to assist with their general detective work – which may be outside her area of expertise.

"*Oui*," says the young woman, "I am qualified as a detective as well as in art specialities. During the absence of *le patron*, when I am not on leave I am to help with whatever is necessary." She does not sound as if she is looking forward to this and is taking time to get over her embarrassment at being told off.

It is precisely at this moment, when there is still a residue of discipline in the air, that René and Fleur arrive together, followed immediately by Faye Benoît, the civilian administrator and sometime assistant in police work. They settle at the big table and quietly sip their coffee, awaiting Pucelle starting the meeting.

"I was just asking Officers Godard and Valéry," she says, "their opinion of whether there is a connection between the death of Monsieur Lindholm and the discovery of Mademoiselle Cartwright – considering that they both happened at the Hôtel des Jardins."

There is silence for a little while as the newly arrived officers consider the question. Fleur, still operating as senior, as well as the most outspoken, gives her opinion as if she has already been asked.

"There seemed a chance," she says, "that the two things might not be related at first. The girl could have just sneaked in. I think we all recognised that. But it soon started to come into focus that there is something very peculiar about the hotel. Something not quite right."

"Specify." Pucelle asks for the detail around that.

"As soon as we began to ask questions," says Fleur, "people started telling lies. It was not that they were unwilling to answer, it was just that they were obviously hiding things. And there are at least two people reported as staying there whom we have not been able to identify. It is a puzzle."

"René," says Pucelle, "your opinion?"

"Same case," says René. "Although we need to stay aware that there could be multiple crimes here. And we do not yet know what they might be."

***

The second visit of the England trip is to see the newly acquired Artemisia painting *Self-Portrait of the Artist as Saint Catherine of Alexandria*, painted around 1615–17, being displayed in the London National Gallery. The gallery had bought it from the art dealer, who had purchased it after its discovery. The National Gallery paid 3.6 million pounds in 2018.

"It's quite similar to *the Allegory of Painting*," says Colette, sighing that it is amazing how a little reading can develop one's mind.

"*Incroyable!*" says Patrice. "Something about the structure, *quoi*?"

"*Oui*, it's almost the same posture of the figure, although this time, she's looking out at us – I wonder what sort of mirror images she used?"

"They're her own arms, aren't they? Strong and capable, not decorative."

"*Oui*. The arms are a continuing thing. And you are getting obsessed with them. But look at her right hand, Patrice, traces of arthritis in the knuckles …"

"And we couldn't see the knuckles properly in the other picture, they were tucked under and over. The time is a bit off," he says.

"*Comment veux-tu dire? Explique.*[150]"

"The *Catherine* was painted first," says Patrice, "in 1615 to 1617, when Artemisia had *22 ans*, and was living in Rome; the *Allegory*, probably painted in London when she had *45 ans*. Yet, it seems to me that the *Allegory* is more youthful than the *Catherine* and, as you say, the *Catherine* might show arthritis."

"Do you really think the *Allegory* is more youthful? I don't think I agree. It's more serious, more, what do you say? More accomplished, masterly, painterly. It's her natural youthfulness and purpose coming through, *n'est-ce pas*? And the hiding of the arthritic fingers? Probably the torture in 1612 – her hands with the Sybille – would have led to appalling inflammation, which she may have suffered all her life. She may have painted through varying amounts of pain always."

Patrice gazes at his wife and considers this new piece of information which he would never have seen alone.

"The accoutrements of the martyr are there," he says. "The palm frond is significant. Have you any idea who Saint Catherine of Alexandria was supposed to be, by the way?"

"*Non.* And I thought that it was Saint Catherine of Siena who was broken on the wheel ... I'd better look her up when we get back to the hotel."

"*D'accord*," says Patrice. "What else about this painting?"

"Nice veil over the top of her left arm," says Colette. "I don't know how she does that! It's fantastic."

"Her draperies are always good. So were her father's. Presumably she got the technique from him. I see that the catalogue says that Artemisia's art followed her life. I'm still not convinced by that; her career was her own creation,

---

150 How do you mean? Explain.

wasn't it? Because she was strong and determined? I guess we'll never know."

"Is it important that we do?" asks Colette. "I suppose we can appreciate and enjoy, whether or not we know the life of the artist, *quoi?*

"Not important for appreciation," says Patrice, "but possibly quite important for attribution!"

Colette opens the catalogue in her hand and reads, out loud, the description the gallery gives of its collection of paintings by female painters:

> "'The National Gallery has 20 works by female artists in its collection and four works by female artists on loan to the Gallery (artists include: Berthe Morisot, Judith Leyster, Rachel Ruysch, Henriette Browne, Rosa Bonheur, Maggi Hambling, Vivien Blackett, Paula Rego, Marie Blancour, Rosalba Carriera, Madeleine Strindberg, Catharina van Hemessen, Élisabeth Louise Vigée Le Brun). There are over 2,300 works in the National Gallery Collection.'

"Twenty-four by female artists, out of a collection of two thousand three hundred," she says, "and four of those are borrowed from somewhere else! What's their excuse? Apart from a list of women painters? Women can't really paint? Artemisia clearly could but it was only because she was raped? How insulting!"

***

Back in the London bed and breakfast, Colette types "St Catherine of Alexandria" into her laptop, and discovers that she was entirely wrong, or her religious teachers were, and that the Egyptian was, indeed, the martyr broken on the wheel. Except she wasn't because divine intervention made the wheel fall to pieces. She was, however, later beheaded.

"She was one of the virgin martyrs," she says, "who refused to marry her persecutor because she had dedicated her virginity to Jesus and experienced a mystical marriage with him. Don't ask me what they used for a ring."

Patrice, fascinated to know, gets up from the bed where he has been idling and looks over her shoulder:

"*Oh, dieu!*" he says as he reads the words *le prépuce de Jésus.*[151] "Oh, yuk!"

"Although," says Colette, "Catherine is supposed to have said that their ring was invisible."

"Oh, good," approves Patrice, resubsiding onto the bed.

"She was supposed to have lived in the fourth century, in Alexandria," continues Colette, "but no evidence of her ever having lived at all seems to have been found. Oh, and she is one of the 'Fourteen Holy Helpers', who are especially expected to intercede for the faithful." She pauses, then adds:

"Ah, that's interesting! Some people think that she's been substituted for the Greek philosopher Hypatia, with a role reversal. Hypatia was persecuted by the Christians because she was a pagan!"

"Ah, well, that's all right, then," says Patrice, returning to his supine position. "What about St Catherine ... of Siena, was it?"

Colette types that in, and learns that her teachers about saints had it muddled:

"Siena was much later, fourteenth century – guess where? *Oui*, Siena. Did a lot of writing and was elevated, with Teresa of Ávila, to the only two women to be Doctors of the Church

---

151 Jesus's foreskin

(whatever that means) – in 1970 by Pope Paul VI."

As she closes her laptop, Colette says that she is hungry and would like to go somewhere nice to eat. After reminding her they are in London, Patrice makes a couple of reasonable suggestions, and they shower and dress.

In the restaurant, a very pleasant Bangladeshi place, which certainly knows how to charge, they discuss the next stage of their journey.

"I was wondering," says Colette, "do you want to go to Burghley House and have a quick look at *Susanna and the Elders*? I thought you might?"

"*Non*," says Patrice, "I think I can wait until another time. I did think about having a look at her ceiling paintings, *An Allegory of Peace* and the *Arts under the English Crown*, at Marlborough House, but we aren't sure who painted what – because Orazio was there as well. Chloë thinks Artemisia did it all, or most of it. But who knows? So that's for another time too, I think."

***

"We need to check on Mademoiselle Horváth and Monsieur Desmond also," says Pucelle as Fleur comes to the end of her description. "*Le juge* hasn't spotted that we haven't done that yet, but he will!"

Clémence is at her computer, looking at the criminal database. She holds up her hand so that everyone can see her, even Yves Mercier, who is lurking at the back of the room as if he doesn't wish to be associated with the others.

"I've got something," she says. "There is no sign of Mademoiselle Horváth, but there are signs of Monsieur Desmond. He, too, has a sealed juvenile record, with no violence, as well as many motoring offences. He is banned from driving for five years, of which three have been served.

He has also been repeatedly arrested by the *brigade des stupéfiants* for abusing *beu*[152] and a few others. Nothing outstanding at present."

"Put it up on the board, quickly," says Fleur, "in case *le juge* comes back."

Pucelle is silent, considering the plethora of information and how she might organise it to see something useful.

***

Florence, in May 2019, is exceptionally hot. Europe is suffering under a large area of high pressure; Paris almost as hot, and *les enfants* are coming home from being educated with exhaustion. This, for the moment, appears to be working to keep Amélie at home in the evenings. The grandparents are hardly venturing out and are talking about returning to Avignon as soon as the children have finished school. At least they will have breezes! Both Agnès and Ralph are faintly homesick. She appears to suffer more from this as her dementia slowly worsens.

In Florence, Colette has booked a double room, although not the one where they spent their previous stay (because the hotel has been renovated over the last twenty years). It is quaint and homely, although without air-conditioning, clammy and airless. They expect to sleep a lot after dragging themselves around the galleries.

On their radar is the Pitti Palace, for the *Judith and her Maidservant*, and the Uffizi, for the *Judith Beheading Holofernes* (the second one, with the gold dress and Holofernes's knee). They have a whole week, and Colette has planned a comprehensive itinerary. Patrice would prefer to stay in the hotel, lying on the bed, popping out to the two galleries he wants to visit. He already knows who will win.

---

152 Grass, weed, marijuana – Verlan (from *herbe*)

They arrive on Monday, when most of the galleries are closed, and treat themselves to a great lunch, and an afternoon remembering their last visit, from the perspective of the bedroom. It is Tuesday when they consider whether they really have the energy to do all the sights, as Colette wants; or very few of them as Patrice wants. They agree a compromise. Patrice will spend most of his time in the Uffizi, looking at the *Judith*, at the Caravaggios, at the Michelangelos and Giottos. Colette will take a shorter look at the *Judith* – just so she can discuss it with him in a vague sort of way – and go to view Michelangelo's *David* in the Accademia, as well as his unfinished sculptures.

While Patrice continues to look at, and think about, the *Judith* in the Uffizi and the one in the Pitti Palace, Colette will take a thirteen-hour tour to Pisa by train. He is horrified by the thought of that, but she is excited by the travel through Tuscany.

"It will be *fantastique!*" she claims. "I'll meet people and I can try out my Italian."

"You don't have any Italian," says Patrice.

"I have a phrase book," she says, "and I have been doing an online course for dummies."

"Wonderful! You should manage all right, then." He keeps the sarcasm out of his voice.

"There's only a certain amount of time I can spend in front of the same painting," she says. "I know, I know. It's your job. At present. But it isn't mine."

Patrice looks dumbfounded for a few seconds but realises that this will make his life easier. At least she isn't insisting on dragging him to Pisa. She hasn't mentioned going to Siena, but she might yet. He will not mention it.

"Will you come with me on the Florence tour, though?" she asks. "Looking at the Baptistery and the Duomo and everything?"

"How long does it take?" he asks.

"One hour and twenty minutes," she says. "Even you can handle that."

"*Oui*," he says, "and I can drop off at the Uffizi if I'm bored ..."

***

She does indeed lose him at the Uffizi, where he feels the need to spend over an hour gazing at the *Judith*, taking in the bloodstains on the breast of the golden dress, the strength of the arms, the arc of blood in Galileo's parabolic pattern. He turns away when he can no longer stand to look. The violence is horrendous, but its rendering is sublime. When women are pushed too far ... no wonder men felt intimidated, castrated.

He spends some of his available time in making a phenomenological description of the Uffizi *Judith*.

The Palazzo Pitti, in its turn, has *Judith and her Maidservant*, the one displaying the neck of Judith, which he had noted previously. He craves sight of the Detroit *Judith* but there is no way he has time to go to America.

He is exhausted when he rejoins Colette at the hotel, chattering on about "Firenze" and what she has seen – he should have been there, he only really saw the Baptistery. Patrice finds he is too tired to eat.

He does, however, have enough energy left to give her his excited reading of the phenomenological reductions of the *Judith* paintings Two and Three.

***

Rome, if anything, is even hotter, and because of this, as well as having only three days scheduled for it, Colette and Patrice restrict themselves to viewing a large print of

Caravaggio's *Judith Beheading Holofernes* (still on loan to Minnesota until 2023) and a real thing in the *maestro*'s portrait of a horse's bottom, in the Cerasi Chapel.

"Do you not think it's a bit crude?" asks Colette as she regards the rump.

"Not at all," says Patrice. He thoroughly approves. "I think it's brilliant!"

"Apparently," says Colette, referring to her guidebook, "there's a story about Annibale Carracci and Caravaggio. Caravaggio was commissioned to make a pair of pictures for a new *patron*, Monsignor Tiberio Cerasi, for his burial chapel in Santa Maria del Polpulo – *The Crucifixion of St Peter* and *The Conversion of St Paul*. The altarpiece, to go in between them, over the altar, was to be painted by Annibale Carracci, the *Assumption of the Virgin*." She waves towards the centrepiece and goes on to say that the first St Paul is not the one they can see here. "It was rejected by Cerasi – it really was rather a mess. This one was the second, which he accepted. As you can see, it shows St Paul's very working-class horse, with its bottom robustly aimed at the Virgin Mary!"

***

As it would take over an hour to travel from their hotel to the airport, it is much easier to travel to Naples by high-speed train, which takes only one hour and six minutes, travelling through admirable countryside. Patrice arranges to sleep through the relatively short journey, avoiding the motion sickness.

They eat a genuine Neapolitan pizza lunch, with olives and artichokes and ham, before going to visit *Judith* One in the Capodimonte museum. Colette looks at everything else while Patrice stands in front of the *Judith* for over an hour, being jostled by increasing numbers of tourists who are, in his opinion, not appreciating it properly.

He dictates his reduction of the Naples *Judith* for Colette to write down as they return, on the train, to Rome for another round with the Italian Renaissance. This avoids Patrice both losing his thoughts and his lunch. He can, though, think of nothing except Artemisia.

25

Clémence spreads all the forensic evidence out on the central table in the *salle squad*. They have already looked at it; there is little enough. Clémence, however, encouraged by Pucelle, is thinking there might be something they missed. The post-mortem report on M Lindholm's body is much as they expected, the wounding having preceded the fall. The brass lamp is in the small amount of evidence, still showing almost its full complement of blood and batter. It has, the *identité judiciaire*[153] has agreed, been wielded with a very heavy hand, but has been wiped of fingerprints.

The team has so far concurred that it must have been swung by a man, but the fresh mind of Pucelle has another thought: Force equals Mass multiplied by Acceleration, so, maybe it could have been a woman, or even a girl. So long as the acceleration is fast enough. Maybe, if it had been swung from high up, that would remove the need for a person of great strength to be involved.

---

153 forensic department

But not Mollie, she thinks. René certainly wouldn't allow his damsel in distress to be accused. What about the others, though? The Chinese woman is skinny, the French girl and the Latvian are both quite frail-looking. Mlle Dorrity, though. The Australian is both tall and strong, an athletic swimmer. What about her?

The team jumps on this idea. Mlle Dorrity is certainly up to swinging a lamp in anger at someone's head. In fact, says Fleur, "She could probably take Lindholm in a fair fight."

***

Pucelle has just finished placating the *juge d'instruction* on the phone. She knows him well enough to believe that he is going to forgive them, because she has thrown him the juicy morsel that they have checked, also, the records of Mlle Horváth and M Desmond, the hotel receptionists. He had, obviously, missed them out of his thinking and so didn't say anything except "thank you".

René looks baffled; this thing seems to be getting bigger and bigger. And he hasn't thought about *pauvre* Mollie once today. Or his bald spot.

***

"I warned you that I'll need to make a side trip to Sweden before we meet Chloë in Helsinki," says Patrice on their last night in the Eternal City.

Colette looks up from her examination of the flight schedules for their journey to Helsinki and supresses a sigh.

"Of course, and we haven't travelled enough recently," she says sweetly.

"I cannot get any further unless I speak to Christer Larsson. He may have had possession of our *Judith* when it was out of sight. If he is still alive, naturally."

257

"Ah, naturally," says Colette, turning the page to find flights from Rome to Arlanda airport in Stockholm.

***

In contrast to boiling Italy, Stockholm is wet; Colette buys an umbrella at the airport. Apparently, the high-pressure zone has not extended to Scandinavia. The Laniers are staying for two nights in the Lydmar Hotel, which is advertised as "boutique" and serving European cuisine. It is in the centre of Stockholm, and close to the address where Patrice has arranged, by telephone, to meet Christer Larsson. Colette is hoping for a boat trip – everywhere in the Swedish capital seems to be a stride or two from the water.

The early air service from Rome arrives at Arlanda at 08.50, having been two and a half hours in the brilliant air, so Colette has almost a whole day to look around while Patrice is busy. Patrice's appointment is at *10 heures* prompt. He can walk to the apartment where M Larsson lives.

"Will you wander around the city while I interview M Larsson?" asks Patrice; they can walk as far as his house and then she can go off on her own.

"I think so," she says. "There are several things I'd like to see. And we can both go on a nice boat trip on Friday ..." Without stopping, she carries on from this to prevent Patrice reminding her, for the five hundredth time, that he gets seasick. He does, but he also thinks boats are too slow and take way too long to get anywhere. "The cathedral, the Royal Palace, the Vasa Museum ... and very good shopping!"

"You hate shopping!" says Patrice.

"I know. But I'll find plenty to do. Do you think you'll take a long time? Or might something happen, and you need to take him out to lunch?"

"We'll leave it open for now," he says. "He may have

more info for me than I expect. Or less. It'll take however long it takes."

***

Christer Larsson's home is in a side street in a less than first-rate area of Stockholm. The apartment occupies the second floor in an antique block, by the dockside, and has no findable lift. Patrice drags his stiff leg slowly up to the flat. There is a light smell of fish on the stairway.

M Larsson answers his own door and ushers the policeman into a tidy but down-at-heel *salon* with shabby furniture and threadbare carpet. This is not what Patrice expected of the owner of a masterpiece, even if he has sold it on. He notes his own prejudices as he enters the flat.

The Swede is as threadbare as his apartment, with thin light hair stretched over his mostly bald head, heavy-framed glasses and a mustard-coloured cardigan. He does, however, have alert blue eyes, which he keeps focused on the detective.

"Good morning, Officer Lanier," he says. "I am Christer Larsson, and I am so glad to meet you." He gives Patrice a firm handshake. "Please, do sit down. I hope my French is easy to understand."

"I also have English," says Patrice, "if that is easier for you ..."

"*Non, non,* either is fine. We Swedes are proud of our language-learning ability."

M Larsson has already made coffee and the set tray is on a small table, close at hand. He asks Patrice how he takes it and provides two cups.

"You want to talk to me about a painting," he asks, "which I had in my possession for some years?"

259

"I do. It is a relatively small painting, oil on prepared canvas, of Judith beheading Holofernes, perhaps by Artemisia Gentileschi."

"*Oui*, of course." Larsson starts to gaze around his living room, as if considering his fixtures and fittings one by one. Eventually, he comes back to eye contact with Patrice:

"You are wondering how someone like me could afford a work of art like that," he says.

"Perhaps your circumstances have changed," says Patrice, "or perhaps you bought it as a copy? I can't pretend to know your situation ..."

"I think you are a kind man," says Larsson, looking as if he needs one. "You want to spare me the shame. But it is all right. I am in the situation where my business failed, my marriage collapsed under the strain, and my son became an addict. It took everything.

"The picture was left to me in the will of my brother, Mats, who was very well off. He knew I liked biblical paintings, and he had come across this one many years ago. It was in the villa of one of his customers, and he was given it, eventually, to pay a debt.

"He didn't sell it on because he liked it. I don't know whether he had it in mind to will it to me, but he did know I'd liked it very much when I visited him shortly after he hung it. He knew that I would never sell it either – except that I did. I had no choice. Although it nearly killed me." He is remembering how that felt, suffering it again.

"Do you know when your brother acquired the work?" asks Patrice. He waits for a short while, sipping the good coffee Larsson has made. The old man thinks, gathering his papery face into more wrinkles. When he speaks, he sounds as if he is mining the information from a long way down in his memory.

"Let me think. I can probably date it to around the

summer of 1976. I know it was very hot. And my brother, Mats, died in the autumn of 1978."

"And you kept it for quite some time?" says Patrice. "Can you locate the year you sold it?"

"*Oui*, easy. It was at the beginning of last year. January 2018. I had nothing else left to sell and my son, Niels, needed money for rehab. This time it was really going to work. So, I sold the painting to the gallery of Edvard Olaveson for six hundred thousand kroner. It took all of it to book Niels into the clinic."

Patrice is reluctant to ask Larsson how went the rehab but, inevitably, must.

"Did he improve?" says Larsson. "*Oui*. I suppose he did. He has nothing to worry about now anyway. He got out of the clinic, against regulations, with a friend. They went to score with a dealer they knew. They both died on the street from taking uncut heroin." A tear creeps down Larsson's wrinkled face.

"I'm so sorry," says Patrice. "Do you feel up to a few more questions?"

M Larsson wipes his left eye with a finger and says that he will manage.

"So, you actually owned this painting between the autumn of 1978 and January 2018, last year, for a total of about forty years?"

"That's right, I think," says M Larsson.

"Do you happen to have any documents for it?" asks Patrice. "I don't suppose you got anything with it from your brother's estate? Or perhaps you did? You will have, I think, a bill of sale from Edvard Olavesen's gallery, *n'est-ce pas?*"

"Oh, *oui*. I have the document which my brother's lawyer gave me when the painting was delivered. He brought it himself; it was most unusual for a lawyer to do that. I think he thought it was worth something, although he'd never heard of the artist. And then, Olavesen's gave me the bill of sale with my money – less their commission, of course."

The Swede gets up from his armchair and goes through a door, coming back after a few minutes, hands holding papers.

"See," he says, laying the papers out on the chair arm, "a bill of sale dated eighteenth January 2018, from Monsieur Olaveson in the Koenigsgat, and the lawyer's signed receipt from when he delivered the painting. It's dated fourteenth September 1978."

"And you had the painting on your wall all that time?"

"I did," says Larsson. "I haven't decorated since it was sold. You can see the marks on the wallpaper where it was hung. It was a superb painting. I am still devastated that it is gone. My ex-wife hated it. I like it because it's about revenge!"

26

Chloë meets them off the aeroplane in Helsinki, where it is at least dry. She goes along in the taxi to the Hotel Seurahuone and waits while they check in. It is morning coffee time, and they go to the bar to introduce Colette to the milky. Patrice and Chloë talk about the provenance, while Colette closely examines the stack of tourist brochures she picked up at the airport. There are many things to see. She decides that if she pretends the fluid in the cup is not coffee but a strange new drink, she does not mind it much.

Chloë tells Patrice that Lumi Salonen is coming to their

hotel at *14 heures* to drive them to the gallery where their painting is. There will be no experts there or, indeed, anyone. Even Lumi will sit in the police car and let them be alone with the picture.

"That's great!" says Patrice. "That is exactly what we need."

"She and Jak are getting a bit agitated about it," says Chloë. "They're still of the opinion that it's stolen and there will be a prosecution. I haven't told them what you said about the provenance not adding up."

"Well done, that could make them freak out. Let's keep that quiet until we have looked again. We will need lunch. Have you found a place which serves nice things, or should we eat here? Colette does not want Rudolph." He looks at his wife, who is almost enjoying a second milky.

"Don't worry about me," says Colette, who has zoned out and is thinking they are talking about something different. "I shall bandage my poor feet and then I'll be fine walking around the city, maybe doing a little boating. Did Patrice tell you he was sick yesterday?" she asks Chloë.

"Oh dear," says the young woman. "He does have a light stomach, doesn't he? *Pauvre patron!*"

***

Colette has left for her big walk when Lumi arrives at 14.00. The Finn has borrowed the chief inspector's staff car, without driver, and drives them at Finnish speed to the gallery in the forest.

It is the same as before, but this time Lumi has the key. She unlocks and lets them into the building, returning to sit in the car, listening to what might be Finnish pop music. Chloë, not above national stereotypes, had expected Sibelius. The hairy-brown-suited man is not present.

The painting, on its easel, is again covered with a cloth. Patrice whips it off, and they both survey the picture which has been on their mind for over four months. It looks brighter than ever, so little damage, so little age.

"It is in such good condition," says Chloë, "it is hard to accept it is four hundred years old. Maybe that is why some people think it's a fake – too modern."

"We know it is old, though, don't we?" says Patrice. They stand still, staring at the fresh colours, superb angles, exquisite grouping of the three figures; what one of Artemisia's letters described as "under a tent curtain, beautifully rendered".

"It must have been protected, *n'est-ce pas*?" says Patrice. "And it would have been if it meant something special to the artist herself."

Patrice walks to a place in front of a window, taking a new perspective, looking, still looking. Chloë looks from the darker end of the room – there are many possible perspectives. The two try all of them. Eventually, they come to sit together on a bench seat somewhere in the middle.

"*C'est tellement magnifique!*[154]" says Chloë. "Have you ever seen anything finer?"

"Not in this lifetime," says Patrice. "Is it too good, do you think?"

"How can it be? For better, we'd be looking at da Vinci or Michelangelo, wouldn't we?"

"Allowing for maturity, do you think Artemisia could have painted it before 1637?" asks Patrice. "She would have had *44 ans*, then, and huge experience. What else did she paint in 1637?"

"I can say the *Adoration of the Magi* off the top of my head. I think the latest *Susanna and the Elders* was around

---

154 It's so beautiful!

then, as well as the *Allegory of Painting*. Maybe *Corisca and the Satyr* and *The Martyrdom of Saint Januarius*."

"All mature works. Either when she was in England or when she returned to Naples?"

"*Oui*." She stops for a moment. "There is a difficulty, though."

"What's that?" asks Patrice.

"After she got back from Rome – and she stayed in Naples for the rest of her life – her painting was, well, mature, obviously, but her style did change. She seemed to begin to paint for the market rather than being the dynamic, passionate artist of her younger days. Age, I expect, but she adopted the more sophisticated, decorative style. I suppose I'm saying her style changed, not suddenly but definitely."

"I don't suppose painting what the market wanted is such a bad thing – she didn't do too well when she went back to Rome, did she? She failed to get the commission for major works that she'd been trying to set up with Cassiano dal Pozzo … she may have been short of money."

"My point, though, is that the style of this is different, isn't it? More an old style but with special maturity?

"Mademoiselle Docteur Garrard says that Artemisia alternated, at this time, between her previous subversive subjects and what would please her *patrons*; even calling her approach to her previous, discomfortable subjects 'the dark Artemisia' and saying that she ceased identifying with the 'victims' and produced, um" – Chloë pauses, recalling the quotation to mind – "'grotesquely inflated heroines', and describing the Potsdam *Lucretia* as 'a bombastic parody of femininity'."

"Harsh," says Patrice. "But we should be able to see if she is right."

"Ah, I think she is," says Chloë. "Her most famous and appreciated paintings were in the past – the Detroit *Judith* is one, 1625 or so. Maybe her masterpiece? A lot of people think so." She reaches down and picks up her laptop case, and places the computer on the bench between them.

"You're looking for a list of when she painted certain things?" says Patrice.

"It's quite hard to keep them all in your head," says Chloë. "The chronology is speculative and there are lots of misattributions and arguables ...and 1630 to 1638 were very productive years for our Artemisia."

Patrice is looking at the list, which has a thumbnail photograph of each of the paintings to which it is referring. He notices that there are several versions of paintings featuring David and Bathsheba, or Bathsheba bathing. They are very definitely nice nudes to look at, but there is little conflict, little drama.

Chloë says that she'll bring up the online version of a 1968 article in *The Art Bulletin*, written by Dr R. Ward Bissell, of the University of Wisconsin. She struggles slightly to quote him, but thinks he wrote:

"'What her last canvases gained in sophistication; they lost in exuberance.'

"He felt her late style was just about represented by three paintings: *Judith and her Maidservant with the Head of Holofernes*, now in Naples, and the Potsdam *Tarquin and Lucretia* and *Bathsheba*. Note that the *Judith*, if it's a late work, can't be the one we have been calling the Naples *Judith from 1612 to 13*, it must be the other one in Naples, from the 1640s. I'll bring all three of them up, if I can, when we've finished the list."

"I've never really taken to the *Birth of John the Baptist*," says Chloë. "It is neither realistic nor very interesting, and the *Saints Proculus and Nicea*, done in 1636 to 37, seems to be horrible and nothing like Artemisia. As for *Saint Januarius in the Amphitheatre at Pozzuoli* it's just, well, ugh."

"Just commissioned works for church," says Patrice. "But you wouldn't put any of the *Judiths* in a church, would you?"

"Absolutely not. There's a *Madonna and Child*," she says, "supposed to have been painted in 1650 or 51, which has a plastic virgin and a plastic child; the virgin's dress is bright red – no nuance at all – and her veil is bright blue and there is a curtain draping overhead, which is olive green. All nearly primary colours which Artemisia hardly ever used!" She stops, realising she is almost shouting. "Mind you," she says after a moment, "the very ugly *Judith, Maidservant and Head of Holofernes* with the same-coloured dress – if it's Artemisia, it has to be juvenilia. It's in the Vatican.

"Judith is very young, which our Artemisia didn't really do – both look like wimps. The head of Holofernes is heavily bearded, as in other versions; but it's dated 1610 and is very similar to Orazio's painting with the same title (which is in Hartford, Connecticut) – so likely a juvenile copying of her father's work. And before the rape in 1611. So, possibly not signifying revenge on Tassi for something he had not yet done ..."

"I was wondering," says Patrice, "exactly how many Artemisia *Judiths* there are. I have only counted four so far: the Naples, the Uffizi, the Pitti, and the Detroit. But you have said she painted another, which is in Naples – but the head of Holofernes, not the actual slaying – and this one you've seen somewhere. So that's six."

"I have read that there are seven," says Chloë, "so if these other two are counted, we are still one short."

"*Alors,* let's look at the other one in the Capodimonte," says Patrice, "and see if we can find another."

"It may distract us though," says Chloë. "It might be distracting us anyway, *n'est-ce pas?*"

"*Certainement*, you are right. I am at the point where I am very sensitive to distraction."

"Are you bored, then?" asks Chloë.

"*Non*," says Patrice, "it's part of the process, I suppose. I'm in some kind of casting-around phase!"

"I've got the other Capodimonte *Judith* on the screen," says Chloë. "Ah, it's lovely! It's dated 1645 – so a late work."

"Very shadowed," says Patrice, "but subtly coloured and ... um, yes."

"And this is the version in the Musée de la Castre in Cannes. See, it is also late!"

They gaze at both of these works side by side on the screen, until Patrice says:

"So, she was still painting subtly and dramatically, although not necessarily doing it for consumption of the public ... these are both very dark – as far as lighting is concerned – although the candle (the homage, I remember!) does work properly as lighting on Judith's face and shoulders."

"She had to make a living, didn't she? Household and studio to maintain, and fewer commissions as 'the dark Artemisia'. I'm not comfortable with the wimpy Madonnas and saccharine saints, or the blowsy beauties. I'm so glad she still had the subversive element underneath."

"These pictures," says Patrice, "are her legacy to us. They prove, don't they, that she was still our Artemisia? And our *Judith* too, if it is genuinely hers ..." He waves towards it and both their gazes leave the screen and settle on the *Judith*:

"She's not wimpy or saccharine or blowsy. She is changed by her task; you can see the light in her face!" Chloë's face is transformed too, something of the light from the picture in her eyes. Patrice, more down to earth, can entirely see what she means.

"Time, then, to examine it as it reveals itself. The central motif is the triad of Judith, Abra and the Assyrian. Let's look at each figure in turn. By the way, when Colette and I were in London, looking at the *Allegory of Painting*, we noticed that the arms of Artemisia are so muscular and workmanlike, so like Judith's in all three of the paintings. Artemisia's arms!"

"Interesting," says Chloë. "And it would, of course, have been incredibly easy for her to look down at her arms as she was painting. Identifying with Judith – who is also doing a job of work?"

"I think so," responds Patrice thoughtfully. "Artist and work synchronised ..."

"There is a compelling reason why it should be," says Chloë, "at least I think so."

"So, on to Judith in general," commands Patrice. "In the 1612 Naples, she is a little younger, less severe than in the Uffizi version. Her hair is almost in the same style in both, but in the Florentine, she has a more severe hairline – cleaner forehead."

"The expression, and the shadowing are almost identical," says Chloë, "but the Uffizi looks less sympathetic, and there is more evidence of the double chin of determination!"

"Ah! Is that what it is?" says Patrice. "*Oui*, I can see that."

"Have you noticed," says Chloë, "that we are ever so slightly further away in the Uffizi?" Patrice gazes at the Judith in the golden dress for a few minutes before agreeing with her. The Neapolitan picture is more intimate. He tries to suspend the fact that he likes it better than the more sophisticated version.

"What about our *Judith*?" he asks, glancing at the room-dominating questioned version, standing on its easel in ascetic Finland.

Chloë swerves to look at it again and cannot help sighing in admiration. The colours are fresher, that is the first thing, and the tiny flowers in the basket she had seen as significant from the beginning have not been faded by passing time.

"Ah" – a long breath – "in this one, Judith seems more serene. Her task almost accomplished. She does not appear to be worried about getting away."

"Perhaps the Lord is going to defend her," says Patrice. "Do not forget it is a bible story, even if not in the actual bible."

"Um. Not a holy picture, though."

"*Non.*"

"Do you think Holofernes looks particularly anguished in either of the canonical *Judiths*?" asks Patrice. "He has his mouth open, and his eyes. He must know what is happening to him. But he's not panicking, nor trying especially hard to get the women off him."

"Don't you think that's because the virtual camera has stopped at precisely that second?" asks Chloë. "What happened next? Had she already killed him, or was there more killing to do? Did she have to saw rather than just slice?"

"Um. I don't know. Maybe we must run an experiment?"

"That would be messy!" says the young woman. She is looking pensive, switching her gaze from the picture to the floor of the gallery and back again. She rises and goes for a walk around the room, ostensibly looking at several other paintings – how dark beside the living colours of the *Judith*. Then she stops, suddenly, whirling round towards the *patron*.

"There's something we didn't see!" she says, in a loud voice, shouting at him. He is surprised and almost gets up himself, before subsiding again on the bench.

"I'm sure there is," he says. "Almost always. What is it?"

Chloë and Patrice walk up and down in front of the *Judith* for a few minutes before subsiding on their accustomed bench to gaze at it. Lumi is still outside but is happily working the telephone, talking to connections in and out of the art world. Patrice has written the details of the fake provenance in the first of two wide columns on his clipboard, and is annotating it with a red ballpoint pen, arrows pointing to the second column where the provable information has been written.

"We can agree," says Patrice, having drawn an arrow between two items, "that the work was likely painted in 1637 and is possibly the painting referred to in Artemisia's letter to Cassiano dal Pozzo in Rome in November of that year. We have no evidence to support it not being sold to someone from the Spanish court and sent to Madrid for forty years, then spending a hundred and sixty years in Barcelona. That brings us up to around 1839, and I think that's where it goes a bit funny."

"*Oui*," says Chloë, "both provenances can't be true. Obviously!"

"So, what happened after 1838?" asks Patrice. "Noting that we have what looks to be a genuine receipt for its coach fare from Paris to Le Mans, although there is no coach fare, before that, to Paris from Barcelona."

"There's a rumour about Herman Goering having his eye on it in 1942 – although he didn't get it," says Chloë. "One wonders why. Because he mostly did get what he wanted, didn't he?"

"I am not totally sure. Hitler might have wanted it too," says Patrice. "They were sometimes in conflict about things like that. It may have been spirited away and hidden. The French must have hidden it from the Germans, originally, mustn't they? The fakeish provenance says it was in a French private collection from 1838 until 1954 and then sold to Monsieur Harper, in London, and sold on, in 1967 – but, according to Monsieur Larsson, his brother received it in lieu of payment of a debt in about the summer of 1976. And he died in the autumn two years later, leaving it to Christer, who sold it last year, because he needed the money – all six hundred thousand kroner of it! Must be a different painting, a duplicate, mustn't it?"

"Christer Larsson says he had it for forty-two years, then?" says Chloë. "But the provenance says only his brother Mats had it until the date Christer sold it."

"That could be all right, though, couldn't it?" says Patrice. "Maybe Mats didn't transfer it officially to his brother."

"He wouldn't have any choice," says Chloë. "He died. You've got the death certificate and the document from Mats's lawyer."

"I have," says Patrice, "and the accompanying document, dated fourteenth July 1976, from Mats Larsson's lawyer, as well as the bill of sale, dated eighteenth January 2018, for the painting, value six hundred thousand kroner, from Edvard Olaveson's gallery in Stockholm. So, what are the holes we need to look at?"

"We're okay until there," she says, gazing steadily at his diagram, pointing to the notations around Le Mans, 1838–1954. "That could be where it goes wrong."

"*Oui*. It's missing from the provenance for seven years from 1954 to 1961, then it appears in London until 1967, when they say they sell Monsieur Harper in London. But it's supposed to only be in Sweden after 1976. So where was it between 1967 and 1976? And we still don't know if Larsson's brother was in London."

"*Non*," says Chloë. "But perhaps Lumi and Jak will find out?"

***

The photograph of the Artemisia Gentileschi painting of the American *Judith* arrives in Patrice's inbox, together with copies of all the documents the lawyers have relied on in America – exactly the same as in one half of the provenance they already have. The painting, too, as far as any of them can tell, is exactly like the one on the easel in the gallery where they have been examining it.

"There must have been two paintings," says Jak. "Either one, or both, could be a forgery, is it not so?" His manner has changed, the enthusiasm gone; he is now thoughtful.

Neither Patrice nor Chloë wish to admit that "their" painting is a forgery, but they have to think one of them is, don't they? They look at each other in puzzlement.

"There isn't much we can do with it now," continues Jak. "It must have been dumped because the gallery, expecting to make a killing exporting it back to Russia, where there is money now, got worried about it being hot. Maybe they had an expert, after all, who thought it was a real Gentileschi. They got it out of Sweden and into Finland, but something must have spooked them before the Russian border."

"So, any wrongdoing is firmly in the past," says Lumi. "Goering stole it and it somehow ended up in the Berlin gallery, who had it copied and sold it twice: once to Mr Harper in London and once to the Soviets. We can follow the progress of the two pictures fairly easily."

"What happens to it now?" asks Chloë. "Our one?"

"Well," says Jak, "it can't be sold. We know it's a forgery. We'll have to return it to where it belonged before all this fraud happened."

"To France," asks Patrice, "because the first wrongdoing was Goering's, when he and his minions stole it from the rightful owner near Le Mans in 1942?"

"*Oui*," says Jak. "The French owner is the one we must return it to."

***

"So," says Jak Kyllo, perching on his desk in the Helsinki squad room, "the provenances of this painting do not match our suspected work from the writings?"

"They do not," says Patrice, whilst Chloë produces their chart with two columns and many annotations in red ink. "There is a period between 1942 and 1961 which is in question. Herman Goering may have picked what we think is our painting up from near Le Mans in '42 and, presumably, made off with it to Germany. We lose track of it until 1961, when a Monsieur Harper of London buys it from a gallery in Berlin. We do not know how it got there but I think we can allow that as a genuine break."

Both Jak and Lumi nod wisely that they agree.

"And what after that?" asks Lumi, in her halting French.

"We have a whole list of owners and paperwork to support them, and it all looks okay," says Chloë. "But here" – she indicates the second column – "we have a different story. Also with receipts and bills of sale."

"They can't all be genuine?" says Jak.

"*Non*," says Chloë, handing him a photocopy of Patrice's diagram.

Jak takes a few minutes to gaze at the sheet of paper covered in Patrice's notes. He doesn't seem to find it too messy to understand.

"Then," he says, "the original provenance which we had, eventually, from the Gambino faction (the experts who presented the painting to us), as a previously undocumented work, found in a waste recycling site in the north of the country, says that after 1961, it was sold from Berlin to

Harper of London, then to an anonymous French collector, to Madame Hersey in America, then to some corporate lawyers in New York. Presumably, it is still with them."

"It can't be," says Lumi. "We have it here; they haven't got it!"

"Please telephone these lawyers, their name is probably on a receipt or something," says Jak.

Lumi returns to her own desk, with the paperwork in an evidence bag, and after searching through the individual receipts, telephones Marwath, Jones, and Leesom in New York.

Their Mr Leesom says they have such a picture; he is looking at it as he speaks.

All the policepersons look at one another mystified, as Lumi asks if the New Yorkers have a proper guaranteed provenance. Leesom says they have. He will email them photographs of painting and provenance.

"If they have the original there," says Chloë, "ours must be a forgery. That's it, then."

"I'm fairly sure," says Jak, "that Russia or, previously, the Soviet Union, has been involved somehow in this. The gallery in Stockholm must have dumped the second painting as too hot to handle, before closing down. I do know, definitely, that the picture we have was dumped in the landfill up in Savukoski. There is evidential continuity.

"Don't forget, though, that Savukoski is beyond the Arctic Circle, and it is only about six hundred kilometres from Murmansk. There's a road, although they're starting to build a brand new route soon, to facilitate communications between us. I'm sure Lumi has told you that our border with Russia can be quite porous at times ... the further north you go, the more porous it is." He begins, with a green ballpoint pen, to make further annotations on Patrice's columns. It is looking Christmassy.

"Perhaps, then," says Patrice, "our picture really did end up in Sweden with the Messieurs Larsson? I wonder whether Mats Larsson had business in the USSR?"

"Why don't you ring his brother and find out?" says Lumi.

***

Leaving Pucelle to do whatever Pucelle is doing, René walks back to *le Trente-Six* from Mme Paston's, where Mollie has continued drawing men's shoes in all kinds of pastel colours – lavender, light green, lemon, peach – when something hits him which he doesn't, yet, understand.

He knows that there is something he should have noticed in the kitchen of the refuge, but he cannot think what it might have been. Something which would help.

***

Patrice gets hold of Christer Larsson on the telephone straight away. The Swede hardly goes out any more, and he is happy to help with the single question M Lanier says he still has.

"Could you tell me," asks Patrice, "whether your late brother was in the habit of having customers in Russia, or the old Soviet Union? What was it he traded in, anyway? I don't think you told me ..."

"I didn't," says Larsson. "Are you saying that Mats did something wrong?" He sounds tentative, concerned.

"*Non, non,*" says Patrice, "not at all. It's just relevant to our enquiries. What did he do?"

"He owned a firm which manufactured and sold tractors and other farm equipment, big, expensive machinery. And, yes, he did have customers in the Soviet Union, the

276

agricultural collectives, their government. It was nothing illegal, though; he had licences and contracts from the Swedish government and everything. Why are you asking?"

"We were wondering whether the painting could have come from a customer in Russia," says Patrice. "And how your brother might have got it back to Sweden, if it did."

"No problem there," says Larsson. "It could have easily come in with machinery needing to be replaced – and it was to pay a debt anyway. So, it's all above board, isn't it?" Law-abiding M Larsson is sounding panicky now.

"Please don't worry," says Patrice, trying to calm the man and assuage his own guilt. "There's nothing to be done now, it's fine anyway!"

"It would be terrible if I had to go to jail," says Larsson. "It wasn't my fault. I had to sell it to save my son. And he died anyway. And my brother." He is openly weeping now. "And I miss the painting too. It brought me much pleasure."

***

They have gathered at *le Trente-Six*, contemplating their next step, looking at Mollie's pictured shoe collection. Clémence spreads the drawings on the big table, and the other three stand around – although Yves isn't proving to be of much use. Pucelle has gone somewhere and not yet returned.

"*Qu'en pensez-vous?*[155]" asks Fleur.

René looks very tired, despite the early hour. He is worried by everything, including his hair receding at an amazing rate, and confused by most of it. The mental picture he has of Mme Paston's kitchen is still in the front of his mind and gnawing at him. Something. But what?

Clémence feels that Mollie must be very familiar with the odd shoes that M Lindholm and M Baker wear. René

---

155 What do you make of it?

angrily asks what that would mean anyway. He confesses he didn't really have any idea why he wanted to talk to Mollie about them. Fleur says something comforting around the fact that detection often turns on little details and little flashes of insight. René tells her he has another one of these *piqûres d'épingle*.[156]

"I think there was something in Madame Paston's kitchen which I should have noticed," he says, "but I don't know what it was. It is driving me *guedin*![157]"

Fleur asks him to describe, in detail, what he saw at Mme Paston's. He sits backwards on an office chair, closes his eyes, moving himself back to the room.

"I went in – after I'd had an argument with their perimeter guard about whether I was a safe male person to let in, and proving to him that Pucelle was actually a police officer; he was suspicious – and the kitchen was warm and bright, just like my mother's really, with lovely smells of cooking meat and spices. Madame Paston was drinking coffee, sitting at a small table. She's plump and homely, much like *Maman*. She was talking to Mollie but, as far as I could see, wasn't getting any words back. I still don't think Mollie can speak, although everyone says she can. She's not speaking to Madame Paston either."

"Where was Mollie herself?" asks Fleur.

"She was standing on a box, over a huge pot, cooking a stew," he says, "probably lunch for the whole house. She looked very content and was rosy with the heat. She looked almost pretty – as well as wearing a clean cotton dress, *comme une paysanne*.[158] I asked if she could stop cooking as I needed to ask her a question.

---

156 pinpricks
157 crazy, mad, bananas – Verlan (from *dingue*)
158 like a peasant, in the peasant style

"Madame Paston said that she would be putting the pot in the oven in a few minutes and could talk to me then. She poured us coffee and we sat with her, watching Mollie work. She still hadn't noticed us; she didn't react to my saying her name, nor to my voice."

"Tell me," says Fleur, "what she was doing while she was cooking. Tell me every little detail, just as you would with *le patron*."

"Let me see." He opens his eyes for a few seconds, then closes them again and resumes in the present tense; he is seeing it as if he is there. "She is stirring with a very large wooden spoon. She seems strong, her sleeves are pushed up. She is stirring it like a country woman, even though she is so young and frail.

"There is a smell of caramelised onions, sweet, and something else." He sniffs as if he can still smell it. "And she is adding cubes of meat, pork, from a chopping board, and browning it in batches. Then, she puts it to the side in a bowl as she browns more. When all this is done, she returns the meat to the pot and adds strips of green pepper from another bowl. She has spices in the pork but I'm not sure what they are – something English?"

"*Non!*" say Fleur and Clémence together. "The English mainly make steak and kidney pie."

"There is a spice thing … what do you call it? Grinder?"

Clémence tries him with "mortar and pestle". He agrees that is what he means.

"*Maman* used to grind Indian spices in it, coriander, cumin, things like that."

"Is that what you are smelling now?" asks Fleur.

"*Non, non,* something quite different. Earthy, smoky, a bit sweet. She's finished frying the pork now. She's gesturing for Madame Paston to come and help her to get the pot into the oven. She gets up and they do it as though they have been doing it together all their lives. I look at the ingredients still sitting on the counter."

"What are they?" asks Fleur.

"There are flat noodles, like tagliatelle but not nested, long ribbons. There are still spices in a dish at the side. I pick it up. Ah, *non*, they are not ground. They are little grey-green seeds, oval, strong-smelling. They aren't going in the stew; they must be for the noodles."

"What's the smell?" asks Yves, first time he's opened his mouth.

"Don't know, can't think," says René.

Fleur is looking deeply thoughtful. Wondering. Thinking about food. Recipes.

"They're *graines de carvi*," she says, after a long time. "They go in rye bread, and sauerkraut too!"

"Of course!" says René. "My mother uses caraway all the time, but not pork, of course. She is Jewish, from Hungary."

"And the smoky, earthy smell is paprika," says Fleur. "Mollie isn't English; she's making *goulasch*. She's Hungarian!"

27

"I am calling Monsieur Zabi," says Pucelle, "to request warrants so we can bring in the Reverend Dr Baker and ask him about the shoes. And why witnesses might have seen him or Monsieur Lindholm, or both, in the Hôtel des Jardins, when neither was staying there."

"You should also obtain a warrant for the arrest of Monsieur Bernard Cloche," says René, "and we must arrange extradition for Monsieur Denthwaite from New

Zealand. I am going to talk to Mademoiselle Horváth at the hotel. She is Hungarian. It isn't beyond the bounds of possibility that she has met, or even knows our Mollie."

Clémence, not wishing to be left out in demanding warrants, wants to arrest Messieurs Renault and Melzer and have them brought to Paris. Something wrong about them, she is convinced.

"And we should put a Europol alert out for Madame Magda Simon," she says. "I don't think we shall find her any other way."

"I am not sure we shall find her at all," says Pucelle. "I am interested in Madame Simon. Or rather in the space Madame Simon leaves. It seems that she does not exist."

***

"But we can't!" says Chloë. She speaks plaintively, in a voice Patrice and Colette haven't heard before. "If we send it back to Paris, as a forgery, it will have to be destroyed in front of the magistrate."

"And that," says Patrice, "is right, according to the law. So it can't be foisted on another buyer in the future."

Chloë and Colette stare at him in horror.

"Can we not search for the original owner, in Le Mans? If they or their descendants are still alive, that is, *quoi*? And give it back to them?" says Chloë.

"*Non*," says Patrice. "You can't even give it back to them for nothing – it's a forgery."

"But neither of you think it is a forgery, do you?" says Colette at length.

"It isn't," says Chloë. "It is genuine, on my life."

"You are very sure of yourselves," says Colette. "Did you decide that before or after the Americans told you they had the real one?"

"Before," says Patrice, looking at Chloë for her nodded agreement. "We always knew, didn't we?"

All Chloë can do, being speechless, imagining the beautiful, meaningful painting going up in flames or being attacked by a man with an axe, is to nod fearfully to fate.

***

René arrives at the Hôtel des Jardins around *17 heures*; he knows that Mlle Horváth works later than that. She is indeed at the reception desk, checking in a new guest. Her hair has been rearranged and is a new colour, but continues to show *preuve de coiffure avancée*.[159] When she has finished with the new guest, she turns to the detective and, smiling, asks him what she can do for him today?

As there is no one now waiting, René asks her to sit with him in the foyer. He needs to ask her a couple of questions. She seems happy with this.

"Last time, when Officer Godard came to speak to you, you said that you did not know about the young girl who was hiding in the basement," says René. "Is that correct?"

"*Oui*," the young woman says. "I had not seen her. The detective showed me a picture. I did not recognise her."

René notices that she does not hold his gaze, just as Clémence had remarked after interviewing the receptionist. This is not an invariable indication that someone is lying, but it is quite suggestive of that.

"Would you be surprised to know that she is Hungarian?" he asks.

She bites back on what she had been going to say, and says nothing until he asks if she has a problem.

"*Non*," she says. "I don't know everyone in Paris who

---

159 Evidence of advanced hairdressing

282

came from Hungary, do I? And I thought you said, or someone from your office said, she is English. Yes, her name is … I don't know … something beginning with *M* – er, Mary, or something?"

"*Non*," says René, "unfortunately, we don't know her name now. I thought, perhaps, you might know it? You are sure you have never met her? You have never heard of her? You still do not know why she was hiding in your hotel basement?"

"*Non*," she says, "I do not know anything."

René watches as she starts to fray at the seams, and picks up the hotel telephone as she stands there, unable to think. He asks the brigadier at *le Trente-Six* to please send a car to take in a suspect whom he has just arrested.

***

The Reverend Dr Gardiner Baker is the next personage to arrive at *le Trente-Six*. He has travelled in under his own power (and God's), and taken a seat, waiting for a policeperson to come down and speak to him. He seems, when Clémence gets there, to be a little impatient at being made to wait.

She greets him politely and introduces herself, taking him into the interview room which she always uses because it is the only one with a wide enough doorway.

She sits him down and says that coffee is on its way. As she finishes the sentence, the door bursts open and a young uniformed officer enters, placing two plastic coffee mugs on the table.

"*Alors*, Monsieur Baker," she starts, "I know you have been interviewed by two of my colleagues, Madame Olivier and Monsieur Mercard, and probably think you have told them all you know."

"I have," he agrees, his French strongly Americanised so that Clémence has to concentrate very hard indeed. "I told your, er, colleagues, everything I knew about Dr Lindholm, that he was of good character, and had no enemies and everything. What else can there be?" He looks genuinely baffled.

Clémence, who has not tucked her chair under the table, looks down at M Baker's shoes. Today, they are apricot and very, very shiny, with no scuff marks or muddy splashes anywhere.

"I am thinking," she says, "about your shoes. Dr Lindholm used to wear shoes very like the ones you have on today: patent leather, very stylish, very expensive-looking … bright colours. They are quite unusual, aren't they?"

"What on earth are you talking about, girl? They are shoes! Why would they be of any interest to the police?"

"Because they aren't just shoes, are they?" asks Clémence. "They are very unusual shoes. I don't know anyone who has seen any like them before. Except on Lindholm and on yourself."

"And that's why Cedric Lindholm fell through the window, was it? Because of his shoes? Is that what you're trying to say?"

"Of course not," says Clémence. "It's just that they are very identifiable. Monsieur Lindholm and you are quite alike: same kind of age and body shape; coiffured hair, probably styled at the same salon; pale suits, too light for winter in Paris; and these shoes … lavender or rose-pink or sky blue or eau-de-nil, pastel but bright." She stops for a moment. "You could be mistaken for one another." She rounds on him and asks a curt question:

"Were you walking in the centre of Paris with this girl, who we now know is Hungarian, at various times in

December and early January?" She passes him a photograph of Gertrude/Mollie/whoever she is. He takes it and looks at it for several seconds. When he looks up he says that he wasn't. It wasn't him.

"Did you take her into a café and buy her food and drinks?"

"*Non*, it wasn't me."

"Did you walk with her and then leave her at the Arc-en-Ciel bar and nightclub in rue Mondoré?"

"*Non*, I did not."

"Are you still saying that you've never seen her? That you don't know her?"

"Yes, I am."

"So, you're saying that it must have been Monsieur Lindholm who our witnesses saw?"

"Because of the shoes?"

"*Précisément*."

Baker executes a deep sigh of frustration, saying there is a good explanation about the shoes. It isn't at all sinister.

"They come from the new American shop," he says, "Metaire, in Montmartre. It is owned by a friend with whom I went to school back in Minnesota. He has developed a new process, a finish which repels dirt and resists scuffing; it works even on very light and easy-to-damage finishes. Cedric Lindholm and I are, were, his experimental animals. We signed a contract to wear these shoes for two years in normal circumstances; we have, we had, six pairs each. Our church receives the fees."

The shoes did not cause Lindholm's death, probably, but they do provide a sure way of identifying Dr Lindholm and himself, and their movements.

When Clémence returns to the *salle squad*, faintly elated at the outcome of her time with M Baker, Fleur reminds her that the shoes are only significant as an identification;

they don't suspect the shoes of anything. Fleur says that M Cloche has been arrested and is being delivered to them tomorrow.

28

Over a dinner of Finnish proportions, Lumi asks how they have got on and, as a tribute to police solidarity, Patrice and Chloë explain their problem with the provenance, keeping the tiny revenge flower they have seen to themselves for now.

"It has some questions," starts Patrice. "Our *Judith* cannot be the picture mentioned in some of the documents I have been studying, because I have evidence that the picture to which they refer was in America during some of the periods already accounted for by that."

"What are you going to do now?" asks Lumi. "Are there any more people to talk to that we can help you with?"

"Probably impossible to say whether it was ever stolen – or even if Herman Goering made off with it," says Patrice, "but we can't rule it out. We cannot see, yet, how it came to Finland. Is there anything you can do from this end, while we consider earlier placements?"

"I think so," says Lumi. "We can certainly backtrack. And because we can do interviews in Finnish and Russian, we can, maybe, find out more than you."

"Russian?" questions Chloë, surprised.

"*Oui*," says Lumi. "Don't forget that we have a huge border with Russia, 1,340 kilometres. Many things cross that, both ways. And, of course, some paintings which the

Germans confiscated in World War II made their way to Russia. It is entirely possible that we could find something interesting. And it's something we Finnish police can help you with!" She looks delighted at this.

Patrice feels that the Finnish woman might burst into "Finlandia", but she restrains herself, *Dieu merci*!

Lumi persuades them not to go back to the gallery; they should probably sleep. She will give their request to involve the department in their investigation to Jak first thing in the morning and collect them at *09.00 heures* at the Seurahuone. Chloë can easily be there, for breakfast if she wants; her *pension* is only around the corner.

***

Colette has had an exhausting day and is pleased that Chloë and Lumi have not returned with Patrice. She herself had lunch and dinner at small restaurants and enjoyed the food, especially the profusion of berries, although they must be frozen at this time of year, must they not? Patrice, who is feeling the cold, thinks they are probably frozen at all times of the year.

He looks exhausted too, when he gets in, and throws himself to rest on the bed. He closes his eyes and tells her that they have alerted the Finnish police to the possibility that their *Judith* might be a copy, and they are ecstatic.

"They probably thought that there would be actual police work to do," says Colette. "Big Interpol people arriving, big art historian arriving, big French *commissaire* of *PJ* arriving ... maybe you have been a bit low-key for them."

"I am low-key," says Patrice. "And that makes it sound like they don't have much crime or excitement, and I don't know if that's true."

"They're bound to have less crime, though, aren't they?" says Colette. "High standard of living, less poverty, et cetera."

"Lot of immigration, though," says Patrice, "and I have no idea how they handle that. If they handle it like we do in France, it will be *horrible*."

"I might ask about that tomorrow," says Colette. "I have made a friend in the café where I had lunch. She is a teacher of French in a *lycée* and I am meeting her again for lunch tomorrow."

"Excellent," says Patrice. "I'm afraid Chloë and I will be going back to the gallery with Lumi Salonen for another round of arguing with Italians. I really don't know how long this is going to take. I'm glad you have found a friend who speaks French!"

***

"We have found out," says Jak, "that Olaveson's was a fence, a route for works of art and culture travelling from Europe and America to Russia, and vice versa. I enquired with colleagues, and they said that it had been known for almost thirty years, since the fall of the Soviet Union.

"It had been raided regularly, but there is too much confusion about provenance – and a lot was lost in the dying days of the Soviet. My colleagues were sincerely surprised when the fence suddenly closed, and everything in both the shop and the warehouse disappeared overnight. They had no ideas about why, but when we asked, they said what it might be worth several hundred thousand euros."

"Their usual level of value was around the middle," says Lumi. "Not rubbish, naturally, but not Titian either. The head of section felt that the Gentileschi painting would be above their usual value. If it proved to be genuine, and worth what some experts thought it was, it would draw attention."

"Does that make any difference to whether you think it might be genuine, *Commissaire* Lanier?" asks Jak.

"It might, if I could allow it," says Patrice, "but I can't. I must treat it as irrelevant, or it will distract me."

The Italian art experts are taking their time to arrive; possibly there is some reluctance to go through it all again – especially when they have all, individually, made up their minds.

Jak and Lumi have returned to their police car, to speak to some more contacts, when Signor Gambino arrives, alone, on fire with youthful enthusiasm, and casting side glances at the Finnish *Judith* as he opens a light conversation with the French detectives. He asks if they have come to any conclusion.

"I am not there yet," says Patrice. "I'm afraid it comes when it comes … in its own time."

Gambino looks as if he were being squeezed and says that it has to be genuine. It just has to be. It is as if it must be so because he wills it. He is completely spellbound.

Chloë makes for the kitchen, intending to warm them with tea. The tension between the two men in the main hall is unbearable. When she returns, several other Italians and the gallery director have arrived. And Lumi and Jak are, again, standing in the midst of them, trying not to answer questions. Chloë wonders what has been said between the *patron* and Monsieur Gambino – both are looking thoughtful.

***

"If the *Judith* now in New York is genuine – and it does seem as if it must be – it is as if our one must be a forgery," says Patrice, "and as such must be returned to France and destroyed in front of the magistrate, so that it cannot ever be resold. End of problem."

Colette, who is now on the side of saving the work of art, rather than what must be, due to the absolute legal situation, makes a small noise of disgust. Alongside her streak of conventionality balances another of anarchy. She is not above perverting the law when it is clearly wrong. She has not, ever, sworn to uphold the laws of the Republic.

Patrice executes a deep sigh and says that there is nothing he can do.

"I am bound by my professional oath," he says. "If I behave according to my own desire, where would it stop? I just cannot do anything else."

"*Non*, you cannot," says Colette. "But I can."

***

"*Ça va?*" says Colette, entering the coffee shop where she lunched with her new teacher friend yesterday. The fiercely blonde Helji is sitting at a table close to the back of the dining room. She stands to welcome the Frenchwoman, smiling broadly, delighted to have a native speaker on whom to practice.

"*Ça va?*" she says. "I am very well. Shall I get coffee now, or will you wish to eat first?"

"Coffee!" says Colette, thirsty. "And I want to talk to you about something important …"

"Ah," breathes the Finnish woman, "something serious?"

"Maybe. Something which you may think is too incredible to be true."

Helji, looking fascinated, asks the waiter to bring coffee for Colette, before settling down and giving all her attention to her new friend.

Colette takes a big gulp of milky before she begins the story.

"Are you interested," she says, "in painting? I mean fine art – old masters and that? Not just Finnish ones; Italy, and Holland and such?"

"Um." Helji seems to be concentrating hard; she had not even guessed what Colette was going to talk about. "I suppose so – I know Monet and Degas, with teaching French. I don't know a great deal about others. I have heard of Leonardo da Vinci."

"*Oui*, of course. My husband, Patrice – I told you he is a policeman, in Finland on a case. It is about a painting which had been found, and he was trying to work out whether it was genuine."

Helji waits for her to continue, gesturing for the waiter to give them a little more time before ordering.

"It turns out that it is not exactly a forgery, it is just a copy. A copy of a genuine painting, with good provenance, which is in New York. So, what we have here, in Finland, is a copy of a great painting, with no provenance, and therefore, no saleable value. It must, under the law, be returned to its last place of origin, which is in France. Unfortunately, French law says it must be destroyed, before the magistrate, so it cannot be sold again."

Helji looks interested, wondering what Colette is asking from her. Suddenly, her face clears; she has it now.

"But it is a copy, a good copy, I suppose. Could someone not enjoy it, without ever trying to sell it as real? Could it not be given to someone who would appreciate it, even though it would have no value attached to it?" Her voice is more shrill towards the end of the sentence. She appreciates beauty more than financial value.

"It cannot," says Colette, "even be given away for free. But there is a person, who had it on his wall for several years but had to sell it because he needed the money – a very sad story; he needed to pay for his son's drug rehabilitation and didn't have any other way to do it. He got very little for the painting, he was cheated. Or would have been if it had been an original. And then his son died. It would give him great joy to have the painting back." Colette stops, not wishing to force the issue too much, leaving it to Helji to decide whether to be involved.

The waiter returns, giving the impression that, if they intend to stay at the table, they need to order something. Helji, still pondering the complications of justice, asks for soup and bread for both.

"You can get the copy to the man who wants it? And there would be some natural justice in that ..." she asks.

"I can," confirms Colette, "and there is. We have extra customs labels and all the documents needed. But we will have no painting to be destroyed. No 'copy' to return to France."

"Will the, what, magistrate, in France look at the painting before having it destroyed?" Helji asks.

"I do not know," says Colette, "although I don't expect that the magistrate will be an art expert. He may not know what he is looking at. Except if that is his habit. And that I cannot know."

"Risky, then," says Helji, "we cannot depend on it. We need a trick which will stop him looking properly at what is in the package. A package, with a painting in it – is it painted on canvas or something else? – is easy. We can easily get one from the art supply shop after lunch. Do you know what size it should be?"

"*Naturellement*," says Colette, giving her the numbers. "But how on earth can we ensure the magistrate does not look at the painting to be destroyed?"

"You could make sure it's run over by a train, or a

luggage cart," says Helji, softly, with little confidence.

"But, if the portfolio is smashed open," says Colette, "they will be able to see that it's just blank canvas, not a painting which could be mistaken for an old master ..."

Helji looks miserable as she contemplates this – if only they could be sure that the magistrate wouldn't open it.

"We could throw some paint at it," she says. "I have a few colours – what colours did your artist tend to use? Do you know?"

"I don't," answers Colette, "but I can find out."

"How can we make it harder to see?" asks Colette, "What if it had had an accident before it was packed? Is that even possible?"

"Sounds a bit far-fetched," says Helji, "but I think there will always be turpentine and other things in an artist's studio – and in galleries for all that. Accidents do happen. Not everyone is scrupulously careful. Sometimes, they are amazingly sloppy ..."

"And we French are very critical and dismissive of people from other countries – even experts!"

***

The two *PJ* officers, and Colette, say goodbye to Jak and Lumi at the airport. Patrice and Chloë are returning directly to Paris, Chloë cutting her holiday short because both she and the *patron* need to report to *le Trente-Six,* as soon as possible, for the conclusion of the Lindholm case. Colette is going to Stockholm to call on M Larsson, to comfort the old man, still much upset.

Her luggage consists only of one small carry-on and a sealed, slim wooden portfolio case, which already has a 'Free export under European Law' sticker on it, as well as the usual 'Fragile' notices. Both items will travel with her in the cabin. She will be in Stockholm less than a day.

Patrice and Chloë have custody of Colette's luggage as well as their own, including a slim board portfolio case. As they arrive at Charles DeGaulle airport, Patrice leaves her to get coffee from a stall. He is desperate for actual French coffee; the milky is inadequate.

***

The magistrate is an elderly white man, with long grey hair, tied back in a bun, bent and wrinkled with the years of destroying beautiful things which just happen to be made by someone other than the supposed maker. His assistant, who executes the destructions, is a young man, wearing jeans and a T-shirt declaring that he is sorry he is late, he didn't want to come.

"Is there a complete chain of custody for this item?" asks Magistrate Lenoir, in a deep, tired voice.

"There is," replies Chloë, keeping her anxiety pushed as far down as possible.

"And are the seals and labels undisturbed?" says the old man.

"*Oui*, monsieur," assures Chloë, now trying to suppress her rising elation; he's not going to open it.

"Very well. I have completed the paperwork. Take the box and give it to the fire." The younger man lifts the portfolio from the desk and goes through the door to the furnace room. Both Chloë and Magistrate Lenoir watch him through the one-way glass as he opens the furnace door and consigns the box to the flames.

"You did not wish to see what it was?" says Chloë, in wonder now that it is too late.

"I cannot bear to destroy beauty," says Lenoir.

It is done.

It is a very long and harrowing job, interviewing M Bernard Cloche, and it requires a relay of four detectives to keep up the pressure. The days of beating up suspects have gone, *dieu merci,* but police are still comfortable enough to keep the lights on twenty-four hours a day and strictly control supplies of food, drink and cigarettes.

René Mercard takes the first shift, and begins by asking Cloche, again, how he knew M Lindholm and the girl in the photograph. René finds himself unable to call her either Mollie or Gertrude now. He sincerely wishes he could find out her name. M Cloche does not know either of the people in question, again.

He now thinks, though, that he did arrive on Thursday not Friday. This is presented as a little gift for René. Why is he doing that? Apparently, he forgot.

"Forgot?" asks René, "But it was Friday in your diary …"

"I was going to stay somewhere else on Thursday night," says Cloche. "Then I decided that I may as well go to the Jardins, they are not much busy, they usually have a room."

"Have you proof that you made a booking at another hotel?" asks René.

"*Non,* I was just going to turn up. No one is busy after Christmas and New Year."

"I see you like little girls." René stops cold, leaving him to think about this until his wristwatch says five minutes have passed. Unlike some offenders, Cloche has not started to splutter and make excuses for himself. He does not say anything. He clearly has considerable experience.

"Did you like the look of Mollie?" René squeezes the name he now knows to be false out against his will. "You like them frail and vulnerable, don't you?" He swallows rapidly, to get rid of the unpleasant taste of the words.

Still no answer; the sex offender appears as silent as Mollie herself. Another five minutes, by his watch. René is getting hot under the collar. He is not a violent man but … sex offenders, child rapists … wouldn't any man?

"Did you beat her?" he raps at Cloche, who makes no sign he has heard. Five more minutes. "Did you put out cigarettes on her arms and legs?" The anger is building up inside René. It feels like indigestion or a huge dinner trying to get out. He is sweating profusely and feels drops sliding down his face. Still no word from Cloche. René doesn't panic, as a rule. He is generally calm and moderately confident. But he has a reckless streak. As he feels his underarms and back streaming, and his stomach turning over, he realises that he has to get out of here. He jumps up, at least making Cloche start in surprise; he hadn't expected that.

René leaves, not even telling the video that Detective Mercard leaves the room at *07.40 heures.*

***

Colette carries the parcel upstairs to the flat. It is not heavy but she needs to be careful not to catch it on the balustrade. She had rented a car at Arlanda airport in order to protect the masterpiece. Colette will pay the bill; this part of the mission is hers, the cost is hers. She has no guilt. She is following her conscience.

The Frenchwoman rings the doorbell. For a few minutes, she thinks there will be no answer, but then hears shuffling and the key turning in the door.

Christer Larsson sees her and smiles. He is pleased, though surprised, at having a visitor he does not know.

"*Bonjour,*" says Colette, "I am Colette Lanier, the wife of the French policeman who came to talk to you about your painting."

"*Allô!*" he says. "Come in, come in."

Larsson doesn't know what to think. If the policeman hasn't himself come to arrest him, why would he have sent his wife? He had half expected the Swedish police.

"I have something for you," says Colette, as she brings the parcel into the living room, placing it, flat, on the central table.

***

"How horrible is he?" asks Pucelle, aware that Fleur and René had both loathed interviewing Cloche at his place of work.

"Horrible," says René, "and he doesn't answer. I didn't think I was so emotionally engaged ... I just had to get out. I couldn't stop myself thinking about her ... um ... and what he might have done."

"Do you think he's guilty?" asks Pucelle.

"I do."

"*D'accord*, my turn." She gets up, pulling off her blue print headwrap, revealing steely curls, and makes for the interview room. There was a time when her team had tried to shield her from this type of interrogation, but she had talked them out of that long ago. Pucelle installs the severe spectacles that she doubts she needs.

They have brought Cloche a cup of coffee, which Pucelle would not have allowed had she been there. He is sipping it, making it last. She tells him she is *Commissaire* LaSalle and that they have not met before. He nods his damned head in acknowledgement. One of a range of responses to Pucelle's unusual presence. She sits down opposite him, and begins her questioning sharply, looking at him over the glasses.

"So, you are a registered sex offender and have a conviction for sexually abusing four foreign girls who had eight to *eleven years*. You went to prison for twenty years and got out five years ago. Is that right?"

Cloche manages to say something that sounds like an affirmative reply without compromising his vow of silence.

"It says here that you like to beat up the weak and frail, vulnerable, right? Makes you feel like a big man, *quoi?*" There is no reply, he just looks at her. She goes back to the beginning, and asks him to confirm his name, address, and place and date of birth. He does not do this, either. She asks him whether he has ever been married. He does not answer, although he smiles in what she might, if she felt like it, consider a sinister way.

"It says here that you had a wife called Léonie, but she divorced you when you were convicted of sexually abusing – what were they called? Ah, yes, Anya who had nine years, Erika who had eleven years, Héléne who had eleven years, and Demi, who had only eight. I have pictures," she says. "Do you want to look at them?"

She throws the file onto the desk and it splays open, displaying the photographs as if they have been fanned out by coincidence. They haven't. This is one of her party tricks, kept for these situations. She cannot help observing Cloche's eye momentarily catching the pictures before looking away. She reaches for the one of the littlest, eight-year-old Demi, an illegal immigrant, whose parents brought her from Mali.

Pucelle starts to describe the child to Cloche in minute detail.

"She's small for her age," she says, pushing back the memory of herself at that age. "She is *renoi*,[160] obviously. Her skin is very dark and shiny. She looks like a black doll I used to have when I was a child too. Do you think she liked black dolls, Bernard? Do you think she had one? Did

---

160 A Black person (Verlan via 'noire')

she want her black doll for comfort when you raped her? When you stubbed out your cigarettes on her sweet black flesh?

"She looks about five or six, doesn't she?" Pucelle turns the photo around so he can see the child. "She has tight curly hair. Is that what turns you on, Bernard? Kinky hair? Look at her little tiny dress, Bernard. Come on, look! It's a little slip. Was she wearing it when you took her to bed, Bernard? Did she have knickers on? She didn't when the police found her. Did you take them as a souvenir? I know men like you do that sort of thing."

Pucelle, stopping suddenly in her recitation, realises that Cloche has moved. He has shuffled on the chair, as if something is affecting him. Perhaps she has broken the shell? She picks up the photograph of the nine-year-old, Anya, who was a legal immigrant with a Slovakian family of four children. She is blonde, still small, but bigger than miniature Demi.

She starts to describe the girl as her rapist might have discovered her, small, frail, vulnerable, white.

"So, you don't mind white girls, then?" she asks, wondering how long she can keep this up; it's harder this time than she ever remembers. "Nice pink cheeks, blue eyes, long fair hair, with a pink ribbon? Do you like that little-girl kind of thing, Bernard? Did she call you '*Papa*'? You never had your own children, did you, Bernard? What is it? Not man enough? Or looking after children too much trouble? If you and Léonie had had any, you would have abused them too, wouldn't you?"

Cloche's face changes as she says this. The shell is at last cracked. He begins to look angry. He jumps up before Pucelle can move, and hits her in the face, hard, with his fist. She presses the emergency button as she falls past it.

***

Fleur takes the shaking Pucelle to the clinic to have her right cheek stitched and her nose taped. Clémence replaces her in the interview room with what they are now calling "the monster".

"*Eh, bien.* Now, Bernard, what are we going to do with you?" Clémence looks at him with loathing; he has just injured her colleague, as well as all the unspeakables they know about. "What is it with you and children? Why do you hate them so much?"

Cloche smiles and says that he doesn't hate them. Indeed, he loves children very much. He loves their delicate fingers and sweet noses; he loves their smooth, unmarked skin and their fine hair. The smile on his face is sickening. Clémence immediately wishes to pay him back in kind for punching Pucelle, as well as for the children.

"*Non!*" she shouts. "Stop that right now! I can easily arrange for you to have an accident on the stairs outside. You know how we police appreciate child sex offenders. Tell me about what you did to Mollie!"

"Nothing," he says. The smile has gone, he is growling. "Don't know her, haven't seen her, never heard of her."

"You've done it before, why not this time?"

He shrugs his shoulders, doesn't say anything. Time for a different tack.

"What is it that you hurt them if you love them so much? Is it the fear that gets you off? Do you like making them scared? Is it the tears? Is it the pleas to let them go? Do you like it when they scream?"

Cloche is looking horrified now. Not ashamed, horrified.

"*Non, non,* you've got it all wrong!" he nearly screams. "It's not the fear at all – the opposite, in fact. I like the courage, the bravery, the way they don't want you to see that they like it!"

Clémence pushes her chair back suddenly from the table and rolls for the door as fast as she can. As she leaves, Cloche says softly:

"And they are so grateful."

*****

René will be interviewing M Renault and M Melzer separately, and because each is being delivered on his own, by the Nantes *PJ* and the Nancy *PJ*, it will require no great organisation to keep them apart. Nancy arrives first, and they put M Renault straight into an interview room. He looks older than his reported *28 ans*, he has white streaks in his hair – more the result of art than ageing.

René confirms his name, address, place and date of birth. He says he has twenty-eight years; René checks that this is true with his identity documents. He asks what Renault does for a living.

"I am a *maître d'école*[161] in Nancy," he says.

The detective leaves him to say more about that, but he does not. He is silent, waiting for a new question. He seems as if he has been through this before.

"Please tell me the dates you were staying at the Hôtel des Jardins in Paris."

"Why?" he asks, "What am I supposed to have done? I haven't done anything. This is *ridicule*!"

"Please answer the question," says René.

"Nights of ninth January until fourteenth January."

"Six nights? Is that correct?"

"*Oui*. I met my friend, André Melzer, from Nantes. We had a good time; we went out a lot. We didn't see anything or anyone!"

---

161 primary school teacher

Ah, thinks René, more information than I asked for.

"How do you know André?"

"Since we began school," he says. "But the family moved away when we had about *12 ans*." He lapses into silence, then volunteers the fact that they had been out on the night of the tenth to eleventh of January.

"We had been out clubbing and didn't get back until *3 heures*. We were told about the accident by others in the hotel lobby. It is terrible."

René permits himself a tiny smile – the same words, again.

"You didn't know, hadn't seen, either Monsieur Lindholm, or this girl in the photo, then?"

"*Non*. I told the girl – not this girl," he says, indicating the photo, "your girl, the officer in the wheelchair. I told her that we didn't know them. And my friend André, he told her the same thing."

"You've been in touch, then?" says René.

"Um, *oui*, of course. We are friends." He looks as if he is wondering whether that was a mistake. Perhaps he hasn't done this before.

"I see," says René. "Look, Pierre, I must ask you all these stupid questions, but I understand about men's friendships. You have a mate, you don't want to say anything detrimental about him." René nods slowly, hoping Renault will start to mirror his movements, if he's sufficiently relaxed, "But you've known him a long time. Is there anything you want to tell me about him before I question him?

"You know the kind of thing; has he a regular girlfriend, or does he play the field? Does he like blondes or redheads or older women, or younger, even? He doesn't like boys, does he?" René gives him a look as if potentially shockable by the latter. Renault is quick to deny the implication.

"*Non*," says Renault, "he's hetero, I've never heard anything else. He likes women, blonde usually, but he's okay with anything at all. He always says he's an equal opportunity womaniser! He's a man of the world – aren't we all?"

"Of course," says René, who is by no means a womaniser, and certainly only holds amateur man-of-the-world status. "Just between us, though, does he like older women? You know, the ones with experience? What would you say were his age limits?"

Renault takes a moment to think about this; René can almost see the wheels turning in his head. What is the best answer to give? If he says "on the young side", what will the detective ask next? If he says the limits are thirty to forty-five, will he be believed, given that he and André are both young and good-looking; both are good catches for any girl. They should be grateful.

"We don't really have limits," he says. "As long as she's good-looking and has a slim figure, and she's up for it, she's fine!"

"Don't object to older women, then?" says René. "Obviously not! And they're so grateful, aren't they?"

Renault looks puzzled; this is not going the way he expected. Is there some other thing at the root of this?

"I think that will do for now," says René suddenly. "I'll need to speak to you again later. This is such a serious case that you will have to wait in the cells. Please take Monsieur Renault away, Brigadier."

***

Monsieur Denthwaite won't arrive until next Tuesday; the New Zealand police are bringing him on a flight which arrives in the early morning. M Melzer, however, is here now, and René wishes to interview him in a carbon copy of his session with M Renault.

Except for his comment that he is an accountant – "I run the accounts department at Maison et Foloff, Furniture Makers, in Nantes" – the first half hour goes exactly as did M Renault's. It is only when they get to "Look, André, I have to ask you all these stupid questions" that it starts to work out rather differently.

M Melzer is more nervous. René estimates that it will not take much to encourage him into hysteria.

"Look, André, I must ask you all these stupid questions, but I'm a man of the world, just like you. I'm thinking about your mate, Pierre. When you have a mate you've known a long time, you don't want to say anything bad about him, I understand that." René nods slowly but Melzer is too tense to start to mirror his movements. "But I think if he did something wrong, you probably weren't involved, were you? Is there anything you want to tell me about before I question him?

"You know the kind of thing; has he a regular girlfriend, or does he play the field? Does he like blondes or redheads or older women, or younger, even? He doesn't like boys, does he?"

It is *Melzer*'s turn to choose and, perhaps because of his inexperience or immaturity – or even his hysteria – he makes the wrong choice.

"*Oui*," says Melzer, "he's always preferred men. It's nothing to me, I'm not prejudiced. They aren't young, he doesn't like boys or anything like that. He isn't a paedo! Being gay isn't illegal."

"Of course not," says René. "I see. So, no girls at all, just adult men?"

"*Oui*, but he wouldn't take me along on any of his expeditions," says Melzer. "He knows I'm heterosexual. But

I don't like young girls, don't think that. I like grown-up women."

"I think that will do for now," says René suddenly. "I'll need to speak to you again later. This is such a serious case that you will have to wait in the cells. Please take Monsieur Melzer away, Brigadier."

29

Patrice arrives back before the *PJ* takes delivery of M Denthwaite from New Zealand, and he girds his loins straight away to have a go at Bernard Cloche. He has already visited Pucelle in hospital and been told that she will be home the following day. Her injuries are not that serious, she is just infuriated that the 'monster' managed to land his punch. She holds that she is usually able to get out of the way. She is bruised but ready to arrange for revenge on M Cloche. Patrice, denying her the possibility, says he will speak to M Cloche himself.

"*D'accord*," says Patrice, settling himself in the chair opposite Cloche. He can do this kind of work, God knows he's had plenty of experience. He just doesn't like it. When he has done this, he will have to go home and take a long hot shower before he does anything else. "I have your record here, and I read that you served twenty years for sexual and physical abuse of four foreign children. You have been free for five years. Is that correct?"

"*Oui.*"

"I am not going to question you about that. You were guilty and you paid what the law required. Notice that I did not say that you paid your debt to society. I do not believe that such debts can ever be paid. No one can make any justification for the things you did.

"What I do want to know is what crimes you have committed since you got out."

Cloche is playing the waiting game, making Patrice come to him. The *commissaire* waits, refusing to say that abusers like Cloche don't stop, the perverse impulse never goes away. Patrice's tactics are to make notes in his notebook computer, and let the accused sit there until his brain fries. It used to be more difficult, when the policeperson had to actually make notes – which the accused could, possibly, read upside down – on an actual notebook. Easier now because the screen is hidden from the other side. The *commissaire* has his old-fashioned police notebook by his side on the table, in case he feels the need to draw some penguins.

Patrice is free-associating, allowing his mind to come up with something useful if it feels like it. He is tempted to write Colette a love letter, to put himself a thousand miles from here, and what he is doing, but he cannot have anything which is important to him to come into this room.

It is almost half an hour before M Cloche begins to move on the chair, shuffling in discomfort. Patrice ignores him and types several words which have occurred to him. He wonders if it is raining outside; there is no window in here. He begins to prepare his intervention. He is after something different from what his team established.

"How many of you are there in the group?"

"Group?" Cloche is taken by surprise enough to answer automatically.

"Your trafficking group."

"I don't ... I'm not ..." Cloche suddenly realises that his silent treatment has broken. He ostentatiously closes his mouth.

Patrice, who is pleased at the reaction, goes back to his free writing. It is almost another quarter hour before he says:

"We know that kids are being brought in from Bulgaria and Hungary to provide for the needs of men who are willing to pay lots of money for sex with young boys and girls. But I am prepared to make a deal with you, because no one has been killed yet, and I don't think you, personally, had anything to do with the organising.

"I'm quite sure it was one of these foreign, probably Serbian or something, gangs who make a speciality of this sort of thing. I think you are probably as much of a victim as anyone – they are taking advantage of your unfortunate sexuality. I, for one, know you can't help it; it's a compulsion." He wonders as he speaks if this is true.

"If you tell me the names of all the men involved, those bringing the girls and boys in, those arranging the meetings or parties, or whatever they are, I'll charge you with aiding and abetting. With your record, you'll get two years in prison, but if we don't mention the sex charge, you'll be out in a year and you can go back to Blois and your business. You probably won't even be beaten up in jail."

Nothing. Silence. Patrice asks the brigadier to return M Cloche to the cells. And have the interview room disinfected.

***

Colette is still at home when Patrice returns for the hot shower he has promised himself. She is still *en vacances*. She remarks on his pallor; he is a bit grey around the edges.

"I'm all right," he says. "I just questioned a child molester. You know how I get."

"I do," says Colette. "Go and shower. I'll make coffee, or do you want to go out for pastries?"

"*Non*," he says, "just stay home for an hour, and talk to you? Then I have to get back to tying up the Artemisia case."

"You are getting to the end of that?" she asks, stroking Sartre, who is laid out on the sofa. "I have nothing else to do. And I think the sun is coming out. We can at least open the *porte-fenêtres*, get some air. While we talk."

***

Pucelle wants to go home. She isn't injured seriously enough to be in hospital; it is mostly her sinful pride which is hurt – although the broken cheekbone is excruciating and she cannot breathe through her nose.

She is satisfied about Patrice taking her place, for the moment, in interviewing Bernard Cloche; she recognises this particularly sleazy character as one the *PJ* generally has to draw lots to avoid. It is good to have *le patron* back, as well as Chloë, of course.

The art historian hasn't spent much time at *le Trente-Six*, but she is definitely a useful part of the team. Pucelle wonders whether the *patron* will expect the girl to take part in the questioning of all these witnesses. Probably not the suspect child molesters, she thinks, but maybe people like the young women around Mollie and any hotel staff they have not yet located.

She lies back on her pillow and thinks about the case. The emergency consultant comes in and tells her she can go home. The consultant is surprised by her unalloyed joy.

***

Monsieur Denthwaite arrives in an ill-tempered phalanx of New Zealand police officers. René is surprised there are so many – there are only four, but four is a lot. Especially when it means paying five air fares from Auckland. The suspect immediately catches René's eye, and focuses his personal ill temper on the detective he has previously spoken to on the telephone.

"I told you," Denthwaite yells in English, "that I haven't done anything and I don't know anything! What the bloody hell is this all about?"

René ignores him and tells the officers, in English, to take him down to wait in the cells; the brigadier, from the desk, will show them. The New Zealander will have to wait until René has had his next scheduled interview with M Pierre Renault, whom he thinks is the weakest link in this case *déplorable*.

"*D'accord*," he says, sitting opposite the younger man. "Are you still sure you don't want a lawyer while I ask the rest of my questions?"

The young man seems more calm now, he has washed his face, and been given coffee and something to eat. He has composed himself into a semblance of confidence. René is sufficiently experienced to know that it won't last.

"*Zyva!*[162]" he says. "Let's get on with this, my time is precious. You have told me that it is impossible for your *ami* to be involved in a conspiracy involving trafficking young girls into France and using them for the purposes of sadistic sex?"

"Uh," says Renault, not sure whether he has or not. René thinks that didn't take long.

"*Oui*."

"Uh, *oui*," says the man, "It could not be him at all. No way. He's not involved."

"But you," says René, "you are?"

---

162 Let's go (Verlan via vas-y!)

Renault starts to get up from the chair, but thinks better of it, and slumps down looking defeated already.

"Um, *non,* I, I, was there, but I didn't do anything …"

The CD player in René's head starts to play the really noisy part of the "1812 Overture" – the part where the church bells begin to ring in triumph.

"*D'accord*, I accept that you didn't do anything. Was it your first time?"

"*Oui,* André invited me to meet him in Paris."

"Did he want to show you what they did?"

"*Oui.* He was trying to help me."

"Help you?" René tries to prevent his eyebrows raising themselves. Failing.

"I haven't been, er, er, that successful with girls. André thinks I should, er, have, er …" Renault turns red in embarrassment. René stares at him, daring him to admit it, sure that he will.

"I've never been with a woman," he mutters, his chin drawn into his neck, no eye contact. "André thought I might manage to do it with a young girl – it is not so frightening …"

Oui, thinks René. He lets the young man rest for a minute before resuming his carefully planned attack, which involves coffee and sandwiches.

As soon as the brigadier has deposited the tactical ammunition on the table between them, René saddles up to resume work.

"I can make a deal with you. I can talk to the *juge d'instruction* and the *procureur*. I can tell them how cooperative you are being, how much you are helping us … and you are, virtually, innocent, aren't you? You just had a problem and your friend wanted to help …"

Renault nods several times, very quickly. He is definitely, definitely innocent.

"But I can't tell them that," says René, "unless you are

really, really helpful. You can tell me the names of the people who were there, in the room at the Hôtel des Jardins. And then we can see about getting you probation. You don't belong in jail, do you, Pierre? You haven't actually done anything."

***

"I understand. I sometimes look around, without intending to, and see these *fillettes*[163] coming out of the schools and how they are dressed, ooh! They have skirts so short they show their knickers, and tops so low they show *leurs mésanges*.[164] *C'est dégoûtant.*[165]"

Patrice suppresses a shudder as he rehearses the excuses paedophiles make. This is a part of a strategy, no more, but he feels that he needs, somehow, to make reparation for using such tactics.

"*Oui*," says Bernard Cloche, perhaps thinking that they are asking for it, but not comfortable in saying that just yet. Maybe this older policeman does, perhaps, understand what he has been through; what many men like him have been through, through no fault of their own.

"They obviously enjoy tempting men, *n'est-ce pas?*"

Cloche doesn't reply, but Patrice thinks he has him on the hook. He wonders how far he should take it this time; it is always a fine line, and Patrice is balancing on the edge of what he considers ethical. He stands up and, for the recording, says he is leaving temporarily. Cloche looks as if he is about to protest, but doesn't. Got you, thinks Patrice.

***

---

163 little girls
164 their tits
165 it is disgusting

311

"Sometimes," says Colette, "you have to do things you don't like – for the greater good." She thinks of handing the piece of stretched canvas, exactly mimicking the size of the *Finnish Judith*, wrapped in a parcel with export stickers on it, to Chloë Valéry, an art expert first, and a policeperson second.

"*Oui*," says Patrice, stretching out on the bed. He has told her very little, not wanting to bring this particularly sleazy aspect of his work home. Colette is sitting at the dressing table, wearing her aqua "Versailles" T-shirt, and rubbing cream into her hands. The screaming bat has gone, *dieu merci!*

"You know that you have to deal with unfresh types," she says. "It's the nature of the job."

"*Oui*," he says again, not wanting to elaborate.

"It's part of the method for holding back the dark."

"Of course. But sometimes you have to not like it. I don't like making him think I'm colluding with him; that I understand him – when I don't,"

"What would be better?" Colette asks. "Letting him go? Banging him in jail without a proper investigation? Madame Guillotine?"

This time, Patrice allows himself to shudder mightily.

"It will all be over soon," says Colette, turning back the duvet and getting into bed.

***

Chloë has been assigned to question Mlle Horváth, along with Yves Mercier, who has a little more experience in questioning suspects. They are short-handed, again, with Pucelle out for a few days with her nose. Mlle Horváth's lawyer has arrived with her. He is half Hungarian and has the ability to translate. This has surprised the team because

Mlle Horváth's French is superb. Collectively, they contemplate what is her game.

"We have already asked you a number of times, Mademoiselle Horváth, whether you recognise this girl who was discovered hiding in the cellar of the Hôtel des Jardins on eleventh of January of this year. Do you still say that you have never seen her and do not know her?" says Yves Mercier, an easy question to start with.

Mlle Horváth stares at him as if she doesn't quite understand. It is a brilliant performance; subtly containing elements of listening, hearing, looking, trying to understand the difficult foreign words, persuaded that she will understand, confident that she won't, nervous, worried, calm.

Whatever she isn't saying, Chloë doesn't believe a word.

The lawyer, *Maître* Annibale Deneice, tells them that Mlle Horváth is still absolutely sure that she does not know the girl in the photograph. She has told them several times. How many times does she have to tell them this? His voice is harsh, aggressive. Chloë, *un peu nerveux*,[166] girds her loins.

"*Merci, Maître* Deneice, are you going to answer all Mademoiselle Horváth's questions for her?"

"Only when she cannot understand them herself. You should note, Officer, that Mademoiselle Horváth's French is not very extensive."

"How does she manage, then, as a hotel receptionist?" asks Yves. "We are under the impression that her French is good, as excellent French is required for such a job."

"Not at all," says M Deneice. "She uses a quite limited vocabulary in that position. There is no legal requirement for perfect French."

---

166 a little nervous

"Is Mademoiselle Horváth aware that this young woman" – Chloë waves the photograph of Mollie in their faces – "is from Hungary?" Both detectives watch the face of the current Hungarian woman very carefully as Chloë says this. Both think they see a glint of recognition, sharply suppressed.

"How can she know that," says the lawyer, "if she doesn't know the girl? That is stupid."

"By the way, monsieur," says Yves, "you are partly Hungarian yourself. Do you know the girl? Is she known in the Hungarian community?" He takes the photograph from Chloë and places it on the desk in front of Deneice. The lawyer takes time to look at it properly.

"I think I may have seen her," he admits. "Do I need an *avocat* now?"

Yves laughs and says that of course he does not. He asks where the lawyer thinks he may have seen her.

"Oh, I don't know," says M Deneice. "Just about, I suppose. She is just a little familiar. I guess I may have seen her at a social get-together. Hungarians are a sociable people. It could have been anywhere." He stops for a moment then bangs the gears into reverse.

"*Non,* on second thoughts, I don't think I know her. She's a type, that's all. A lot of Hungarian girls are similar. Why, Mademoiselle Horváth is not unlike her ..." He stops when he realises that is a mistake. Mlle Horváth looks at him as if he were a slug in her *salade*.

"I am wondering," says Yves, "whether either of you might recognise the girl if you saw her in person? Sometimes, a photo can be misleading. It isn't a good photo anyway; it's too dark. Perhaps we should take them around to Madame Paston's refuge and let them meet her?"

"We still won't recognise her," says Deneice. "We don't know her."

"*Très bien*," says Chloë, "I think that will be all for now. Please tell your client that she can go. But that she should not leave Paris until we tell her she can. This investigation is far from over."

30

When they have gone, Chloë and Yves rush for a pool car and get to Mme Paston's a full fifteen minutes before the Hungarians, waiting unobtrusively outside. They were unsure how long the others would take as they do not know what lines of communication exist between Mollie and Mlle Horváth. The *PJ* watch from the car; the two are in the refuge for about another half hour, and then come out with a couple of bags and Mollie, who is linking arms with Mlle Horváth.

Chloë, who seems to be in charge, has not asked for uniformed back-up; she thinks she and Yves can arrest the Hungarians. Anyway, the brigadier would have asked for the authorisation she does not have.

They get out of the car and to the doorway as fast as they can. There is a small walled garden in front of the house, which would require leaping over in order to escape. None of the three do this – and they are caught. It is Chloë who tells them all three are under arrest. Her first.

***

Although Patrice has taken over as main questioner of the abominable Cloche, he is to have a go at Herr Doktor

Ascher, who has now arrived from Switzerland. The German Swiss has come in response to a direct request from the *juge d'instruction*: to help with enquiries. M *le Juge* has personally assured him he is not a suspect, but a witness. He has come in without a lawyer; presumably he has no lawyer in France. The team is delighted that he has come voluntarily; there is no extradition from Switzerland.

Patrice has asked for coffee, the "good" coffee from the bistro, in line with Herr Dr Ascher's pretentions as a highly respectable university professor. Patrice has few German language skills, but the professor speaks both excellent French and English.

"Monsieur *le docteur*," Patrice begins, "I have to ask you about the incident on the very early morning of Friday the eleventh of January of this year at the Hôtel des Jardins. You were, of course, staying there with your wife, Heidi. I realise that you have been questioned on the telephone – by Sergeant Mercard – but the case is progressing, and I am also now free to conduct it personally."

"I see," says Herr Doktor Ascher. "I am not surprised by this. I did feel that it would require a more senior detective to speak to me in person. It is to be expected."

"*Merci beaucoup*," says Patrice. "I wouldn't want you to think that we are closing in on you!" He laughs; of course he's not closing in on such a respectable figure. The Herr Doktor laughs heartily, he is content with this, and quite calm.

"May I ask you, just for the record," says Patrice, "what is your discipline at the university?"

"*Mais certainement*. I hold the chair in psychology, and have done so for a number of years."

"*Merci*. And before that, you held a full professorship in psychology at the University of Minnesota, Twin Cities, is that correct?"

"It is."

"I don't quite know, what does 'Twin Cities' mean?"

"There are two separate campuses, Minneapolis and St Paul, about three miles apart. I have taught at both of them – they're parts of the same university."

"I see. I am familiar with the system in California – University of California Los Angeles is UCLA, and there are UC at Irvine, UC at Davis, et cetera."

"*Oui*, of course."

"Why did you leave there, Herr Doktor?"

"For two reasons," says Ascher. "My wife wished to return to Switzerland, and I was, happily, able to gain a promotion. There is much prestige in occupying a chair at a European University, still."

"*D'accord*. Now, Herr Doktor, I need to ask you a few more questions. You understand that I am trying to help you. I'd very much like this case to go away. *C'est une grande nuisance!*[167] I know that you could not possibly be involved, and you have done nothing wrong. But there are some things I need to ask, so I can be sure of them. I'm sure you understand?"

"*Mais certainement*," says Ascher again, magnanimously. "I will tell you anything I can."

"I don't really know how to ask you this," says Patrice, "given what I've just said." He looks at the Swiss, as if in perplexity. "In fact, two of the other witnesses, Monsieur Cloche and Monsieur Melzer, have said that you were in the hotel on that night, that you were, with them, in one of the rooms, er ..." He turns a page of his notepad and says, "Room 307. What can you tell me about that? Are they lying?"

The man's face turns white and tense and his lips thin to a severe line. His pale eyes travel to the upper right-hand side.

---

167 It is a great nuisance

"Of course they are lying! I wasn't there. Not that room anyway." Patrice says nothing for a while, letting the man twitch on his chair. Ascher's confidence is slightly dented, not completely shattered. The Swiss quickly thinks of a plan.

"*Non, non,*" he says, "not in that room. What was going on in there, anyway?" Slight roses appear in his cheeks, and his voice, from being strangled, changes to being entirely calm in a few moments.

"We do not yet have a full picture," says Patrice. "We are trying to piece together what happened. There appear to have been several men, including Monsieur Cloche and Monsieur Renault. And, presumably, Monsieur Lindholm, the preacher who exited through the window ... as well as at least one young woman, well, girl, about *10 ans*. Whose name we do not yet know."

"Wait a minute, Monsieur *le Commissaire*, exactly what crime are you investigating here? The murder, or something else?"

"The murder," says Patrice, only half lying. "Someone bashed Monsieur Lindholm over the head and killed him, then ejected him from the window of Room 607. We have clear forensic evidence of this. We have a DNA match from the *identité judiciaire*.[168] I am investigating who, amongst the people in the room, could have done it, could have had some motive for doing it."

"It wasn't me!" says Herr Doktor Ascher. "I haven't killed anybody! I didn't know this Lindholm person. I was in another room. I never saw Monsieur Lindholm until he came past the window. I was on another floor ... there are people who can tell you that ..."

"So, it is true that you were in the hotel that night, but nowhere near the victim, Monsieur Lindholm?"

---

168 forensic science service

"That is right," says Ascher. "Someone can be a witness for me – maybe Herr Cloche or Herr Renault? They both saw me on the third floor. As did the girl. Her name is Mollie, I think."

"So, you do know Monsieur Cloche and Monsieur Renault, then? And are you telling me that was the room where the girl was? Am I understanding you correctly? In Room 307, where Messieurs Cloche and Renault, and a few others were?"

"*Oui, oui,* there was nothing about murder there. We were having a drink and a bit of fun. The girl was a prostitute, by the way, and sixteen. She was very easy-going. She liked fun and a good laugh. You, you know what they are like, all that type of person … they can be very tempting." He becomes breathless, remembering, sculpting the facts to suit his story.

"I do, and they often pretend to be older than they are too," says Patrice, suppressing a sigh, and not looking forward to being depressed this evening. "I know there's been a lot of talk recently about the age of consent. Of course we don't have one, as such, in France. But the liberals are getting upset at the moment because the government, in trying to give some kind of protection to these younger sex workers, has left it more open than they think it should be. All on account of those two eleven-year-olds last year.

"Of course, France has always maintained that a 'victim' has to be proven to have fought back before what they call sexual abuse can be classed as 'rape' – which carries a sentence of *20 ans*, while otherwise, it's only sexual assault and only carries *10 ans*. All nonsense, of course; they should go and live in Nigeria, where the age of consent is just eleven years."

The Herr Doktor does not speak but is nodding vigorously in agreement; this is getting better and better …

"My wife happens to be one of the *gnian-gnian*[169] liberals who is very annoyed about all this age of consent stuff. She says that the government has let vulnerable girls down – they tried to set the age at *15 ans* but only succeeded in having to drop the plan. Apparently, surprise or coercion can be 'characterised by the abuse of the victim's vulnerability, the victim doesn't have the necessary discernment to consent.' My wife and her friends think that 'offenders' will be able to get away with a lighter sentence if coercion can't be proved." He thinks, Please forgive me, Colette.

"You are right," says Ascher. "In Switzerland, the age is sixteen, but in Austria, Hungary, Germany, Portugal and Italy, it is fourteen years. It's fifteen in Greece, Poland and Sweden. Otherwise, it's sixteen only in Great Britain, Benelux, Spain and Russia. I ask you, is that sensible? And you might recall that, in the United States, different states have different local ages ...[170] Although they do tend to think marriage is important – and, of course, there is no such thing as marital rape."

"Um," says Patrice, shrugging his shoulders. "Now, you've told me that Monsieur Cloche and Monsieur Melzer were with you and Mollie in Room 307. And that Monsieur Lindholm, the dead man, was not. I'm wondering who else was there? So that we can get a proper sense of everyone who cannot possibly be implicated in the murder. I'm sure you will recall all the names? A scholar like yourself?"

"Um, *oui*," says Ascher, looking very much as if he is thinking deeply. "Ah, there was a man from somewhere on the other side of the world, Australia maybe? His name was Michael, I remember. Tall and blond, rangy. Strong accent. I don't think he told me his last name, and I doubt

---

169 namby pamby
170 This is not strictly true!

I told him mine. He was a little, er, rough, lower class. Let me think." He stops, marshalling all his resources, deciding whether any or all of them would help or hinder him.

"There were two older men," he says, "grey-haired, obviously respectable, well dressed. Their names were Albert and Max, one of them was from Bordeaux, I think, but I don't remember which. And there was another young man with Melzer, a car name, let me think … *oui*, Renault! They were together, they definitely knew each other."

"And just Mademoiselle Mollie, the *poule*, no other women?"

"*Oui*," says Ascher, "that is all. I should leave now. I took the liberty of making an appointment to see someone in Paris while I am here …"

Patrice stands up and stretches to his full height, towering over Ascher, who is taller but still sitting.

"*Non*, Herr Doktor," he says, a new voice from which the understanding has been stripped by revulsion. "That is not going to happen. You cannot leave. I am arresting you on suspicion of the sexual trafficking of children, and of sexual assault. You will be held in *garde á vue*[171] for twenty-four hours, in the first place, for further questioning by the examining magistrate, which may be extended to forty-eight hours, and further, by written notification from the district procurator. You have a right to a lawyer. You will not be available to meet anyone."

Ascher begins to splutter. There is no way he expected this, he is far too eminent, far too clever. He can form no words which make any sense. Patrice asks the brigadier to take Ascher away and, as he goes through the door, says:

"Just one more thing, Herr Doktor. Did you not lose your job in America for gross moral turpitude? Did they

---

171 police custody

not tell your new employer you slept with first-year students?"

***

"There's a phone call for you, *patron*," says Clémence as Patrice returns from questioning Ascher, thinking Got you! She says it's the Reverend Professor Milton D. Hafflinger calling from Minneapolis.

"*Merde!*" he says. "I am up to my neck in professors today! Still, I got what we wanted from Herr Doktor Ascher."

He goes into his private office and settles by the telephone. It is Mrs Greta Smith on the line, the reverend executive director's executive secretary, and she says she has the main man for him. He thanks her politely.

"Good morning!" says Prof Hafflinger (it is, in St Paul). "I understand from Mrs Smith that you wish to speak to me about the Reverend Dr Lindholm."

Patrice, who is surprised by the call, confirms that he did, he does.

"It is, specifically," he says, "about a telephone call Monsieur Lindholm made on his cell phone on the twenty-ninth of September 2018 to your number. Madame Smith said that it was probably to you, and that would be why it is not logged. I am asking you if you can enlighten me as to what that call was about?"

"I have to tell you," says M Hafflinger, "that calls made directly to me from missionaries in the field are outside the church's usual communication systems. They are calls for spiritual guidance and, therefore, confidential. Generally, I should refer you to Dr Gardiner, who was Dr Lindholm's supervisor in Paris. But, on this occasion, I am prepared to speak to you about it because Dr Lindholm has passed,

322

and because the call occurred in very special circumstances."

"*Bien!*" says Patrice. "I am grateful for your cooperation; it may make all the difference to the investigation of Dr Lindholm's death."

"That is what I am hoping. Dr Lindholm called me on that occasion because a conflict with his normal work had occurred. As I'm sure you are aware, he was appointed to our Paris church in order to work, explicitly, on the conversion of Muslims. He had worked briefly in the Middle East and knew quite a bit of Arabic. But something had come to his attention which was not about that, it was about something very different."

"And that was?"

"What he believed was a circle being set up to traffic and exploit young girls for sexual purposes." The cleric seems shocked and upset by having to discuss this with Patrice; his voice has taken a turn for the quiet. "Cedric Lindholm was horrified, as you might expect – he was a very moral man – but he needed to talk with me about whether the Holy Spirit was calling him to do something about this new thing, or whether he should confine himself to his normal work with Muslims."

"So, this was nothing to do with Muslims, and he was seeking your permission to add it to his portfolio, so to speak?"

"You are correct that this was nothing, directly, to do with Muslims, although he did suspect that he might find a connection eventually. The words you use – about adding it to his portfolio – are strange to our experience. And asking permission is not appropriate either. He wished me to discern with him whether the Holy Spirit was calling him to a different piece of work. But, essentially, you have it."

"Tell me," says Patrice, "what he told you about this trafficking ring?"

"Do you think that it was because of this he was killed?" asks Hafflinger.

"It may be," says Patrice. "I need to know everything I can before I can form the picture of the crime, or of the crimes, we are investigating. Tell me what he said to you, *s'il vous plaît.*"

"He knew he had not to ask permission, that is between him and the Holy Spirit, and it is according to his own discernment. But I prayed with him and assured him of my support." He pauses, although the air on the phone does not go completely dead; Patrice can hear his breath.

"He said that it had come to his attention that there was a young girl who appeared to be on her own in the city. He had spoken to her, although he could not get any answer. He felt that, perhaps, she could not speak – although she may have been a non-English or non-French speaker. She was not an Arab, so that was no use either. He thought she was about ten years old. He suggested, having communicated somewhat by gestures, that he take her to the police, but she ran away from him on that occasion.

"He saw her around and took care to speak to her again. She was, apparently, elusive and ran away any time he mentioned taking her somewhere – even when he promised her safety. She did let him buy her food and coffee, but police or social workers seemed out of the question. Eventually, he followed her and she went to a bar and nightclub in the city centre. He spoke there to a Chinese woman who said she was taking care of the girl and that she would be safe."

"Did he believe her?" asks Patrice.

"No," says Hafflinger, "and he did not feel comfortable with that. He asked the Chinese girl where the other girl had come from, and she told him some kind of vague story about her folks bringing her from England but she had run away because they were cruel to her. There seemed no point, according to, er, Sue, I think he said, in trying to find them, she would be better on the street. In the meantime, Cedric had developed a theory that Mollie, as they were calling her (they did not seem to know her real name), was vulnerable enough to be the victim of sex trafficking.

"I encouraged him, I have to say, to do what he could. These things are very evil; there are many evil men about who will abuse children. I know this, it seems to be getting more and more prevalent. Or else, we are finding out more. If I had discouraged Cedric, I would have felt responsible. What would have happened if I had told him not to get involved?"

"*Oui*," says Patrice, "if you had not encouraged Monsieur Lindholm to do something, you would have been partly responsible. I am glad that you did. Even though it may have led to his death ..."

"That is what I am concerned about now," says Hafflinger, "that I may have contributed to his death. Although I know he is now in heaven with Almighty God and his saints. Do you think someone in the trafficking ring killed Cedric, Mr Lanier?"

"It would seem possible," says Patrice, "but I am not there yet. Please tell me what Monsieur Lindholm was thinking he should do about all this. Did he tell you?"

"He was going to make enquiries," says the executive director, "trying to find some solid evidence before calling in the police. He was spending time around the nightclub and the centre of Paris, where this Mollie and Miss Sue seemed to be based. Perhaps he thought this hotel he fell from was implicated – but he never told me that. I only spoke to him once, at the end of September. He never called again. I thought he must have sorted it out."

"Well, thank you for calling, and for all the information," says Patrice. "It is very helpful."

"Before I go," says Hafflinger, "could you tell me when we may have Dr Lindholm's earthly remains shipped back to the US? We want to arrange a proper Christian burial, of course."

"I think it will be quite soon now, Dr Hafflinger," says Patrice. "As soon as the *procureur de la Republique* charges those responsible. I will make sure that we let you know as soon as possible."

"Thank you very much," says Hafflinger.

31

"Monsieur *le Commissaire*," says *le juge d'instruction*, when the whole team is settled in his office. René looks as if he has been up all night (which he has). Patrice looks fresh as if he has slept well (which he has not). Fleur is drinking coffee and playing with a pen as if it were a cigarette. Pucelle looks as if she has been thumped with a baseball bat. Clémence and Chloë sit as far away from one another as it is possible to get. Yves Mercier is eyeing up the delectable Roxanne from a chair behind Clémence.

"Have you decided whether we have one crime here or two? Or even three or four?" Zabi smiles sweetly and waits, just as sweetly, for Patrice's answer.

"Our latest estimate is that we have two crimes, which are related, Monsieur *le Juge*," says Patrice. "One, the murder of Monsieur Lindholm by hitting him over the head with the brass lamp; and one, involving the girl who is likely not called Mollie, which appears to be a sex-trafficking situation and may be the sexual abuse or rape of children. There will be several crimes there."

"*Bon dieu!*" says Zabi. "And where are we in the separation of these hideous crimes?"

"They are connected," says Patrice. "What we do not exactly know is the precise link. In the interim, perhaps Madame LaSalle can tell us about her interview with Monsieur Bernard Cloche, who we think may be the organiser of the sex ring. He has a previous serious conviction for rape of four young girls, for which he served twenty years."

Pucelle takes her turn to describe what has been said, and Patrice follows up with what he experienced. René talks about the younger men, Messieurs Melzer and Renault, as well as M Denthwaite from New Zealand.

"*Commissaire*," says Zabi, "are you intending to charge Monsieur Cloche with assaulting an officer in pursuit of her duty? Madame LaSalle does not look well."

"I am," says Patrice, and indicates that Clémence is next up.

"I talked also to Monsieur Cloche," she says. "I have the transcript here." She flourishes papers, enough sets for everyone to read, fastened together with a treasury tag. She doesn't want to talk about it. "He told me how he loves children. He described how he loves their courage when they are being abused. It was very nasty. I took the opportunity to threaten him." Clémence looks both ashamed and repelled.

Chloë, feeling pity for her colleague for the first time, pitches her own onions into the stew:

"Officer Yves Mercier and I talked to Mademoiselle Szonja Horváth," she says, "the day receptionist at the Hôtel des Jardins. And her avocat, *Maître* Annibale Deneice. She was engaged in pretending that she doesn't speak good French. Which is untrue. Deneice would not let her say anything, but said that neither of them – he is another member of the Hungarian community – know Mollie. I believe that they do." She stops speaking and looks over to where Yves Mercier is sitting, no longer gazing at Roxanne Stein, and then says that she and Yves had arranged a trap for them:

"I know I should have got permission from the *commissaire*, or you, Monsieur *le Juge*, but I felt we needed to take advantage of the opportunity. Both Mademoiselle Horváth and *Avocat* Deneice went to Madame Paston's and left with Mollie Cartwright. All three are now in *garde à vue*, waiting to talk to Monsieur *le Juge*."

"You have arrested Mollie?" asks Patrice, ignoring the fact that everyone is addressing the magistrate.

"Sorry, *patron*," says René. "There is a piece of evidence that you do not know."

He explains how they worked out that Mollie is Hungarian and that Chloë has suspected a link to Mlle Horváth at the Hôtel des Jardins.

Zabi looks a little baffled by the speed of all this and asks where they are now?

"I think," says Patrice, "that we are on the brink of a solution; one big one, or several smaller ones. I have also interviewed Monsieur Cloche, who is at least one half of the organising team for the sex trafficking, and Professeur Ascher, who is likely to be the other. The Herr Ascher gave me virtually everything I needed to charge him and all the other members of the ring. Pucelle, Fleur, René, Clémence, Chloë and Yves have talked to the other people who were there that night and obtained the necessary corroboration. As we," he says, nodding to Chloë and Yves, "have still to talk to the Hungarians and, possibly, the friends of

Mollie – who may also be involved – we are not quite there yet. But we shall be by tomorrow!"

"Whom do you think I need to examine first?" asks Micah Zabi, indicating that Roxanne should make a note.

"Cloche and Ascher, first and second," says Patrice. "Then Mademoiselle Horváth and Mollie – although we still don't know if Mollie is examinable by any usual means. The others could possibly be seen in a group; whatever you decide, Monsieur *le Juge*."

"*Merci*," says Zabi. "I am glad you are moving towards the closing act. And congratulations on using every member of your team so efficiently."

Patrice, whose mind has mostly been full of Italian mediaeval art, shrugs off the compliment. All success is due to the team.

***

Colette is delighted to be home. Sartre has missed them and been a little confused at their comings and goings. This is beyond his usual experience; he is a dog of firm perspective.

She gives him a cuddle, sitting on the sofa, and then they go out onto the veranda, to welcome the spring. Having lately been in Helsinki, Colette is experiencing Parisian spring all over again. It is cool but sunny; *merveilleux*.

She turns around in a circle when she hears Patrice coming in through the front door. He is popping home for a break; deep in interviews which, he says, will solve his crime. She goes back into the flat, followed by the Bedlington, to drink the coffee her husband has started to make.

It is still too cool to sit on the veranda, so they make do with the sofa and open *porte-fenêtres*. The flat is full of peace, and calm, and elegance.

"What's up?" asks Colette, knowing he wouldn't have come home from work unless he was stressed.

"Just this case," he replies. "We're almost there. I wish it was finished."

"It will be," his wife replies, "very soon now. You know exactly where you are, and it's only that you have to tie off the ends …"

"And tuck them in," he says. He goes to bring their coffee; he didn't stop for pastries today.

"Who is it going to be today?" she asks.

"Mademoiselle Horváth, the hotel receptionist," he says. "I doubt she's actually in the sex ring, but she does, I'm sure, know much about it. And she's definitely connected to Mollie. I'm having the other three young women in too – but leaving the rest of the team to talk to them and try and work it out. Happily, I am passing the men involved, on my nice lists from Monsieur Ascher and Monsieur Melzer, to the examining magistrate. So, I don't have to see them again until trial."

Colette is pouring coffee, adding hot milk.

"That's good," she says. "You can forget about them until you have to give evidence from your notebook."

"Except," says Patrice, "that my understanding of what happened is still not perfect. But after the special session I am arranging for tomorrow, it probably will be."

"Ooh. That sounds exciting. Have you decided, yet, who is the murderer?"

"*Oui.*"

***

In the witness lottery, Fleur has drawn Signe Zvenieks, the Latvian girl whom some of the team think is probably a prostitute. She speaks good French, and admits it, which is a relief. Fleur asks her whether she thinks she will need a lawyer.

"*Non*," says the Latvian, "I have done nothing wrong." She is very sure of this, very confident.

"I see," says Fleur. "Will you admit that you are a part of a conspiracy, centred on the Hôtel des Jardins and which also involves your friends, Chang Su-Ming, Marie Lagrange, Julie Dorrity, and the child known as Mollie Cartwright?"

The Latvian looks much harder than she really is and Fleur, who knows many of the street girls around the city, cannot believe she is a *poule*. A dancer or nightclub singer, *peut-être*.

"I have done nothing wrong," she wails. "I wasn't even there!"

"You weren't even where?"

"Uh, anywhere. I have done nothing wrong!"

"If you are so sure," says Fleur, "that you have done nothing wrong, why don't you tell me about the plan?"

"Plan? I don't understand very good," Signe sniffles, abandoning her admission to good French. "What is 'plan'?"

"Your plan featuring Mollie. You told us, when we questioned you, that her name is Mollie. But it isn't, is it? And she is not English, is she? Apparently, she is Hungarian. Did you know that?"

"*Non, non.* How would I? You're confusing me now. My French not good. I don't know. I didn't do nothing wrong!"

"I will be holding you," says Fleur, "on charges of criminal conspiracy, and of assisting a perpetrator before and after the fact. You will be held for twenty-four hours in the first instance and may have access to the public defender should you wish. Take her to the cells, officer!"

*****

René's interviewee is Chang Su-Ming, the bartender from l'Arc-en-Ciel. Because she has met him before, her insouciance is palpable. She is shown in by the uniformed officer and takes a seat without being asked.

"*Bonjour*, monsieur!" she says. "*Ça va?*"

"*Bien*," says René. "I must ask you some further questions. We know," he says, resting his chin on his steepled fingers, elbows on the table, "that there is, in the centre of Paris, a ring of people, men, who are trafficking young girls, even children, for the purposes of rape and sadistic sexual abuse. We know this. What I must ask you is how are you involved?"

Chang Su-Ming looks levelly at him. She is beautifully made-up; her skin pale and shell-smooth, her eyes shadowed with peacock-green, matching her cheongsam, embroidered with a golden dragon.

"I am not involved," she says, "in anything like that." Her voice is calm, she has no nerves. She folds her hands. She will say no more.

"We know that you are," says René. "We have already spoken to Mademoiselle Zvenieks, who has incriminated all of you. You are the leader, with Marie, Signe, Julie, and Szonja Horváth, from the hotel, all in it up to your necks."

She gives him a look that would have rendered him dead, had looks been able to kill.

"I have done nothing wrong," she says.

"Were you in Room 307 of the Hôtel des Jardins on the night of the tenth and eleventh January last?"

"I was not."

"Are you aware of any of your little group who were in that room on that occasion?"

"I see no reason to suppose that any were," she says. "Why would they have been? We do not know anything about it. Signe must have been mistaken. Perhaps she is unwell?"

"Are you saying she is mentally ill?" asks René.

"*Non*, she is just confused. She must be thinking of some other place. What did Julie and Marie say?"

"They have not yet been questioned. But I imagine one of them will break and tell us the truth. Or Mademoiselle Horváth will. We know she is in it too.

"Are you aware," asks René, "that Monsieur Lindholm, who went out of the window, was not part of the sex-trafficking and child-rape plot? He was trying to investigate to stop it?"

He immediately spots something pass over Chang Su-Ming's eyes, a little falter, a little doubt.

"*Non*, I know nothing. I have done nothing."

"I must tell you that I am charging you with criminal conspiracy to commit homicide, with the possibility that you will be later charged with that homicide. You are entitled to a lawyer if you wish for one. Please take her to the cells, officer!"

***

Clémence is to examine the young French girl who is called Marie Lagrange. Chang Su-Ming has insisted on there being a responsible adult present, as the French girl is of diminished learning capacity. A middle-aged woman from social services has been called. The detective asks Marie to confirm her name, address, and place and date of birth. She is fifteen and originally comes from Normandy. She seems young, even for *15 ans,* and Clémence realises her learning difficulties are quite severe. She certainly seems vulnerable.

"I have to ask you, Marie," says Clémence, "whether you are part of a conspiracy with Mademoiselle Chang, Mademoiselle Zvenieks, Mademoiselle Dorrity, Mademoiselle Horváth, and the girl known as Mollie?"

The social worker looks fierce.

"Conspiracy?" Marie repeats. "What is 'conspiracy', please?"

"Did you join with them in a plot to destroy or interfere with the plans of some men who were trying to hurt young girls?"

"*Non.*"

"Were you there in Room 307 of the Hôtel des Jardins on the night of tenth to eleventh January 2019? Were you with your friends?"

"I don't remember. Where is Hôtel des Jardins please?"

"In the rue Mondoré, the continuation of the rue Palmier, where you live."

"I do not know it."

"You don't know where it is? Could you have been there and forgotten?"

"*Oui.* I don't always remember. I have done nothing wrong."

"*D'accord,*" says Clémence, "I shall have to speak to someone about this. The officer from by the door, and Madame Chalois from social services, will stay with you until I come back. You are quite safe."

She rolls her wheelchair out of the interview room with the wide door and takes the *ascenseur* to the *salle squad*.

Fleur, who is back from interviewing Mlle Zvenieks, looks askance.

"*Nous avons un problème,*" says Clémence. "Marie Lagrange has learning difficulties and may be unable to plead. I think she may have been a potential victim, as well as Mollie. But she doesn't seem to have anything she can tell us. Just the 'I have not done anything wrong' – which they have all obviously learned by heart."

"Don't arrest her," says Pucelle. "Can we keep her in the cells until we are finished with the others? *Oui,* for her own safety. Keep her under guard but feed her and everything. I don't think we can release her. Perhaps social services; you had someone with her, *n'est-ce pas?* But don't just let her walk out."

"Can I stay and chat with her awhile?" asks Clémence. "You never know. Maybe she'll tell me something. Or is that exploiting her disability?"

"I'm not too bothered about that," says Pucelle. "Be nice to her, I'm not suggesting we continue their abuse. But I'm conscious that I owe a large debt to Monsieur Lindholm – we must find out who killed him, and why."

*****

Patrice and Fleur are interviewing Mlle Horváth, Mollie, and Annibale Deneice, the *avocat*, together. It is not clear that M Deneice will function as their lawyer. As a person accused of removing a witness from a place of safety, he may well need an advocate himself. This is the first thing Fleur asks. The *avocat* says that they don't need a lawyer; they have done nothing wrong. Which is an extremely odd thing for a lawyer to say.

"I don't completely understand how this thing works," says Patrice, "although I believe that Officers Valéry and Mercier set a little trap for you by deliberately letting slip the information that Mademoiselle Mollie Cartwright, as we knew her, was staying at Madame Paston's women's refuge. You went there immediately, and they arrested you leaving with Mollie." He gestures towards the child in acknowledgement that she is here.

"First of all," he says, "may we know what your real name is, young lady? And how many years you have?"

"*Non,*" says Szonja Horváth, "she still cannot speak."

"I think you can tell me her name, though, can't you, Mademoiselle?"

"It is Sofija Horváth. She is my sister. She has twelve years." The receptionist squeezes the information out between tight lips.

"Who then," asks Fleur, "is responsible for planning this conspiracy? We are assuming that someone of you found out that there were men, with convictions or suspicions of this kind of exploitation of children, who were setting up a trafficking and abuse scheme for their own use. And that you wanted to prevent it.

"So, you took steps. Maybe you, Szonja, got a job at the hotel which had been chosen – or …" Fleur, looking at Szonja Horváth, realises that it is the wrong way round. "Or, when you got the job, you suspected what was going to happen. Did you bring in your sister then?"

"I find that very hard to believe," says Patrice. "Bringing in your own sister to be trafficked? How could you?"

"We thought she would be safe," says Szonja. "Because she can't tell anyone anything, we thought they would not kill her." Her face collapses, as if defeated. As sometimes happens with inexperienced criminals, the flood gates quickly open. "I knew before," she mumbles. "I met Dr Ascher when I was a psychology student in Zurich. He … told me he was in love with me. I was stupid. I believed him."

She pauses, tears fall, she wipes up, gets a stronger voice from somewhere. "I thought we would be together forever – he wasn't married, his wife was dead." She takes a very deep breath, working up to something big. "Then he started to do some things …things I did not like." She reaches up and pulls off the beautifully styled wig, revealing rucked, burned skin all over her head.

All five persons in the room gasp at the sight; it must have been extraordinarily painful, tragic, life-destroying.

***

Chloë, as the newest member of the team, is left with interviewing the Australian, Julie Dorrity, expected to be the easy one. Mademoiselle Dorrity seems easy-going and, with the habit of world travelling attributed to Aussies, Chloë is confident that her own English will suffice. The Australian may well have some French anyway. Chloë had been expecting Yves Mercier to join her in the interview, but he has suddenly gone down with belated *Trente-Six peste*.

"G'day!" says the Australian, cartoonishly. "How are you?"

"Well, thank you," says Chloë, indicating a chair.

"I have a few questions to ask you, Miss Dorrity," says Chloë, "about this conspiracy we have learned about, with Mesdemoiselles Chang, Zvenieks, Lagrange, Horváth, and the girl known as Mollie?"

"Conspiracy?" asks Dorrity, looking dumb. "Some kind of plot or something?"

"*Oui*," says Chloë. "Did you join with them in a plot to destroy or interfere with the plans of some men who were trying to hurt young girls?"

"No."

"Really? I think you do know of such a plot and think that, if you did, you would try to stop it. It's only right, isn't it? To try and protect children who will be harmed, or even killed?"

"No, er, yes. Yes, I suppose I would if I did. Know, that is. But I didn't."

"Do you mean that you would have done something if you had known of the plot?"

"Yeah. 'Course I would if I knew. But I didn't. I haven't done anything wrong." Return to the repeated phrase.

"Tell me, Julie, if you knew that there were some adult men, one of whom already has a conviction for multiple child rape, and another who was dismissed from his job teaching young people, for suspected sexual abuse, and they were plotting to set up a sex-trafficking ring, bringing young girls and maybe boys too, we don't know yet, in from abroad, so they could be passed around from one to the other – and sexually abused and beaten and have their flesh burned by cigarettes – wouldn't you want to help them?"

Julie Dorrity looks as if she is going to be sick, and before Chloë can offer her a receptacle, she is. On the floor, and over her white embroidered sweater. The *PJ* asks the uniformed officer if he can get someone to clear it up. It smells strong and bitter, the bile of a very nervous stomach. Chloë gives the Aussie some water but refrains from asking anything else until the vomit has gone from the room.

Patrice, coming from interviewing Szonja Horváth and company, sees the officer with the bucket and asks what happens? He asks the uniformed officer to get permission from Mlle Valéry for Patrice to join her. The officer hands him the sick bucket before doing so.

Patrice enters and takes a chair out of the young women's sightline.

"I'm sure you would want to help them," says Chloë. "I'm sure you're a good person. So, I must ask, what exactly did you do? When you found there was a plan to pass around Mollie and Marie Lagrange? And ruin any life they had left? When you got to know that these grown men were going to use them for sex, and hurt them in body and soul? Maybe they were going to kill them? What did you think?"

Julie Dorrity is weeping now. She cannot speak; she has been deeply affected by what Chloë has said. But Chloë's ruthlessness hasn't quite finished.

"We all have a duty, don't we? To protect those who cannot protect themselves. Anything else is a betrayal of the vulnerable?"

"If I may ask a question of Miss Dorrity, Officer Valéry?" says Patrice into the quiet.

Chloë nods.

"Did you hit Monsieur Lindholm with the lamp and throw him out of the window of the room?"

"Yes," says Julie Dorrity, "I did. I hit that man – I don't know which one of them it was – on the head with the lamp. Then Mollie and I pushed him out of the window between us. She isn't strong enough. But I am. I am not sorry. Someone had to do it."

***

"I did not expect this," says the Interpol man, transferring his angry gaze repeatedly from Patrice to the report.

"What did you expect?" asks Patrice benignly. He himself has expected Duchamps to jump at him as he reads the thing. He knows perfectly well that it is not what he is looking for.

"An analysis of the documents and bills of sale," he blusters, "some extraction of the information of the provenance ... a definite conclusion about the authenticity of the painting. A yes or no. What did you think I wanted?" He collapses into his executive chair, looking defeated.

"What I have produced," says Patrice. "A pheno-menological account of the picture in question, using all the documents provided to me."

"But this is just a lot of stuff about the other paintings around the same subject," says Duchamps. "It hardly mentions the provenance at all. It doesn't clearly trace where the picture has been, or prove that it is, or is not, what it seems to be."

"I think you have misunderstood my method," explains Patrice. "I am not trying to prove anything in particular – I am trying to give you a plausible story from the evidence you have provided. And I have concluded that it is plausible that this is a genuine Artemisia Gentileschi; it is also plausible that it is not.

"And it is entirely irrelevant at this stage because the painting, called the Finnish *Judith* in my report, was anyway destroyed by the magistrate on its return to France."

"Then it is over." Duchamps looks defeated. How else could he look?

32

They have allowed Julie Dorrity a break and are now oiling the wheels with coffee and pastry. She seems relieved to talk, although she still doesn't know they have killed the wrong person.

"We had to get Marie out of there quickly because we felt she was in danger of her livfe. They seem to have thought, at first, that Marie wouldn't be believed if she spoke to anyone – because of her mental age – but she is able to speak of some things. I got her out in time."

Chloë is devastated by the lengths these young women went to try and fix this, and how, by making a single mistake, killed someone innocent.

"How did you know," she asks, "that Marie was in danger?"

"Because I was in the room above," says Julie Dorrity. "I was listening on a baby monitor. And I could follow the way things were sounding. Marie had been allowed to leave the room for a pee, and the men were talking – the German very loudly – about whether she could be trusted with their secret. The German said she couldn't; he was boasting that he was the psychology expert. He said that she wouldn't understand that she shouldn't tell what had happened in the room, and that someone would believe her. It would all be over before it had hardly begun. And, he said, it was regrettable because it was a very good plan. He was cold; it sounded like a business transaction.

"I left the room and went downstairs. Marie was in the corridor, frightened. She had picked up the feelings of danger, even though she hadn't followed the speech. She was very upset. She had been assaulted by one of the men already, and had her arm twisted behind her back by another. Mollie was waiting upstairs in 607. I went straight in to get her out."

"You can tell us, then, which men were involved, and what they did?" says Patrice.

"I can," says Julie Dorrity. "Better, I have an audio recording of their session."

"And you were registered as occupying Room 407?" says Patrice. "So. You are Magda Simon of Reims?"

"I am."

***

"It is time to wrap this case," announces Patrice to the collected team sitting around the large table in the *salle squad*. "It is only one case, although several crimes. I have, here, the transcripts of interviews which have been carried out. This is our opportunity to make sense of the whole thing, as a group.

"I should be grateful if you would begin, Pucelle, with the very beginning, which is *January the tenth*, at the Hôtel des Jardins."

"*Oui*," says Pucelle over hands folded on the table in front of her, "but I need to say something first which comes before that date."

A ripple of surprise runs around the table.

"I have to confess something of which I am ashamed." Her husky contralto is still cracked. "I made an assumption, which was not only uncalled for but incorrect. Because of what I already thought I knew about Monsieur Lindholm – I suspected that he was behind the fake terrorist incident at Notre-Dame, although that still is not proven – I was only too ready to implicate him in a sex-trafficking and paedophile ring. This was wrong. I am very sorry." She bows her head, as if waiting for criticism.

There is none. Anyone would have done the same.

"*Se déplaçant le long ...*[172]" says Patrice, "if you could just give us the outline of what happened ..."

"Monsieur Lindholm descended from the window of Room 607 at the hotel into a snowbank, having been brained with a brass lamp applied to the back of his head. Mademoiselle Julie Dorrity has confessed that she was the person who wielded it, although she was helped to push him through the opened window by Mademoiselle Sofija Horváth, a girl of *12 ans* who was in the room.

"The killing of Monsieur Lindholm was not planned but was the consequence of a conspiracy of a number of young women to put a stop to a sex-trafficking ring which was holding an event in Room 307.

"We can prove the names of the conspirators, of whom there are four, as Szonja Horváth, Chang Su-Ming, Signe

---

172 Moving along ...

Zvenieks and Julie Dorrity. Two others implicated are Sofija Horváth and Marie Lagrange." She stops, without further comment, as René takes the floor.

"I think we all think," says the detective, "that Sofija Horváth and Marie Lagrange were involved but as victims. At any rate, Sofija has only *12 ans*, and so is too young, and Marie has pronounced learning difficulties and is likely to be found unfit to plead." This comes out as part of René's mission to protect the weak and vulnerable.

Fleur Olivier takes up the baton regarding the trafficking circle:

"The men involved in this horrendous matter" – she suppresses her natural snarl – "are of various ages and inclinations. We might think, because one of the men is a homosexual, that the group intended to expand into the exploitation of young boys, but we have no evidence which suggests this.

"Monsieur Renault was there, he admits, because he had had no experience with females. He was being taught by the others – perhaps as a form of reparative therapy..." She does snarl now, looking as if she has a bad taste in her mouth. "He and his boyhood friend, Monsieur Melzer, may not have been concerned with the organisation of the matter – they may have been just customers. We do not know.

"What we do know is that there are two organisers, Doktor Ascher and Monsieur Cloche. Both have previous records; the former never charged but evidence still available, the latter having served *20 ans* in prison for proven crimes against little girls." The taste in Fleur's mouth gets worse, from her expression. "Monsieur Denthwaite is part of the ring – although, it seems, not an organiser. He has admitted to one count of rape of a minor." She looks over at Clémence and gives a little nod that she should continue.

"We cannot locate anyone else from the hotel or otherwise in the trafficking group at present – although it may be that some of the other guests were on their way there but had not quite made it when Monsieur Lindholm did the flying bit. We are keeping Monsieur Juliane and Monsieur Sansone under light surveillance for the moment, with no great hope."

Chloë, faintly intimidated by the professional team, reminds herself that she is the detective who got Julie Dorrity to confess, and tells them, in a quiet voice, that they are unsure of whether *avocat* Annibale Deneice, the girls' lawyer, might be involved somehow, and that there seems a chance that Mlle Barnier, the seamstress from the Jura, might also have been on the perimeter of the plot.

"We have at last got our heads around who was where on the night of the tenth to eleventh of January," says Chloë, "and the room where the partying happened was 307, a suite – all the 07 rooms are suites – but when any of the men, this was the plan, made a connection with one of the girls, he was to take her to his own room."

"That wouldn't work for Melzer and Renault," says Fleur. "They were sharing."

"*Oui*," says Chloë, "but there were many other rooms available that one of them could use. And Mademoiselle Horváth could have one made up for him on request."

"But, about 307," says Clémence. "It was the suite into which Magda Simon was booked but never used. Julie Dorrity, aka Madame Simon, actually used a different room – 407 – with a baby monitor, which she brought in herself. She heard what was going on in 307 and took herself up to 607 by the fire escape to wait for them. Unfortunately for Monsieur Lindholm, he was there already, although Mollie had been pushed into the suite and the door locked, and Ascher had disappeared into the bathroom to make preparations. Julie hit Lindholm with the lamp and she and Mollie threw him out of the window. Mollie was in shock. They left the room, leaving Ascher still in the bathroom."

"But," says the *commissaire*, wrapping up, "nothing is ever simple, and we must be vigilant in the event that there are tendrils which may trip us in the future. I should, though, like to thank all of you for your hard work. It has been a most abominable thing, and we have all suffered the consequences. We have made errors, we always do, but we have done much careful work. I am, as always, available to talk through anything which is troubling you. Please come and see me when you are ready to talk."

***

"I don't know," says Patrice when he is at last home. "It is very peculiar. We have solved several cases, and two lots of people will go to jail eventually. There will be much litigation about the sex trafficking, and some of them may even get away. The *proc* and Zabi both reckon the case is good – as do I after listening to Julie Dorrity's horrible recording – but one never knows what tricks will be used in the defence."

"You've all done what you can, though," says Colette. "You did everything that was necessary. Even though you were away part of the time. Are you feeling guilty about doing the work for Interpol when you think you should have been working this horrible case?"

"*Non,*" says Patrice, "I thought the *divisionnel* had fielded a substitute, Monsieur Bonnetain. I couldn't have known that it wouldn't work out. When he seemed to have disappeared, I begged Pucelle to return. The team did a wonderful job, though. They got their heads down and did solid, dreary, and eventually horrifying police work. They shook the tree until the fruit dropped. I am incredibly proud of them!"

"I know," says Colette, who does know. "What about the murder case, though? That must be open and shut, mustn't it?"

"*Oui, certainement*, although probably manslaughter – they did plan something but certainly not to kill Lindholm. They didn't know that they were killing the wrong person. But that is problematic. Saying that – and I did say that to the team – infers that if there were a 'wrong' person, there would have been a right person. And, perhaps, that right person could have been chosen from amongst all the men who were in the room with those two little girls. I don't like that much!"

"I can see," says Colette, "but I wonder why you changed your minds about the idea that it must have been a man who pushed Monsieur Lindholm?"

"It was strange," says Patrice. "I was thinking about the other case. About Artemisia's workmanlike arms. Julie Dorrity, a champion swimmer, has arms exactly like her. And she, too, knows how to use them in revenge. But for her it was revenge for Szonja Horváth and all the other students Ascher had damaged, not herself."

Epilogue

juin 2019

"We didn't think it would be him," says Patrice, the sense of déjà vu enveloping him. There is no snow now, it is full spring, but the body lies almost certainly where the snowbank which received Monsieur Lindholm had been.

The *commissaire* is waiting for Dr Rousseau again, as he had on the early morning of *janvier 11,* but not feeling cold, so not in such a hurry. Marc Rousseau arrives and says, again, that the body is dead. Although not, this time, brained as well. It looks like a simple jump.

Patrice, who thinks it is anything but simple, considering all that has gone before, waits for the time of the post-mortem. It will be at *18 heures* this evening, when the pathologist has finished dealing with a big traffic accident involving some foreigners and, naturally, their diplomatic representatives.

There is little point in arguing about this. Rousseau always sets his own peculiar preferences, so the death certificate and report of the death of Monsieur Cloche can only be a postscript. Patrice had, in some way, expected that there could be another death, although he would have been in a dilemma as to how he knew.

If he had made an instinctive choice, it would have been Dr Ascher – the real leader of the ring. But no, maybe Cloche's previous experience of a paedophile's stay in prison had made him not wish to repeat it. Or, just maybe, he had been sorry. Patrice would like to think even the worst of us can find redemption.

The pathologist instructs his assistants that they can remove the broken body as Patrice wonders how he managed to get here, while on his way to prison. René, who has been standing at a little distance from the body, comes over with two young prison guards, both looking pale, one worse than that.

"He kicked Jean here in the balls," says René, "as they were loading him into the transport outside the court. They did not expect him to make a break for it." René pronounces this as if to say that Cloche would not have got away from him. "They thought he was relatively safe if there were no little girls around."

"Shows how wrong you can be," mutters Patrice. "He ran quite a way to get here, didn't he? Desperation, do you think?"

"He really did not want to go to prison again," says René. "Well, anyway, he won't hurt any more *petite filles*." He knows that there will have to be an enquiry both tedious and painful. But at least the abominable Cloche is no longer in the world.

The *commissaire* watches as the body is loaded into the medical examiner's van and taken away. There is a chance, now, that Herr Doktor Ascher will be convicted for the crimes of both – a jury will likely consider someone has to pay and they have no one with whom they can share the responsibility. Patrice sighs: they will do what they will do. Time to go home at last.

***

Pucelle is outside *le Trente-Six* when Patrice arrives back from his home visit. They go without consultation to the seat on which they always sit. They ask each other how they are. They are well.

"I am told that you came in after the Notre-Dame burned ..." says Patrice, folding his hands on his knees, much as she always does. "Was it that you wanted to look through your window?"

"I did," she says, the rasp in her voice testifying to her ordeal in the Paon case, seeming so long ago now.

"I had to see whether I could still be in the office, the fire seemed so significant; *j'étais dévastée.*[173] Something I saw all the time, an anchor, perhaps? Suddenly, ahh!"

"I know," he says, lapsing into silence to be alongside her. After a while, he says:

"Did you want to see me about something?"

"Coming back permanently," she says. "You know it was only a leave of absence I took. Monsieur Robert has been in touch about something he really wants me to take on outside of Clichy; another of those 'only you can do it' things. So, it's necessary for me to come back formally before I go off back undercover."

Patrice looks and feels disappointed that she's not coming back to his team right away, but thinks that it's better than nothing. After Robert's latest incredible demands have been met, he could well get Pucelle back permanently. He must, however, not depend upon it.

"*D'accord*, what is the case? Can you tell me?"

"Not so much," she says. "I don't know everything yet. It will be in Paris. My special skills are required (whatever they are), although not Russian. I am now engaged in a study of *vodou.*"

"*Bon Dieu!*" he says. "Whatever next? Does he go out of his way to find you weird cases? Will you be safe?"

"That is one of the two things I am authorised to ask you, *patron*. Will you give me personal supervision during

---

173 I was devastated

my undercover work? This is because I do see certain dangers; there is some possibility of physical and spiritual vulnerability, of course, but I am in most peril, if any, of risking my mental faculties. I believe that you can help me with all of this. Will you?"

"If I can, *mais certainement*. But I have no experience as a spiritual director. The idea makes me go cold all over!"

She looks at him sadly, conscious that she has few options if he says no.

"But you are my friend," she says. "The person I trust most in the world."

"*D'accord*," says Patrice. How can he not validate her trust?

FIN